D1385517

David Thewlis rose to prominence in 1993 when starring in Mike Leigh's film *Naked*, for which he won the Cannes Film Festival Award for Best Actor. Other notable film appearances include *Seven Years in Tibet*, *Kingdom of Heaven*, *The Big Lebowski*, *The Boy in the Striped Pyjamas*, *War Horse*, *The Theory of Everything*, *Anomalisa* and *I'm Thinking of Ending Things*.

He is known for his portrayals of Remus Lupin in the *Harry Potter* film series and Sir Patrick Morgan/Ares in *Wonder Woman*. He was nominated for an Emmy Award, Critics' Choice Television Award and Golden Globe Award for his role in the TV series *Fargo*. He also wrote and directed the BAFTA-nominated short film *Hello Hello Hello*.

Shooting Martha is his second novel.

Also by David Thewlis

The Late Hector Kipling

SHOOTING
MARTHA

DAVID THEWLIS

WEIDENFELD & NICOLSON

First published in Great Britain in 2021 by Weidenfeld & Nicolson
an imprint of The Orion Publishing Group Ltd
Carmelite House, 50 Victoria Embankment
London EC4Y 0DZ

An Hachette UK Company

1 3 5 7 9 10 8 6 4 2

A CIP catalogue record for this book is
available from the British Library.

ISBN (Hardback) 978 1 4746 2153 3
ISBN (Export Trade Paperback) 978 1 4746 2154 0
ISBN (eBook) 978 1 4746 2156 4

Typeset by Input Data Services Ltd, Somerset

Printed in Great Britain by Clays Ltd, Elcograf S.p.A.

MIX
Paper from
responsible sources
FSC® C104740

www.weidenfeldandnicolson.co.uk
www.orionbooks.co.uk

For Hermine Poitou – of course

'Making this movie is like trying to complete a crossword puzzle while plunging down an elevator shaft'

Spoken to the author by Marlon Brando, Australia, 1995

PART ONE

CHAPTER I

After his lunch of burnt lamb, cabbage and corn, he turned out the bathroom light, curled up on his side on the tiled floor and spoke with his wife, who, being dead, listened closely.

He told her how poorly the work was progressing, he told her about his lack of sleep, his crippling indecision. He told her about the footsteps on the ceiling, the flies in his mother's old bedroom, the suffocating dreams. After ten minutes he pushed himself up onto all fours. 'Martha,' he concluded, 'it looks like this could go on all night. I won't be home till the morning. Shall I wake you, or will I leave you to sleep?'

Nothing.

And then, out of the silence, some small thing. Distant footsteps, perhaps, moving closer. More silence. Out of the darkness, two gentle knocks. Jack held his breath.

'Mr Drake?'

He froze. 'Who?'

'Mr Drake?'

'Where?'

'Hello?'

'Who is it?'

'They're ready for you, Mr Drake.'

Mr Drake. That meant something, it seemed. Jack dabbed the wet corners of his beard with his woollen cuff. 'Coming.'

Unexpectedly, the door opened a few inches and one small part of a small, pale face began to emerge.

'I said coming! I didn't say come in.'

The small, startled piece of pale face tucked itself back in and away.

'I'm sorry, Mr Drake, it sounded like—'

'I don't care what it sounded like. I said I'm coming. What's your name again?'

'Alexander, sir.'

'Where's Nora?'

'Nora Flynn?'

'Yes, Nora.'

'She's downstairs.'

'Tell her to come upstairs.'

'But she sent me up to tell you to come down.'

'Well, go down and tell her to come up.'

'She asked me not to let you say that.'

'Did she?'

'Yes, sir.'

'So what are you going to do?'

'I don't know, sir. What should I do?'

Jack pressed his beard into shape and put on his spectacles.

'Don't ever get married.'

By the time Jack reached the top of the stairs and looked down, both bodies were still spinning slowly at the end of their ropes. He paused on the second landing, assessing the comings and goings of the irritatingly nervous rabble awaiting his appraisal on the floor below. None of them dared look up. They knew they were likely to have something dropped on them if they watched as he made his way back down the staircase after a long lunch.

He approached the edge of the first landing, where he could get a better view of things: if he reached out from here, he could touch the ropes; they had been rigged from the scaffold bolted across the second landing's cast-iron banister. Now that he was close enough to smell him, Jack gazed at the top of Conrad Ripley's head with utter disdain. There were few people in this world whom Jack cared for less than Conrad E. Ripley, and yet here he was, hanging from Jack's ceiling in a faithfully reproduced pair of Jack's father's red paisley pyjamas, spinning slowly in the rolling shafts of dust and no doubt pre-occupied not with the immense gravity of the matter in hand, but rather with the timing of his next drink.

Arriving at last at the ground floor and feeling suddenly adrift in the vast entrance hall, Jack absorbed the inevitable attention of his crew without looking any one of them in the eyes: fists clasped behind his back, he walked to the base of the tableau and took in the enormity of how little he had been listened to when he had asked for a dignified yet provocative re-creation of his father's suicide.

The scent of Moroccan musk and the singular click of her vinyl heels alerted him to the arrival of Nora Flynn, no doubt clutching her notebook and pencil, ready to identify, itemise, tabulate and outsource. She knew him well, of old, better than most, and was paid accordingly. She knew not to speak until spoken to, at least not in front of the others: it was a different story when she got him alone. She was a short, rather feeble-looking woman in her early sixties, but was known as a keen arm-wrestler and had taken on and ruffled many a bulky spark in her three decades in the film industry. A previously delicate and pale complexion was now, after basking in continental locations, tough and overcooked; her once red hair had long ago burned down to ashes and, though still girlishly long, for the last fifteen years had been clipped up and back and settled out of sight beneath a signature tweed cap.

'So?' she said. Her pencil was already poised over the page.

Jack said nothing. He cast his eyes further afield in search of his cinematographer, Solomon Monk. Feeling himself beckoned, Solomon put down his coffee and shuffled over.

'So?' said Solomon. He was the oldest soul in the room and suffered the posture and weary demeanour of a television gardener.

'This looks fake,' said Jack

'Fake,' wrote Nora.

'I know,' said Solomon. 'I've got to agree. And I've done my best, I really have.'

'And what am I supposed to do about all this?' said Jack, gesturing at the tangle of straps, ratchets, buckles and tape hidden behind the back of the real Ripley. While the prosthetic was suspended by an authentic noose about the silicone neck, this was not possible with the man himself, though Jack would have liked to give it a good try: Ripley was tethered to the rope by means of a triple-stitched harness buckled about his pelvis and shoulders, and what passed for the noose was in fact a gimmick designed to detach and fall away at the smallest hint of real pressure. Now that Jack had begun his review, Ripley ventured to open one eye in what he thought might be a deliciously comic effect, should anyone be looking his way. Nobody was.

'What do you mean?' said Solomon.

'This, all this. All this paraphernalia round the back.'

'Oh, we can hide all that. Shoot from the front.'

'I don't want to shoot from the front. I want to circle all the way round, and I want her . . .' Jack indicated a willing and enthusiastic-looking woman in her mid thirties, 'I want her to cut him down.'

'You want *me* to cut him down?' said Eve Parnell, stepping forward, licking the last smear of egg grease from her fingers and shifting her silicone pregnancy bump a few inches to the left.

'Not *you*,' said Jack. 'I want *Eleanor*, your character, to climb up, cut him down and then take her dead husband on her shoulders, fireman-style, and carry him to the floor. How's she going to do that with all this shit on show?'

'Fireman-style?' said Eve, confused, clutching her prosthetic bump like it shouldn't be hearing any of this.

A stocky little mastiff of a man known to all as Rex FX stepped forward to join the growing throng of concerned lackeys. 'You didn't say anything about cutting him down. He's too rigid. He's not designed to be cut down.'

'Nor is he designed to hang, by the looks of things,' said Jack.

'But they . . . that's how they hang . . . they . . .'

'That's how *who* hang?'

'Them . . . y'know . . . people who . . .'

'I've seen hanged men! Real ones! What do you think we're talking about here? Don't bullshit me, Rex.'

Solomon took a deep breath and ventured in. 'Well, we could shoot the prosthetic in the wide and, er . . . come in for the . . . when she . . . come in close and . . . we could—'

'Solomon, listen,' said Jack, placing two fingers over the old man's mouth. 'In fact, all of you listen, including all those of you hidden behind monitors and dollies and doors. All those of you in other rooms and outside, in the garden, on the roof, in your cars and caravans. All those of you who aren't even here today. Listen to this: this is not a game. I know you've all had a splendid hoot out on location, where you could scatter and escape scrutiny, but we're here now, and we're here for the next four weeks, and there will be no more dicking around and just trying to make do. And I'm sure you've heard rumours that they're going to pull the plug any day now. That Mr Drake's

7

not really up to snuff, that he's lost his way, or his mind, or his self-respect, what with his poor wife, and "Oh dear, what a shame. What a pity. And have you seen him first thing in the morning? Isn't that the same pair of trousers, the same shirt every day for two weeks now, and wasn't he wearing the same thing at the read-through?"' He paused. Some poor bastard in the corner was trying not to cough, afraid he might be marched off out into the garden and shot.

Jack continued pacing around the vast hall to the other side of the grand piano. His lunch had been meagre; this was dessert. He settled now – magnificently, he imagined – next to a suit of Tudor armour. He'd had it moved into the hall from the library so that it could bear witness to his father's lurid demise; if it could be suitably burnished, he might even go for a shot of the horror reflected in the breastplate. He was not done, though now the tone was to be softened and supplicatory.

'I know it's an unusual job for most of you. For some – Nora and Solomon here, who've been with me, as you know, for two or three centuries – it's a walk in the park.' Nora and Solomon stole a glance at each other. 'I just can't tolerate people not pulling their weight. People not listening, refusing to listen, not realising that they were supposed to listen. It's not a breeze chiselling out one of these things. We all know that. So why make it harder by not making it easier?' He looked around the gathered congregation and cocked his ear, as though the question were not rhetorical. By now, having paced out a full circuit of the room, he had arrived back at his point of departure, the base of the double hanging. One of Conrad Ripley's slippers – red paisley, to match the pyjamas – had fallen to the floor. Jack bent over to pick it up and placed it, with mock tenderness, back onto the actor's dusty yellow foot.

'What do you think of all this, Conrad?'

'What do I think of what?' said Ripley, suspicious.

'Of all this.' Jack was smiling, as though his answer might set things in order.

'What is all this? All this what?'

'Well, I don't know. This is your first scene playing the corpse, and putting aside scenes three, seven, twenty-nine and fifty-two, you'll be a corpse from now on, for the rest of the shoot. How are you feeling about that?'

'I'm not sure,' said Ripley. Was it possible the concern was sincere?

'Well, what is your opinion of this puppet?' Jack continued, pushing the foot of the figure so that it swung out and back, nudging Ripley on its return.

'It's hardly a puppet. I think they've done a splendid job.'

'You don't think it looks fake?'

'No, I think it looks real enough.'

Jack took a step back, the better to appraise the tone of Ripley's red face. 'Do you? Real enough for what?'

'For its purpose.'

'And what is its purpose?'

'To look like a hanged man.'

'Just a man?'

'Well, your father.'

'But it looks nothing like my father looked.' Jack pushed the dummy again, this time a little harder, so that it swung like a pendulum.

'You said you didn't see how your father looked. You didn't see it.' The dummy crashed back against Ripley's shoulder, causing him to steady himself in his harness.

'Well, he certainly didn't look like that,' said Jack. 'Do you know how I know?'

'How?'

'Because it looks like you.'

'Well, yes.'

'And you, Conrad, look nothing like my father.'

'Then why did you cast me?'

'Good question. I really can't remember. Perhaps I was drunk.'

'You don't drink.'

'That's right. But you do, so . . .' Jack grabbed Ripley by his slippered foot and squeezed the toe till the actor winced. 'So, Conrad, what will we do?'

'I'm not talking to you.'

Jack turned to the increasingly baffled crew. 'Does anyone have an idea of what we should do about all this?'

Silence.

'Very well, I have an idea. I'll tell you what we'll do. We'll do this.' And suddenly he was off, marching across the room with an impressive gait and surprising speed, pushing aside the gathered mob, swinging round to the other side of the piano, and before anyone realised what he was up to, he had, with alarming ferocity, wrestled the two-handed great sword from the metal fists of the armoured knight and was now marching back, double the speed – running, really – with enormous strides, leaping the last few feet. He began to strike at the prosthetic with all the gleeful abandon with which, one would imagine, he would have enjoyed striking the real Ripley. He hoisted the enormous blade high above his shoulders and brought it crashing down time and time again against the dummy as if it were an elaborately fashioned and extremely expensive piñata. 'We'll do this!' he cried, at the top of his voice. 'And this, and this, and this,' and with each demonstration of what it was that he would do, he did it, smashing the hapless figure over and over till the entire thing began to fall apart.

Conrad Ripley was not at all happy with this turn of events. 'What are you doing?' he yelled, as one of the legs separated at the knee and fell to the floor. 'They said I could keep that. Rex, didn't you say I could keep it?'

Jack was now lashing out with such blind rage that several members of the crew began to wonder if they shouldn't risk their lives and step into the fray.

'I have a collection,' whined Ripley.

A hand flew across the room and landed at Nora's feet. Finding the horrid thing a little difficult to stomach, she kicked it further across the floor, where it came to rest beneath the sound trolley.

As at last he began to weaken, Jack seemed to lose control of the sword until it began bouncing off the eviscerated silicone corpse and twice in a row smashed into the side of Ripley's knee. 'Watch what you're fucking doing, you maniac!' cried Ripley. 'You're going to kill me! Rex, Solomon, get me down.'

Nora was scribbling furiously in her notebook, tearing out pages as she went, handing them out on all sides. Eve Parnell had stood frozen throughout the ordeal, her hands to her face and her mouth agape; she was only now beginning to move again, reassuringly stroking her poor bump.

Eventually Jack collapsed to the floor, letting the sword clatter and clang as he thrust it out and away, where it could do no more damage. Larry Cox, head of props, scooped it up and handed it to his assistant, Bob, for possible maintenance. The lower half of the silicone corpse was so critically damaged that the pair of paisley pyjama trousers dropped from the buckled and spinning torso, landing on Jack's heaving back. He snatched them off and flung them across the floor, where Barbara Fish, the wardrobe mistress, scooped them up and tossed them to her assistant, who folded and bagged them up for doubling in the event of soiling the hero pair.

For the second time that day Jack found himself on all fours, monitoring his own progress. He called out to his first assistant director, Charles Ball, the poor man tasked with keeping order and decorum on the set. 'Charles, where've you been?'

'I'm sorry, sir,' said Charles, astonished at the scale of the devastation wrought upon a set he had left pristine only ten minutes before. 'I had to take a call.'

Jack pushed himself up to standing and dusted himself down. 'Charles, listen. We're going to have to revisit all this. I've realised I can't get the camera far enough back. We'll have to knock this wall down.' He gestured at the enormous wall dividing the main entrance hall and the library.

'We can't knock that down, sir.'

'Not now,' said Jack, walking over to the wall in question and patting it like a good horse. 'We'll do it at the end of the shoot. The whole wall can come down so we can get the camera right back there,' now gesturing through the door to the back of the library.

'What I'm saying,' said Charles, 'is that I don't think you can knock that wall down. You know, technically. I think it's a—'

'It's *my* fucking house, I can do what I want! What is wrong with you all?'

Most of the crew were by now trying to creep softly away.

'Has anybody else got anything negative to say?'

'Yes, me!' said Conrad E. Ripley, who had just finished removing the final strap of his harness while rearranging the crotch of Jack's father's pyjamas.

Jack turned. 'Yes? Go on.'

'I quit.'

'Good, 'cos you're fired.'

'Good, 'cos I quit.'

'Good, 'cos you were shit.'

'Goodbye.'

'Goodbye.'

And with this, Ripley began walking from the set, yanking

off the paisley top, exposing his pink and chunky upper body, something no one wanted to see and would hopefully never see again. Hopefully. Maybe. Who knew? It wasn't the first time Ripley had quit. He'd done it three times on the first day.

Half of Ripley's hopeless doppelgänger turned gently on its thread, pop-eyed and legless, tongue out on its silicone chops. At Solomon's behest the plugs were pulled and the dummy became nothing more than a formless silhouette. Everyone who hadn't already called it a day began now, silently, to disperse, while in the background of all this new dark, a solitary Jack Drake could be seen mounting the staircase to return to his childhood bathroom, where his dear wife Martha might perhaps speak to him through the pipes.

CHAPTER 2

Three different kinds of jam in eight different places on two strips of carpet that covered almost half the floor. Marmite on the skirting board; butter on the light switch, half unscrewed; on the mantelpiece, three plush dogs and a one-eyed duck; on the windowsill, two dead daddy-long-legs; and outside, on the window ledge, a dense paste of pigeon shit and a cracked heart-shaped ashtray filled with brown rain.

In the middle of the room, on a three-legged stool, sat little Freddie Dean, six years old, his weary green-eyed, chapped-lipped, purple-slippered mother painting an almost perfect pipevine swallowtail on Freddie's upturned, smiling and seemingly flawless face.

'Tell me something else about butterflies,' whispered Betty, and Freddie turned the page of his best big book and gasped.

'They can taste things with their feet.'

'Goodness. Imagine that,' said Betty, dipping her brush into a puddle of blue.

'What if *we* could taste things with our feet?'

'What would we taste, Freddie?'

'We'd taste socks.'

'I wouldn't like that.'

'Who would?'

'Some people would. Mrs Farley would.'

'What would she say?'

'She'd say, mmm, socks, delicious.'

'Do how she'd say it, Mama, do Mrs Farley speaking.'

This was one of Freddie's favourite things about his mother: she could do Mrs Farley speaking. And not just Mrs Farley; she could do almost everyone on the street speaking and everyone they met in the shops and on the bus and even the people on the television. She could do animal sounds – mouse, kitten, cuckoo, bat, a little bee – and sometimes the sounds of things that weren't even alive, like water poured slowly from a bottle into a tall glass, a steam train, a squeaky door, drains, distant thunder. She could do Donald Duck better than Donald Duck. She could even make it sound like there was a tiny excitable woman trapped inside her belly, begging to get out.

'Go on, Mama, do Mrs Farley speaking.'

So Betty appled her cheeks and peeled her lips, baring as many teeth as she could manage. 'Well it's funny, isn't it, Freddie,' said Mrs Farley in her reedy Midlands twang, far, far back in Betty's throat, 'because it looks like I couldn't be happier, like no one could ever believe how wonderfully excited and jolly I am, but if you look closely, you'll see that my head is always tilted to one side, like I'm thinking you could do with a good wash, and you might notice that my hands are often balled into fists, like I want to punch all sorts of people on the chin.'

Freddie's eyes were as wide as they were wet. 'Mrs Farley, did you know that butterflies can taste things with their feet?'

'Well, yes, I did know that, Freddie, as a matter of fact, because you see I do know most things. But did you know that I can also taste with my feet?'

'No you can't, Mrs Farley.'

'Yes I can. And I can also walk around on my tongue.'

Freddie was now twisted with giggles, rushing a tiny hand to his tiny crotch to still his tickled bladder.

'And stop laughing, boy,' barked Mrs Farley. 'It's bad for your teeth.'

'Do Mr Compton speaking, Mama. What does he say?'

Betty deflated Mrs Farley's chilling rictus and folded it away into Mr Compton's dopey, droopy beagle face. Mr Compton was obviously from somewhere frightfully posh and seemed utterly bewildered to find himself adrift in Betty's body. 'What do I have to say about what, young Frederick?' he said. 'Don't ask me such difficult questions. You know that thinking is not my favourite part of the day.'

'What do you think about this butterfly?'

'What butterfly?'

Freddie rolled his eyes. 'This butterfly on my face that Mama painted.'

Mr Compton pulled in his chin. 'Oh, it's a butterfly, is it? I thought it was a birthmark. I wasn't going to mention it. Didn't want to embarrass you, old chap.'

'How's Mrs Compton?'

'Yes thank you, indeed. Why not?' said Mr Compton, beginning to dribble and flutter his eyelids from thinking too much, it seemed. 'That's most kind of you, I must say. By the way, have you seen my nose? It can do this, look.' Betty stared at Freddie for almost a minute, making Mr Compton's nose do nothing at all. And the more nothing it did, the harder Freddie laughed.

Then came the knock at the door. First the knock and then the knocking. The laughter stopped.

'Do Papa,' said Freddie. 'Do Papa!'

'I can't do Papa. My head's not big enough,' said Betty, and Freddie just couldn't believe his ears, and his mouth opened up so wide that he could have swallowed his own face, so much so that he almost began laughing again, but then the knock came back. Only this time it sounded more like a kick. Papa certainly was impatient sometimes.

Betty set down her brush and sponge and straightened the mirror before smudging a thumb of blue beneath her own eye and licking and sniffing the palm of her hand for last night's gin.

Freddie was already at the door on tiptoe, fumbling with the latch. He could spy his father through the glass of the door:

'Come on, Fred, can't you do it yet? Where's your mother?'

Betty was still taking stock in the mirror. She seemed to have a face that bore solemn report of recent tears, or else forecast the onset of imminent woe. Sometimes she would realise that she was perfectly happy and that there was no need for such a face. At other times, times like right now, for instance, well, it seemed that the face just about fitted the bloody bill.

'Mama, it's Papa, and I can't reach.'

'I'm coming, chicken.'

Before she could hand her son over for the weekend, she needed to know what sort of man was at the door, and so she ushered Freddie up the stairs to finish packing his bag. Dropping the latch burned in her chest, like throwing the safety off a revolver.

There he was, full weight on one leg, one arm raised above his head, gripping the top of the door frame, the other out to the side, fingering the hinge, as though blocking her escape. His T-shirt boasted *Gorganic Records* and pulled down hard over his eyes he wore a grey baseball cap promoting *Sid née Syd*, one of his new artists, no doubt. Behind him, on the other side of the road, a purring red Jaguar with a young woman at the wheel. He'd mentioned her. Friends had mentioned her. She was mentioned in magazines. A thousand hairstyles a week, it seemed. Well there she was, nodding and throwing that apparently beautiful head up down and around in time to something incessant.

Paul sniffed. Not smiling.

'So.' Betty smiled. 'You're early.'

'Not really.'

'We said eleven.'

'You said eleven.'

'You said fine.'

'Fine,' said Paul.

'It's ten.'

'So?'

'So, you're early.'

'Not really.'

She could feel her chapped lip beginning to tremble.

'New car?' she said, keeping things moving along.

'It's Edie's.'

'You're letting her drive?'

'It's her car.'

'Is she old enough?'

And that was the end of that.

'Fred!' he yelled. She could feel the heat of it on her cheek.

'Freddie,' she said.

'Fred, come on.'

'It's on his birth certificate.'

'We're late,' he yelled.

'You're early.'

Freddie fluttered down the stairs, landing on one foot, throwing his arms out to the sides and spinning so that his hair ended up stuck to his beaming blue cheeks.

'What's that?' said Paul.

'What?' said Freddie.

'On your face.'

'My nose,' said Freddie. 'Haven't you seen a nose before?'

18

'Don't be cheeky. Show me.' Paul knocked the hair out of Freddie's eyes.

'It's a pipevine tailswallow.'

'Swallowtail,' said Betty, taking hold of his hand.

'Yes, a swallowpipe tail. . . What is it, Mama?'

'A viper swine tail pipe.'

'Be serious, Mama.'

'We're going to my father's,' said Paul.

'And?' said Betty.

'And look at him.'

She looked at him.

Freddie looked at the ground.

Paul looked at Betty looking at Freddie looking at the ground. Behind them the engine of Edie's red Jaguar kept ticking over.

'Leaving your engine doing that for just one minute . . .' said Betty.

'Don't start.'

'. . . for just one minute produces enough exhaust to fill how many balloons, Freddie?'

'A hundred and fifty.'

'What happened there?' said Paul, stepping forward, taking Betty's face in one hand and turning it into the light of the hallway.

'It's paint,' she said.

'Under that,' pushing his thick thumb into where the cheekbone met the socket, clearing the blue paint in one go. Beneath was a small, livid discoloration.

'I did it getting the bike up from the basement.'

'It's true,' said Freddie, not liking the look of his papa's big thumb.

Paul turned his attention to the hallway behind her and began chewing on something that hadn't been there before. He did that sometimes, chewed on nothing, as though he was fooling anybody. 'Who broke the mirror?'

'I did,' said Betty.

'How?'

'What's it got to do with you? Can I have some gum?'

Paul crouched down to look his son in the eye. Freddie flinched, clearly unaccustomed to such a manoeuvre. 'Fred, look at me.'

'I am looking at you.'

'How was the mirror broken?'

Freddie's chin began to quiver. Then his eyes began to sink beneath a brimming pool of tears. Then his cheeks burned so hot and red that his lovely blue butterfly turned puce. 'Sean did it, with his head.'

With this Paul sprang back up and pushed past them both to take a closer look at the splintered glass. There was blood in the cracks. For fuck's sake, there was even a dyed black hair. Betty pulled her son close into her lap, baffling his ears with the soft wool of her cardigan. The man she had once loved, who had loved her in return, was now inside the flat, kicking anything in his path to the other end of the hall: bags, boots, wooden trucks, piles of magazines, balls, books, and then on, into the living room, more bags, smaller bags, bigger boots, beer cans and bottles, cushions, cloths, odd socks, broken candles, fag packets, a clock, a plastic trumpet, a rolled note, a photo of feet. '*Exactly!*' he shouted, and '*Fucking perfect!*' then on and round and up the stairs, Betty and Freddie following, Freddie in Betty's arms by now, his wet face bleeding blue onto her hot neck, and on into the bedroom, one leg of the bed broken, causing it to list to one side, drunken lamps leaning back, underpants on top of the radio, lipstick on the window, pot plant with a wig, Paul throwing open the battered doors of the plywood wardrobe, men's shirts and jackets cowering in the dark, yanked out by the scruff of the neck. 'I fucking knew it!'

'Don't.'

'He's moved in, hasn't he?'

'Stop it.'

'Hasn't he? The twat's moved in!'

'He just stays sometimes.'

'Liar!'

'Let's not do this in front of Freddie.'

He picked up a broken stool. 'Was this done in front of Freddie?'

'No.'

He kicked the bed, breaking the other leg. 'Was this?'

'No!'

She held the shivering boy tight, one arm round his back, the other under his bottom, legs bending at the knee, clinging on between calf and thigh. Paul was coming in, one hand on Freddie's shoulder bone, scratching his neck, the other across his panting belly, pulling, squashing him. Her hand against his spine, tears and spit running to her breast, fingers pressed into buttocks. Paul tugging at his hip, the other hand now in his ribs. Betty beginning to let go, for fear of tearing the boy in half. Freddie clinging on, terrified, as if in open water, fingers clutching. The waves closing over. Paul in full possession now, hissing, twisting, blowing down the door, barging the walls out of the way, kicking the floor down the stairs, holding the child in front of the bloody broken mirror. 'Was this?'

'No.'

'Was this done in front of you?' he asked Freddie. 'Did you see Sean do this?'

'Paul, for God's sake!'

He put the boy down, then pointing him at the purring red Jaguar and patting his wet behind he screamed, 'Go!' and beautiful Edie, alerted by the commotion in the doorway, sprang out of her warm car to meet the poor soul halfway. 'Get that paint off him,' yelled Paul. Edie, grinning in oblivion, scooped the boy up in her tattooed arms and swung him round, and, feeling perhaps, at last, a way to shore, Freddie let her. She pulled open the back door and ushered him inside, where he climbed up onto the smelly leather and stretched himself out, staring at the soft white ceiling, stricken, as though electrocuted.

Shaken by his own rage, his chest swelling for want of full breath, Paul turned back to Betty and managed to utter, 'You've lost him.'

Betty's nose was bleeding. 'You can't.'

'How many warnings have I given you?'

'You can't.'

'It's over.'

'Paul.'

'I'm doing it.'

'Please, I—'

'I don't have a choice.'

She began to crash her head into the hardest part of her fist.

He said nothing more. It wasn't the first time he'd seen this; it was what remained of their love. This was the sound.

And then, just as it seemed that chaos had had enough of both of them, a tall, black-haired man in tight grey jeans and hobnailed boots came speeding down the street and, in attempting to dismount Betty's bicycle while maintaining a basket filled with popcorn and lager, smashed into a neighbour's ornamental wall, fell off to one side and skidded on his leather elbows nearly two feet across the wet pavement.

'Perfect timing,' said Paul as he watched Sean Porter, with a bloody nose of his own, scuttle about on the cold stone, eager to gather all his bags and cans together, the wheels of the bicycle still spinning.

'What's going on?' said Sean.

'Have you moved in?' said Paul.

'What's it got to do with you?'

'If you think you're living in the same house as my son, that has a lot to do with me.'

'Sean, go inside,' said Betty.

'Your nose is bleeding,' said Sean, finally making it to his feet.

'So is yours,' she said, wiping her own on the cuff of her cardigan. She looked out across the street to see Edie, leaning over into the back seat of the car, scrubbing at Freddie's face with what looked like an old glove. 'What's she doing?'

'She's wiping that muck off his fucking face.'

'His fucking face? That's how you describe your son?'

'What's happened?' said Sean.

'Never mind, love,' said Betty. 'Just walk away. Paul, tell her to stop doing that. She looks like she's hurting him.'

'I told you weeks ago,' said Paul. 'If this cunt moves in, you're not seeing your son. Your son will be taken away from you.'

'By who?'

'By me.'

'Don't call me a cunt, Paul,' said Sean.

'Don't call me Paul.'

'What should I call you?'

'Don't call me anything. Don't even address me.'

'Don't even address you? Fucking hell. It's the Pope.'

'Sean,' said Betty, 'I don't need your help.'

'You heard her,' said Paul. 'She doesn't need any help from a thick cunt like you.'

And so Sean smashed Paul smack in the middle of his face with a cold can of San Miguel, his cap flying off into a nearby bush. Paul, half blinded, lashed out with a backhander at Sean's dyed black head, but, failing to rattle his adversary, was met with that very head coming back at him like a wrecking ball, bending Paul's favourite two teeth against the roof of his mouth.

And that was it. Off they both went, down onto the puddled kerb, splashing and kicking. Next door's window thrown up and open; marching music on the television; a gummy old face in a vest; coughing; a bulldog leaping out, snapping at the skirmish like a crazed referee. Paul, desperate for his son not to see his father's bloody, sobbing face stamped hard against an iron grid by the heel of a drunkard's dirty boot, called out across the street, 'Go! Go!' and Edie, her eyes blazing with guilt and panic, revved the engine.

Betty leapt out through the gate, jumping over the heap of men. 'Don't you fucking dare!'

And Freddie's face against the tinted glass, his screech trebled by the screech of the tyres, 'Papa, stop it, stop it, Sean! Mama, no, Mama!'

'Stop!' howled Betty. It echoed against the street's cold bricks, so that the whole hellish city could hear. She was almost upon the car when suddenly it shot away, like a startled animal, snarling, furious, never coming back. She raced to the other side of the street, snatched up the bicycle and pedalled until she thought her legs would break, the sound of the wrestling men and the marching music fading with every block. Clattering through red lights and screaming horns, the car speeding further and further away, smaller and smaller, until it was almost nothing at all, a scarlet dot, a droplet, gone, thrown around a corner. And the silence then, save for her heartbeat and breath. Save for the lingering clamour of Freddie's fear and the black rubber wheels rolling on the wet asphalt until the city tipped over and she fell.

CHAPTER 3

It was peculiar, this thing that Jack Drake was doing; anyone would have thought so, but somehow he couldn't bring himself to do anything other than this. He was sitting in his mother's old bedroom, which had recently been converted into his editing suite; on the desk were three large monitors hooked up to various hubs and terminals. From this set-up he was able to edit audio samples from a multitude of sources: films, TV and radio drama, home movies, phone calls, interviews. He then assigned any one of these samples to a specific note upon the electronic keyboard situated to the left of his desk, so that with enough skill, imagination and wanton desperation, he was able to form new, never-before-spoken sentences – and that was how he managed to bring his dear Martha's voice back to life. And as if all this were not peculiar enough, he saw fit to perform this near miracle beneath the heedful gaze of Martha's artfully decapitated silicone head, which she had been gifted after playing Anne Boleyn in a production of *Anne of a Thousand Days* at the Royal National Theatre in 1998.

It would have been a great success were it not for the fact that most of the time it left him feeling hollow and perverse. When all was considered, Martha felt further away than ever.

'Don't worry,' said Martha, for example, in her native San Franciscan, a snippet of consolation lifted from a short film shot in Palermo in the mid nineties. This was middle C.

'Jack,' said Martha. Easy enough to find on any number of voicemails. F sharp.

'I'll never leave you,' this originally spoken to a cat in a forgettable adaptation of *The Maltese Falcon* in 2010. San Francisco again. E flat.

And hence, 'Don't worry – Jack – I'll never leave you,' an exquisitely crafted, consistently accented, well-modulated untruth created to evoke a sense of . . . what? Indeed.

To stitch together something more substantial with anything approaching a narrative – with nuance, revelation, contradiction and wit – could take an entire week and require the virtuoso fingering of Franz Liszt, and so it was often the case that Jack settled for an old movie – Martha taking a swim or a shower – or a simple voicemail from recent history; for example:

'Jack, I've just landed. I'm walking to the car. Has it been raining like this the whole time? Anyway, I'll see you in about an hour, darling. I love you.'

Well, maybe not so recent.

He turned his head to her head, wishing her styling were not quite so Tudor. He'd tried kissing it a few weeks ago, but that had not been his finest moment and he'd almost put it back in its box. He returned to the screen where her living face was paused: an Italian film in which she'd played an embittered nun. He could recall a day of burning in the ruins of an eleventh-century convent on the outskirts of Florence, Martha miserable in her heavy black cotton costume, trapped beneath the blazing lights and loathing the director for his delusional passion for his slender allegory.

'Don't worry – Jack – my darling – I'll never leave you – I promise.' Brief soft laughter perhaps, and then, 'I'll always

– love you.' No, no. Now it sounded morbidly remote. But he couldn't turn it off. He couldn't pull the little plug. How else would this accursed film of his be finished if he didn't somehow hang on to her increasingly cold hand? It wouldn't. And that was unthinkable.

He stretched himself out upon the floor and stared at the ceiling, as his mother must have done for countless years after the death of his father. High on the white wall, above where his mother's bed had once stood, was a modest bronze and hickory crucifix, its poor Christ looking as if he were about to sneeze. He'd tried talking to that in his time, but found it too tiny to take seriously.

His mother's bed had been carried off by the art department to store up in the attic, until Eve Parnell, the actress playing her, requested that it be moved into her dressing room so that in her down time she could lie upon it and immerse herself in the residual aura of Eleanor Drake. Eve was also keen to wear as many of his mother's original clothes as possible – this, as she was too fond of boasting, did not preclude underwear. Jack, after some initial scruples, had given his permission. She'd then asked for the privilege of her actual wedding ring, but Jack would not hear of it. He told her his mother's ring had been passed to Martha, who'd worn it right up to the day of her death. When Eve asked where it was now, he claimed not to know. He told her it was an awful mystery, since the left hand had never been found.

There were no further questions.

He closed his eyes to see how far Martha had drifted. Deeper and deeper into the shadows, it seemed. He could glimpse only the side-lit parts of her: a fading shoulder; a turning cheek; a flash of her bright mouth whispering, then dimming, her breast rising and falling, her feet in water. When he opened his eyes, Nora Flynn was standing over him with her notebook and pen.

'We have a problem,' she said, and took a seat next to the head, which didn't seem to bother her at all.

'Thank God for that,' said Jack.

'Conrad Ripley has walked off the picture.'

'Oh.'

'I mean for real this time, no doubt about it. And don't say he can't . . .'

'He can't.'

'. . . because apparently he absolutely and definitely can. He's finally out of contract, after all the delays with . . .' and she nodded at Martha's head.

'He's using that?' said Jack.

'He's saying he can't work with you.'

'He hasn't *worked* with me. He hasn't *worked* with anyone. I don't know what the fuck he's been doing. No one told me he was a drunk.'

'*I* told you.'

'You said he liked a drink, not that he couldn't stand up after four o'clock. It's the worst decision I ever made.'

'Well, he's walked.'

'Well, good, let him walk. I'm surprised he can. We'll find someone else, someone better, someone cleaner, thinner. Someone who looks more like my father.'

Nora consulted her notebook. 'Joseph Doriss is going to be available.'

'Who the hell's Joseph Doriss?'

'He was mentioned early on, but he was busy. You liked him. You said he had the look.'

'*Does* he have the look?'

'He has *a* look. Looks a bit like Dirk Bogarde.'

'Joseph who?'

'Doriss.'

'I don't remember him,' said Jack.

'He's in a play at the Court. I've read one or two passable reviews. It finishes Saturday.'

'Well, let's go see him.'

Nora pressed the low D on the keyboard and the room was filled with the sound of Martha softly sobbing. She moved behind Jack and rested her hands upon his shoulders.

'Should I be worrying about you, Jack?' she said.

'I'm fine, Nora, thank you. Everything's going to plan.'

'We could just not carry on, you know.'

Jack looked up at the sneezing Jesus. 'I know.'

She removed her hands from his shoulders. 'I meant with the film.'

'Oh.'

'It's not too late.'

'Yes it is, Nora. It's far too late,' said Jack. 'And I don't know why.'

CHAPTER 4

Upon hearing of Betty's recent troubles, her father, Harold Dean, expressed little concern, distracted as he was by the ravages of a recent stroke that had closed one eye and considerably reduced the number of fucks he could give. A silent man for much of his life, he had now completely lost the power of speech – though 'power' seemed a fancy word for anything he'd ever possessed in the first place.

Ruth, three years older and two inches shorter than her sister, had been lumbered with navigating their father's cumbersome chair across the puddled potholes of the Whitechapel Road as they headed east to Shanty's Pharmacy to buy pads, cloths and germicidal grease.

Clearly this was not a day when Betty had given any thought to how she might appear to the outside world. Her hair was high and tangled by a night of fevered scratching. She'd accused Sean of giving her lice and he'd accused her of giving him a stye; a rambling confrontation had ensued, mollified only by a midnight trip to the fridge for what was left of the rum. Then they'd squabbled about whether or not rum should be kept in the fridge. Another fifteen minutes passed trying to rebalance the bed on its broken legs, until they propped it up on two piles of books. Eventually Sean fell asleep and Betty tried to call Paul four times, twice on his mobile, once on the home number and once at his studio. Each time she left messages she doubted he would understand, drowned as they were in the wet acoustics of her sobbing. She crept downstairs and looked out onto the road for an hour and smoked three cigarettes, even though she'd given up four nights ago. She cleared some space on the sofa and slept for maybe three minutes before being woken by the sound of a helicopter, and later by Mrs Mason coughing behind the wall, which set off Mr Thackery's dog, which must have woken Sean, because after that the radio switched on upstairs and it was all Blind Willie, Blind Lemon, Furry Lewis, Howlin' Wolf, all 'My woman done left me', and 'I woke up this morning', which would have been fine if she'd ever managed to get any fucking sleep in the first place. And then the sun came up like a blister and it was half seven, so she tried Paul again, hoping to catch Freddie before he left for school, but both phones just rang out.

This had been happening all week and it was getting to the point where she was going to have to go round, but Sean told her to drop it and now Ruth was saying that the very worst thing she could do was turn up at the school. That it would be too confusing, too heartbreaking for Freddie.

'Well I should think it's confusing and heartbreaking not to be able to speak to his mother for all this time. It's never been like this, Ruth. It's never been as cruel as this.'

'I know, darling.'

'So what do you think I should do, if I don't do that? You're literally saying do nothing.'

'I'm not saying that.' Ruth caught sight of herself in a car window. A poncho and a beret were a lousy idea. What had she been thinking?

'Well I don't know what else you're saying. You're no help.'

And Betty went up her sleeve for a fresh ball of kitchen roll, scraping it over and over across her nostrils. All the way from Ruth's front door she'd had to breathe through her mouth, her lips lolling open, plump and slippy, like a baby, not even minding if she dribbled. Now she had to cling onto the back of her father's chair for fear her legs might give way from so much drama.

'Are you all right?' said Ruth, making sure her dad wasn't slipping down and thinking of something to say to Betty that wouldn't just provoke more waterworks. They should both try being Ruth once in a while; that wasn't exactly a breeze either.

'Course I'm not all right,' said Betty.

'I don't know, it's hard to tell with you.'

'What does that mean?'

'Well, you know . . . actresses.'

'Oh fuck off if that's it,' shrieked Betty, and trotted off up ahead, just far enough to look like she wasn't with them, but not so far that she couldn't come back to borrow some money for fags if they passed a shop, even though she'd given up again after the three she smoked last night. 'I can't fucking believe you sometimes,' she shouted back, into the wind. 'This is an emergency.'

'Don't swear in front of Dad,' said Ruth.

'Fuck Dad,' she said. Then, 'Sorry, Dad,' and then, 'if you can hear me.'

'The problem is,' said Ruth, 'you should never have let Sean move in.'

'He hasn't moved in,' said Betty, stopping.

'Well, he has.' Now they both stopped, and Harold started slipping down.

'Only since you've had Dad to look after. When I'm finished at the theatre, he won't need to be there.'

Without looking, Ruth hooked her hands under her father's armpits and heaved him up. 'Does Paul know?' she said.

'Does Paul know what?'

'That Sean's been looking after Freddie.'

'No, he thinks you have.'

Ruth kicked the chair back in line and set off walking, faster now. 'Well, don't ask me to lie for you if he calls me.'

'Has he called you?'

'No, but I'm just saying that if he does . . .'

'Well, don't go making it worse.'

'I'll make it worse if I lie. Doesn't he know what's happened to Dad?'

'Of course he knows.'

'But does he know he's out of hospital?'

Betty looked down at her father, as though she'd only just realised this herself. 'No.'

'So when he hears that Dad's out of hospital and that I'm looking after him, and he knows that you're at the theatre every night, then he's gonna presume, rightly, that Sean is looking after Freddie and he's gonna go fucking nuts, Betty. So don't involve me by getting me to lie.'

'Have I asked you to lie?'

'And he's gonna find out from Freddie anyway, unless you've asked Freddie to lie, which you probably have.'

'No I fucking have not. And I haven't asked you. Have I, have I asked you?'

'No, but if he calls me . . .'

'Fucking hell, all right, make things worse then, Ruth.' And Betty folded her arms, twelve again, and spun around to look in the nearest window, which, brilliantly, was filled with toys.

'I'm not making things worse,' said Ruth.

'Well, you're not making them better.'

'It's not my job to make things better. Why's that my job?'

'I didn't say it was your job.'

'I don't even have a job right now. I'm turning pupils away.' Ruth taught Hammond organ and yoga, sometimes to the same people, sometimes on the same day, in the same room, but that had become impractical recently with Harold slumped in the corner reminding them all how futile and forlorn were their attempts to elevate themselves.

From somewhere in the depths, poor Harold emitted a rare sonorous grunt. Ruth, kicking on the brake, took a tissue from her pocket and wiped his glossy chin from behind.

'This is my job now, doing this sort of thing; and this is nothing compared to some of the things I've had to do the past three weeks. You don't even want to know.'

Betty looked over her shoulder before turning back the whole way. Her father's face terrified her.

'It's all right for you,' said Ruth, 'swanning off every night, thinking you're just great. Everyone clapping how fucking great you think you are.'

'Swanning? It's my job. I'm a professional actress. That's what I do.'

'And that's what I'm saying – that's your job, and this is mine. And it's fucking excellent, isn't it, Dad?' said Ruth, leaning over her father so that he could see her upside down, scaring him. 'And aren't I fucking good at it, Dad?' Her beret fell into his lap and he snatched it up, throwing it into a nearby doorway. Betty smiled, bent over, picked it up and settled it tenderly back on her sister's head.

'I'm sorry,' she said, but Ruth didn't think she was and so didn't smile and thought to herself that a lot of the time Betty couldn't act for toffee.

They continued on in silence. Eventually Betty spoke up, offering a new tone. 'There's only another week to go with

34

this play,' she said, 'then that's it. I've got nothing after that. I'm unemployed, again. I'll be able to help.'

'No you won't, 'cos you'll be too busy with all this shit. The thing is, Betty, I think he's got a point.'

'What the fuck do you mean by that?'

'I mean he's got a point. I wouldn't want Sean looking after my kid.'

'You don't have a kid.'

Ruth took a moment to resist getting into a whole new fight. She let it go. 'All right, I wouldn't want a fuck-up like Sean looking after *this* kid,' she said, nodding at their father.

'So now you're on Paul's side? He let that bitch drive Freddie away at ninety miles an hour. She went through two red lights.'

'You told me Sean was stamping on his head. What was she supposed to do? Let Freddie see a thing like that?'

'Have you seen her on the cover of that magazine? She's wearing a plasticine fucking bra.'

'I'm surprised Paul's not pressing charges.'

'God, you love Paul. Why don't you go and live with him? Marry him?' They were right outside the chemist's now, blocking the door, putting off other customers.

'I'm just saying, I think he's got a point,' said Ruth.

'He doesn't have the right to take Freddie away from me. 'Cos that's what we're talking about here,' said Betty, struggling for breath now. 'He's not fucking about, Ruth, he's seriously talking about taking him away, proper, for good. Like that's it. Like I'd never see him again. Doing it in court, moving abroad. His label's bought offices in New York. He reckons that's what he could do, and I don't know that he couldn't.'

'Well, get rid of Sean,' said Ruth, turning the wheelchair around and entering the chemist's backwards, pushing the door open with her bum.

35

'No! No, I won't get rid of Sean. I don't have to do whatever you and Paul tell me to do.'

'Oh Betty, you're willing to jeopardise being with your son because you won't admit to yourself what everyone else can see for a fact.' Ruth and the chair and the bags and Harold were all the way in and the door began to close. 'That Sean Porter is a complete fucking arsehole.'

Betty stayed outside, gazing at a plastic leg in the window. It wore a grey sock and a brown shoe. She thought of butterflies tasting things with their feet. She turned to look out over the road at the enormous blue hospital rising up from the bones of the old Georgian hospital where she'd been born and where, thirteen years later, her mother had died. First she smelled and then she saw half a cigarette, half squashed but still smouldering, on the pavement outside the bookies. She picked it up, looked at it, squinting, as though assessing its vintage, before sucking it all the way down to the filter in one go.

CHAPTER 5

                    YOUNG JACK
What's wrong with Dad?

                    ELEANOR
He's sleeping.

                    YOUNG JACK
He's not in your bedroom.

                    ELEANOR
No.

                    YOUNG JACK
I knocked. There was no answer.

                    ELEANOR
He's in the end bedroom.

                    YOUNG JACK
I knocked. There was no answer.

                    ELEANOR
Well, he's sleeping, sweetheart.

                    YOUNG JACK
        He didn't look like he was sleeping.

                     ELEANOR
        You went in?

                    YOUNG JACK
        That room smells awful.

'Cut!' shouted Jack, taking off his headphones.

Eve Parnell looked around as though woken from a dream, theatrically unsettled to be called out of the scene. She set a large red leather-bound Bible down on the table, dug her fingers under the stiff seam of her pregnancy bump and yanked it a little further to the left.

Jack walked over and took her softly by the arm, his mouth close to her ear. 'Don't call him sweetheart,' he whispered.

'No?' said Eve, softly.

'No. My mother would never have called me sweetheart.'

'OK.'

Jack smiled and let go of her arm, keeping his voice low. 'I know it's just the wide, but . . .'

'No, it's fine.'

'It's the wrong . . . Remember how recently she . . . It's not as if she's comfortable with . . .'

'Not at all comfortable. Horrified.'

'Completely horrified. Certainly at the beginning. I mean, she wasn't . . .'

'Used to . . . any of . . .'

'. . . a sociopath. She wasn't a sociopath.'

'No, not at all. Do you think I'm . . .?'

'Let's go again.'

'Jack?'

'Yes?'

                        38

'Does the parrot have to be in the room for this?'

'This is the room he was in.'

'I know, but . . .'

'Let's go again.' He gave her hand a light squeeze and walked over to Billy.

Billy was thirteen but looked ten. He was playing Young Jack, who had been twelve at the time but looked more like nine. There was something in his face, something bewildered and morose, that reminded Jack of the good old days. He was a fine young actor and didn't really know it, which was perfect. Jack rested his hand gently on Billy's shoulder and spoke softly. 'When you say it smells awful in there, don't do too much. Don't pull a face. Do almost nothing. You're not . . . you don't know yet that . . .'

'That he's dead,' said Billy.

'Yes, that comes later. For now you just think your mother's behaving a bit oddly.'

'Something's not right?'

'It's called dramatic irony. Let's go again, all the way to the end this time.'

Solomon requested another flag be placed between the table and the window. Laura, on boom, redirected her cables to the other side of the track. Billy's mother, Phyllis, was lurking in the shadows, nibbling a Ryvita, edging ever closer to one of the carpenters. It didn't matter which one – she liked them all. After Lil from costume was happy with Eve's bump, and Vladimir, the parrot, had been pacified, Charles called for quiet, synchronised camera and sound, took the nod from Jack and, in a calm, assured and well-modulated Cornish accent, said: 'Action.'

CHAPTER 6

'Paul, it's me. I'm gonna try to get through this without crying, and I'm definitely not going to shout or insult you, so please keep listening. I don't know if you listened to any of my other messages – I've left about ten now – and maybe you don't care and just deleted them, since I know a few of them started off not the best – too angry – and I hope you might, after all this time, understand why that might be the case. And yes, some of them, particularly the ones at night, might have been a little drunk – well, there's no "might" about it – and were perhaps a little nastier than they needed to be. But you know, we all like a drink now and then. You like a drink now and then, you're no saint, and I see in the papers that your new lady likes a drink now and then, we all do, especially when things aren't going so well, and sometimes when things might be going wonderfully well, and perhaps that's the case with your new lady, Edie – I'll call her Edie and be respectful, since I know that's her name. She seems to be everywhere right now, so well done, and I don't mean that in a bitchy way, and yes, I have been reading all about her, and not in a stalky way, but because as far as I understand, my son, our son, Freddie, is spending more of his waking hours in her company right now than in the company of his mother, and that can't be right, can it, Paul? Can it? Anyway, I'm not going to go on about her. This isn't really about her, but you take my point. My point is: just imagine how that might be making me feel. How you felt about Sean and Freddie, and now you're doing the same thing, the other way round. I'm not saying that she's moved in, and maybe she hasn't moved in, I don't know. I'm sure she's got a lovely house of her own, with all the money she must be making, so well done, and maybe you've moved in there, but you better not have done, because I'm assuming that I'd know where to find my son if I just decided to come round to get him. Not that I'm saying I'm coming round to get him. I do admit that I waited outside your house a few nights ago, but then I pulled it together and realised that wasn't the best sort of thing to be doing and that if you caught me there, there might be a scene, and that if Freddie had seen me there in the bushes, it might have freaked him out. I'm joking, by the way. I wasn't really in the bushes. You don't have bushes. But then again, I didn't see you, and I didn't even see any lights on, so maybe you have moved into hers, but I can't imagine that you'd have done that, and where is that anyway? I can't imagine it's anywhere near the school. Paul, come on, it's been over a week now, and I know you hate me, but it's just fucking cruel to keep this up. Sorry for saying fuck, but . . . fuck, it's cruel to Freddie, so forget about me, it's not about me. It's about Freddie and what he must be thinking. What are you telling him? He must be asking, so what are you saying? What is *she* saying? Does she try to explain that sort of stuff to him? I fucking hope not. Sorry again. I know nothing about her apart from what I see, and I can't say that I like what I see. I don't mean that in a bad way, but she seems a bit . . . Anyway, I won't say it, and she must obviously be doing something right to be doing so well for herself, unlike me, who's not. Not really. I'm fine. Anyway,

I'm rambling, and I've got to go. I'm at work and they've called the half and I still haven't got my costume on. It's the last night. It's a shame, 'cos you never came to see it, and I think you might have liked it actually, Paul, despite everything. It's right up your street. I play five different parts, and Ruth says it's the best thing I've ever done. And Dad's out of the hospital, so that's good. Well, it's not good, it's fucking awful, but anyway, you don't want to hear about that, not now, anyway. Paul, I'm gonna go. I have to. But please call me back, or at least call me back and put Freddie on so that I can explain to him why he can't see me at the moment. And lots of love to you, and your new lady. Edie; I'll call her Edie. What does Freddie call her? It's funny, 'cos her name is hidden inside his. I don't like that. I don't like any of this. Does he like her? Does she make him laugh? Does she? Does she make him laugh? Does he like her? I don't like her. I fucking hate her. I think she's a cunt. I think you're both cunts. Sorry, I've got to go.'

CHAPTER 7

The crew had been given the weekend off and the house was deserted – save for Jack, who had spent the day alone, sleeping till eleven. He passed the afternoon drifting in and out of rooms. He stared into the eyes of half-remembered portraits – a brigadier general in gold epaulettes, a smiling duchess with a canary, a leering cardinal. In the green-walled vestibule he found the portrait of a young girl he had once loved, and though she had lived far away – upon a mountain apparently, in another century – it was to her he would nightly unburden his soul. Yes, the house now, and even back then, seemed to him a vast and ominous repository of fitful spirits.

In the sixties his father had been a considerable cheese at the BBC, a producer of arts documentaries. Sir Huw Wheldon had been a dear friend. David Attenborough, Alistair Cooke, John Schlesinger were all regular visitors. Orson Welles had once spent the night on the library floor. Young Jack had sneaked in to watch him snore and with tiny trembling hands stolen the stub of the great man's cigar. He still had it and kept it in a small Victorian tulipwood jewellery box at his house in France. His father had had a passion for arcane curiosities, and while it was he who had given the house its character, the money was Eleanor's, or rather her father's: he had made his fortune importing luxury rugs and ceramics from North Africa.

Besides the easy wealth, she also inherited her father's religious zeal, born of unreasonable fear. Or at least that was Jack's theory, since her faith seemed to have brought her so little comfort: she used to spend almost as much time on her knees as on her feet, never letting her blood-red leather-bound Bible out of her sight. She had kept a modest black wooden rosary in every room of the house, even the larder; Jack could see one of them now, dangling from a golden nail to the left of the painting of the girl on the mountain. To its right was a framed black-and-white photograph of his father arm in arm with the composer Leonard Bernstein.

Over, under, in between and within all this history sat the prosaic and often brutish apparatus of the cinema. With everyone gone, the clamour of the living set had given way to the low buzz of bulbs and the gulp of plumbing. Every floor was now patrolled by these dormant machines: the snuffed lights, the microphones still listening in their sleep; the camera hunched beneath a black sheet; the screens and speakers; the padded banisters; the yellow ladders; the never-ending serpentine wires winding in and out of rooms, lurking in knotted piles next to steel boxes, their red lights blinking, as though the whole building were on life support. All Jack had here, now, in his parents' ill-fated home, was a creaking brass bed and six suitcases filled with clothes, books and whatever else had not been sold from his and Martha's Kensington house to afford the telling of this lamentable tale. This elaborate exorcism.

It's the first time I've been out for months, thought Jack, as he made his way towards St John Street in search of a taxi. March had been the month of Martha's breakdown. April took her away. Dull roots, dried tubers, all that. Back then he'd walked around Clerkenwell after dark – long after dark – the small hours, as they were known for some reason, but for Jack they had lumbered, enormous and dense, like pulling a hundred black rubber tyres through the twisting city streets. He had not wanted to see people. He had no taste for the shape of things and so he walked the back alleys, the narrowest passages, lest he catch a glimpse of a lighted window, and the life there inside. But then, gathering courage, he'd walk out to Smithfield to watch them heaving the stinking carcasses from the trucks. The thick smell of it down there, right by Snow Hill, where they'd drawn and quartered poor William Wallace's corpse, and sometimes a slow walk, through St Bart's hospital courtyard and down to St Paul's, down to the river to sit beneath the bridge and listen to the water grind to a standstill. Why had his father not thought of the water?

'It's the first time I've been out for months,' he said.

'We've been out on location,' said Nora, as they climbed the stairs to the Circle Bar.

'I mean out like this. Washed and combed.'

Nora glanced at what she could see of his hair and his mangled beard. 'And how does it feel?' she said.

'Like a fucking film set. Just look at them all. This would never happen in real life.'

He was wearing his hat for the first time this year. Martha had never approved of it and thought it a grand affectation. She had accused him of aping Bertolucci, and yes, it was true that he had once dined with the Maestro in Venice and had spent an agreeable evening comparing ailments, and it was shortly after that that the hat, a navy Borsalino, had first appeared. Besides this he wore a grey wool jacket, white shirt and a striped green-and-gold tie, which he imagined to be rather schoolboyish, a little Hockney perhaps, though his spectacles leaned more towards Eliot or Joyce. The black cashmere overcoat had been stolen, many years ago, from the private wardrobe of Peter O'Toole. Nora, for her part, had shown up in a green cape and knee-length chestnut boots. Her grey hair worn down for once and her large thick-rimmed spectacles giving her, Jack thought, the appearance of a paler, more provincial Annie Leibovitz.

'You look rather fetching,' said Jack.

'Really?' said Nora, sardonic and nonchalant, though privately charmed, for she cherished such crumbs. 'You too.'

She had purchased the programme, so that she could remind Jack of what he had once considered promising in the face of Joseph Doriss. Jack had glanced briefly at the posters outside and had not been encouraged. He was already regretting having made such a sartorial effort, since he did not now foresee remaining beyond the interval.

'You didn't say it was *The Devils*,' he said.

'Have you seen other productions?'

'No, but I know Ken Russell's film.'

'You didn't like it?'

'I thought it was the best thing Ken ever did, but I'm not sure I want to see a litter of millennial hipsters desecrate the memory.'

'Joseph Doriss is forty-two; he's hardly a millennial.'

'Well, I'm sure it'll be a splendid night out for a good Catholic boy.'

'I'm sure it will,' said Nora. 'Do you know where we can find one?'

Jack took off his hat and messed up his hair. 'What do you want to drink?'

'Red wine. Organic if they've got it.' And she wandered off to find a shelf to lean on.

Jack struggled to claim a place at the bar and found himself wedged between a woman who reeked of cheap primrose and a tall, intoxicated scruff with a bruised face and what looked like a small white pillow feather lodged in the back of his dyed black hair.

'Mr Drake?' enquired a sweating mustachioed baby of a man, suddenly making an appearance on Jack's left. 'Is it Mr Drake, the film-maker?'

'It is,' said Jack, and continued pushing his way to the front of the queue.

'I'm a great admirer of your work, Mr Drake. I've seen almost everything.'

'Well, you've seen more than me,' said Jack. The man had to think about this and looked for a moment like he might go away, but then he was struck with new inspiration.

'Are you working on anything at the moment?'

'Yes, I'm trying to get noticed by this barman.'

'Ah yes, marvellous,' chuckled the man, nodding his baby's head frantically up and down. 'I meant a new film.'

'Oh, I see,' said Jack, and took a small step back to tread on the man's foot. 'I'm terribly sorry, sir.'

'Oh, that's all right. I'm honoured.'

Jack looked around for Nora, who was sitting on a stool immersed in the programme. The final bell rang out and the bar began to clear.

'So?' said the man.

'So what?'

'Anything new?'

'Excuse me,' said Jack, giving up on the drink and making his way over to Nora.

'I was sorry to hear about your wife, Mr Drake.'

Jack carried on walking.

'I met her once. She was delightful. Poor woman. And poor you, Mr Drake.'

★

47

For the next two hours, without interval, Joseph Doriss was Urbain Grandier, a seventeenth-century French priest accused of witchcraft and calling upon Satan to stage the corruption and abuse of a convent of Ursuline nuns, who were consequently thrust – torn and bloody wimples first – into a turbulent procession of religiously ecstatic orgies, torture, sodomy, cruciform rape and forced enemas. Heretics were stretched, hunchbacked nuns pissed into the orchestra pit, and Joseph Doriss was stripped, shaved, flayed and throttled and his broken, naked body burned at the stake. At which point, against a Boschian backcloth of burning villages, a howling nun was strung up on a gallows built from human bones and lifted high into the air, her veil seemingly steaming beneath the blazing lights of the gallery. She then plunged to the ground at such terrifying speed, and with such a sickening dead thump as she smashed into the boards, that the entire audience gasped for fear something might have gone wrong. But then, in the next moment, the raving nun scrambled to her feet, wriggled out of her noose, tore off her habit, and wrapped her horribly scarred naked body around the bleeding, burning priest as though she were going to devour him.

At this point, something strange happened. A few rows in front of Jack, the intoxicated scruff with the bruised face and the dyed black hair stood up in his seat and began gesticulating towards the stage and cursing, though it was difficult to hear him above the pounding industrial din and deafening hysteria blasting out. In attempting to climb over the legs of his neighbours, the man fell flat on his face, wedging himself between their knees and the backs of the seats in front. After a little commotion he reappeared and continued his journey, still agitated, still cursing. On stage, the priest was cooking nicely, thanks to the novel use of spinning scrims and back projection, as several other nuns gathered at his blackened feet, fondling

48

and slobbering. The black-haired clown finally made it to the end of the row; he slumped heavily against the exit door, which gave way, swallowing him whole.

The audience, momentarily distracted by this drunken slapstick, resumed their enjoyment of the artfully staged immolation. It was then – as the flames died down and the unearthly glow of the distant conflagration faded – that a solitary nun, the same nun who had dangled so convincingly from the rope, now re-dressed in a clean white habit, was picked out in a fixed spotlight, looking as if, after all the lunacy and filth, she were the last pure thing left on earth. As she began to softly sing, a flickering shadow fell upon her delicate face, and in that solemn moment, Jack was transported.

For there in the diffused beam, like the Blessed Mother in Titian's annunciation, was Martha. Only Martha.

And as Jack waited for the moment to pass, knowing that it was a cruel trick of the light, the moment did not pass, but rather sustained and grew ever more intense, until it felt as if it would never end and the entire theatre might be drifting off into deadly space. Those were Martha's eyes, Martha's lips, and it was Martha's voice singing so softly this aching lament. The last light dimmed and the song faded and the silence settled as the curtain gently landed. And when it lifted again, and all the actors joined hands, sweaty and breathless, grinning and bowing, there she was, the pale young woman who had just now brought Jack, trembling, to the edge of his soul. She was the only one not smiling.

'Well, goodness me,' said Nora, sinking her second glass of Prosecco in Joseph Doriss's dressing room. 'What a business. And that's a true story?'

'Apparently,' said Doriss, still half naked, his wet bald head glistening in the light, too close to the ceiling.

He'll never do, thought Jack. Far too tall. The man's a brute. Eve could never carry him.

'And that girl, the nun at the end, plummeting from the ceiling,' said Nora. 'Crikey.'

'Betty,' said Doriss.

'We all thought that was it,' said Nora, a little tipsy. 'Like when you hear about those accidents in the circus.'

'No, she does that every night. She's well padded.'

'She was one of my favourites,' said Nora. 'And you, of course. My God, you've got to be fit.'

'What did you think, Mr Drake?' said Doriss. 'Did you enjoy it?'

Jack, who had been staring at the wall, open-mouthed, put on his hat and smiled. 'Enjoy is not the word.'

'He loved it,' said Nora. 'You should have seen him at the end. He could hardly stand, could you, Jack? I had to help him up. He was shaking.'

'I was shaking, Joe,' said Jack, smiling as much as he could, declining another glass of water. 'Well, thank you very much. We must be getting along.'

Doriss, a little panicked, put down his drink, pulled on a robe and began towelling his head. 'I'd love to take a look at this script, sir. I'm free, of course, now this is over . . . I mean, if you thought me suitable.'

'We'll get it over to you,' said Jack. 'Nora, we'll get it over, won't we?'

'First thing,' said Nora. Jack already had one foot out the door and his hand on the knob.

'First thing,' he said.

'I'll make sure,' said Nora.

'I can't wait,' said Doriss, beaming.

'Goodnight,' said Nora, 'see you soon,' closing the door

behind her and setting off down the steep stone stairs, hanging onto Jack's coat for balance.

'Why did you say that?' said Jack. 'Have you seen the size of him?'

'But he's very good.'

'He's good, but he's taller than he is good. And balder. It'll never work.'

'Oh fuck,' said Nora.

'And you're drunk,' said Jack.

'I know,' said Nora. 'I should have eaten something.'

They wobbled down another two flights before Jack stopped on the landing. 'I wasn't going to say this, but . . .'

'What?' said Nora.

'But you know what I'm going to say.'

'You're going to say what you weren't going to say.'

'And you know what that is.'

'I think so,' said Nora. 'So say it.'

Jack took a deep breath and looked to the ceiling. 'I'll do it myself.'

Nora whooped, threw her arms up in the air and then around his neck. 'Yes, yes, yes, yes, yes, yes, yes, fucking yes, yes, yes.'

'All right, stop that.'

'I've been praying.'

'Well, there you go.'

'On my bended knees.'

'We have no other choice,' said Jack. 'We can't stop filming and there's nothing left to shoot.'

'You were born to play your father.'

'I hope that isn't why I was born,' said Jack. 'That would be very . . .'

'And if it wasn't for your father, you'd never have been born to play your father.'

'. . . disappointing.'

Nora was smiling so much that she began to hiccup.

Suddenly, from the staircase above, there came a great commotion, raised voices and pounding feet. And then Joseph Doriss, wearing only a pair of white underpants, barefoot and with a bloody nose, came charging down the stairs with the dyed-black intoxicated scruff close behind, trying to get a hold of him, his hands slipping off wet skin. 'You do that again,' screamed the scruff, 'and I'll crack your fucking head open.'

'It was part of the play,' yelled Doriss. 'It happens every night.'

'Are you fucking kidding me?'

And as they carried on down, turning the corner, so Jack and Nora trotted down with them.

'And why would I do it again?' said Doriss. 'It's the last night!'

'It's your fucking last night, I know that,' screamed the scruff, and got in a good kick to Doriss's back, so that he went crashing into a wall.

Nora gasped.

A woman's scream from up above. 'Sean! Sean, stop it. Leave him.'

Doriss regained his balance and leapt down the next flight, with the scruff in raging pursuit. As they disappeared around another corner, Jack and Nora gave up, but then another louder call of 'Sean!' Deafening. 'Fucking pack it in!' Even louder. She appeared on the staircase above, before flying past and crashing down; but on finding her man far out of sight and sound, she finally gave up and collapsed in a heap on the cold stone steps, her white veil spattered with blood and the whole thing a deal grubbier than it had appeared on the stage. She put her head in her hands and began to sob.

Here she is again, thought Jack. He looked to Nora. She could hear it too, he had no doubt.

'Do you hear it?' he said.

Nora may have nodded. 'Poor woman,' she said.

Jack watched as a tiny white pillow feather drifted down from the ceiling and came to rest on the black cashmere shoulder of Peter O'Toole's stolen overcoat.

And here she is again.

CHAPTER 8

The church bells did not wake her; nor Mrs Mason's emphysema; nor Mr Thackery's bipolar dog; nor Sean, at ten, hammering the bell into the brick; nor the snoring of the man in the bed beside her. She awoke briefly at noon, sickened by a dream of talking meat, and by then the man was gone. She couldn't remember if it had been Father Mignon, Father Barré, Cardinal Richelieu, or Louis XIII himself. No matter: he had not woken her, and for that she was truly thankful.

She carried on sleeping until three, and by then she had missed seven calls from Sean and one from Paul. Sean had left seven messages, all of which she deleted without listening to; Paul had left none. She realised the bed was broken again when she felt her heels touching the floor. She barely managed to make it to the bathroom, where, thwarted by a full and unflushed toilet, she threw up in the bath. Afterwards she lay on her back, naked, watching planes passing over through the cracked and sooty window. For the next half an hour she squatted at the top of the stairs, peeling the fake scars from her arms, legs, breasts and buttocks, rolling the rubber cement into small red balls and flicking them across the carpet. Finding nothing but margarine and an onion in the fridge, she cycled to the shop and bought cheese triangles, popcorn, liquorice shoelaces, a Cornetto, twenty Benson & Hedges, toilet roll, *Elle* magazine, two apples and a carton of milk.

Back at home, she tipped it all onto the bed and watched *Dial M for Murder*. In *Elle* she read that Edie Krauss was born in Geneva, detested plastic cutlery and liked nothing more than scuba-diving in the Red Sea. On her way back from the kitchen with the Cornetto, she noticed a prosthetic silicone hump with dirty flesh-coloured Velcro straps lying in the corner of the bedroom. It was signed with a Sharpie: *To Betty, I love you . . . You have to give a little back, so here's my little back. Second 2 nun — ha ha ha — Rebecca. Miss u little Devil xoxox*

She picked it up and put it on, but the smell unsettled her so she took it off and left it outside the bedroom door. She finished off the popcorn, smoked two more cigarettes and fell back asleep for the rest of the night. At ten, Sean rang the bell again. It did not wake her.

On Monday morning, Betty got up at seven and started cleaning. Flushing the toilet, scrubbing the toilet, slopping out the bath with sponges and a bucket. She washed every cup, plate, bowl, pan, glass, knife, fork, spoon and ashtray she could find and then swept the floor. She hoovered the cobwebs from every corner, dusted the window ledges and razored the wax from the kitchen table. She found a screwdriver and a bottle of glue and fixed the legs on the bed. She put new bulbs in all the lamps and changed the sheets. She watered, sprayed and fertilised her Easter cactus, her Chinese money plant and her creeping fig. She sat on the floor with her legs crossed and breathed in the way she had been taught at drama school. She called Paul. Paul didn't answer. She called Ruth, who didn't have time to speak since she was busy bathing their father. In *Tatler* magazine she read that Edie Krauss had an Irish wolfhound, dabbled in Kabbalah and had once had dinner with Barbra Streisand.

Betty cycled to the shop and spent eleven pounds thirty-eight on water, oatcakes, four oranges, seedless grapes, a tuna steak, two courgettes and a pointed cabbage. On the way back from the shop, her agent called.

'Congratulations,' said Arnold Plack.

'For what?' said Betty, stopping at the traffic lights.

'On finishing the play.'

'On being out of work.'

'I hear the party was a little wild.'

'I don't remember.'

'I heard it rivalled the debauchery on the stage.'

The lights turned green and Betty set off, steering with one hand, her shopping bouncing around in the basket. 'Well, there you go,' she said, not really wanting to talk about it.

'Yes. Anyway, listen,' said Plack. 'Two words: Jack Drake.'

'Yes,' said Betty.

'*Blue Dog*; *The Ruins*. Heard of him?'

'Yes.'

'*Broken Tomorrow*; Jack Drake, yes?'

'Yes, Arnold,' said Betty, pulling over, realising this wasn't going to be a quick call.

'Well, he was in on Saturday night, to see Joseph Doriss, actually, but you seem to have rather caught his eye and he wants you to go in and meet him on Wednesday.'

'Why?'

'I don't know. They're being a bit mysterious. I got a call first thing this morning from Nora Flynn, his producer stroke assistant stroke writing partner stroke editor or whatever, I don't know. A lot of stroking. Anyway, I've given her your email and she's sending something over that she wants you to learn by Wednesday, and she'll give you all the details of where and when, et cetera.'

'OK. Is it a film?' asked Betty, almost smiling for the first time in what felt like weeks. Perhaps she'd smiled on Saturday night; she couldn't remember.

'I presume. It's Jack Drake. He don't do television, darling. Actually, he hasn't done anything for the past four years, but apparently he's back shooting something right now, so let's wait and see. Can I leave all that with you?'

Back at home, Betty cooked the tuna with the cabbage and courgettes and washed it all down with a tall glass of water. She cut ten grapes in half and ate them on top of five oatcakes. She took a shower and watched a documentary on Goya.

The email came through some time after nine. There were two files attached. The first contained an address and a list of precise instructions as to when and how she should present herself. The second was not, as she had expected, a script, nor even pages to be learned, but rather an audio file. The quality was poor, as though recorded by accident. A man, clearly seated close to the microphone, could be heard sniffling or stifling a cough. Further away, a wistful-sounding woman delivered a peculiar and rather disturbing speech. Her accent was American, a little slurred.

Betty, suddenly finding it difficult to breathe, searched her bags and pockets for one last cigarette. She had until Wednesday to learn it.

Having endured the usual struggle of lugging the bicycle down into the basement, it was even more of a nuisance when the chain fell off as she strained to drag it back up again. An hour later she leaned it against the postbox, where it couldn't be seen from the window, and crept up the seventeen steps of Paul's apartment building. Crouching down, hiding from the camera, she rang the bell: her arm reaching up and groping with a greasy black finger for the right button, the passing people in the pretty street thinking something unsavoury was afoot. She grinned, put the dirty finger to her lips and shushed them as if it was all a bit of a hoot, which it certainly wasn't since there was no answer and her heart was breaking right there beneath those lovely trees.

CHAPTER 9

Behind the imposing Victorian townhouse in the parish of St Bartholomew, at the end of the garden, beneath a stately lime tree and surrounded by bone-white birches, was a small guest house that had been converted into a studio by Jack's mother, in the days when she'd nursed aspirations to be a sculptress. It was now being used as a small ad hoc production office while principal photography took place in the main house. Nora Flynn ushered out the gaffer who had just finished setting up the lights: 'Thank you, Stanley, I will take care of things hereafter.'

Nora Flynn wasn't sure about all this. She pressed the earpiece close against the drum and sat down on a painted white wooden chair. Then, staring directly into the main camera mounted on a tripod at the other end of the room, she said, 'Are you seeing me?'

'Yes,' said Jack softly in her ear. 'I have a very clear picture.'

'Is it the right distance?'

'We'll see. I'm going to turn off the main lights now.'

'Go ahead,' said Nora.

The overhead fluorescent lights clicked off and Nora was left in complete darkness. A few seconds later, several pre-positioned LED lights were switched on. She put a hand up to her face, dazzled. 'Sorry,' said Jack in her ear. 'Hold on.' The offending light was slowly dimmed. 'How's that?'

'Fine.'

'Turn your head to the left.'

She did so.

'Now to the right.'

She did so.

'And now back, looking at the ceiling.'

She tipped her head, feeling the warmth of the lights on her throat.

'And now to the floor, slowly, eyes downcast. Hold it there.'

She stole a look at her watch. It was nearly noon.

As Jack took young Billy aside to discuss the details of the afternoon's work, he heard, to his great dismay, the click clack click *fucking* clack of Billy's mother's buckled blue shoes. He had informed his assistants and runners that they should do their very best to discourage her at all times, and that he found it near impossible to mould her only child and bend him to his will if she insisted on presenting her ghastly beak at every opportunity.

Billy watched closely as Jack twisted a lever, pressed a catch and pulled on a small ring until the base of the camera could be lifted off. He then unscrewed the lens and removed it from the body. He placed all the components gently on a soft cloth on the table between them. 'So this is the actual camera,' he said, and smiled. 'A Leica M5.'

'M5,' said Billy, eager to please.

'That's not messing around. A Leica M5. One of the best cameras in the world at that time. Now my father gave me this for Christmas.'

Billy moved to pick up the camera, but Jack gently pressed his hand away. 'Don't touch anything till I've shown you exactly what everything does. You can do great damage if you handle it incorrectly. I'll show you how to load it with film. I want you to do this on camera after lunch.'

'What do you mean?' said Billy

'I mean in shot,' said Jack. 'I want to see Jack, Young Jack, loading it for the first time after his father shows him what to do. So how this is going to work is . . . I'll show you how to load it, then we'll turn over, slate it, and then shoot you loading it, without practice. And if you screw up, it doesn't matter, we'll just keep rolling. But I need to show you first how not to do any damage, because it's extremely valuable. Do you understand?'

'Do you understand, Billy? Don't break Jack's lovely camera,' said Phyllis. The prospect of her son breaking Jack's treasured possession seemed to amuse her enormously.

'This lens alone costs over two thousand pounds,' said Jack, trying to ignore the idiotic creature, but then Phyllis snorted, as though she'd never heard anything so ludicrous in her entire life. Jack turned around to look at her over the top of his specs. 'Mrs Rigby,' he said.

'Phyllis.'

'Phyllis, would you mind granting Billy and me a little privacy. I understand that you are here as his chaperone—'

'I'm his *mother*,' said Phyllis.

'Indeed, but you are not required to remain at his side for every moment he is not in front of the camera. That is not how it works.'

Billy looked mortified and pushed his twisted fingers through his hair, staring wildly at the inside of the camera.

'In order for Billy,' continued Jack, 'to create, what should be a very complex character, I need him to explore without inhibition, and I suspect he finds that difficult when his mother is there monitoring his every word and action. I know I would.

I know I did. Indeed, it has much to do with what this film is about.'

'I understand,' said Phyllis, looking suitably chastened. 'You're saying give you both some room. I say that to his father all the time, don't I, Billy? "Give me some room, Ted," I say. "I feel stifled." I'll go and talk to the make-up ladies, see if they've got any beauty tips.'

'Oh, they've got hundreds,' said Jack, 'Not that you need any,' and if that didn't see her off, nothing would.

Phyllis smiled her gummy smile, ruffled Billy's hair, said, 'See you later,' and trotted off, click clack.

His hands now trembling, Jack gave up trying to reassemble the camera and set it down on the table. 'Anyway,' he said, 'we'll come back to that this afternoon.'

'OK,' said Billy, and he began to get up from his seat.

'Wait,' said Jack, placing a hand softly on his arm. 'We still have to talk about the other scene; this next scene. We still have time to make a start on it before lunch. How are you feeling about it?'

Billy sat back down. 'Well, fine,' he said. 'There are no lines, so . . .'

Jack looked the boy in the eye with unnerving intensity, concerned. 'There are no lines, but it's a key scene, isn't it?'

'I suppose so,' said Billy.

'It's a turning point,' said Jack. 'Finding out that his father is actually dead, and that his mother has been keeping this a secret, not only from him, but from everyone, it seems. That's unusual, isn't it?'

'Mmm,' muttered Billy.

'How would you feel if you found out that your mother was hiding your father's body in the loft, the shed? Can you imagine that?'

Billy's face turned pink as he attempted to suppress a smirk.

'It's not a joke,' said Jack, leaning back in his chair, aghast, desperately disappointed. 'It's not funny. It wasn't funny. Do you understand? This *happened*.' He was beginning to visibly sweat.

'Really?' said Billy, genuinely, for he couldn't be sure.

'You think it didn't?'

'You're not exaggerating a bit?' His face was still pink.

'No!' barked Jack, loudly enough to turn the heads of nearby crew. Nora appeared in the doorway. Jack rose up with such force that the table shot back across the wooden floor. 'We can't do this if you don't believe it's real!'

Phyllis appeared in the doorway next to Nora. Nora stopped her from going any further.

'I do believe it,' mumbled Billy, his lip beginning to quiver.

'It's not fucking *Spider-Man!*' screamed Jack, for the benefit of everyone upstairs and downstairs, and he kicked his chair so hard that it took off and tumbled across the room, coming to settle – rather unbelievably – back on all four legs. So furious was he with this outcome that he charged across the room and kicked it again, harder, higher, further, until it did what he wanted and broke into pieces.

Betty had been told to approach the house from the rear. Following the instructions, she located a green gate set in an ancient wall at the far end of an overgrown alley and found – just as the email had said she would – a thick white button in the old style, hidden underneath a knot of ivy. It wobbled when pressed. She did not know who had written the directions, but the mischievous tone of the missive had set her at ease. She was dressed all in black, as per the instructions. Her hair was pinned up and folded as close to her head as she could manage: all those months of cramming it nightly beneath a tight wimple had not been wasted. She wore no make-up.

As she waited, she thought she could hear someone calling out in distress from somewhere behind the gate. Eventually a handsome, rather urbane young man who spoke as if it were 1935 swung it open. He welcomed her in, congratulated her on finding the place, thanked her warmly for her patience and warned her to take the greatest of care as he led her down a mossy path of broken flagstones. He showed her into a fascinatingly cluttered outbuilding at the back of what appeared to be a very austere townhouse. She was handed a bottle of water and encouraged to make herself comfortable. He assured her that someone would be along in no time, and that his name, by the way, was Alexander, and it had been a delight to make her acquaintance. And with one last charming smile, he was gone.

Left alone, she sipped her water and slowly began to appraise the nature of the room around her. There was a video camera mounted on a tripod, pointed at a simple white bentwood chair. What struck her as peculiar were the number and the serious nature of the lights. The room looked as if it had been set up for an elaborate photo shoot, rather than the usual natural daylight of a simple casting tape. She had suffered through enough of them to know there was something overblown about this set-up, as though it had been constructed with the sole purpose of unnerving and intimidating.

She took another sip of her water and ran some of what she had been asked to learn, still baffled by the meaning of it. She stood up to look across the garden to see if anyone was approaching; finding no sign of life anywhere in sight, she relaxed a little. On one wall of the room she could see a series of cork boards, swatches of material and strips of colour charts pinned on them. There were photographs of grand old houses and their gardens, interiors of what looked like school halls and dusty classrooms. Another board was filled with pictures of old film cameras and projectors. On a table beneath the boards sat several folders, including some that looked like leather-bound portfolios. She opened one up and saw dozens of coloured pencil sketches modelling what appeared to be a broad selection of 1970s outfits, once again with swatches of material stapled to the pages: faded denims, green-and-yellow polka dot in cotton and silk, red paisley flannelette. Another folder was filled with pictures of crockery, cutlery, vases, candlesticks and other small furnishings, once again in the style of the seventies.

She did not linger. The next folder, a large portfolio, took her by surprise and quickly turned her stomach: it featured photographs of corpses in various stages of decomposition. Some of the photos were close-ups of decaying extremities – a blackened foot, a degloved forearm, a blistered and pustulant hand over-brimming with grey maggots. There was a series of what she recognised to be Victorian post-mortem photographs, showing a departed loved one – usually a child, often a baby – posed, fully clothed, buttoned up and beribboned, alongside the rest of the living family, all solemnly gazing into the camera. And towards the end, images of executions, with a particular emphasis on hanging.

Betty felt nausea overcoming her. As she closed the book, loath to see any more, she was startled by a terrible cry ringing out from the direction of the big house: she looked out across the garden and saw a young boy screaming, running out of the back door, fleeing in a wide-eyed fever. At this point black automatic shutters began to groan and shift, moving slowly down the several windows to conceal the light of the day outside. For about half a minute Betty found herself in complete darkness; then a small lamp in the corner of the room clicked on and in the distance she heard someone shout, 'Cut.' And then laughter and applause. She walked back to her seat, sat down and finished her water in one great gulp. Suddenly the door at the far end of the room opened and an elderly woman with grey hair stuffed beneath a tweed cap came in and walked over to the camera.

'Hello, Betty, sorry to keep you waiting,' she said, smiling, crossing to the sofa, offering her hand. Betty stood up and took hold of the hand too close to the fingertips, making their greeting a little awkward. 'My name is Nora,' said the woman.

'Pleased to meet you,' said Betty.

'Why don't you take a seat?'

Betty took a step back towards the sofa.

'On the white chair,' said Nora, making her way to her own black chair at the side of the camera. Betty did as she was told, noticing for the first time the large microphone suspended directly above her.

'Say something,' said Nora.

'What do you want me to say?'

'That's fine,' said Nora. 'That seems to be working nicely. Are you all right to begin?'

'I'm not sure I understand what it is I'm supposed to be doing,' said Betty.

'I thought it had been made clear in the instructions,' said Nora.

'You want me to perform the speech, as it has already been performed?'

'Yes.'

'Note for note.'

'Note for note.'

'Not to interpret it? Not to make it my own?'

'No, otherwise Mr Drake would have simply sent you a transcript.'

'So more like an impersonation?'

'Yes.'

'The same accent?'

'Yes.'

'It's Californian, I think.'

'Very good.'

'North California.'

'Mr Drake is interested in your ability to listen, to reproduce. Is there a problem?'

'It's just unusual.'

'We're perfectly aware.'

'I didn't have long to prepare.'

'That's understood. If Mr Drake likes you, if you are given the job, you will have to get used to having little time to prepare.'

'What is the job? No one has told me.'

'If you get the job, then you will be told the job.'

'I see. Who is speaking?'

'That isn't important for now. Any more questions?' Nora's tone clearly implied there ought not to be, and so Betty left it at that and began to arrange her hair. From out of the darkness behind her, Nora produced a hat. A wide-brimmed fedora. 'Don't worry about your hair. Put this on.'

She pressed her finger to her ear and listened.

'Pull it down further at the front.'

Betty obliged.

'More of an angle. Down a touch to the left. Good. Now you may begin.'

Betty composed herself, choosing to address some imagined listener just off to the left of the camera, someone she could not see. Then she began. Softly at first, as it had been learned:

'The lipstick on the back of my hand,' said Betty, raising her hand level with her face, 'had already worn into the cuffs of the blouse—'

'Stop,' said Nora. 'Your hands should remain in your lap. If she refers to her hand, as she does here, there is no need for you to show us your hand. Take that as a general instruction. Your eyeline is good, the voice is good, but do not embellish with any gesture. You are essentially a talking head.'

'I see,' said Betty. Though it was a very uncommon note, she had conceded by now that this was a very uncommon situation. Once more she composed herself, making sure that the offending hand was now pressed firmly into her lap. She began again:

'The lipstick on the back of my hand had already worn into the cuffs of the blouse. They must think I'm a dirty one. Therefore I must be a dirty one. Therefore I must roll in the hot street and on the wet floor of the public bathroom. I wiped a finger across the lid of my drooping eye and sucked on the blue. I wondered if anyone had fallen in love with me yet. I wondered if anyone could tell that the style of my hair was new. I sat there in the corner, quiet as a louse, with one arm leaning on the cold table, with my green glass at my elbow and nipple. For the old silk was such that the nipple showed through. I longed to be approached by some intriguing stranger; someone not quite pleasant. I longed to be talked to as though I didn't deserve to be told the truth. I didn't care if it was a man or a woman. I didn't care about age. I didn't care about any of these things, simply because I had always cared so much about these things. The only important thing was that whatever happened next should in no way resemble what had usually, all my life, happened next. I didn't even care if it hurt.'

Betty moved her head for the first time, but did not touch the hat, for fear she would be scolded. Instead she tilted her face back just a little to gather the response of this odd woman who sat in the shadows behind the camera.

'Do you smoke?' asked Nora, smiling benevolently for the first time since she had greeted her at the door.

'I'm trying to stop,' said Betty.

'Do you have cigarettes with you?'

'Yes,' said Betty.

'Could you smoke one now, while we talk a little further?'

'Of course,' and Betty reached into the darkness to where she

68

remembered leaving her coat. She fumbled for the packet, took one out and lit it.

'Don't worry about the ash,' said Nora. 'Just flick it on the floor.'

Betty nodded and took a couple of quick drags just to get things going.

'You did that superbly,' said Nora. 'You have a very good ear.'

'I've always been good with accents,' said Betty, nodding.

'I will not keep it a secret any longer that I am in touch with Mr Drake as we speak. He can see and hear everything we do. He would like to pass on his thanks for agreeing to this, and to say that you have moved him a great deal. More than he might have expected.'

'Thank you,' said Betty.

'But could you now finish your cigarette in silence?'

'You don't want—'

'Don't say anything else. Just take your time and finish smoking. You may extinguish it on the floor and then leave. I won't say anything. At some point later in the day, perhaps this evening, I will contact you and explain things a little further. But for now, just smoke and relax. You're among friends.'

It was the most absurd little speech Betty had ever heard, and she was glad she'd been asked to remain silent, for she had no idea of how else she might respond to such a declaration. She noticed that the camera's red light was still on. Nora did not move but sat very still, gazing at the floor, her hands folded upon her brown tweed skirt, as though in prayer. Betty elected not to rush. She understood that this moment carried just as much importance as the speech. She took another pull on the cigarette and allowed the smoke to drift from her mouth in a rolling cascade, imagining that this might be useful or interesting to him.

Suddenly Nora stood, walked further into the shadows, opened the door and exited. Betty placed the cigarette carefully onto the tiled floor and crushed it beneath the toe of her boot. The camera's red light was now extinguished. A few seconds passed before she heard the hum of the black shutters as they rose to reveal the dull grey glow of the day outside. She gathered her things, walked out of the room and back down the mossy path of broken flagstones towards the green gate.

Jack took off his headphones. He stood and walked slowly down the darkened corridor, past his childhood bedroom, to the musty brown bedroom where his father had lingered. He walked over to the window and drew aside the curtain for the first time in forty years. Down there in the alley the young woman made her way along the overgrown path towards a blue bicycle chained to the lamp post he had once, many, many years ago, failed to climb.

As she pedalled away, he walked back to his mother's old bedroom and, taking a cardboard box lined with a small white towel from the cupboard, gently placed Martha's Tudor head inside.

CHAPTER 10

'Pox,' said Paul.

'Pops,' said Freddie.

'Pox,' said Paul.

'Pops, pops, pops,' said Freddie. 'I've got chicken pops, Mama. I caught them off a chicken.'

'Is that what Papa told you?' said Betty. She could see Papa's dark arm barely there at the edge of the screen, but still there – just to show her, just to let her know.

'He says I got them from a boiled egg,' said Freddie, and he bent towards the screen in such a fit of giggling that he went out of focus. He was in a maddeningly ebullient mood and looked just awful. Apart from his face, neck, hands and arms being spattered with hundreds of hot red spots, his hair was cut short and combed so neatly, so severely that with his blue plaid blazer and his well-pressed button-down collar, he looked like a little news-reader. 'It's an ear-cut, Mama,' he'd said at the start of the call.

'You mean haircut,' his father had said.

'No,' said Freddie. 'Ear-cut, 'cos now you can see my ears.'

'That's right, darling,' Betty had said, smiling through her disappointment. 'We've never seen your ears before. I didn't think you had any. Well, thank goodness for that.'

They had called without warning, after all this time. Out of nowhere came her darling's beaming, ravaged little face and his playful voice all split with mischief and spilling giggles. Unfortunately Betty was horrendously hung-over, barely awake and still wrapped in her ragged dressing gown. Before answering the call, she'd stuck her head, in a panic, beneath the cold tap, declaring she was just out of the shower. She'd closed every door between the bedroom and the kitchen to muffle Sean's hacking cough, so that it might be passed off as one of Mrs Mason's bronchial eruptions.

'That's why I couldn't see you,' said Freddie, 'in case you caught my chicken pops.'

'Is that what Papa said?'

'Isn't it, Papa?' said Freddie.

The dark arm moved, but had nothing to say.

'I've had it, darling,' said Betty. 'Papa knows that.'

'You might get it again,' said Freddie.

'You can't get it twice.'

'I didn't want you to see him like this,' said the dark arm, leaning in a little.

'I *want* to see him like this,' said Betty. 'I am his mother.' She was trying her very best to maintain civility, though her stomach was churning and her skull felt as if it were packed with roasted plasticine. 'I might have been able to make him feel better.'

The arm grunted.

'I was all right, Mama,' said Freddie. 'And Edie made it go away at the photo shop.'

Betty bristled. 'Did she?'

'She took every pop away, like magic.'

'What do you mean?' said Betty.

'At the photo shop,' said Freddie, a little too impatiently for Betty's taste. 'And then she gave me twice as many, three times

72

as many,' he giggled, 'so that you could hardly see my face at all and I was just one big pop. It was funny, wasn't it, Papa?'

'Mmm,' mumbled the arm.

'Do you know what we did then, Mama?'

'What, darling?'

'We did dot-to-dot. She put numbers on the pops at the photo shop, and we joined them up and did different letters and numbers and the . . . What were the stars called, Papa?'

'Constellations.'

'Well,' said Betty, 'that sounds wonderful. Very imaginative.'

'So funny, wasn't it, Papa?'

She really wished he would stop saying that.

'Very funny,' said the arm.

And he could fucking shut up.

'I have a red plastic comb now, for my hair,' said Freddie.

'Great.'

''Cos you like red plastic, don't you?'

'Yes,' said Betty.

'It's your favourite plastic.'

'It is.'

'Have you been in Edie's car, Mama?'

'Not *in* it, no,' said Betty.

'It can park itself. And the roof comes off.'

'Well, she should get that fixed,' said Betty.

'What?' said Freddie, frowning and pouting.

'But does it have a basket to carry things in?'

Freddie ignored this. She could see his mind racing, his body fidgeting, never still, like he didn't want the talking to stop. He looked to the ceiling for more news to tell. 'Oh, and I met some new children. Sasha, who's seven, and Guinness, who's six, like me.'

'I'm sorry,' said Betty. 'What's that name?'

'Guinness,' said Freddie.

The arm moved a little and then settled, a touch further into the shot.

'And is that a boy or a girl?' said Betty.

'A boy, of course. And we might be going somewhere very hot when school is over, where they have real elephants just walking around in the street. And Edie has a good house and it has a puzzled monkey tree, and she has a very, very, *very* big dog called a Irish wolfhound and its name is . . . What is it, Papa?'

The dark arm mumbled something incomprehensible.

'What is it, Papa?' said Betty. 'I didn't hear.'

'Giacomo,' said Paul.

'Giacomo?'

'Yes.'

She thought she might have managed a smile if she hadn't felt so extremely, so profoundly, so irredeemably fucking hopeless and depressed. She had waited for so long for this call to come, and now here it was, and she could think of nothing worse.

'Mama?' said Freddie.

'Yes, darling?'

'I have to go to the toilet.'

'OK, love, you go and—'

'So I'll say goodbye.'

She hadn't expected that. 'Oh.'

'Big kisses, Mama,' he said, blowing them with one hand while balancing his descent from the chair with the other. Both hands flew to his crotch as he skipped from the room, singing, 'Bye, Mama, bye Mama, bye bye.' And then he was gone.

The dark arm slowly shifted till it filled the screen, then moved back and away. A purple shirt and a new necklace. Then his face, one eye still black and puckered. All his breath pushed down through the nose. The lips thin and closed, not about to speak, it seemed – waiting for her, she supposed – but she didn't know what to say and so they just stared at each other like that for a while.

'That's that, then,' she said.

He smiled, for no other reason, it seemed, than to rub her face in a couple of raw red holes where two of his favourite teeth had once lived. She nodded. He nodded. It was awful.

'So . . .?' she said.

'So . . . he's still there.'

'Who?' said Betty, genuinely puzzled.

'Bukowski,' he said.

'No. Who? What? Sean? No.' Well, that went terribly.

'I can hear him. He hasn't stopped coughing this whole time.'

'That's Mrs Mason,' said Betty. 'Next door.'

'You're fucking Mrs Mason from next door?'

'Emphysema.'

'Don't insult me, Betty.'

'I'm not,' said Betty. 'Where's this hot place you're thinking of going? With the elephants?'

'We're not thinking. We're going.'

'Not without my permission.'

'I don't need your permission,' sneered Paul. 'I don't know why you're making all this so easy for me.'

'You call this easy?' said Betty. 'Taking a child from his mother?'

'*Saving* a child from his mother,' said Paul. 'And if you want to get legal about it, then let's get legal about that rolled-up tenner on the table behind you. Nice touch. I can see you've thought all this through.'

Betty turned around, though she didn't really need to, and anyway it didn't really matter because here came Sean lumbering down the stairs, quoting *Goodfellas*, oblivious no doubt, probably naked, and just as the door opened, Paul's smirking, black-eyed, toothless face disappeared and the screen snapped back to desktop – a pipevine swallowtail – and Sean shuffled in. He'd managed to put a sock on.

The two sisters were seated next to each other, waiting to hear news of their father, who had been wheeled away down the corridor two hours ago. It was impossible for them not to be reminded of those same sounds, those same slow hours, when, in their early teens, they had waited for news of their mother: she had also been wheeled away, but down darker corridors, glaring at the ceiling, her face in bitter shock at what her trembling body had visited upon her. Back then, the girls had sat in a room like this, in hospital silence, until a man in a brown suit and broken spectacles had appeared, with the practised face he used for such occasions, and the voice he used, and uttered the words he had spoken time and again. And that was that, and there was nothing further to say. And so they'd phoned their father, who had not, till then, thought the situation sufficiently critical to keep him from his work, and he'd picked them up in his dusty black taxi, which reeked back then of tobacco and Old Spice, and driven them home as they listened to the traffic reports. Yes, it was impossible not to be reminded of all that now.

Harold had fallen from his bed in the middle of the night, and Ruth had soon realised that he was now completely paralysed from the neck down, and that this was a significant and sinister change in the already miserable weather of their life together, and so she called first an ambulance, and then her sister, who had been suspiciously eager to offer her services.

'The Lunar something,' said Ruth.

'Sunbeam,' said Betty.

'The Lunar Sunbeam and the Coachman Mirage.'

Betty nearly spat out her coffee at the memory. Ruth placed her hand on her sister's knee as she rocked forward, unable to suppress her laughter. 'You'd think we were off into space,' said

Betty, 'not to the middle of a muddy field just off the M25.'

'With no toilets.'

'With no toilets.'

As it happened, they had elected to deal with this particular crisis by reliving their childhood holidays, recalling a fonder father, a delusional, hapless father who had done his best to show his family the high life by pulling them around Britain in various exotically named caravans.

'And Mum always wanted to go and see the stately homes and castles,' said Ruth, 'where everyone was tortured and decapitated.'

'Nice,' said Betty. 'That was always a pleasure.'

'Do you remember going to Tewkesbury Abbey to see that box of fucking bones?'

'The Duke of Clarence.'

'We'd gone all that way, and they weren't even there,' said Ruth, shaking her head.

'And Dad not wanting to do any of that, ever,' said Betty.

'Dad just always wanting to go to Loch Ness to look for the monster.'

'Which was never there either.'

'And he spent a fortune on those binoculars,' said Ruth.

'Fucking hell,' howled Betty, and Ruth had to nudge her not to wake the old woman sleeping on the opposite chair, who might have died about an hour ago by the looks of things, which made them laugh even more.

A doctor emerged from the doorway where they'd last seen their father go in. He looked around, looked over at the sisters, decided they didn't seem to be whatever it was he was looking for, turned and went back into the room. The silence settled. Betty wiped her eyes, and Ruth got up to buy another coffee from the vending machine in the corner of the room. Betty held out her cup and smiled.

Another hour had gone by, and Betty had explained the torment of her call with Freddie, Paul's threats and Sean's stupidity. Ruth listened, saying little, letting Betty hear for herself how it all sounded when spoken out loud. But then, at four, she still made a phone call to Sean to make sure he was all right and to tell him that she didn't know when she would be home – and no news yet, and thanks for asking, and lots of love, and Ruth sends her love, and Ruth made her take that back, literally, down the line. They sat in silence and looked at the old woman for another ten minutes till they seriously thought about alerting someone in a position of responsibility.

Betty then told Ruth about her day in Clerkenwell and the phone call she had received later that evening and the offer of the job, and the nature of the job, which now baffled Ruth as much as it had baffled Betty upon first hearing the details.

'Martha Lear?' said Ruth.

'The actress,' said Betty.

'I can't place her.'

'You'd know her face. She's American.'

'But what's she got to do with this freak?'

'She's his wife,' said Betty. 'Was his wife.'

'Oh, right,' said Ruth. 'You missed that bit out. Well, that doesn't make it any less creepy. In fact, if anything it makes it creepier. And she's dead?'

'Yes,' said Betty.

'When did she die?'

'Recently. A few months ago.'

'How?'

'I looked it up. She killed herself. She threw herself under a train.'

'Under a train?' said Ruth, appalled.

'Under, in front of, I don't know how it works, it didn't say.'

'That's horrible.'

'And this woman,' said Betty, 'this Nora, the woman I met, she says that Jack Drake is asking me to do this as some sort of experiment. That's how she put it, like she was trying to give a name to something that obviously didn't have a name, 'cos no one's ever heard of such a thing, obviously.'

'So you'd have to sit at home waiting for his calls, and put on her voice so that he can imagine that he's talking to his dead wife?'

'They'd be video calls,' said Betty, 'but shot professionally, with expensive lighting – because he's a director, don't forget – so I'd be lit like I'm in a film, to look like her, and I'd be dressed and made up like her. Like if I was playing her in a film.'

'And what would you say?' said Ruth.

'I'm not sure. I think he'd write things, or maybe I'd just have to listen. They've already sent me links to all this research, so maybe they'd want me to just make it up. I don't know. I don't think they know that yet. Like they said, it'd be an experiment.'

'This,' said Ruth, taking a deep breath to remind herself that this was potentially very funny, 'is the most bonkers thing I've ever heard. So they'd put all these lights and cameras in your house? Have they seen your little fucking house?'

'Well, that's the bit I haven't told you,' said Betty, smiling now. 'That's the really mad bit.'

Ruth lit up and perched on the edge of her seat. 'Oh, go on then, I can't wait for this.'

'It wouldn't be at my house. I'd be living in another house.'

Ruth put her hand on her sister's arm, spooked. 'His house?'

'One of his houses,' said Betty, nodding.

'How many has he got?'

'I don't know. I think he's a very rich man, Ruth. He's making a film in one of them. That's where I went the other day.'

Ruth was getting lost. 'What film?'

'This film he's making in this other house, that belongs – that belonged – to his parents; the house he grew up in. Nora explained all this, 'cos I had all the same questions as you.'

'So you'd be living in his parents' house?' said Ruth.

'No, 'cos that's where he's living now, while he's making this film.'

Ruth sighed, exasperated.

'But he has another house,' said Betty. 'That's where I'd be living. That's where they want to put all the lights and cameras. That's where I'd be doing the calls.'

'Right,' said Ruth, 'and where's that house?'

'France,' said Betty.

'France?' said Ruth.

'The South of France!' said Betty.

'The South of fucking France?' shouted Ruth, and the old woman woke up with a start, not dead after all.

All three women took a moment to catch their breath. Ruth looked like she'd never close her mouth again. 'Money?' she said.

'I'd be getting a minimum of ten thousand pounds, more if it goes well, to be paid on conclusion of the, er . . . assignment, I think they're calling it. Arnold has said he'll forgo his ten per cent since it's not really what he'd call a proper job, which is nice of him.'

'And . . .' said Ruth, mouth still hanging open, taking her time, 'when is all this supposed to happen?'

'As soon as possible,' said Betty. 'They wanted me to go before the end of the weekend.'

'Oh come on,' said Ruth. 'And what have you said? Have you said yes?'

'Of course I haven't said yes.'

'France,' said Ruth, simple as that.

'I know, but—'

'You've never been to France.'

'I've hardly ever been out of the country,' said Betty. 'Thirty-six – I've been abroad, what? Twice?'

'So, here's your chance.'

'I know, but—'

'And don't go worrying about Dad, 'cos either he comes home with me tomorrow, in which case it's business as usual, or they keep him in, in which case, I get a break. Either way it won't affect you, just like it never does. And I don't mean that like I'm having a go.'

'It's not Dad,' said Betty. 'I mean, yes, Dad, but . . .'

'But what?' said Ruth. 'And if you say anything about Sean, I'm gonna hit you with that vending machine.'

'Freddie,' said Betty, exasperated. 'Freddie. I can't just go flying off to France with all this going on.'

'With all what going on?'

The old woman was now fully alert and looking between the two of them like she too wanted some answers.

'I haven't seen him for over two weeks.'

'Listen,' said Ruth. She took Betty's face in her hands and gently squeezed. 'Paul's not going to let you anywhere near Freddie as long as Sean's around, and you have no intention of getting rid of Sean. This'll take you away from him. It'll show Paul that you're making an effort to get Freddie back.'

'How would flying a thousand miles away from my son show that I'm making an effort to get him back?'

'Because you'll be flying a thousand miles away from that twat,' said Ruth, letting go of Betty's face. 'Tell Paul that's why you're doing it.'

'I'm not doing it.'

'You said the other day that the only reason Sean had moved in was so that he could look after Freddie for as long as you

81

were working at the theatre and I was looking after Dad. Now you've finished at the theatre, Dad's back in hospital, and Freddie's with Paul, so why is he still around?'

'Sean's not the issue. It's Freddie. I need to be here, to see him.'

'You won't see him if you don't get rid of Sean. Christ almighty, Betty, how many circles do you want to go round in? 'Cos you're making me dizzy.'

The old lady, having heard enough, stood up and left. The doctor re-emerged from the doorway. He looked around, looked up and down the corridor, looked over at the sisters, and this time evidently concluded that they were what he was looking for after all and walked over, consulting his notes.

'Are you ladies all right?' he said.

'I am, she's not,' said Ruth.

The doctor ignored her.

'Your father is comfortable,' he said, 'but we're going to have to keep him here with us for the time being. He's sleeping now. Would you like to see him?'

'I've seen him sleeping,' said Ruth, collecting her things together. 'How about you, Betty?'

But Betty was already on her feet, pulling up her hood and heading for the door.

On the empty streets in the hushed dark an hour before sunset, Betty's old bicycle was the only sound. The loose chain clanging and the basket rattling and the saddle squeaking, and Betty breathing through her aching neck and burning chest, her hangover sailing on a second wind. About a mile from home, she rode through a red light and suddenly, out of nowhere it seemed, a police car pulled out of a side street and blocked her path and the window came down and a mean-looking woman with tight brown hair like a thrift-shop bonnet told her that

82

she'd seen what she'd done, that she shouldn't have done it, and not to do it again, and when Betty said sorry and promised she would never, the woman leaned a little further out of the window, and the man in the seat beside her leaned over to see, and the mean woman said, 'Because you *will* die.' Emphasising 'will'. 'You *will* die,' she repeated. Then they drove off, leaving Betty to lament the lack of subtlety in today's law enforcement.

It was a ridiculous encounter, but it was all she could think about for the next mile, and when she arrived home, she threw her bike against the wall, unlocked the door – *youwilldieyouwilldieyouwilldieyouwill* – and up the stairs to the bathroom, which smelled like her father's taxi, and noted what looked like a pint of spit on the mirror. She sat down to piss and found an empty bottle of tequila in the toilet. She didn't bother to take it out. As she climbed naked into bed, Sean turned over, groaning. As she settled on the pillow, flat on her back, he pulled her towards him and ground his groin into the side of her hip.

Her eyes closed and everything was perfectly still except for her heart, which raced like a piston. She dared not open her eyes for fear of seeing the ceiling an inch from her face. The weight of it all. A gentle coughing behind the walls. Another noise. A mosquito perhaps. And then the sour odour of rising ammonia, and the foul tang of sulphur, and the wet hip, warm at first, then a hot splash, up and over her belly, puddling at the buttocks, and the groaning beast, letting it all out. The Loch Ness fucking monster here at last in the bed beside her, pissing for longer than seemed possible. The yellow stink of the sheets turning grey. Torrential. Oblivious. Already tepid. Freezing soon. Cold enough to set her teeth a-chatter. And when it was over and he turned away, she opened her eyes. Her face turned to salt. She folded back the sodden sheet and placed her feet upon the bedside rug, the stinking flood following her all the way to the edge of the mattress, dribbling down the backs of her pimpled legs.

Down in the kitchen – wet flesh shining in the glow of the gas ring, left on after lighting a fag and a candle, with the mirror from the hall propped against the kettle – she turned the gas down low and tilted her face, her cheeks half in shadow. And with a mouth full of smoke, she began: 'They must think I'm a dirty one,' softly, in the broken tones of Martha Lear. 'Therefore I must be a dirty one. Therefore I must roll in the hot street and on the wet floor of the public bathroom.' She blew out the candle. Faint gaslight and the tip of her cigarette. 'I wondered if anyone had fallen in love with me yet. I longed to be approached by some intriguing stranger; someone not quite pleasant. I longed to be talked to as though I didn't deserve to be told the truth. I didn't care if it was a man or a woman. I didn't care about age.' Her red mouth across the crack of the mirror. 'I didn't care about any of these things, simply because I had always cared so much about these things. The only important thing was that whatever happened next should in no way resemble what had usually, all my life, happened next. I didn't even care if it hurt.'

PART TWO

CHAPTER I I

Dear Miss Dean,

Forgive my candour, but I do not wish to know you. I have heard your voice only briefly and have now put it from my mind. Since the nature of this stratagem will be one of illusion, we must not begin in such a way as would undermine the integrity of that illusion, and therefore I feel it is better that we do not communicate directly.

Forgive me that I do not consider it fitting to express my deep gratitude to your face. Let me say this: your performance the other day was passable – and for that I commend you – but please do not be complacent. It still requires much dedication. To this end, I believe Miss Flynn has already put you in touch with a splendid coach. Until I feel you are worthy, I shall request that you maintain a plausible silence, since all the initial work will be upon establishing a viable system focused on the visual challenges of this conceit, which are manifold. Much of this need not concern you, and I will not waste time explaining details that will be made apparent upon your arrival.

Finally let me say, in all humility, that I do not know if this will work, and you must prepare for the eventuality that I may, at any moment, call the whole thing off, in which case you will be asked to leave and return home. This might not be your fault: I may simply be asking the impossible. Some might say it would not be the first time. My condition at present, I should explain, may be characterised as volatile; but then were it not, we would not find ourselves in this situation.

I have said enough.

Goodbye, Miss Dean.

Yours,

Jack Drake

It was Saturday evening, two days after her night at the hospital, one day after she had defeated Sean in a fight he had no stomach for – so severe was his hangover, so complete his humiliation and so devout his contrition. She had told no one: not Sean, not her agent, not even Ruth. Her calls and texts to Paul and Freddie had gone unanswered and so she had withheld the news of her departure, deciding that for now the only thing that mattered was that she should put herself first, and hold her nerve.

Jack Drake's email had been sent, perhaps with considered precision, a few minutes before take-off, and therefore Betty had the entire two-hour flight to assess the disposition of this man and the wisdom of her decision. It was heartening to hear that he characterised his condition as volatile. How enlightened, she thought, how quaint: perhaps they could find some common ground in this regard. Otherwise she found his tone utterly patronising and considered it a little rich that she should bide her time waiting for him to decide whether or not she was worthy. Wasn't the real issue whether or not *he* was in any position to pass judgement on anything at all, since this stratagem he spoke of – this illusion, this conceit – seemed little more than some astonishingly elaborate masturbatory subterfuge, conceived in the mind of an ageing ghoul. Either way, she was happy to give it a try, and had never flown business class before. She asked if she could have another glass of wine, and they said, '*Oui, bien sûr*,' and she said, 'Cheers,' and '*Merci*,' for she had learned that much and pronounced that one word with such a perfect accent that people were puzzled when she failed to respond to further, more native platitudes.

Even given the considerable depths and dimensions of Betty's self-loathing, she was not incapable of pride and self-esteem. She knew that there were some things at which she excelled, and it was with the application of this rare confidence that she managed to keep her head above water. Even though she felt it was of no real use, since the head in question – her head, the head of Miss Betty Dean – had already drowned. These were the sorts of things she was thinking as she looked out of the window, curious as to the whereabouts of the charred bones of her dear doomed priest, Urbain Grandier, and where, in all the thousands of fields down there, was that cow who found cheese such a fucking laugh. She was a little drunk, yes, quite a lot now, in fact, and they should never have let her into that lounge, because how many of these warm nuts was she allowed to ask for?

It was a dazed Betty who shuffled through customs and baggage reclaim, trying to translate every sign and poster from lessons she had slept through at the back of the class twenty or more years ago. She was charmed to be greeted by a gaunt, unshaven, dishevelled man of about forty, holding a large card reading *Elizabeth Dean*. He shook her hand, said, 'Georges,' lifted her one case and backpack onto a trolley and with a mumbled 'Please', indicated that she should follow him. She did so, smiling politely, noticing the man's pronounced limp, though he seemed in no pain.

It was night outside the terminal, but the air was wonderfully warm and, despite the dense fug of jet fuel and diesel, there seemed to Betty a solid fragrance of something sweet and clear. She could feel her excitement growing by the minute and wanted to catch Georges's eye to share it with him somehow, for while she was overcome with deliciously nervous anticipation of something possibly glorious, she was, at the same time, beset by a curious sensation of overwhelming loneliness. How she might communicate any of this to a complete stranger who seemed to speak little of her language she had no idea, but she was willing to give it a go. After all, she was a trained actress.

In the event, not a word was spoken until they reached the car, when, opening the back door and pushing forward the passenger seat to allow her more room, Georges gestured with his hand and once more mumbled, 'Please.'

'*Merci*,' said Betty, and climbed inside, sitting back and spreading the flat of her hands across the fine leather and smiling to show that she appreciated the quality. It was one of the fanciest cars she had ever been in and seemed not at all in keeping with the man's slovenly demeanour.

'Air conditioning,' said Georges, indicating a panel of coloured dials between the seats.

'Wonderful,' said Betty, 'yes.' She turned one, though she had no idea why or what it did. '*Formidable*,' which she remembered from films. Yes, she had always been very fond of that one. '*Absolument formidable*,' she went on, surprising herself.

Georges smiled for the first time, said, '*Bien*,' and closed the door.

In the few moments she had alone while Georges walked round to his own door, enveloped in the rich hush of this perfumed automobile, she muttered, 'Fuck me, Betty. What the hell are we doing?' and, still a touch drunk, she laughed, childishly, through her nose.

As they pulled out of the car park and onto the *autoroute*, banked by twinkling hills and wide-open stretches of dark woodland, Georges picked up a large white envelope from the seat beside him and passed it to her. 'For you,' he said. 'From Madame Nora,' and he turned on the radio, which was tuned to some kind of unsettlingly discordant jazz.

Betty watched his eyes in the mirror: they remained fixed on the road ahead, appearing kinder and more child-like than she had previously thought. As they travelled on, passing dimmed shopfronts and traversing a series of wide roundabouts, she thought of attempting a few questions, but could not find the words, and felt frustrated and, curiously, a little sad that he might think her rude. Eventually she took up the large white envelope and opened it, flicking through pages and pages of printed notes and information. There were several unlabelled black discs, either CDs or DVDs, it was difficult to tell. There was another smaller envelope containing two hundred euros in various denominations, together with some documentation that required a signature by the looks of things. And in yet another envelope – stiff-backed and containing a plastic sleeve – were about fifteen photographs of Martha Lear, taken, it seemed, in recent years.

Betty had of course studied many and varied pictures she had located online, but these photographs were different: no film stills, no red carpets, no posed, formal studio headshots. These were obviously more personal, private photographs, taken by someone intimate and trusted. In many Martha was smiling, in others laughing helplessly, dressed in simple outfits – T-shirts, shorts, bathing costumes – half undressed in some, and in one, the last one in the pile, naked, in black and white, taken from the back, seated by a large swimming pool, a drink in one hand, a cigarette in the other, her face turned with her chin resting on her dark shoulder, her hair pinned up and a pair of sunglasses allowed to fall to the tip of her pretty nose. It was astonishing. It might have been Betty. It almost looked like it might have come from the photo shop, as Freddie would say. She wanted to say something to Georges, but she didn't know how, and she didn't know what. Overcome with a sudden feeling of foreboding, she put the photographs back into the envelope, and the envelope into her backpack.

It had been about half an hour by now, and the music had stopped for some reason, without her noticing, and the engine hardly made a sound. She looked out of the window and could see almost nothing. They had left the lit roads and now seemed to be winding down a much narrower lane, which in a short time gave way to another even narrower, and then another, and then another, until dark leaves brushed and rustled against the tinted windows and the car had slowed to a silent crawl. In the distance she could see a solitary light in a small window. The light flickered slightly, as though from a guttering candle.

'Are we here?' said Betty.

'*Oui, madame*,' said Georges, bringing the car to a standstill. '*On est arrivé.*' He let out a gentle sigh. '*Enfin.*'

CHAPTER 12

Now that the beard was off his face and gathered, rather obscenely, around the glistening plughole of the tan basin, Jack Drake's head seemed a good deal smaller. It was certainly smoother, colder, pitifully younger and more chillingly reminiscent of his triple-chinned and plump-cheeked father, which was, after all, the whole idea. He hadn't expected this. He hadn't anticipated the fear he now felt looking himself in the eye and seeing the old brute cut down from his rope and set back on his feet on the floor of his bathroom.

'We have them in three different sizes,' said Lil Sipple, the timid costume assistant. 'We thought these were the best – a bit on the small side – but it's up to you, I mean of course it is. What do you think?'

Jack had already considered the inconvenience, not to mention the assault upon his dignity, of directing a film while made up, head to toe, as his father's decomposing corpse – finished off nicely with a pair of robust seventies sideburns and those wretched red paisley pyjamas. As he stood before his mother's mahogany cheval mirror, brought down specially for the fitting, he wondered why on earth his father had chosen such gaudy apparel for his final trip. Neither Jack nor his mother had ever seen the pyjamas before. Had he bought them expressly for the occasion? And what of the occasion? Why hanging? thought Jack, not for the first time. Why had he not drowned himself as he had so many times promised to do? 'I'll hurl myself from Blackfriars, just you see. You'll find me in the Serpentine one of these days,' if dinner was overcooked. 'Wait till I'm face down in the Hampstead Ladies' Pond,' if he'd suffered a bad haircut.

No, this hanging was premeditated and vicious. What spite had so infected him that he should have his corpse introduced to the world of the living with such histrionics? And right there in the middle of the entrance hall, dangling from the banister: not in some upstairs chamber, not in the cellar, not in the guest house, not from a bough of the old lime tree. My God, he must have despised me, thought Jack. Not that he'd seen it, but his father wasn't to know. After all, he'd done it on a school day, shortly before home time. He'd certainly despised Jack's mother – but then not half as much as she had despised him. And all for the love (if that was what it had been) of Mary Marsh.

Miss Marsh. Mrs Mary Marsh. Was she worth it, Dad? thought Jack; was she worth the price of the rope? Was she worth those pyjamas? Did Mary Marsh buy them for you? And still you persisted in loving her – if that's the right word. Was it ever the right word? Should it even be a word, since there was so much confusion as to what exactly it referred? They had been arguing about it for millennia, it seemed. Why not forget it? Why not forget about love? Look where it's got us, he thought, look where it's got *me*, pulling down the ridiculous red flannelette trousers.

'Alginate, Mr Drake, sodium alginate,' said Rex FX, stirring vigorously a viscous baby-blue porridge in a shallow navy bucket.

'I know,' said Jack, sitting bare-chested on a plastic chair, eyebrows and lashes Vaselined, ears plugged, hair greased and squeezed beneath a latex bald-cap.

He had no intention of spending the entire next four weeks lying around on his own film set, holding his breath. He'd make himself available to himself for the close-ups, but for anything wider, he'd decided to shoot a prosthetic carcass. Yesterday they'd cast his entire body; this morning it was his head. He was having no fun.

'It's actually derived from brown seaweed,' said Rex, now pouring a little more water into the mix and beckoning his assistant, Neville, to prepare to scoop.

'Yes, yes,' said Jack. 'I've seen this done many times.'

'I'm sure you have,' said Rex.

'My wife's head was cast endlessly.'

'I'm sure it was.'

'She claimed to be one of the most decapitated actresses in the business . . .'

'God bless her,' said Neville, scooping up the first gloopy handful.

'You can actually eat it,' said Rex.

'. . . Marie Antoinette, Lady Jane Grey, Mary Queen of—'

'So don't worry if any goes in your mouth. It's good for you.'

'Is it?' said Jack, dubious.

'Yes, but I wouldn't recommend swallowing it.'

'Very interesting,' said Jack, before the first blob of blue slop was slapped against his forehead, slipping slowly down his nose, and then another plop over his left ear, and a barrage of clammy globules slathered across his cheeks and chin.

'Close your eyes,' said Neville, before closing one for him with another buttery dollop, a thick gummy pudding, far colder than anything ought to be. 'It's perfect now, just what we're looking for.' Another slab went on over the ear, and the same dense slop on the other side, and Jack could no longer make out anything Rex and Neville were saying.

'I can't hear you, Rex,' he said. 'I can't hear anything now,' and their voices faded into the far distance. And as his mouth was stopped with another fat handful of glop, he felt himself slowly sinking to a calm bed on the dark bottom of a deep and silent lake, with Rex and Neville somewhere high up above, shifting around on the surface, nattering away about this suffocating blue blubber now encasing Jack Drake's entire head. He could tell from the weight that they had begun to apply the wet bandages to the outside of the mould. He could feel the warm splash of plaster on his back and breast. His now enormous head felt like a wasps' nest, as heavy as an old leather medicine ball.

He swallowed, and then swallowed again and again and again, till there was nothing left to swallow and his tongue dried up as he peeled it away from the roof of his mouth. He could hear other voices arriving in the room, and far-distant laughter, and the slight vibration of the floor beneath his feet. They had stopped touching him now. Just one last pat on his head like he'd been a very good dog. The waiting had begun; maybe ten minutes now. He sensed them all walking away, concerning themselves with other matters. A soft, low rumbling, faint, mumbled incantations, as though from another world entirely, as though he were formed of some other substance, as though he were the only spirit at a seance. Yes. It was difficult not to think of the grave.

Nora didn't really want to spend her free Sunday with Jack; she'd rather have enjoyed some quality time frolicking on Primrose Hill with her crippled basset hound, Jack (no relation), but she'd spent Friday night and most of Saturday in France ensuring that everything was in place for Betty's arrival and now had to deliver her report. She had made available all pertinent materials, furnished several clothes rails with appropriate outfits; she had laid out cosmetics, jewellery, wigs and accoutrements. She had locked away what was private and brought out into the open that which should now be brought out for the purposes of whatever the hell it was that Jack had in mind. Nora didn't really want to know, and yet Jack himself, it seemed to her, did not really know. She had met with Georges Guerin, a local photographer and aspiring cinematographer, who had been recommended to Jack through a mutual friend, and who seemed to Nora a perfectly amiable sort of chap: clean, punctual, knowledgeable, reliable, and willing to take on the task of accommodating Jack's demands without too many questions. He was happy to facilitate the technical requirements of the task as well as applying himself to general maintenance: cleaning, shopping, driving, etc. Nora had chatted away merrily in his native tongue, even flirting a little, much to the poor lamb's discomfort, she had thought. He would reside in the guest house.

Having reported back to Jack, she found him now surly and reticent, unwilling to talk too much about the peculiar scenario, as if it were something seedy and distasteful. Well, she couldn't argue with that, nor did she want to: she wanted to get away before lunch.

'By the way,' she said, 'Bernadette Lowe can't shoot till next Monday now.'

'Who's Bernadette Lowe?'

'You cast her to play Mary Marsh, remember?'

Jack didn't answer. He was still picking small bogeys of blue rubber from behind his ears.

'Shaving that beard's taken years off you,' said Nora, smiling fondly. 'Maybe things can level out now. Now you've got what you wanted.'

'I don't know what I want,' said Jack, gazing at the sky.

97

'I hope that's not true. You know that's why I'm happy to go along with this caper.'

'Don't call it a caper,' snapped Jack.

'Well, whatever it is. As long as it helps you finish this film. That's all I care about.'

'We'll finish this film,' said Jack, firmly, leaning forward and staring now not at the sky, but down at the mossy flagstones beneath his feet. Thinking that was the end of it, Nora turned to go, but then: 'There won't be any more drama,' he said, almost a whisper. 'I promise. Not now Martha's back.'

CHAPTER 13

A slim blade of sunlight, slicing beneath the shutters, had been ticking towards her all morning: upon the shelf and wooden floor, up across the wall and wardrobe, down along the chest of drawers, and now it cut into the unlit lamp on the nightstand, surely only minutes from her pillow. She would wait, she had decided, till it crept across her throat, and that would be the sign, for she needed a sign; she needed the will of another thing to tell her it was time for the curtain to rise and the play to begin.

Last night Georges had walked her to the front of the house and by the light of his phone had guided her a short distance down a narrow corridor to the room in which he had been told she should sleep. He had set down her bags and, with the minimum of fuss, bid her *bonne nuit* and then left by the front door, though curiously she had not heard the car depart. She had used the toilet in the adjoining room but had been far too tired to notice much about anything, and had certainly not bothered to clean her teeth or wash herself. They must think I'm a dirty one, she had thought, therefore I must be a dirty one. It was the last thing she remembered thinking.

What did she know of where she was in the world? Only

that she had been driven inland from Marseille airport for what felt like half an hour. She had been given no itinerary regarding the exact address, nor even the general location, but really, she thought she should be thankful she had not been bundled into the car boot, gagged and blindfolded. She felt that the whole peculiar pudding thus far had been a little over-egged in terms of mystery, but that surely everything that happened from now on, after she threw open this door and walked out of this room, would reveal with crystal clarity the truth of why she had been brought here.

For now she harboured a sinking feeling that the whole thing would be a disappointment, the situation mundane, the intrigue a sham and the task itself – this business of impersonating a dead wife for the morbid stimulation of a debased husband – so ludicrous and impractical that it would fall apart in the first hour and she would be back at the airport before sunset. But then she heard birdsong right outside the window, as though the most melodious creature in the whole of Europe had alighted upon the ledge and told her to pull herself together – 'Try to enjoy yourself for once in your life, you miserable old bag' – and so she unzipped her suitcase and looked for something suitable to put on.

The first thing that struck her, as she ventured out in a simple white cotton dress and a pair of red plastic flip-flops, was that it had been a calculated decision to have her pass her first night here in the most unremarkable room of the house. No matter that it was the finest room she had ever slept in, with an exquisite chandelier, stone walls and a hand-carved wooden bed that looked like something she had once seen, as a young girl, behind thick red ropes in Hampton Court. Last night's narrow corridor opened up, little by little, into a much wider corridor, and on, down a small flight of six or seven white stone steps and into an open hallway with polished cobbles that in turn led to a large kitchen with high, wide ochre walls and wine-red terra-cotta tiles – slightly damp, as though recently mopped – and white marble counter tops recently scrubbed and fresh yellow lilies in a green glass vase, with pearls of water still drying on the shining leaves. There was a shocking amount of fruit in a bowl as big as a bicycle wheel, fruit she'd never seen before, prehistoric-looking things in new colours. The sun was pouring in and over everything in a bright hot torrent of light, like there was far too much of it, even shining in hidden patches where shadows should have been, like it really didn't give two monkeys what you were used to back home because this was France, and the South at that.

She opened the fridge and just laughed in its face and told it to fuck off with all that food, and took the same attitude with all the cupboards, and shook her head and tutted at the powdered baguettes on the wooden board, and at the blocks of blue and pink and turquoise cheese beneath the bell-shaped cage, like cheese in a zoo, not to be teased. She began to laugh and carried on laughing at the fact she was laughing, which made her laugh all the more. She decided she should make her way out of this most delicious of kitchens, since it had clearly rendered her completely delirious.

She averted her eyes from the terrace, which looked, from the little she had glimpsed, the sort of place one might want to spend the next ten years of one's life. She could see that there was a series of long rooms all leading one into the other in a colourful procession of considered ostentation. She walked softly now, recalling her dancer's training, her head slowly turning, tilting her chin up and then down, then up and to the side, her mouth agape, as though in a gallery, for that was how the first room presented itself, its white stone walls almost entirely covered in paintings and photographs. There were enough faces staring out and down to populate a small village. As well as dozens and dozens of beautifully framed paintings, oils, water-colours, there were simple pencil sketches, studies in pastel and charcoal, elaborate illustrations, botanical, anatomical, torn from old books and fixed with thick pins to the mortar. Deeper frames held dried flowers, pressed flowers, pinned insects, precious stones, hand-made maps, mounted rosaries, small bones and skulls. Displayed on shelves, plinths, cabinet- and tabletops were fossils, clocks, small bottles, broken china, antique pencils, burnt-out candles, piles of wire spectacles, telescopes, kaleido-scopes, a large oak kinetoscope, a birdcage filled with Polaroids of roses, large seashells filled with small seashells, and oyster shells filled with beetle wings. There were rugs on the walls and rugs underfoot, fat soft sofas piled high with books and papers, an old green guitar in a shabby green chair. In a glass display case next to the mantelpiece, twenty, maybe thirty, maybe forty old cameras, and upon the mantelpiece, in pride of place, a stuffed yellow parrot on a branch beneath a bell jar, and engraved upon a brass plate, the name Bartholomew. Betty looked closely at its talons, at the beak, then into the black glass eyes, and saw herself bent across the small hill of its gaze.

Then, just as she felt ready to turn and behold the splen-dour of the garden, there was the sound of something heavy falling and crashing, and a man's voice cursing. It came from somewhere beyond the doors at the far end of the room, the tall, important-looking doors. She walked towards them, more afraid than she would have liked, for she had thought she was alone. There came the sound of heavy footsteps crossing the hard, wooden floor, the slamming of a door, then more foot-steps, crunching, as if on gravel. In the still further distance, the slamming of another door, a car door, the sound of the engine firing up, and the tyres on the gravel, before the car was driven away at speed. Betty ran into the next room and climbed up onto a window seat to see a small red car disappearing down the narrow lane, away from the house. The other car – the elegant sedan in which she had arrived – was still parked in the drive.

She climbed down from the window, turned to face the room and immediately noticed large fragments of broken porcelain on the surface of a small table and scattered across the floor. This room was lined with bookshelves so high there was a ladder leaning up against the ceiling. There was a densely cluttered desk, a large leather globe and what looked like a harpsichord, and many more framed paintings and lurking curiosities.

A pair of heavy blue doors led into yet another room, which was almost completely dark, save for an eerie grey glow emanating from the far end. In the glow she could make out the silhouettes of two women sitting in complete silence. She could not see their faces, but their hair seemed dishevelled, as though they had been fighting, and one of them held her head at such a strange angle that Betty wondered if she were even conscious. She felt her entire body turn cold, and all the sun in the kitchen, and all the sun in the garden, and all the sun in the whole of France suddenly felt like a ball of ice.

'Hello,' she called, and as she stepped slowly across the threshold, she accidentally kicked a shard of the broken porcelain that had fallen into the darkened room. Still the two women did not move. She could see now that all the shutters in the room were closed, and that the source of the glow was some kind of small screen attached to an articulated stand, and that much of the room was filled with such stands. She could make out the silhouette of a camera. She drew nearer to the backs of the chairs where the two women were seated, but now it seemed that one of the women was not seated after all, but was perhaps more like a very short woman standing, and then, as she drew closer, well, that didn't make any sense at all.

'Hello,' said Betty, blood pounding in her ears. 'Hello?' she said again. She switched on the torch on her phone, illuminating the faces of the women, and let out a loud scream. She ran back out into the light of the other room, gripping the frame of the door, trying to catch her breath, wanting to go home, because she didn't like it here any more, and there was no need for this sort of thing, and what *was* this sort of thing? and 'What the fuck!' she screamed as loudly as she had ever screamed anything.

Until I feel you are worthy, I shall request that you maintain a plausible silence, Jack Drake had written, *since all the initial work will be upon establishing a viable system focused on the visual challenges of this conceit, which are manifold. Much of this need not concern you, and I will not waste time explaining details that will be made apparent upon your arrival.*

Well, she had certainly not maintained a plausible silence. She could well understand that the visual challenges were manifold, but she felt it would not have been such a waste of time explaining a few of the details rather than waiting for them to be made apparent upon her arrival, because she had found some of these details to be very fucking concerning indeed.

Here was what was clear so far. She could only imagine that it had been Georges racing away from the house in his dinky red car, which suited him much better than the black sedan. She therefore imagined that it was Georges who had mopped the floors and scrubbed the counter tops and dressed the flowers in the vase. She might therefore presume that it would be Georges who would be taking care of the manifold visual challenges, only maybe he could have mentioned something about that the previous night: since he seemed perfectly capable of saying 'please' and 'please' and 'air conditioning', he could perhaps have got round to explaining that he would be 'responsible for establishing a viable system concerning the resurrection of the late Mrs Drake, who, let us not forget, did in fact take her own life by stepping into the path of a speeding freight train.

Yes, let us not forget that, *madame*,' he could have said. 'And by the way, *bonne nuit*. Sleep well.'

For fuck's sake. Betty was furious. She was not the healthiest of women at the best of times and was not too young to suffer a heart attack. It would have been a preposterous way to go, discovered stiff and blue on the floor of a French chateau, terrified to death by a cracked mannequin and a cheap hairdresser's training head balanced precariously on a Regency plant stand. This was the most ludicrous job she'd ever heard of. Her agent would be hearing from her forthwith.

Betty had walked all the way to the far end of the garden, the sharp grass pricking her feet, and her poor English heels and toes were scalded when at last she finally made it to the hot tile perimeter of the enormous pool. She had, she realised, been foolish to kick off her red plastic flip-flops on the terrace; she could see them now, in the distance, like bloody footprints on the shining white steps. The pool had long ago been covered in a parched tarpaulin, and the tarpaulin in leaves, and the leaves in the dirt and dust of other seasons. She had dug her fingers beneath the thick rubbery seam, breaking her last good nail, but had been unable to reach the shallow brown water below. She'd dragged a chair into the shade of a nearby fig tree and spread the several pages of Nora's notes beside her on the grass. Finding no alcohol anywhere in the house, she had filled a tall glass with some kind of iced minty cordial and scattered a handful of raspberries onto a saucer. What she really desired was to close her eyes, but she knew that she could no longer put off the job in hand.

The first few pages were a general introduction to the house: a basic floor plan, a list of dos and don'ts, and be carefuls, and be mindfuls, and be not forgetfuls. They told her where things were and why they were where they were, and to put them back where she had found them. There were lists of essential phone numbers, places to shop, places to eat – though most of that would be taken care of by Georges. Ideally she should try not to leave the house, for a call might come through at any hour of the day or night, though obviously every effort would be made to establish a schedule or at least give fair warning. In that regard, it would be understood that if she could not answer a call, she might have other obligations, but it must be equally understood that her principal obligation was to be of service to Jack.

Betty took a deep breath, a gulp of her drink and popped in a raspberry. Regarding Jack, it must be stressed that she should call him Jack, and only Jack, at all times from now on and to never address him in any other voice other than 'the Voice', which was hereafter written throughout with a capital V. Nora suggested that Betty could wear whatever she wanted, as long as it issued from Martha's closet, and that a selection had been made, and that this was to be found in the upstairs bedroom, opposite the statue of St Bartholomew, which was also, by the way, where she should sleep from now on, and that it went without saying – but say it Nora must – that Betty should treat this room, above all the rooms, with the utmost respect. Regarding her hair, she should make every effort to maintain it in a presentable and plausible condition. To this end wigs would be provided and indeed were to be found in the aforementioned bedroom, in the cupboard labelled *Wigs*. Betty was to be discouraged from consulting the internet, since much of the biographical and almost all of the personal information contained thereon was either laughable and flawed or else completely fallacious, and often libellous. She was furthermore warned that she was not at any point to attempt to improvise until Jack considered it to be a viable option. She was required to keep her own opinions and prejudices to herself, and furthermore she was under no circumstances to question anything while on camera. If there were any problems, she should contact Nora by phone, text or mail.

As far as possible she would never be asked to do anything with which she was uncomfortable or to which she was morally opposed.

In summary, she was not to discuss anything that passed in this house with anyone outside of this house, other than Nora herself; not even Jack. *For you must remember,* wrote Nora, ver-batim, *for Jack Drake, Betty Dean does not exist. Nor has she ever existed, nor will she ever. No offence.*

Martha, is everything all right? I haven't heard from you x

As instructed by the notes, Betty had found her new phone – Martha's new phone – upon the desk in the study, which, apparently, was what Nora was calling the room with the broken porcelain urn and the harpsichord. Having swept up the mess, she now sat at the desk grappling with the rules of this lunacy. On her own phone, a message from Nora said, *This is Nora. I will send you messages on this phone and not the other phone – Martha's phone. Jack will never send messages to this phone and will only communicate with Martha on Martha's phone. Martha's phone is for Martha only and is not to be used by you.*

On Martha's phone, there were three messages from Jack. The first, asking if she was all right, and saying that he hadn't heard from her, had been sent in the morning, and it was now nearly four in the afternoon. The second message said, *Martha, I've been in fittings and tests all day. Very strange. Bade farewell to my beard. Not sure how I feel about all this. Do you think I've made the right decision? I don't know what else I could have done x*

Was she supposed to reply to this?

The third message said, *Martha, why aren't you checking your phone? Just tell me you're all right. Tell me you're not mad with me x*

Betty typed, *Sorry, Jack. Couldn't find my phone, but here it is, in the study. Of course I'm not mad with you x*. She pressed 'send' and immediately felt like she should take a long shower, which she probably should anyway, considering that she hadn't washed since London, but the point was just . . . Well, as it so often was these past few days, it seemed, the point was just *What the fucking fuck?* She couldn't stop saying it. Sometimes it was an expression of surprise and enchantment, but more often it was an expression of revulsion, incredulity, exasperation and bewilderment, as it was right now upon watching herself take the first dirty step into Jack Drake's dirty and diabolical world.

Unable to find a light switch in the darkened room, she had opened up one of the shutters just enough. Just about perfect, she thought, with that scented beam of golden light sliced into six by the wooden slats. She lifted the wig from the cracked mannequin and placed it upon her own head. Taking advantage of one of the many grand mirrors in the house, she took a close look at herself. A shadow curled across her nose and cheek, carving her jaw and pouring ink into the eye's cold socket. 'Hello, Jack,' she said, in Martha's slurred yet lyric drawl. 'I'm dead, my dear. So I don't know what you think you're up to. I thought I'd made it perfectly clear. That train, I thought, had made it perfectly clear.' She smiled. 'Is there something you forgot to tell me? Is there something I forgot to do, Jack? Well, it's too late now, Jack, and all this nonsense won't help. *She* won't help. *She* won't get us anywhere; this ugly bitch in a ten-dollar wig. Goddammit, Jack, you must be desperate.'

CHAPTER 14

Vladimir, the yellow parrot, had been a little skittish and was making things difficult for the sound department with his constant complaints and his wild impersonations of Jack, shouting 'Cut!' every few minutes. Eventually he had to be written out of the scene and escorted to the guest house.

The first shot of the day had seen Jack as his recently throttled father – grey-faced, in crimson paisley – hauled feet first up the steep staircase by Eve Parnell as Eleanor Drake, prosthetically pregnant, sweating and grunting, while muttering something sinister from the Book of Job. As Jack removed the back and elbow pads, slipping on a plain black robe, his mood lifted. In the morning he'd apologised to Billy and presented him with a 1930s Rolleiflex, and invited Phyllis, the boy's mother, over to the monitor to explain the difference between butterfly and Rembrandt lighting, which had made her smile, and when she sat down in Jack's chair to finish her cup of tea with as many as three digestives, Jack had not flinched. Nora was encouraged. After all her hard work – her weekend flight to France, her conscription of complicit stooges, her elucidation of the strategy, her coercion of the sop – it seemed that all had been to a good end. As the crew began to lug much of their equipment up to the top bedroom, Jack could be seen leading the way, taking two, sometimes three steps at a time, and Nora wondered if Bergman had ever attempted such a thing.

As Solomon and his team worked to adjust the lighting of the room, Jack had decided to contemplate the next scene lying on his back on the hard single bed – the same place where his father had once lain, contemplating nothing, but slowly turning from one strange thing into another, in the open air, in plain sight, at home, feet up, in a musty narrow room with arabesque rugs and brown wallpaper rich with thistles and wasps.

What his mother had been thinking by subjecting her husband's corpse to such degradation had been, for years, beyond Jack, but now – as he lay there in his father's considerable sideburns, mouth open, eyes closed, breath held, listening, perhaps as his father had listened – who was to say? As a boy he would stand at the end of the corridor, straining to hear. Sometimes it was only tears, other times a low hum, a hushed murmur, a song even. But other times – when he could hear, when it was difficult not to hear, when it was dreadful to hear – such things she said, such abominable, irrevocable things that he had not always understood: unearthly howls, the sound of dragging, slapping, kicking, hissing, sniping. Sounds that didn't have a name, formed in the throat, at the back of the nose, on the roof of the mouth, at the edge of the gum, deep in the gut, in the socket of the eye. How was all this to be explained to a trembling boy who was hungry for the blame, for after all wouldn't everything have been fine had he not interfered, had he kept his nose out, declined to play the sneak, his camera uncapped, all set to tell tales and show Mummy what a fiend his father had been? *Here, look at Miss Marsh, Mummy. Miss Mary Marsh. And her supposed to be my teacher. Teaching me what then? Well, look at this, Mummy, look at this picture, and look at this, and this. What is he doing here? What are those called? Why does her face do that? Is she all right?* Christ, what a nest he'd poked. What a rope he'd tied with his skulking and ratting. And the worst of it was, it wasn't over – for here he was, at it again, peeping again to prove to the world what a prize squealer he was.

'Jack, can I have a word?' said Eve. 'Am I disturbing you?'

'No, no,' said Jack. 'I was just relaxing.'

'Well, that makes a change,' she said, 'for you.' She sat down on the corner of the bed, setting down the red leather-bound Bible she had taken to carrying with her at all times. Jack pushed himself up on his elbows to rest his head against the brown wall. 'I wanted to talk about the scene,' she said, smiling, for she liked Jack, and she liked the role, and she liked being an actress, and last night she'd met a new man who'd promised to take her to Brussels when all this was over.

'Of course,' said Jack, smiling too, for things were looking up, despite his realisation that he had effectively murdered his own father. This was not really news. He supposed it was why he'd written the script in the first place.

'Because,' began Eve, 'it's the first time we're going to see her in here, with him, and we don't want to give too much away.'

'No.'

'We need to leave her somewhere to go.'

'Absolutely.'

'Because she's going to . . . My God, by the end . . .' and she rolled her eyes and whistled.

'Indeed,' said Jack, swinging his legs round to set his feet on the floor, fixing his eyes on the backs of his dead man's hands. He lowered his voice so only Eve might hear. 'It's not continuous with her having dragged him in here,' he said. 'She's not out of breath. She's composed.'

'Yes,' said Eve.

'She feels betrayed, obviously,' said Jack. He rested one hand flat and soft on her silicone bump. 'She has life inside her.' He squeezed. 'Millimetres beneath.'

Eve wanted to talk about babies then, and how she'd always—

'And yet,' said Jack, pulling away from the bump, 'with Mary he . . . Mary Marsh he . . . Miss Marsh to Jack. Jack's teacher.'

'I know, his fucking teacher!' said Eve.

'Can you imagine?'

Eve shook her head. Deeply saddened.

'She'd never imagined this sort of thing was possible,' said Jack. 'She was naïve. And that's what you should be . . . Especially here, at the start.'

'She was going to do it,' said Eve, wide-eyed, nodding vigorously, loving all this.

'What?' said Jack.

'I think . . .' and she thought about it a little more, until she was sure. 'What if she was going to do the same thing?'

'What thing?'

'She was going to kill herself. She was waiting for the baby to be born, and then she was going to . . . not necessarily hang . . . pills, whatever . . . wrists . . . gas . . . to show him.'

Jack shook his head. 'It would have been against her beliefs.'

'So would this,' said Eve, pointing to Jack's cold grey hands, warming to her theme. 'This isn't in the Bible. It could work.' He wasn't dismissing it, and so she continued. 'Even if it's not explicitly stated.'

Jack stood up and began pacing.

'She's just so fucking furious. He's beaten her to it. Isn't it partly that?'

Jack looked up. 'He's stolen her thunder.'

'Exactly.'

He paced all the way to the door, turned, and paced all the way back. 'No,' he said, abruptly. 'No, that's a dreadful idea.'

His phone chirped. 'Absolutely dreadful,' he said, and pulled the phone from the pocket of his robe. Without his spectacles he held it at arm's length to focus. Eve couldn't help but notice that he'd received a text – from Martha. There was her picture on his phone.

He opened it. Read it. Smiled. Put the phone back into his pocket.

'Is everything all right?' said Eve, frowning.

'Yes, fine, fine,' said Jack. 'It's just Martha.'

'Right.'

Silence.

'She wants me to call.'

'Oh?' said Eve. 'Where is she?'

'She's in France.'

'Oh,' said Eve, and if she looked concerned or baffled, Jack didn't seem to notice. 'And how is she?' Eve said, and smiled, for she liked Jack, and had liked Martha, in her way.

'Oh, she's fine,' said Jack. 'She's doing really well now.'

After lunch, Nora discovered Jack sitting with the sulking parrot in the back room of the guest house. He was scribbling on sheets of yellow paper with a stubby black pencil sharpened at both ends, while gripping another larger, longer white pencil in his teeth. When at last he noticed her, he pushed the papers, all in a mess, across the desk, then, letting the white pencil drop to the floor, he wiped the slick of spit from his lips and chin and said, 'Send these.'

'Send these,' repeated the parrot.

CHAPTER 15

It was Wednesday. Betty had been studying Martha for over a week. Since accepting the job, she had watched many of Martha's screen performances; she had analysed various talk shows, press conferences, radio interviews; she had been granted unusual access to numerous home recordings, wherein Martha, usually a little drunk, sometimes prompted, spoke candidly, wittily, honestly, often emotionally. Throughout all this Betty had identified and made thorough notes on many aspects of accent, attitude, gesture, posture, tone and temperament. She had observed precisely how Martha crossed her legs, when she crossed her legs and why she crossed her legs. Or at what point in a conversation she pushed the hair from her face. At what point she would scratch, where she scratched, with which hand, with which finger; how that finger was ringed, clipped and painted; the shape of her mouth as the scratch was applied, and how many twitches of the finger were necessary to defuse the itch to her satisfaction, and how that satisfaction was expressed. When she rested her closed fist against her temple as she listened – often defensively – it was almost always with the middle knuckle of the ring finger pressed against the cheek, pushing up the thin flesh there in three, sometimes four fine folds. Never five, hardly ever just two. At the same time her thumb rested in the hollow beneath her ear, lifting forward the lobe, the index finger pointing away from the rest of the hand, up into the hairline.

When Martha held a tumbler, she would wrap three fingers round it and tuck her pinky back into the palm. Wine glasses were always lifted by the stem, two fingers round, ring and pinky folded back, thumb straight, resting against the tip of the middle; her head ushered forth to meet the rim at the lower lip before tilting both the glass and the head at the same time, the eyes briefly closed. Cigarettes were held snug at the base of the first and second finger and posed at rest, palm up, burning tip towards the floor, causing the smoke to rise through and around the hand for a dramatic effect she clearly enjoyed. The ash was tapped with the pad of the thumb. She would punctuate a well-made point or a witty riposte with a sharp flick of the head, tossing her chin skywards while artfully curling her lip to dimple one cheek. If ever she suspected her interlocutor of posturing, she would turn her face fully to the side, offering them one wide-open eye, while the far eye was squeezed shut, with comic panache, unashamedly piratical. Eyelashes, often false, were invariably held or delicately pulled between pinky and thumb, the corners of the mouth dropping down. Betty's mother had done something similar. Indeed, there was something of Betty's mother haunting the mask and countenance of this tragic woman.

By the end of her second day and night in France, Betty had begun to feel a curious sympathy for her subject. An immense pity, and she didn't know how or why. And of course, in summary of all this, it was difficult not to hear Freddie's sparkling plea: *Do Mrs Martha, Mummy, do the dead lady. What would she say? How would she say it?*

★

After her first night sleeping in Martha's bed, Betty awoke abruptly: she had bled heavily upon the fresh white sheets. This was both a horror and a relief, for at least it was the last time she would have to consider Sean and could therefore focus upon the job in hand. The bedroom was perhaps the purest, prettiest room of the house. Nora had called it Martha's room, but one must assume that it was also Jack's room. The walls were white, as were the nightstands and lampshades, as were the floorboards, rugs, chairs, drawers, mirrors and shutters. Even the books upon the white shelves were bound – for art's sake, one must assume – in white.

Two things stood out therefore against all this. The first was a dour painting in a dark, knotty frame hanging on the wall opposite the bed, in such a position, at such a height, that made it impossible to overlook. It was a beautiful piece of work, but as unsettling as anything else she had seen in the house thus far. According to a spidery scrawl, the painting dated from 1895 and was titled *L'Étranger*. It was about two feet by three feet, painted in a vaguely impressionist manner, and depicted a slight, blowsy-looking woman seated at a table in a dimly lit bar, a green drink at her elbow. She was just about wearing a diaphanous black-and-scarlet blouse through which one could discern a plump purple nipple. A slender cigarette balanced precariously between her fingers looked like it might tumble to the floor at any moment. Her dark eyes were smudged blue, too heavy for her face, so low they drooped in thick uncomfortable intoxication. Across the table and creeping up the wall the artist had painted the glowering shadow of a man (or was it a woman?) wearing a top hat, askew, which gave the painting a sinister air.

The room's second anomaly was a large white crucifix: a startled ivory Jesus on a white wooden cross, hanging on the wall directly above the bed, giving it the appearance of a deathbed.

The blood upon the sheets seemed to serve a similar purpose.

It was Wednesday, and still she had not engaged with Jack face to face. She had exchanged a few cursory, exploratory texts that had never passed beyond platitude, and had twice been summoned to what she now thought of – a touch melodramatically – as her chamber of execution. There, her new friend, silent Georges, adjusted lights and flags before falling back into the shadows to fuss with the camera while Betty sat fully made up, wearing one or other of Martha's dresses, invariably instructed, as in Clerkenwell, to say nothing. It was not apparent if Jack lurked on the other end of these sessions. He had made no attempt to reveal himself. Betty had fallen into the routine of dressing in Martha's clothes most of the time, if for no other reason than that in every single respect they were better than her own, and it helped her to walk, figuratively and literally, a mile in Martha's shoes. The same was true of wigs. There was such a diverse selection that it was difficult to choose. In the more intimate home recordings, Martha's hair was shorter than Betty's, and therefore difficult to reproduce. Otherwise she found herself adopting looks from various films, even though that rarely made her feel close to the vibrant core of the living Martha, which burned more vividly when she was captured in the home tapes.

Then, earlier that morning, just as she had suspected that a call would never come, Martha's phone had rung and Jack's surly face had lit up in her hand. In the event she had been too distressed to answer and so allowed it to pass to voicemail.

'Martha, it's me. I got your message.' He sounded meek and frail; not nearly so imposing as she had imagined. Perhaps he too was suffering the glaring absurdity of the masquerade. He went on: 'I'm sorry, darling, not to have called yet. Things have been so hectic here. I'll tell you all about it. Please forgive me. I'll do my very best to call this evening. I love you.'

It sounded completely unaffected. It sounded precisely like a man, albeit a rather timorous one, calling his wife and apologising for not having found the time to call. It seemed remarkable to Betty that it should sound so commonplace, and caused her confidence to swell to think that all might be achievable.

Certain troublesome roles in Betty's professional past had required her to remain in character for much of her waking day. While this often perplexed or infuriated those around her – and while she could well concede that such excess might be perceived as at best an eccentricity, at worst a tedious affectation – she often found it curiously liberating. And so it was not only Martha's clothes and jewels and piled-up hair that she had taken to wearing for much of the day; it was also Martha's curiosity and her jealousy, her petulance and sarcasm, her small excitements and her sordid disappointments, her hunger, her hygiene, her relentless fatigue. It was not Martha's voice that concerned her: for Betty, that was the easy part, that was merely the putting together of the lips and blowing, and she had dispensed with the spurious services of a voice coach after the first session, finding her too officious and clinical, with no feeling for the elocution of the heart. For Betty, what was tough was knowing so little, feeling so little – and therefore it was not merely a matter of living *with* Martha, *within* Martha, but living *as* Martha, following every impulse to its place of rest. And yes, of course it was a distraction and an anaesthetic, since it gave the impression of re-lieving Betty of the pain of her own problems. But at what cost if she was then burdened with the more complex and perhaps forever lost problems of Mrs Martha Lear?

And what, after all, had been these problems? If Betty was spending her days asking herself the question vital to the success of her enterprise – *Why does Martha do what she does?* – then the next natural step was to confront that other terrible question: *Why did Martha do what she did?*

And so it was with all this in mind that, later that evening, Betty found herself taking the slow walk down the long corridor to the chamber of her execution – fully made up, fully dressed, fully baffled, in strange readiness – for her first face-to-face encounter with the man who was responsible for . . . well, what?

CHAPTER 16

These past few days of simply watching her – gawping at her really, even in wonder, for he had not been wrong about her potential – had left him feeling horribly empty. It had felt like peering at some poor suffocated thing trapped under glass. It was too silent. The microphones had been muted for risk of overhearing trifles, or some whispered profanity. She had been presented as little more than a shifting face, turning and tilting this way and that, like a clockwork automaton in a dark room, of which nothing could be discerned. Speechless, fixed in the narrow light, no room to breathe, no room to be. As limited in her abilities to engage as that dreadful waxen head on a stick. It would not do. So now she must speak.

Jack had chosen not to sit in the gloom of the editing suite, but with tablet, headphones and no spectacles to find a comfortable corner in the downstairs living room, beneath the Venetian lamp, in the leather chair. Not that it mattered where he sat or what he looked like, thank God – he was still his father's cadaver – she would be spared the sight of him. At the agreed hour, seven o'clock precisely, he called, and, tapping the tablet's black screen with his bitten fingernails, he waited, until finally, after almost one full minute, the screen blushed, feeling suddenly radiant and warm in his ashen hands.

There she was. There was no doubt about that. Out of the dark at last. Up until now she might as well have been in the room next door, a small white bird in a locked black cage. Now she could be seen. Still tucked loosely in the necessary shadow – but Martha often sits out of the sun, he thought; she feels faint in close heat, a devotee of the shade, and so shadow is good – they had worked it out, and there she was. 'You look as beautiful as ever,' said Jack, and she smiled proudly, a little cocky, as though it were expected, and that was all fine, for that was Martha, nicely done.

'Thank you, Jack,' she said, as she had always said it, and Jack's heart skipped a beat. He held the screen a little closer to his face, fussed with the headphones.

She always took herself off there, to her favourite room, whenever they would talk like this, for it afforded her the finest views in all the house: on one side out and far down into the garden to the fig tree on the edge of the pool; out on the other to the small copse of laurel at the front, the long lavender-edged path in case of visitors; and through the tall church doors on the southern side: the light, the sunflower field and Cézanne's mountain.

'Did you sleep?' asked Jack.

'Hardly at all. It was too hot,' said Martha. 'And there was a mosquito in the room.'

Jack hesitated. 'Hardly at all' was new, was *hers*, and he had written 'a pair of mosquitoes', but no matter: one was good, better, in fact.

Martha passed briefly into the thicket of shadow in search of matches. She lit a cigarette, as suggested. 'It's still too hot,' she said, the timing her own. 'How is it in London?'

'Rain,' said Jack. 'All through the night, and all through the afternoon.'

'Ha,' she snorted knowingly, with a hint of mockery. She took a drag on her cigarette and pulled on her eyelash, and Jack's heart skipped again. Remarkable.

This was the room where Martha would nap in the afternoon, read her books, play her piano, learn her lines, write; the room with no bones, nor shells, nor stuffed birds. Martha's room. And there she was, lounging, leaning on one elbow, her legs crossed over the arm of her favourite chair. Sarah Bernhardt's chair from the Théâtre de l'Odéon. 'If I sit in this thing long enough,' she was fond of saying, 'then maybe . . . who knows?'

'So how's it all going?' she said now. 'Any better?'

'A little,' he said, 'a little. Eve's very good, as usual. The boy's fine, but he needs to focus. His mother's there every fucking minute. I'm surprised she hasn't walked into shot to wipe his nose.'

Martha laughed, though he hadn't specified it. Since when was she so easily amused? That would need attention.

'Bernadette Lowe arrives next Monday,' said Jack.

'Who's that?'

'She's playing Mary Marsh.'

'Ah,' said Martha, smiling. 'Should I be worried?'

'Of course not. You know me. Why would you say that?'

'It's fine, Jack,' she said. 'I trust you,' and she chuckled, though not in quite the right way.

'I know you do,' he said, resting the tablet down on his knee. He waited. It was her move.

'Jack?' she said, at last, scratching at her shoulder with her pinky.

'Yes?' said Jack, with a sly smile.

'I'm very proud of you, you know.'

'Are you?' said Jack. 'For what?'

'For what? For everything. I'm proud to be your wife.'

'Oh Martha . . .'

'I just wanted to say that. I never say it, and I think you ought to know.'

'Well, thank you,' said Jack, modestly.

'And that I love you. And that if anything should ever happen to me . . .'

'Nothing is going to happen, Martha.'

'I didn't say anything bad,' and she laughed. This was all delivered particularly well, and to the letter. Typical Martha. Never asked for a prompt.

But she was still laughing. A little too long now. 'Sorry,' she said, and that was uncalled for, and still laughing, or rather trying not to laugh, as though something had amused her. He didn't like this.

'Everything all right?' he said, but he wasn't sure who he was saying it to. Fatal. Fatal.

'I'm sorry, Jack, yes,' said Martha. 'I'm just a little giddy.'

Making it up now. He felt like they'd let go of the boat.

Silence.

He waited. Nothing. Tapping the glass. It was her move.

Nothing.

This was a nuisance.

'Martha?'

'Yes?'

'Ah,' he said, 'you're still there. I thought we'd been cut off.'

'I wish I could see you,' said Martha.

What now? Where had this come from?

'I know,' said Jack, wearily, 'but it won't be long. Another few weeks.'

'I mean now,' said Martha. 'I wish I could see you now. I presume you can see me.'

Hadn't Nora explained anything? Of course he couldn't be seen. What did she think this was? Christ, he knew it – first time out of the fucking gate. 'Yes, I'm sorry about that,' he said. 'It's a technical thing. I'll sort it out.' He wouldn't sort it out. He would do no such thing.

'Only because I miss you,' she said, too sulky, 'and it's strange just talking to a voice in the dark.'

Completely off book now. She'd gone rogue. And yet it was still Martha, still that drawl, that cool eye, that flick of the chin. Still that old feeling, in fact, that familiar frustration.

'Well, never mind, eh?' said Jack. 'Nothing to be done now.'

She just sat there, slouched, petulant, smoking, watching the smoke rise. Silence. It was her move. And yet once again, nothing. Not a peep.

'Is there something you want to say?' said Jack.

'What?' said Martha, like she really hadn't heard him. Kicking one foot up and down till her slipper fell off, landing with a clatter on the ashtray. She had studied well.

'I thought you . . . that you might . . .' He took a deep breath. His brow was beginning to prickle.

'What?' she said again. This was a thing now, it seemed.

'I thought you'd said there was something else you wanted to say.'

'Did I?' she said.

'I thought so,' said Jack, sternly.

'No,' she said, and leaned over the side of the chair to crush the cigarette out in the dark, her fingers caught in the brief glow. Sitting back up, 'No,' she repeated.

He stared at her hard for a long time. He didn't know what to say. If she wasn't going to carry on, they had reached an end. The rest would make no sense.

'Well, let's just forget it, Martha. That's it. You've frozen,' he said.

'Jack, there's no need to be—'

'You're frozen, Martha. I have to go. If you can still hear me,

124

I love you, goodnight.' He didn't allow her one more syllable. He closed it down.

He pulled off the headphones and felt like smacking the tablet to the floor, but instead he turned it face down upon his lap and discovered himself stroking the back of it, allowing his breathing to settle. The feeling was familiar. If it really was Martha, she would have called back by now. Nothing infuriated her more than being hung up on. She would have called back and he would have answered and they would have persisted a little while longer. He took his small pad from the table and made a note. He sat there in the soft glow of the lamp, resolved to leave it at that. Somewhere far off in another room, a tap was dripping.

He looked down at his grey hands and his grey feet and saw only the hands and feet of his father, and became lost in the dancing paisley of the pyjama leg, just as his father would often seem lost, obsessing over the pattern of some rug or tile. He recalled a time, a small moment, not long before his father's death, when he had observed him through a crack in the door, his father looking bemused at all the things in the room, as if he recognised them only from a dream and wasn't sure if he should cherish them or smash them to pieces.

'Well, that's not good,' said Nora, on the other end of the phone. 'Shall I speak to her now?'

'I thought everything had been explained,' said Jack. He was walking towards the meat market, headed for the river.

'Everything *had* been explained. I wrote ten pages.'

'Then why did she think she was going to see me?'

'I may not have explained that,' said Nora.

'She was just saying whatever came into her head.'

'Well . . . you know . . .'

Jack pressed the phone closer to his ear, waiting. 'What?'

'Martha could be a troublemaker.'

He marched on, picking up the pace, forcing Nora to listen to his breathing and how fast he was walking. Nora listened. She could hear the keys in his pocket. 'Sorry,' she said.

'I said I didn't want to have to talk about her again.'

'Betty?'

'Don't say her name!' yelled Jack. 'She doesn't exist, she has never existed, she will never exist. Isn't that what I said?'

'I told her that in near enough those exact words.'

'And yet here we are talking about her.'

'Well, there are bound to be some things we need to talk about.'

'You talk to her. Tell her to knock it off,' said Jack.

'Apart from that, though? Everything else?'

'She looked very good,' he said, grudgingly. 'The hair needs attention. The voice is . . .' He thought carefully. 'A miracle,' he said. 'That's why I'm so annoyed. Tell her it's not a game.'

'Right,' said Nora. 'What should I tell her it is?'

'Tell her it's life and death,' said Jack, and he hung up. Nora didn't mind being hung up on. He suspected she rather enjoyed it. She would not call back, and if she did, he would not answer. That was their understanding.

These streets were too wide. It was getting dark. He would take himself off to smaller, narrower streets, and stay there a while.

CHAPTER 17

'And this is Georges,' said Betty, holding up the phone. 'Say hello, Georges.'

'*Comment?*' said Georges, turning from his work to see Betty skipping towards him, happier than he'd ever seen her.

'This is my sister, Ruth,' she said.

'Ah?'

'Say *bonjour. Elle s'appelle Ruth. C'est ma sœur.*'

'Listen to you, *ma sœur*, you've only been there four days,' said Ruth.

Georges waved at the screen. '*Bonjour,*' he said, and smiled, though he could see little but a grinning head the size of a grape, bidding a squeaky *bonjour* back. Betty kept the camera on him for a little longer, since, to the delight of both women, he was stripped to the waist, struggling with the pool's grubby tarpaulin, sweating, streaked with earth, and just so heartbreakingly, gorgeously coy they both burst out laughing, causing him to turn back to his work, adorably embarrassed, at which point both Betty and Ruth felt a touch childish but didn't really care, because this was France, for Betty at least, and the sun was beating down.

'Are you fucking kidding me?' said Ruth. 'He lives with you?'

'It's just me and him,' said Betty, beaming. 'He lives in the guest house.'

'Oh . . .'

'Which, before you start feeling sorry for him, is bigger than both our houses put together, look . . .' and Betty skipped further down the garden, beyond the pool, through a copse of walnut trees to show Ruth the elegant white wooden out-building at the end. 'She thinks you're dishy, Georges,' she shouted, holding up Ruth's little red grape of a face as she passed.

'Betty!' shouted Ruth, eight hundred miles away.

'*Comment?*' said Georges.

'It's all right,' said Betty to Ruth, 'he doesn't understand.' And then, back to Georges, 'She thinks you're a dish.'

'A dish?' said Georges, who might have known what a dish was but saw no sense in this talk and wished that Betty would go away for now.

'Yes, never mind. You carry on,' said Betty. 'I've asked him to get the pool up and running. Four days I've been here, and no pool.'

'Oh God,' said Ruth, one hand to her face.

'I know, dahling,' said Betty, a perfect Celia Johnson. 'Can you imagine?'

'You poor dear.'

'Utterly unbearable. These people are heathens. I shall simply die.'

She had already shown Ruth the main house, darting giddily in and out of rooms that she hadn't yet explored, including a total of six or seven bedrooms she vowed she would sleep in one at a time, now she'd got over the whole thing of sleeping in Martha's bed. Besides, that painting and the crucifix were beginning to spook her. She now took her sister's tiny smiling head out and round to the other side of the house, towards a large pair of shabby-looking doors that opened on an old brick extension, clearly more ramshackle than the rest.

'I think this is some kind of old garage,' she said, stepping through the doors, holding the phone, using her sister's shining face to light the way.

'Sean came round,' said Ruth.

'Did he?' said Betty.

'He thinks you've blocked his number.'

'I have. What did he want?'

'To know where you were. I said I didn't know, but the further away from him, the better.'

'And what did he say to that?' said Betty, searching for a light switch.

'He sulked,' said Ruth. 'And when I went to the toilet, I caught him with my phone, looking for texts from you, so I kicked him out. Literally: pushed him to the door, opened it, and kicked him.'

Betty laughed. 'Good for you,' she said, finally finding the switch, lighting up a ridiculously cluttered old garage. It was difficult to walk any further. 'Oh my God, look at this.'

'Hoarders!' said Ruth.

'Rich ones, though, eh?' Betty said, and gazed around in fascination.

'And have you spoken to Freddie?' said Ruth.

Betty didn't answer for a while, but carried on exploring.

'Betty?' said Ruth.

After a long silence, Betty finally mumbled, 'No.'

'Are they not answering?'

'I haven't tried, to be honest.'

'You haven't tried?'

'No.' She'd had enough of this crappy garage.

'Not at all?' said Ruth.

'Not at all,' said Betty, and she stared at Ruth defiantly, her lip quivering suddenly, out of nowhere, daring her sister to ask her next question.

'Why not?' said Ruth,

'Because I don't care,' said Betty. 'They can call me. When Paul realises what a pig he's been, they can call me. When Freddie realises how cruel he's been, they can call me.'

'He's six, Betty.'

'Well, he's not three. He's a bright six and he should know better. I raised him to know better than that.'

'Oh my goodness,' said Ruth. And something about that 'Oh my goodness' reminded Betty of their mother.

'I can't do everything, Ruth. You're the one who told me to do this . . . to come all the way out here and get involved in all this . . . well . . . y'know . . . It's hard.' She was sniffling and dripping now, wiping at her eyes and nose with the back of her wrist. 'It's not a piece of cake. You've got no idea. I can't do all this and be the world's greatest mother.'

'I don't understand,' said Ruth.

'I know you don't. Nobody does.' She placed the phone on the ground, face up so Ruth could see, and threw her head back as if she had a nosebleed before throwing it violently forward and wedging it between her knees, hands clasped behind with fingers interlocked. And in this position, she began to sob. This went on for some time. Ruth said nothing.

When at last Betty had calmed down and raised herself up, blowing her nose and patting her hair into some sort of shape, she looked back at the screen to apologise. Her sister was gone. The phone had been set down and balanced to give a still view of the kitchen. Ruth was nowhere to be seen. All Betty could see was her father, positioned at a distance in the centre of the shot, isolated, unaware he was being observed, slumped in his chair, mouth open, eyes agog, oblivious. She had been on the phone to Ruth for almost an hour and had not once asked about him. She supposed this was precisely her sister's point.

She stood up and twisted herself around and beneath low-hanging old chairs and the broken plastic wheels of a small tricycle. She blew dust from an ancient typewriter and rattled a hundred marbles in a painted green tin. She kicked down a pile of magazines and poked at thick cobwebs with the tip of a tattered parasol. Then, behind a ragged red blanket hanging on two hooks from the buckled ceiling, she saw something curious. It wasn't the same make as her own bicycle; the saddle was black, not tan, the pedals were rubber, not steel, and the tyre walls red, not white. But it was a near-identical blue and had a basket filled with pine cones. On closer inspection she saw that the tyres were flat but not punctured and the chain was dry but not snapped. She located a working pump behind a polystyrene dog, and a set of cloths and spanners on a low shelf, and took it all out onto the grass, in the afternoon sun, to see what she could make of it.

Nora had contacted Betty the day after the contentious first call to tell her not to be such a little madam and that Mr Drake had been considerably distressed by her disregard for the rules. Betty had protested that she could not do the job to the best of her abilities, that there was scant hope of reaching her full potential, if she felt so constrained. She went on to explain that this ridiculous conceit of feeding her written lines had made her feel exploited and cheap, and that she thought that suppressing her imagination and removing the element of creativity from the procedure would only stifle the potential for it to be authentically cathartic, as she believed Mr Drake wished it to be. To which Nora had countered that Betty had no idea how privileged she was to be given this opportunity, working with the internationally acclaimed film director Jack Drake, and her just a snotty provincial theatre actress whose biggest asset was a

131

knack for mimicry – akin to any common house parrot – who just happened, by a trick of the light and a quirk of genes, to vaguely resemble Mr Drake's poor, poor wife, who, in Nora's opinion, had she been alive, would never have sanctioned such a fiasco. But then Betty pointed out that if Mr Drake's poor, poor wife had been alive then there would be no call for such a fiasco since she could have done all this herself. At which point Nora hung up in a fury, firing off warnings and rebukes down to her very last breath.

There had been two other calls since that first excruciating charade. These were also scripted, though utterly banal, and since nothing had been so objectionable, nor risible, as her forced declarations of love and adoration in that first call, she had behaved herself and toed the line. These subsequent calls had been fleeting, and Betty believed they bored Drake as much as they bored her, offering him little stimulation and less comfort. And it was, by the looks of these new pages, to be the same story today: more vague allusions to this enigmatic film of his, more moaning about the crew and how much he missed his beard. It was all very pitiful and Betty had no interest in allowing things to continue in this manner. The next call was scheduled for seven that evening.

Betty pushed the newly pumped and polished bicycle up to the end of the steep gravel drive and set off. She pedalled along for nearly a minute before she saw another house; she could see the front door at the end of a long path banked on both sides by row upon row of small olive trees. As she paused to see what sort of people might live there, she saw a cloud of dust rise from the road and heard the high-pitched snarl and whine of a fero-cious motor, followed by the startled headlights of a battered little car, a quaking block of ginger rust, just about hanging on as it made its way up the hilly path. As it drew closer and closer, Betty stood aside to let it pass, but instead it slowed to a crawl and crept towards her suspiciously before creaking to a stop between the pillars of a broken gate. The engine was still coughing. Betty was a little afraid that the whole thing might explode. Then the dusty window stuttered down and the alarming face of a rather breathless-looking woman appeared. She had very wild yet tightly curled silver-grey hair and wore perfectly round spectacles with thick black frames. In the back seat, Betty could make out an agitated and equally breathless baby.

'*Bonjour*,' said the woman, grinning. Her teeth were shocking.

'Hello,' said Betty.

'You're American?' said the woman.

'No,' said Betty, 'English.'

The woman's face lit up. '*Ah, vous êtes Betty?*' she said, and grinned even wider, as if she had just performed a magic trick.

'Yes,' said Betty, smiling back, bewildered.

'I am Isabelle,' the woman said, 'and this is Tomas,' pointing to the disgruntled baby.

'*Bonjour*,' said Betty, '*Bonjour, Tomas.*' The baby ignored her. Betty waited for the woman to speak again, but she just stared back at her, breathing heavily and smiling. 'How do you know my name?' said Betty.

'Your husband told me about you,' said Isabelle.

'My husband?' said Betty, shaking her head.

'Well, I don't know, your boyfriend.'

'Who are you talking about?'

'Georges. I met Georges yesterday. He told me it.'

'Oh,' said Betty, until she had something better to say.

'Georges,' said Isabelle mysteriously, 'is the funny man.'

This was news to Betty. 'Georges is not my boyfriend.'

'Well, OK,' said the woman, dropping her smile for the first time and looking a little irritated that Betty should not accept her version of the story. Baby Tomas scowled at Betty through the back window. 'OK, he is not your husband, he is not your boyfriend, but you are together in the house, no?'

'What did he tell you?' said Betty, concerned.

'He told me what you are doing.'

'Which is what?' said Betty, feeling that the conversation had taken a difficult turn.

'Oh,' said Isabelle, 'I don't want to cause trouble. I'm just saying hello . . .' And she started to rev the engine. The baby began to wail.

'Well, it was nice to meet you,' said Betty, above all the noise, not sure what any of this was about.

'Hey, Betty,' said Isabelle abruptly, revisiting her smile, 'it is nice to have people at the house again, no?'

'I suppose,' said Betty, 'yes, it must be.'

'After all the trouble.' Isabelle pulled the corners of her mouth down like a clown. She looked a lot like a clown.

'Yes,' said Betty.

'Poor people,' said Isabelle. 'Poor Martha, eh?'

'I know,' said Betty, though she wondered if she did.

'Poor Jack,' said Isabelle.

'I know,' said Betty, though really she did not.

'Poor little one.'

'Little one?' said Betty.

'I know, terrible,' said Isabelle, rolling her eyes in those big round glasses. 'Listen, Betty, I don't have the time now. Tomas has not the time for this. He is the busy baby.' And she laughed, wrestling hard with the car to pull it into gear.

'OK,' said Betty, smiling and waving. '*Au revoir.*'

'*À tout à l'heure,*' called Isabelle, working the engine back up to full snarl. With that, she and the furious Tomas lurched forward and roared away, leaving Betty astride Martha's blue bicycle, in Martha's blue dress and Martha's flat blue pumps covered in dust, still waving. Look at me still waving, thought Betty, look at me, like a simpleton in a clever foreign film.

And then – *little one?*

CHAPTER 18

'My father had never given me anything,' Jack said, and paused. He stopped and rewound the scene to the opening wide shot of the boy sitting at the table with a single lamp illuminating his face and hands. As soon as the shot began its slow track in, he tried again. 'It was the only thing my father ever gave me.' As it became apparent that the boy was struggling to load his camera with film, Jack cued in a simple piano and carried on, speaking softly, almost a whisper, his mouth close to the microphone. 'If I questioned it at the time, it was the wrong question, and therefore my answer . . .' He stopped and pulled away from the microphone, frustrated. Cursing, he began the whole sequence again. The wide shot of the boy assembling the camera and the slow track in. 'The first thing I ever loved, before I was aware of the wounds it could inflict, was the smell of the thing, the chemical stink of it, the fetid acetate, the leather and the brass. My father had taught me to take it apart and load it, like the weapon it was, ready to shoot, take, capture, cut. I loved the language of it. It seemed, to me, a perfect thing.'

He paused the playback. 'A perfect thing' had been interrupted by a strange noise coming from one corner of the room. Earlier that morning, before anyone had arrived, he had been sitting in the vestibule, staring at the painting of the girl on the mountain, and a small antique ink pot had tipped on its side and rolled off the table onto the rug. It was the third time in recent weeks such a thing had occurred. It was the sort of thing he thought he remembered witnessing often as a little boy, but in the intervening years he had written off such memories as childish imagination. And yet here they were again, these things, falling, rolling, tipping over and dropping of their own accord. He played back the last few words of the narration, but there was nothing on the recording, and once more his whole skull flushed cold. How curious it was that he should now find it so chilling to hear nothing. And how completely foolish he felt as he hurried to the door, switching on the lights and throwing open the curtains. If this thing could move a pot, he mused, or cast a book down from the shelf, or slam a door, blow out a candle, if it could turn on taps and hurl a bird against the window, then could it not also play with the neurones of his brain, and cause him to lose, as he had done the other day, the ability to tell the time from a common clock, rendering the hands and the face nonsensical, reducing the digits to gibberish?

He took out his phone and typed a message: *Martha, what are you doing? I miss you. I feel foolish for saying it. I wish I was there with you. I must go back to work, but I feel sick to my stomach. I can't do this. No one will care. Will we talk tonight? X*

He sent it and watched the screen, assured that she would write straight back as was Martha's way. Within a minute came her reply.

Jack, you are foolish for saying it. There is nothing you cannot do. I believe in you. I am out on my bike, going into town to buy wine. I saw Isabelle. Her baby's a freak! Of course we will talk. 7 again? X

Jack kept his eyes on the screen long after he'd read the message. He felt the insides of his mouth bloody from chewing on his cheeks. He loved his wife. He knew that. He remembered that. He could never tell her what to do. It had always been thus. She knew that. They both knew that. She was on her way into town on her bike, to buy wine. Well, that was splendid. Who was Isabelle? A neighbour, he thought. He kept himself to himself. Martha was more sociable. And Isabelle had a baby. Good for her. He swallowed more blood and shook his head, minutely, back and forth, back and forth, before looking at the time to see that lunch was over.

For the rest of the afternoon, thirty-five professional adults focused all their specialist abilities on facilitating the flight of Vladimir the parrot in the role of Bartholomew: starting from the telephone table in the main entrance hall, up two flights of stairs and to the farthermost door; land, pause, push open the door, then hop up onto the chest of his decomposing master and tell him to wake up, wake up, over and over. Vladimir was not an easy bird to work with, and by the end of the day everyone despised him.

'I still can't see you,' said Martha. 'Is it always gonna be like this?'

'I'm afraid so,' said Jack. It hadn't taken her long. They'd only been talking for two minutes, though a little tediously, it was true.

'Well, that's a big fat drag,' said Martha, taking a big fat swig of her wine. She was really on form tonight.

'I'm sorry,' said Jack. 'It's the way it is.'

'Everything's the way it is,' said Martha. 'That's the problem. But this not seeing you, Jack – it's a pain in the ass. We might as well just talk on the phone.'

'But I can see you, Martha. And that's what matters, isn't it?'

'It matters to you.'

'And that's what matters,' said Jack, perhaps a little too firmly. He checked himself and took a breath. 'And besides, you wouldn't want to see me, the way I look right now. It would frighten you.' She should know what he was referring to, but he knew she did not.

'Don't be so hard on yourself,' said Martha.

'Seriously,' said Jack, 'it would frighten anybody.'

She had nothing to say to that, but fell into a silence, looking around, as though something in the room had distracted her. He let the silence run, waiting to see if she had any intention of returning to the script. He suspected she did not. She was just smiling at him now, almost leering; a little bored, a little condescending; one eye losing the battle with its thick lashes to remain open. He'd seen it many times. She had one arm out to the side and her fingers spread dramatically on the cushion of the chair. 'And I'd really like to be able to move around sometimes, instead of being strapped to this fucking chair.'

'That's your favourite chair, Martha.'

'Ha.'

'And you're hardly strapped to it.' They had to be careful. 'I don't think you should have any more to drink, Martha.'

'I know what you mean,' she said, nodding slowly.

Nora's little talk had obviously had no effect; in fact, quite the opposite. She seemed more determined than ever to kick everything apart.

'You never ask me anything,' said Martha. She was off again. 'It's all about you and you. The two of you. Don't I matter?'

'Of course you do.'

'So ask me something.'

Jack was impressed; she'd learned this somehow, from somewhere, this *it's all about you and you*. She'd said it before, long ago, he was sure of it. 'Like what?' he said.

She threw her head back and then brought it slowly forward, as though it had nearly come off. Jack smiled. 'Oh come on,

Jack Drake,' she slurred, in her fabulously raspy drawl. 'The famous Jack Drake. Don't tell me you need help with your imagination.'

And the way she licked her lips, and that proud, almost arrogant arching of the back. He pushed his page of scribbled script to one side and leaned forward, smiling more, his eyes brightening. 'Tell me what you did today.'

'I told you, I dug my bike out of the garage – which is a fucking mess, by the way, mister – I rode it to get wine and back, saw two animals on the way, a horse and a baby. I mean two animals and a baby, who, by the way, was soooo pissed, and a horse in the field next to Isabelle's, and a rabbit at the side of the road, which was dead and half eaten away at the leg. Then I . . .' She paused, thinking, her red eyes on the floor. 'No, I can't say that. Er . . . yeah, that's what I did today. And now I'm here talking to you.'

'OK,' said Jack, 'well, there you go. You paint a nice picture, I'll say that.'

'Do I like animals, Jack? You never told me.'

What was she talking about? Why did she have to make everything so nerve-racking? 'Why would I need to tell you something like that?'

'You're right, you don't,' she said, pulling herself together, "cos in fact I know, because . . . Well, why wouldn't I know? I'm sorry. I shouldn't talk like that. I drank too much.'

'I think maybe you did,' said Jack, sitting back, ready to close this one down. Too much was at stake. 'Maybe we should say goodnight.'

But then she sat straight, pushed herself up from the arms and tucked her now bare feet beneath her on the chair so that she was kneeling, like she was just getting started. Very Martha. Why wouldn't it be? This was, after all, Martha, and she didn't want to say goodnight. 'Do animals . . .' she said, and paused to consider, 'feel disappointment in each other, Jack, the way humans do?'

'Well . . .'

'Or is that what makes us human, the fact that we can feel immense disappointment in each other?' She poured herself another glass of wine.

'I don't know,' said Jack, cautiously. 'What do you think?'

'I wonder if they ever go through the trauma of sensing that someone they once liked, maybe even loved, is now turning into someone they don't respect.'

'Why do you say that, Martha? Where's that coming from?' Jack was chewing on his cheeks again.

'Do animals, birds, fish, whatever, fall in and out of love?'

'I believe they can.'

'In that case,' she continued drowsily, 'can a fish, Jack, listen, can a fish love another fish, but then one day imagine that they do not in fact love that fish and that they now love another fish, only to realise at some later date that they did actually love that first fish more than they would ever love another fish for the rest of their lives, and therefore feel that their existence is overcome with a feeling of regret that they sometimes imagine to be like that of humans? Does this ever happen?'

Jack had a choice: he could wrap it up right now, cleanly, respectfully, and begin again tomorrow with some new ideas, new possibilities, or he could roll up his trousers and take a few tentative steps into whatever foaming torrent she was clearly up to her eyeballs in. 'Well, Martha,' he said, and wished in that moment that she could see the bewildered delight on his face, 'I've never thought about such a thing.'

'Well, think about it now, because I think that does happen, because I have looked at fish, I have looked closely at fish, and that is going on.'

'Precisely that?'

'It's going on, Jack. Get used to it, you bastard.'

'Wow, Martha, OK.'

'I'm sorry,' she said, and swung her legs back into a sitting position, briefly dipping out of the key light, to put on her shoes, he thought.

'That's fine, Martha, I'm not angry.' Could she tell? He needed her to know. Did she care?

'Poor Jack . . .' she said, reappearing, though beginning to stand.

'Are you all right?' he said, for she looked a little white.

'Poor me . . .' she said, leaning in to pick up her drink.

'Don't go, Martha. Where are you going?'

'Poor little one.' She turned away from the camera and walked slowly, carefully, all the way to the far door, and then as she disappeared round the corner, no longer in shot, in a loud English accent, 'Georges!' and louder still, 'Georges? You can turn it all off now. I'm done.' And the slamming of a door.

Jack tore off his headphones in a terrible panic. What was the matter with her? Why couldn't she . . .? Not in a flash, but with a dull, woolly click, her name came back to him and he lifted up his foot and stamped it down onto the rug, a ludicrous gesture. He shook his head and smiled. As he stood and stretched and brushed himself down, he looked to the ceiling, and forgave her.

CHAPTER 19

Betty was upside down in the bed; her head where her feet should be, and her feet, living the dream, trying out the pillows. It wasn't the first time, and she rather liked it. There was an empty bottle of Bordeaux on the nightstand. From this angle she was able to look directly up at the twelve-inch Jesus: this morning he seemed in more pain, his brow more lined and his eyes clenched tighter than usual. There seemed to be, dancing around his bleeding head, a soft and celestial light. When Betty closed her own eyes, the lights were there inside her head, pulsing red on the backs of her lids, and when she opened them again, Jesus seemed more dazzled than ever, and then suddenly, wonderfully – and yes, religiously – she was struck with a revelation: water. Sunlight tripping upon water, upon the wall. The pool. The pool was ready. Exhumed and coaxed back to life by beautiful Georges! Magnificent Georges!

Nora had not set out any of Martha's bathing costumes for her to wear, which was understandable, since bathing had been out of bounds, but now Betty had tried on three and still found nothing that thrilled her. She was searching for a particular costume that she had seen in a photograph taken here not too long ago, but when she found what she thought was the one, she was disappointed to see it was far too big for her – which was odd, since all the others had been too small, if anything. Perhaps it was not Martha's. But then she found another of a similar size.

With a growing sense of unease, she began to explore some of the other dresses that had not been set out by Nora, stored in a smaller side cupboard. It was the same thing again: at least three that were far bigger than any of Martha's. It was then that Betty realised these were maternity dresses, and upon further exploration, she discovered, among the underwear, a number of well-worn and stained nursing bras. Holding one of the bras against her cheek, she began to shake; she felt tears rising up, and a burning in her nose, and salt in her throat. She saw Freddie, no bigger than a rabbit, lighter than a boot, soothed in her arms, pink and drugged with morning milk, sleeping through a thunderstorm, his first smile in the second month, his first thank you, his first joke, his first . . . She had to kneel down where she stood. Then she sat back and bowed her head, eyes wet, shut tight, and stayed like that for a long while till she felt she might tumble over. And then she did tumble over, hunched up against the wardrobe door, the blue bra still balled up in her fist and her only child loose in her heart, kicking up a fuss, making her feel like the saddest woman in the whole of France, which she was: she had no doubt about that.

Now she was in the kitchen, in a bikini and a kaftan, hands deep in the cutlery drawer, rattling it all furiously, lifting up fish slices and spatulas in search of what she thought she re-called seeing in there the other day. And there it was, caught between a sieve and a whisk: a long, slim blue-and-yellow rub-berised spoon for a little mouth, a jaunty, winking turtle on the handle. And hadn't she seen a red ball in the garage, and a pot of blowing bubbles, and yes, that plastic tricycle hanging from the ceiling. She'd thought nothing of it at the time, for surely children came to visit, nephews and nieces, the children of friends. There were babies and toddlers in some of the framed photos standing on the table in the hall, but none of these, she suspected – though she didn't know why – were the *poor little one*, of whom Isabelle had spoken, and who was apparently bigger than a mere baby if the tricycle was any indication. So why had none of this been mentioned? Why had Nora kept it from her? And stranger still: if she searched online for 'Martha Lear, baby, child, son, daughter', why did she find nothing but the fictional children of a fictional Martha?

She set off in a muddle, beetling about the house, upstairs, downstairs, inside and out, in search of two things: Georges (perhaps he could explain) and a hidden child. Not the child itself of course, but other signs and symbols of the child's existence. Georges was nowhere to be found, though both cars were parked in the driveway. She thought he might be hiding from her, so fearsome had she been the previous night. The door and shutters of the guest house were locked, and if he was inside, no amount of knocking brought him into the light. Back in the main house, she called up and down corridors, but to no avail.

Turning the focus of her search to the possibility of a child, she swept from room to room scanning every nook and corner for primary colours, again to no avail. It wasn't until she got down on the floor, crawling about the rooms on her hands and knees, that she found, beneath various pieces of furniture, three large, brightly figured jigsaw pieces, the chubby wheel of a tiny vehicle, and what appeared to be the dial of a toy telephone. Suddenly, struck with the idea that if there were a child living at the house, then there would surely be a room for the child, she remembered how, while giving Ruth her virtual tour, one of the doors at the end of the landing had been locked. It had felt unimportant at the time; she'd assumed it to be off limits,

145

which did not seem excessively prohibitive considering she was permitted to sleep in the master bedroom.

Recalling a trick she had learned from an old boyfriend (a freelance plasterer and an accomplished thief), Betty borrowed a couple of colour gels from one of Georges's lights before racing upstairs to slip the lock. The room, alas, did not reveal a hidden nursery but rather a mundane, utilitarian dump room. Nevertheless, her curiosity at its concealment drew her over the threshold and through its contents. After a few minutes, inside a buckled shortbread tin, she found a smaller tin filled with small keys, and, remembering that there were a great number of antique drawers, chests, cupboards and bureaus scattered around the house, all of them locked, she spilled the lot of them into the pocket of her kaftan and set off downstairs, for now she was enjoying herself.

After half an hour of trying every key in every lock, with varying degrees of success, she had found little to interest her. For the most part, drawers were crammed with legal papers, bank and credit statements, yellowing invoices. Much of the time she could not see why the drawers and cupboards had been locked in the first place; more against housebreakers, she thought – fraudsters, identity thieves – than against herself. She did happen upon a few more curious baubles: a jack on a spring, out of its box, a tiny clockwork chicken, and a small bag of coloured balloons. From the back of one drawer she pulled out a smartphone, old and cracked, but not so old it was not worth pocketing for future trespassing. Finally, in the lower compartment of a large Art Nouveau bureau in the office, she found two leather box files filled with over a hundred photographs, alluring enough for her to carry back to the bedroom to be studied at leisure. But first she felt compelled to track down Georges, who might well save her a lot of time with a simple explanation. Besides, his absence was now beginning to spook her.

She found him at last, sitting in the dark in a hitherto undis-
covered screening room, watching a film, half turning his head
as she crept through the door but too engrossed to acknowledge
her presence. She took a seat at the back of the room, happy not
to disturb him. For a while she gazed more through the screen
than at it, so distant were her concerns from whatever was happening in the story. It was the sort of film her mother would
have loved, some kind of Elizabethan tragedy with glowering
shots of the River Thames, sweating archbishops, clench-fisted
cardinals coughing blood and horses in armour with sinister
hoods. And now the Tower of London, cut out in black against
the twilight, the tranquillity of an isolated courtyard, a small
gathering of hunched men in dark robes and a young woman
in a once-elegant dress, kneeling, trying to read from the Bible
through tears, fat droplets splashing down upon the page.
Martha must have been about twenty.

'Wash me thoroughly from mine iniquity, and cleanse me
from my sin,' she said. 'For I acknowledge my transgressions:
and my sin is ever before me. Against thee, thee only, have I
sinned, and done this evil in thy sight: that thou mightest be
justified when thou speakest, and be clear when thou judgest.
Behold, I was shapen in iniquity; and in sin did my mother
conceive me . . .'

The music rose and soared above the words. The book was
taken from her, and with her own hands she tied a white silken
blindfold across her eyes. The camera panned across various
faces looking on, misshapen by despair or villainously gleeful,
and then a close-up of Martha, steadfast in her faith.

'Will you take it off before I lay me down?' she said, discussing
the fate of her head with the hooded executioner. He assured
her he would not. Martha then knelt and groped at the air
before her to feel for the block, and, failing to find it, cried out,
'What shall I do? Where is it?' At which point a white-faced

old man stepped forward to soothe her and helped rest her head in the hollow. 'Lord,' said Martha, more tears now darkening the blindfold, 'into thy hands I commend my spirit.' And with this the enormous axe was smashed down into the meat of her neck and split her small head from her tender shoulders. There was a bed of straw upon the floor to soak up the blood. A low bell began to ring. The sound of ravens taking flight, distant thunder, the whole business. The body lifted and carried to the doorway. And now the lonely head seen from a distance. The dark men leaving, as though that was what happened. Only the head now, and more music, harps and fife, clarions and crum-horns. Another shot of the Thames as it began to rain. *The End.*

Wonderful, thought Betty, just what I needed.

Georges lingered, watching the credits to the very last name before standing and, with appealing solemnity, turning on the lights. His eyes were moist and he took a tissue from his pocket to press against his face. Betty remained in her chair. '*Bonjour, Georges,*' she said, smiling, pulling tight her kaftan to conceal the bikini, lest he get the wrong idea.

'Good morning,' said Georges.

'*C'était Madame Martha?*' she said. '*N'est ce pas?*' This was a favourite of hers – *n'est ce pas.* She felt that even if she had been born in France it was the sort of thing she would say all the time, so now that she *was* in France she did her very best, whenever the opportunity arose, to do precisely that.

'Yes, yes,' said Georges, 'she was the lady. *Très jeune.*'

This was about the way it went these days. Nothing of great substance had passed between them this first week, and when they did communicate, over food, shopping, the practicalities of the lighting and calls, they had fallen into this routine of her speaking dismal French and him reciprocating in equally dismal English. So far it had worked, or so they imagined. Sometimes they had no way of checking, and the rate of success could only be truly assessed by a third party. However, Betty was a little concerned that some of the things she now had to say to him might strain the system to breaking point. '*Elle est ton amie?*' she said.

'Who?' said Georges, putting away his tissue and taking a seat across the aisle.

'Madame Martha.'

This seemed to confound Georges, and he shook his head as if he had never heard anything so strange. 'No, no, no, not at all. She is not at all.'

'But you know her? *Tu la connais?*'

'I not know her. Not meet her. Never.'

'*Et Monsieur Drake? Jack? Tu le connais?*'

'We speak, now,' said Georges, 'on phone. In French. He speaks French. But I never meet.'

'OK,' said Betty, and thought about this. It was not as she had imagined. How much had he been told? '*Et l'enfant?*' she said. '*Tu connais l'enfant?*'

'*Quel enfant?*'

'Never mind,' said Betty, not knowing the French for never mind and so holding up her hand, indicating he should give her a minute, which, judging by his eager nod, he seemed more than happy to do, for the conversation seemed to be unsettling him. 'Isabelle?' she said, after a while. '*Tu connais Isabelle?*' She was getting sick of saying *connais*.

'Isabelle?'

'The neighbour,' said Betty, pointing in the vague direction of where she thought Isabelle lived. She was wrong, which didn't help. '*Isabelle, la dame, là-bas, avec les cheveux fous et le bébé, comme ça,*' and she pulled out her tongue and scowled, which seemed to scare Georges.

'Ah!' he said. '*Le voisin.*'

'*Le voisin?*' said Betty.

'*La dame*, the lady in next house, there,' he said, pointing in the right direction.

Betty swung round, getting her bearings; it was difficult in the dark room. 'Yes, yes, in the next house.'

'Yes,' said Georges, and waited, smiling.

'You speak to her? You tell her what we do here?'

'I say we make camera tests for a film. Like Nora Flynn say tell her.'

Betty wondered if this was true, if he really had said that. If Nora really had told him to say that, and if that was what he really believed. He must be very confused. She drew a deep breath. 'Also,' she said. '*Aussi . . .*' Speaking French with a hangover was killing her. '*Aussi, un autre chose. Tu as dit que je suis ta femme.*'

Georges looked appalled. 'No.'

'*Oui*,' said Betty, nodding her disapproval. '*Tu as dit ça, apparemment.*'

'No, Betty, no. I see her. She come to the door and is very . . . very . . . She look everywhere. Very . . .'

'Nosy?' said Betty.

'She ask many questions. She say who is the lady? I say Betty. I say my friend.'

'Yes, girlfriend. You say girlfriend?'

'I say *copine. J'ai dit c'est une copine, pas ma femme. J'ai dit copine, je te promets.* She is idiot with the *cheveux fous et le bébé, comme ça*,' and he pulled an excellently spiteful face. '*Je suis d'accord*, the *bébé* is horrible, like this,' and he pulled a different, more obnoxious face, which was also excellent, and Betty snorted with laughter; something she hadn't done since she arrived. She wiped her nose where she thought there might be some snot and laughed even more, before pulling a grotesque face of her own. They remained there, in the dark of the screening room, seeing who could do the best impression of the irascible Tomas.

★

This was the first time in her life that Betty had floated on her back in a private pool. Completely alone, in complete silence, gazing up at the sky, and the sky gazing down, and the far-distant tops of the immense poplars glittering, and strange new birds hovering, and if she turned her head just a little she could see the mountain she saw every morning. Never the same mountain twice. And as she lay there, drowsy from the heat, hardly breathing, her heart hardly beating, hardly needing anything, she was almost happy. She had decided to be Martha for the afternoon. But now that Martha had let her down by shuffling what was and was not known, Betty chose to let her go for the day, feeling that one could only take so much of being pawed by a ghost.

Sometimes one had to lie life on its back in a cool blue pool and, since no one was looking, allow the sky to have its way.

CHAPTER 20

It was the hottest day of the year, and Jack Drake should have been dissecting the brain of a rat, but his stomach had weakened in the night and he could not face the sight, nor the stench of blood in that already fetid schoolhouse, and so had fled one horror, only to stumble into the theatre of another.

There were so many windows in the house that it was easy to keep one of them unlocked without attracting the attention of his parents, who had no reason to suspect his skilfully executed absences. He was, after all, a good boy, everyone thought so, and so in he crept through the open frame, landing like a breeze, shoes off, on the polished tiled floor of the scullery. Knowing he had the house to himself, he would have strolled blithely to his room had he not heard something strangled and bestial issuing from the ceiling. He paused, imagining that some animal had made it inside somehow. Then came another muffled, spluttered, indefinable release of . . . what? Something relished and then admonished. Something guttural and frustrated, followed by a forlorn gasp. He had no idea what to make of it and was fixed to the spot at the foot of the stairs. He had heard similar sounds in TV and cinema advertising, a woman exaggerating the delight of eating a fabulous cake. Was some woman eating a fabulous cake with his father in a room at the top of the stairs? It was certainly not his mother, for his mother could not abide cake.

He had to hold onto the banister as he ascended, one huge step at a time, pausing on the first landing to meet eyes with Bartholomew, who looked just as gobsmacked, his beak hanging open, stunned into silence. As he reached the second landing, he saw the door of the guest bedroom ajar; the sounds had levelled out into a kind of chesty harmonic hum, with the word 'yes' sneezed out haphazardly. Enough was enough, Jack had to see it.

That Jack's father should be relaxing in a hot, sunlit bedroom in the middle of a Tuesday afternoon was unusual enough; that he was currently completely naked, engaged in some kind of sexual congress with Miss Marsh (who earlier that very morning had read to the class the opening three paragraphs of *Animal Farm*), was beyond Jack's comprehension. Strangely, among the many and various thoughts kicking and splashing around inside poor Jack's head that afternoon was that he should not, under any circumstances, be spotted by Miss Marsh in case she might report him to Mr Parsons for bunking off the rat dissection. The fact that Miss Marsh had one of her breasts squashed against his father's lips did nothing to dispel this concern, though it did, of course, ignite other worries.

Before now Jack had only heard of sex; he had no concept of what it really looked like. He had seen topless women in tabloid newspapers, and the occasional bottomless woman in magazines found near the railway lines. But none of these girls were having sex; they were only showing you the bits they had sex with. But when it came to intercourse, which was what Jack assumed was going on here, he was clueless. His first impression was that it looked far more painful than he'd imagined. His second impression was that it made him want to cry and cry

153

and cry. And so he walked himself away from it, blocking his ears, chewing on his cheeks, sliding his socks across the wood all the way to his room, throwing himself down onto the bed, almost within the bed, there to live inside in the dark with the bugs and the springs.

And that was when he saw it. Up there on his best shelf: the heavy, deadly, fully loaded Leica. He took it down and cocked it, sliding back along and up and in the name of his mother – 'If the ISO is eight hundred' – working out his settings, pressing his teeth tight together till his jaw began to throb – 'If it's six feet from the door to the bed' – then twisting the focus ring, and if he could keep it at eight . . . 'But what if the sun goes in?' And he could hear them again, snuffling now, Miss Marsh whistling like a fucking kettle.

He dropped to one knee and assessed his light, twisting the aperture wide open. As he snapped the first frame, he remembered his father telling him that one of the great advantages of the Leica M5 was how wonderfully silent it was compared to other cameras on the market. Jack fired off another six, setting the shutter at one over one-twenty-five so as not to blur the movement of the bed and its passengers, who, to his horror, were vibrating with such abandon that he might have to increase it to one over two-fifty, which was risky. He took a shot of four quivering feet, three bare, one black-socked. A brown bra beneath the toe of his father's boot. A pair of spectacles he recognised as belonging to Miss Marsh were now mangled in the skirmish, with one lens sticking to the sweaty red flesh of his father's buttocks. Miss Marsh's breasts, completely out of control, and very likely out of focus. He had ten pictures now and, confident he had his kill, he crawled away on his elbows and knees, and the feeling of the cold polished wood against his exposed belly was a feeling he would remember for the rest of his life.

It wasn't until he reached his own room that the whole thing described itself to him in hindsight, and slowly, almost gently, he threw up across the floor, sliding backwards as he did so to allow it to puddle and spread. It was really very awful. That was what he remembered most of all, many years later: it was really very fucking awful.

Jack considered how low he could place the camera if he were to have Billy crawl towards it, and how far back they could go, and at which point the shot would die. They would have to build a track to the side; he asked old Solomon to join him on the floor. Jack relished the fact that all he was really doing here was bringing a much bigger camera into the same room – for yes, it had indeed been in this very room – but why not? he had thought. Why shoot it somewhere else and spend countless thousands making it look like the very room? It was a wonder his mother had not cleared it out years ago. Perhaps she'd had her reasons to preserve it like this, as some sort of bleak museum, her personal self-torture chamber, a warning to the future. It was jarring that the staging of his father's infidelity was such a spectacular business, with two twenty-foot scaffold towers rigged up in the garden outside the window with im- mense silks, 18K Fresnel lights and a high-end crane brought in specially for the next two days. For something they had all wanted to keep so quiet at the time, Jack really was making an enormous song-and-dance about it now.

'This must be a strange one for you,' said Solomon, flat on his stomach, peering along the floor with his hand over his eyes, as though scouring the horizon.

'No stranger than the rest of it,' said Jack, nonchalant, his cheek now pressed to the wood to see if there were any reflec- tions to exploit.

'How's it going to work?' said Solomon.

'How is what going to work?'

'Well, you'll be on the bed in the all-together—'

'Don't say all-together,' said Jack.

'Naked,' said Solomon. 'You'll be on the bed, naked, with Bernadette.'

'What's the question,' said Jack, raising himself up onto his knees.

'Well, you know,' said Solomon, and winked.

Jack had expected better of him. Apparently everyone on the crew was looking forward to a day of toe-curling awkwardness. Thankfully it was the first day Jack did not have to be painted like a cadaver, the first day he didn't have to put on those ludicrous pyjamas. Instead he was wearing a dressing gown over track pants and vest. Beneath that, as everyone knew – and seemed so childishly thrilled about – he was naked.

'Explain,' he said.

'Will you be going to the monitor between takes?' said Solomon.

'If necessary,' said Jack.

'In the all-together?'

'I told you not to say that.'

'I'm sorry,' said Solomon. 'It's what my mother used to say.' He paused and looked up to the ceiling, remembering something. 'And she used to call my whatsit my taily.'

'Your whatsit?' said Jack.

'My taily.'

'Your taily?'

'Don't,' said Solomon, in a panic, 'don't say it. Never say it.'

Jack had not met Bernadette Lowe but had cast her on the strength of a taped reading she had given to Nora. After the reading, with the camera still running, Nora had engaged Bernadette in polite small talk to give Jack another facet of the woman, and it was then that he decided that Bernadette was perfect for the part, since he could not bear the sight nor the sound of her. Just like the despicable Miss Marsh, Bernadette had been raised in Dublin, and it was her mellifluous brogue – as well as her hard, bony face and her stone-grey eyes – that had clinched the deal. All that was missing was the slicked black hair and the nostril mole, but that would soon be taken care of.

'Good morning, Mr Drake,' said Bernadette brightly, a little too confidently. 'Sit yourself down,' she said, patting the seat of the old chesterfield.

'Good morning,' said Jack, pulling the belt of his terry-towelling robe tight around his waist. 'I just wanted to pop my head in and say hello. I'm afraid I was indisposed for the casting, but I wanted you to know that I loved the tape.'

'I loved doing the tape,' she said smoothly, clearly accomplished at this kind of perfunctory chat.

'I wanted to make sure that you're comfortable with everything and to see if you have any questions, any thoughts.' Jack cursed the betrayal of nerves in his voice. 'Obviously, today is what it is, but, looking ahead to the dialogue scenes next week, at the school, if you have any thoughts about that . . . But really, to make sure that you're relaxed about today.'

'Oh God bless you, Mr Drake.'

'Jack.'

'Jack. That's very kind,' she said. 'The truth is, I don't get asked to do this lark very much – not any more. Bed scenes, I mean. I'm not so young as I once was.'

'Who is?' said Jack, mustering a chuckle and rocking back on his buttocks.

'And I was in two minds, to be honest, but then when I heard it was with lovely Conrad, I was like, oh God, that'll be a gas!'

'Right,' said Jack, rocking forward on his buttocks and stopping.

'We worked together maybe . . .' she put a finger to her pursed lips, 'maybe six, seven years ago.'

'You and Conrad?' said Jack, feeling the morning's porridge on the move.

'Yes,' said Bernadette. 'Me and old Ripley. Old Raspberry Ripley we used to call him, on account of all the raspberries, the filthy fucker.'

Jack had no idea what she meant by that, but laughed anyway. He was trying to picture her naked on top of him – or trying not to, he wasn't quite sure.

'We did this awful piece of shit at the Criterion Theatre, and he had to bum me every night. Me with my knickers down and him with his prosthetic cock out. And I'm telling you, Jack, it could have been a fucking nightmare, but old Ripley was such a scream. When I heard he was doing this, I just thought, oh fuck it. Go on then, Bernie, why not get the old girls up and about one last time, for Conrad. I fucking love that man.'

In the room's silence, Jack heard the muffled hilarity drifting up from downstairs. They were surely talking about him.

'Well, you see,' he said, and took a long pause while he began biting off the nail of his thumb, 'the thing is, Bernadette, I don't really want this to be a laugh.'

Bernadette's smile vanished. 'Of course not. I didn't mean . . .'

'It's one of the gravest moments of the film.'

'I get that, I do.'

'And to be honest,' he continued, the tears rising in his eyes, 'rather personally traumatic, if you can understand.'

'Absolutely. Nora explained how this whole thing was sort of autobiographical.'

'Not sort of.'

'Not even sort of,' she corrected herself.

'No.'

'Just autobiographical, end of. So this woman I'm playing . . .'

'Mary Marsh,' said Jack.

'She was your teacher. You must have . . .'

'I despised her. Once I threw a horseshoe through her window at three in the morning.'

'That should be in the film. I love that.'

'Her house is not a location. We don't have the time.'

'Oh God, though, I get it, Jack.' She put her hand on his. Her flesh felt ominously cold.

'It wasn't at all funny,' said Jack.

'Of course not. I didn't mean it would be a laugh. I just meant that these scenes can be excruciatingly awkward and I just wanted to reassure you that . . . even though I'm obviously still nervous . . . I wanted to reassure you that it'll be fine, and that I'm comfortable with Conrad, so there won't be any problems. *Of course* we'll take it seriously. I mean, I've read the script over and over, and Jesus, no – it's hardly a comedy. I just meant—'

'It's fine,' said Jack.

'As long as you understand that,' said Bernadette. 'Does Conrad know it's me? I expect he must. I didn't get a call sheet, but I expect he—'

'No,' said Jack.

'No?' she said, her voice rising an octave. She clapped her cold hands together. 'He doesn't know? Oh my God, he's gonna *die*.' And then, realising that she might have gone too far, 'I'm sorry, I don't mean that in a funny way. I mean he's gonna die . . . seriously.'

The ten-minute warning had been called. Jack was sitting on the stairs, staring down a fly, biting off what was left of one thumbnail, when he heard the dreaded click clack clack click of Billy's busybody mother tottering over. 'Excuse me, Mr

Drake,' said Phyllis. 'Jack, I can call you Jack, can't I? It's been nearly two weeks. All this Mr Drake is a bit—'

'What is it?' said Jack, gathering his robe together at the throat.

Phyllis sat beside him on the step. 'Well, I wanted to ask you, Jack, what is the nature of this scene today?'

'Haven't you read the script?'

'Not all of it. They only let me see Billy's bits, but even Billy won't show me this one, so I was wondering what was going on. It's just that one of the riggers . . . Is that what you call them, riggers?'

'I suppose so,' said Jack.

'One of the riggers – Bruce, I think it was – told me it was a closed set, and I said what does that mean, and he told me because there was nudity, and I said, "Oh crikey," and then he said that you were going to be nude, and I said, "Oh double crikey!"' She put her hand over her mouth.

'Yes,' said Jack.

'Well, how does that work?' said Phyllis. 'And where does Billy fit in?'

'Billy won't be nude. He's watching.'

'What's he watching?'

Jack looked at his watch, hoping she might take the hint. 'Well, of course it's not Billy watching. I mean Young Jack is watching.'

'What's Young Jack watching?'

'He's watching his father.'

'You?'

'His father.'

'Doing what?'

Jack took a moment. 'Fucking,' he said, and left it at that.

Phyllis looked at his fist as it clutched the neck of his robe. The word hung in the air and she seemed then to look at it in the space between them. He wondered if they were going to have a problem. He wasn't sure if he could bear it. And then Phyllis's mouth seemed to double in size as a crimson smirk took over her face and her sticky lipstick came unstuck and her teeth broke out into the light and back went the whole lot with the rest of her head, like she'd never heard anything so fantastically hilarious in her whole life. She gripped his knee with her sharp green nails and simply said, 'Priceless, Jack, fucking priceless. You're a fucking legend. Good luck with that,' and off she trotted, click clack click clickety clack.

Billy was wearing his school uniform and went straight to Jack so that he could fashion the tie in the precise thick, loose knot only he could reproduce.

'I've heard we're shooting things out of order,' said Billy.

'Yes,' said Jack. 'Is that all right?'

'Sure,' said the boy, shrugging his shoulders. 'I'm used to it by now.'

'We've had some problems,' said Jack, 'with Bernadette. Did you meet her?'

'I saw her in make-up; she seemed very annoyed about something.'

'About the mole,' said Jack, enjoying the word.

'The mole?'

'She's pissed off about the nostril mole,' he said, enjoying both words.

Billy frowned, but didn't seem to need any more information than that. He moved on. 'Jack, you know when I have to throw up?'

'Yes.'

'I'm not sure I can do that. I can make myself cry, but I—'

'Thick vegetable soup,' said Jack.

'Ah,' said Billy, delighted by the revelation and then almost

161

immediately disgusted by it. 'That might make me *actually* throw up,' he said, laughing nervously.

'Well, there we are,' said Jack. 'Now listen . . . Bernadette's also pissed off at . . . Well, she's a little uncomfortable, shall we say, about doing this whole thing with me. She thought . . . Well, it's a long story, you don't need to know. You're OK with everything, aren't you?'

'What do you mean?' said Billy.

'With the whole naked thing,' said Jack, putting his hand on the boy's shoulder. 'With me being naked.'

Billy looked at him askance, with the same expression of revulsion as when Jack had mentioned the soup. 'You?' he said, and blushed. Bernadette had pulled an almost identical face; it was uncanny.

'You've read the script,' said Jack, taking his hand away.

'Yes, but . . .'

Jack looked down at the wooden floor, at the warm tone of the oak, and the practically transcendent grain, and wondered if he shouldn't have been a carpenter. Perhaps if his father had given him a hammer instead of a camera, things might have been different. Everyone might have died a little sooner, he thought, a little quicker, a little happier.

Why on earth would you not have something like that removed, thought Jack, whatever the cost? A dark mole, as black and pitted as a large peppercorn, on the top of the upper lip, directly beneath, almost inside, the left nostril. He had watched it for countless hours as Miss Marsh's mouth moved up and down, up and down, reading to the class from whatever book she thought might take their minds off it for twenty minutes. You just wanted to throw your handkerchief at her. How had his father borne it? How could Jack bear it now? This prosthetic facsimile of the dreaded thing, glued fast like a squashed bug on

Bernadette's sweating lip? Strange that she was sweating when her naked body was so intensely clammy sat atop his own, their pelvic bones positioned as far apart as was possible while still giving the impression of penetration. Her nipples were covered with circular plasters. That was fine; they wouldn't be needed. They had also established that it would not be necessary to kiss. Enough rhythm to set the headboard knocking would suffice. The rest could be done with eyes closed and some trained breathing from the diaphragm to simulate ecstasy and release. With any luck they could get it in one take.

'It feels like it's falling off,' said Bernadette, patting the mole into place with the tip of one finger. Barry, the focus puller, was winding up his tape measure, final checks had been called, it was too late now to come in again with the glue. Jack needed to concentrate, and so should she, if she could find the time to stop sulking. The gushing, bright-eyed Bernadette of earlier that morning had long ago left the building, leaving this fierce harridan in her place. The wig was perfect, the mole immaculate; Miss Marsh, Mary Marsh, Mrs Mary Marsh was back in town and Jack was in hell. Why had he ever thought this was a good idea?

'You know I worked with Martha, years ago?' said Bernadette.

'Did you?' said Jack.

'We did Chekhov's *Three Sisters* at the Bristol Old Vic.'

'I see,' said Jack. Why on earth did she think this was a good moment to bring that up? They were about to put the board on.

'Stand by,' shouted Charles. 'Roll sound.'

'I really liked her,' said Bernadette. 'I thought she was gas.'

'Sound speed.'

'Yes, she was,' said Jack, 'she was gas,' taking a deep breath and closing his eyes.

'Roll camera,' shouted Charles.

'Rolling,' said Solomon.

'We really got on,' said Bernadette. 'How is she?'

Jack opened his eyes and let out the breath and took in another.

'Mark it!' said Charles.

'One, take one,' said Ron.

'Oh, didn't you hear?' said Jack, grabbing Bernadette by her stone-cold bony hips as they both began to bounce. 'She's dead.'

'Action!' yelled Charles.

And off they went.

CHAPTER 21

Every morning now, for the past week at least, Betty had woken up twice: first as Betty, then, mere seconds later, as Martha. It was not unduly disconcerting, and as the days wore on, she was happy to allow Martha all the time she needed in preparation for communion with her husband.

But this morning, something had changed: as Betty awoke and took in the light and the hour, she realised, with a sting of horror, that Martha had already been up for some time. How else to explain waking not in the bed, but on the chair by the window, sitting upright, fully dressed, a freshly extinguished cigarette smouldering in the ashtray? When she opened her mouth to speak – 'What the hell?' – it was Martha who said only 'What?' and left it at that. It wasn't until the woman who usually passed for Betty stood up and took herself into the bathroom, wedging Betty's head under the cold tap, that Martha tucked herself away into a patch of passing shade, grateful to be stood down, for she had not slept so well.

Having changed into one of her own dresses and breakfasted on buttered warm baguette, hot black coffee and strong cigarettes with a red-eyed and sullen Georges, Betty made her way up the rough dust path towards Isabelle's front door, with the box of photographs, bound tight with string, bouncing around in the basket of her bicycle. A large, hirsute man wearing only a pair of striped shorts – Isabelle's husband, apparently – struggled to explain that Isabelle was not at home, but could be found, every Monday, selling her pots/pets/pâté/plates – his accent was like boiling tar – at the market in Pontelle, the same small town where Betty had bought the wine at the weekend, a twenty-minute cycle away. By the time she arrived in the town, she had to sit down for a few moments on a small bench before entering the market square, for fear of collapsing. She hated Georges's cigarettes and should never have said yes to three in a row.

Isabelle was seated beneath a white canvas canopy with Tomas, who was sleeping, or trying to, beneath a smaller white canopy, beneath a tiny white hat. His tongue was out on his chin like a small dog. He looked furious to be almost asleep. What was wrong with him? It wasn't until Betty took off her own hat (a perfectly tattered panama found in the garage) that Isabelle recognised her and sprang to her feet. 'Betty!' she called out across her stall, leaning over to offer her kisses, causing Betty to meet her halfway, fearful of knocking over the display of colourful bowls and plates. 'I am so happy to see you,' she said. 'Tomas, look who has come to see us.' Tomas couldn't have cared less; he didn't even open his eyes.

'It's all right, don't wake him,' said Betty. 'I wanted to ask you something.'

'Yes?' said Isabelle, taking off her perfectly circular yellow sunglasses and replacing them with her perfectly circular black prescription spectacles, as if they were more suited to answering questions. 'I am ready.'

'When I saw you the other day,' said Betty, 'you were talking about Jack and Martha.'

'*Oui,*' her expression passing to full stern now.

'You said poor Jack and poor Martha.'

'*Oui.*'

'Then you said poor little one.'

'*Oui,*' she said.

'What did you mean? Who is the poor little one?'

'The child,' said Isabelle, 'the poor little boy.'

So it was a boy after all, just as Betty had supposed. She lifted the box from her basket, untying the string, to see if all her other suppositions fitted. 'You mean Martha's son?' she said, setting the box down on the stall between them.

'Yes, of course,' said Isabelle.

'What was his name?'

'I don't know. I forget. I never see him so much, but I know Clara.'

Betty had taken three photographs from the top of the pile, ready to present, but now she held them back, pressing them against her breast. 'Who is Clara?'

'She looks after the boy,' said Isabelle. 'The nanny, I think you say, when Martha works . . . worked.'

Betty took a moment to think about this. 'But the boy was definitely Martha's son?'

'*Oui.* Why?'

'And this is him?' said Betty, showing the first of the photographs: Martha lying on the grass, close to the pool, a bonny black-haired boy of about six beaming at the camera, one tanned arm around his mother's neck and the other out and open with fingers spread, as though presenting the distant mountain. Martha was wearing the same blue dress Betty had woken up in. She too was smiling and animated, one foot lifted off the ground, caught in mid kick.

Isabelle looked at the photograph over the top of her spectacles. 'No,' she said, and smiled. 'No, this is not the boy.' She took off her spectacles altogether and studied the picture in detail.

'Oh,' said Betty, deflated. She'd found five photographs of this particular boy. Three of them with Martha, two with other adults, other older children, all at the house, taken, she had assumed, over the space of three or four days, judging by the continuity of the hairstyles and the changing outfits. She had been certain she had it right. 'Are you sure?'

'Yes,' said Isabelle, handing the photo back.

Betty passed her the other two, as though it would make a difference. 'And these,' she said, 'definitely not him?'

'*Bien sûr que non,*' said Isabelle, examining both of them in turn. 'It is the same boy in all of them, and he is not the boy.' Just before handing them back, she stopped and took a closer look at the last photograph. 'Ah,' she said, pointing. 'Yes. But this one, this is him. This is the boy. Martha's boy.'

'Where?' Betty leaned in to look as Isabelle indicated a small figure in soft focus in the far background. Another boy of about the same age, sitting in a chair, scowling, arms folded, his face in shadow beneath a black cap and his legs covered by a towel.

'This little guy,' said Isabelle, chuckling. 'He doesn't look too happy, does he?'

'Are you sure?' said Betty. She didn't recall seeing this child in any of the other photos.

'Yes,' said Isabelle, 'because look.' She pointed to another hazy figure standing behind the boy. 'This is Clara, the nanny. I know her.'

Clara was a sturdy-looking woman who appeared to be in her late twenties, with long light-brown hair, wearing shorts and a vest; also unsmiling but not quite so surly as the boy. Betty began to shuffle through the other photos in the box to see if there were any more images of these two. She could find nothing. 'Did you know Jack and Martha well?' she asked.

'Jack not at all, and I only meet Martha maybe twice. Say

hello, how are you, yes, no, maybe, OK then, nice to see you, goodbye, like that, but she spoke good French.'

'And who is this boy with the black hair, playing with her?'

'My God, Betty, you are like a detective,' said Isabelle, laughing. 'I don't know. I never saw him.'

'Sorry,' said Betty.

'Why don't you ask Jack?'

'I will.' Betty began to gather all the photos back together, tying the string to bind the box.

'He never comes back after his wife kills herself here.'

Betty placed the box into the basket of the bicycle and turned back to Isabelle. 'Here?' she said. 'She killed herself *here*?'

'Of course.'

Betty wasn't sure why this shocked her as it did. She'd supposed that the suicide had been committed in Britain. 'Here?' she said. 'In Pontelle?'

'Near the house,' said Isabelle, nodding. 'Through the woods. She walked into the tunnel and lie down, they say, on the track, with her head . . .' She paused, checking that Betty was ready. 'And the train, it go . . .' She made a cutting motion with the flat of her hand across her throat, augmenting the gesture with a sharp, sibilant exhalation through stretched red lips, her horrible grey teeth coming out to smile in mock horror.

Betty was suddenly nauseous. She put her hat back on, snatched up her bicycle and wheeled it away from the stall at speed, bouncing it across the cobbles, the bell on the handlebars like a broken alarm going off in her brain. What a stupid fucking woman, she thought, this Isabelle, to say a thing like that, to tell it all like that, like an appalling joke, like gossip. Pushing the bicycle ever faster down the hill, she jumped up on the saddle and pedalled as hard as she could till it felt like the wheels might buckle and send her crashing into the asphalt. She could hear the brim of her panama hat flapping, the box of photos bouncing around in the basket, and thought of the boy brooding in the back of the shot in his black cap and the towel across his knees. What was it about him? There was something she could not find. In the far distance, across the fields, through the twisted vineyards, the olive groves and the shimmering haze, she saw a silent train slide slowly over the horizon, swallowed whole by the hillside.

Nora was not answering her phone, nor was she responding to texts or voicemails. Betty had not mentioned the specifics of her concerns, only that there were issues about which she wished to speak, which stood in the way of her performing the job to the best of her ability. In truth, she was incensed. How was she expected to inhabit this woman, to talk on such an intimate level with the husband of this woman, if such a critical facet of her existence had been concealed? If this woman – whom Betty had been tasked with resurrecting – had been a mother, and if her husband – whom Betty had been tasked with appeasing – was a father, then why was this never mentioned? Nothing infuriated Betty more than being treated as though taking her work seriously was a thing of small concern: Jack Drake should understand this better than most.

But then Betty suspected it was Nora who pulled the strings of this particular puppet. Why send her to live in this house, have her sleep in Martha's bed, dress in Martha's clothes, walk around in Martha's life, but then withhold something so fundamental? Would Betty be the woman she was if she were not a mother? Of course not, and maybe it was because Nora herself was not, as Betty suspected, a mother that she did not consider the matter important. Or had the order come from higher up? In which case, why? Was Betty to be only a caricature, a doodle of this dead woman? Or was Jack interested in something a little deeper, more credible, more accomplished? If what he needed was not an actress but a compliant ventriloquist, then he should go back to his dead-eyed mannequins.

The phone was old and badly cracked, but after a brief charge, it was brought back to life. There were few photos of any interest, and none at all of the boy. There was a fascinating video (shot by Jack, judging by the off-screen laughter) of Martha dancing wildly, drunkenly, but rather beautifully to what a quick search revealed to be 'Lulu's Back in Town' by Fats Waller. Betty was so taken with it, and for a few moments so delightfully distracted from her anguish by the silliness of it, that she watched it three times in a row, quite forgetting the tragedy of the poor creature spinning and dipping within it. The screen's cracked glass only added to the intoxicating dizziness of the footage. The fragmentation of this giddy woman in this moment of wonderful foolishness.

This was another thing that Betty resented: not being allowed to drink, banishing alcohol from the house when it was another part of Martha not to be disregarded. She picked up her own phone and sent Nora another text, bombarding her now: *And another thing. I asked Georges to buy some wine in this week's shopping. I believe that Martha liked a drink as much as, if not more than, I like a drink, therefore I would like a drink as much as, if not more than, Martha would like a drink. I promise only to pour it into Martha's mouth, even if I am the one who must pay the price of the hangover. I am prepared to make this sacrifice in the name of authenticity. Fair? Let me know ;)*

She didn't expect Nora to take that in good humour, but by now, honestly, fuck her. Betty knew Jack wasn't about to fire her – she was doing too well, she could feel it – and she would, from now on, only push things further, so fuck the old cow if she couldn't take a joke.

Then a simple idea occurred to her. It seemed so simple she

felt she might never have thought of it. She went into the contacts of the cracked phone and searched for Clara, and there she was, of course she was, why shouldn't she be? No surname, just Clara. Then into Clara's texts, to explore further. It was there that she found him: the boy, the son, the simple name. Oliver. Oliver Drake. Nothing revelatory – only times and dates, brief, commonplace questions – but he was more than a rumour now: now he had itemised needs, favourite meals, places to be, things to see. And in the middle of all that there were three photographs of him, full face, well lit, in focus. Betty forwarded all three to her own phone so as to see him clearly, to look him in the eyes. As in the other photo, he appeared to be a surly child, with a plump and sulky lower lip and a tendency to hide behind a thick fringe of hair, pressed down and flattened by the ubiquitous black cap. Each photo was surely taken against his will, as though the camera offended him. It was a distressing thing to see.

But what distressed Betty most of all was the look in his eyes, or rather, the eyes themselves, for just as Betty's eyes were sometimes Martha's eyes, so Oliver's eyes were – in another lifetime – Freddie's.

CHAPTER 22

For so much of their married life they had spoken in this absurd fashion – face to face, far apart, different towns, countries, continents – until it became as natural to them as any other unnatural thing. Before life-size screens, upon candlelit tables, they would eat the same meals and talk for hours, hardly aware at all that they were not really, not actually, not physically together. When they were done, they would say good day or night, blow a fond kiss, blow out the candle and with a light tap of the finger turn each other off. Leaving one alone in the room, as one had always been, of course.

In which case, did it matter if this was not really Martha? For had it ever been really Martha, when the real Martha was also capable of vanishing so completely, so cruelly?

This woman whom Jack did not care to name, though her name was now, in recent days, too easily within his grasp, had pulled off, unprompted, something magical, and now he must concede that the floor was hers. Nora, the previous afternoon, had made a fresh appeal for him to resolve the situation, but this had more to do, he thought, with Nora's disdain for the woman than it did with a sincere concern for his own well-being, as if she feared, in her melodramatic fashion, for his sanity.

The truth was that the young woman had displayed remarkable ingenuity, moving him to tears, moving him to almost forgotten planes of simple delight and laughter with her dancing, in the same room, the same moves, to the same music, spinning and dipping, so thrillingly close to falling with every step, in the same green linen dress, her hair in the same messy stack, a false eyelash dropping and sticking to her hot pink cheek, her bare feet shifting and twisting on the white wood floor, slipping as she howled, kicking a cushion into the curtains, singing in tune, in time, but the wrong words, ridiculous words, but still from the heart, exactly like Martha. From the first note to the last, when she slumped down breathless on the sofa, every move was Martha, every sigh and groan, every squeak and whistle, every wink and hiccup was Martha.

And then suddenly it was over as she marched towards the camera, laughing, blowing kisses, then turning it off with that same light tap of the finger. At the end of a maddeningly unhappy day, Jack had fallen asleep with a smile on his lips, and slept deep and long, had not dreamed, nor been woken by dreadful knocking and footsteps on the ceiling, and had made it through to the morning without screaming out in suffocated silence. Things were looking up.

He was finding it difficult to concentrate. Everyone could tell. He was shuffling around the set, back in the red pyjamas, back in the mask and soft slippers of a dead man, and yet more alive, it seemed, than any other day in recent weeks. He was smiling at nothing, gazing at dust in a beam of light, asking people to repeat themselves, and was often unable to address the question in the haze of his distraction, and when asked again if he was all right, he would say yes, yes, I was just thinking of last night, of Martha last night, dancing, you should have seen her. Did you ever meet her? Oh, you would love her. She's extraordinary . . . and sorry, what was it you asked me again?

Eve Parnell, having witnessed this the week before, was more prepared than others. 'I'm sorry, Jack,' she said. 'It only occurred to me last night to ask, was your mother on medication at this point?'

'No,' said Jack, 'not at all.'

'So she's lucid, so to speak, when she's saying all this?'

'Well, that's a question of semantics,' said Jack, 'but it has nothing to do with medication. It's grief, is it not? It's rage, it's revenge, spite, contempt.'

'I see,' said Eve, repeating, 'rage, revenge, spite and contempt. In that order?'

'What?' said Jack, looking at the floor. A slug had crept up from a crack in the boards.

'I was learning it last night and thought one must resist any inclination to make it at all funny.'

'It's not funny,' said Jack, pulling back from the slug.

'No, I know,' said Eve, 'of course not, but it could be, if one—'

'It mustn't be,' he snapped.

'Definitely not,' she said.

He seemed back to his old self all of a sudden. He called out to a runner for another coffee and, taking hold of the script, marched off up the stairs, expecting Eve to follow, which she did, amused at his irascibility in such a comical costume – and right on cue, one of his red slippers, catching on a nail, was left behind on the stair, without him even noticing it was gone. One must resist the inclination to make it funny, she repeated to herself, though sometimes it was difficult, since this entire project bore all the hallmarks of a farce.

'How did it go yesterday?' she said, as Jack cleared the room for rehearsal.

'How did what go?' said Jack.

'You know, the rumpy-pumpy.'

Jack turned to her, appalled. 'What's wrong with you, Eve? What's this urge to make everything stupid?'

'Sorry,' she said, bowing her head. It was true: it was an urge. 'I just wondered how you got on with Bernadette. She can be tricky.'

'She can,' said Jack, and left it at that. The runner arrived with his coffee and they both sat down on the edge of the hard, white-sheeted single bed. Eve went into her bag and pulled out her red Bible, ready for action. 'The silicone father won't be here for another week,' he said, 'so you've got me again, as you might have noticed.'

'Oh,' she said. 'Another week?'

'It'll be here in time for the hanging, and that's it.'

'Oh,' she repeated.

They sat for a moment in the new silence. Eve riffled idly through her Bible.

'Good,' said Jack at last, and opened the script to Scene 68. 'Shall we take a look?'

'Let's,' she said, and moved a wooden chair into position as Jack lay down on his back on the bed, his hands crossed upon his chest. As he fidgeted to make himself comfortable, he raised his head to look at his feet.

'Oh,' he said.

'What?' said Eve.

'I've lost a slipper.'

'So you have.'

'Never mind,' he said, leaning back and closing his eyes.

Eve rolled up her sleeves and wrestled with her silicone bump, patting her dear darling imaginary little baby into position. She took her deepest breath. There passed a brief silence, and then . . .

'You're staying right where you are,' said Eleanor Drake, for

Eve had taken a moment to compose herself in the posture of Jack's unmedicated mother.

'Stop,' said Jack, his eyes still closed. 'I want you to say it to yourself; don't even whisper, just speak it to yourself, silently, slowly.'

'Oh,' said Eve. 'Don't speak at all?'

'Only in your mind. And before that, take a few moments to see him, here, dead. Dead for days now.' Jack began to whisper, fading away with each word. 'Think about that. I'll shut up and you sit with the body. See how that feels.' And with that they both fell silent, and in the silence Jack too was called upon to see how it felt to lie there, once again, on the same bed, in the same room, in similar silence to the silence of his father.

Eve looked nothing like Jack's mother, but there was something about her, something disappointed; something gentle, yet bitter, tender, yet resentful; somewhat like his mother before all the bother, before all the fucking and hanging and hiding the corpse. Suddenly, out of the stillness, Jack felt his mother's red leather-bound Bible set down upon his father's red paisley chest. 'You're staying right where you are,' said his mother. 'I know what you're thinking. You're thinking you've gone too far this time, Eleanor. But it's your fault, Sam. It's you who's gone too far.' Had she ever said any of this? Jack doubted it, but it would do for now, and Eve had already learned it. 'Don't look at me like that,' she went on. 'This is where you live now.' Stupid joke; he'll cut it. And maybe the next line: 'We have some talking to do.' Without doubt. In fact, he thought, I'll cut the lot. This never happened. It never happened back then, so why should it happen now? Every time someone opened their mouth, Jack wanted desperately to shut it. People didn't speak like this. Only silence meant anything, but what, he had no idea. It was agony, lying here dead with so much to do. He could not wait for the evening's call. Only the calls were real.

For the first time, he had prepared nothing. Even the previous night he had mailed through a few pages, which she had dutifully printed out, only to tear them up on camera right before walking over to the record player. For a brief moment, he had been furious. Then the music had begun. The shoes were kicked off, the wine poured and the cigarette lit, and within half a minute all had been forgiven, and so this evening he had sent nothing, only a brief and tender message on where she might find her precious ring.

The night before, the lights and camera had been moved from Martha's room to the music room, which was fine; that was Martha's choice, not his. But now they had been moved once again, and this time to the bedroom. The call had been accepted, but by whom was not clear, for he could see that the room was deserted, the wide lens showing a simple shot of the empty bed with clean white sheets folded back, white pillows plumped and the white ivory Jesus on his white wooden cross nailed up on the white stone wall. Well, what was he to make of this? He felt his mouth so dry it almost hurt to peel his lips apart to breathe, and his heart pressed down on whatever nerve rigged the ignition of a dull nausea. He was seated in his usual chair, beneath the usual lamp, in the corner of the library, with the tablet upon his knee, but for some reason he found himself suddenly up and on the move, across the floor, out through the doors and into the hallway, lighting the dark walls of his childhood home with the white glow of his French bedroom, all the time checking that Martha had not yet made her entrance. He took a seat at the top of the landing, his back against the wall, his legs out before him, as a child might sit, and, placing the tablet flat on the floor, with a light tap of the finger he turned it off.

He was still wearing his father's red pyjamas. He had taken

to sleeping in them on the hard single bed in the narrow room at the end of the corridor. He knew it would be considered queer and macabre, were anyone to find out, but there was no reason they should, and little did he care. Jack liked to think that by wearing his father – by putting his father to sleep where his father had slept and spent the first few days of his death – he might shape him into the sort of father who could forgive his son, and in turn help Jack become the sort of son who could be forgiven. It was a long shot, but sometimes, in the middle of the night, when the footsteps on the ceiling were booted and restless, he took some comfort in what might be perceived as the first scratchings of redemption.

Why were they to meet now in the white bedroom? It wouldn't be the first time. Martha would often call early in the morning or last thing at night, but at eight in the evening? And why would she tease him like this by accepting the call and not appearing? He took himself off to the second landing and into the editing suite so he could call her, life-size, on the big screen, so he could see what they were talking about here, see things clearly, assess the bigger picture. With his hand a-quiver he clicked on 'call' and waited, and sure enough, after a few breathless moments, there it was again, the clean white bed, freshly unmade, and a candle now, burning low on the night-stand. The main light dimmed slowly, almost imperceptibly, with ceremonial suspense, as at the opening of a play. Then a key light picked out a pillow, throwing all else into shadow, and here she came, on from stage left, passing close to the camera, blacking out the frame for a small second, too close to tell how she might be dressed, or not. A bare arm hung in the gloom. A pale hand with curled fingers. The cherished ring's procession of perfect diamonds blazing. A cigarette was lit and a flash of red tongue and lips. It had been a long time since Jack had felt like this: all his breath held fast in his breast, all the blood rushing through his flesh. Two small hoops of smoke were sent across the bed, and then Martha, her body draped in white muslin, spread herself out in the faint glow, her face dappled and downcast, with a white silk scarf tied about her head. Her pale bare shoulders catching in the candlelight.

'Good evening, Martha,' said Jack, and took a breath.

'Good evening, Jack,' she said.

What to say then. What was there to say?

'Have you anything to tell me?' said Martha.

Jack blushed, as though she could see him. 'What should I tell you?'

'I don't know,' she said. 'Something I've never heard.'

'Something you've never heard?' he said, and laughed. 'Like what?'

'How do I know?'

'Well, how do I know?'

'For example,' she said.

'Yes?' he said.

'For example, why do we never talk about . . .' She stopped.

'Why do we never talk about what?'

'Why do we never talk about . . .' she said, and stopped a second time. She took a long drag on her cigarette.

'What?' said Jack, smiling. She let the smoke trail from her lips, up into the light.

'You know,' she said.

'Sex?' he said.

'Sex?' she said, frowning. 'No.'

'No?' he said.

'No.'

'Oh.'

'Oliver,' she said.

'What?'

'I said, why do we never talk about Oliver?'

Jack said nothing. For a long time he said nothing at all, but only looked at her as she gazed at him from the shadow, as still now and cold as the white stone wall.

'Because,' he said at last, and paused. 'Because he isn't born yet.'

And with the lightest of taps from his trembling finger, he turned her off, and she vanished.

He was alone once more. Alone in the room, as he had always been, of course.

CHAPTER 23

Every time Paul's new sweetheart Edie Krauss made a move out there in the world, Betty Dean would receive an alert and knew where she was or where she had been, where she planned to go, with whom, how, when, why, wearing what (or who), how long she stayed, what and how much she ate and drank, who did her hair, who did her face, who trained her, who sprayed her, who gave her the shoes and jewels and what she now weighed, compared to the last alert (usually less). And now this morning here she was in a billowing feather dress, iridescent in the Sri Lankan sun, feeding something delicious to a small elephant, assisted by an adorable boy of six or seven – the news site didn't know precisely who, but perhaps a nephew, or a secret son, but perhaps not, for in the next paragraph it was conjectured that that small bump in the feathers was very likely to be her firstborn, already finding his or her light on this flying visit to the Pinnawala Elephant Orphanage. Paul was not mentioned and was nowhere in sight. Freddie looked as happy as Betty had ever seen him as his hand rested on the beautiful girl's beautiful shoulder, and as for Betty, well, it was difficult not to smash the phone on the edge of the cistern (for during this interlude she was seated on the toilet).

There followed a trivial exchange of texts. Paul assured her that he had indeed been present and was in fact cropped from the shot as was standard with these hacks. Betty stoically accepted this and wrote back that she supposed nobody wanted to see the toothless lover of a fuckable sex puppet. Paul did not reply for another hour. Betty apologised for her language and hoped she had not brought trouble into paradise. Still no reply. She sent her congratulations on the small bump in the feathers, and if Freddie was a good boy, was he allowed to rub it? Three minutes later, Paul insisted that Freddie had not been told of Edie's condition. Betty went on to praise Paul's preference for communicating significant details of their – and Edie's – son's life via the tabloid press, and that while she understood his desire to punish her in increasingly ingenious ways, did he really think it befitted a man of his standing to stick her heart up on a spike in a public square? That one did not receive a reply, and she was happy to leave it at that and get on with the day.

What distressed her most of all was how this made her feel about Freddie. It was a simple thing to despise Paul for his ruthless disregard, or Edie for her facile celebrity, but it was chilling to feel resentment towards her own child for that hand casually resting on the beautiful shoulder, and for that smile of all smiles lighting up his face. It felt like she was seeing him only days after her death: how quickly he would forget her, as if he'd never known her and would never miss her as long as there were pretty girls and jungles, and poor elephants to be fed. And if there was something writhing inside that bump, then wouldn't that also rip him from her and stick him in place? A new brother or sister to suck up all his love. She had no family to offer him. Her dead mother confused him and her dying father terrified him. She'd read that Edie's mother and father had met and now worked together in the Large Hadron Collider near Geneva, and that her brother was one of the world's leading

183

authorities on Artemisia Gentileschi. Her baby, thought Betty, will probably step out singing 'O mio babbino caro / Mi piace, è bello, bello', with Paul biting the cord in two with his new gold teeth, while Freddie . . . She had to pause and remember to breathe. She could feel the kernels of cancer popping with each new thought.

When she had conducted her extensive study of Martha's quirks and feints – how, for example, when vexed by suspicion, she would draw a finger along the shore of her hairline, or how, when briefly entertaining a prospect she was about to confound, she would tap the tip of a fang with the pad of her thumb – when Betty compiled this inventory of affecting gestures, it was impossible to miss and therefore not covet, if only for professional considerations, the ring.

It is in my study, my darling, precisely where we failed to look. I have kept it for you in the lacquered black box in the locked bureau. The key is beneath Bartholomew's heel, and I am once more down upon my knee.

After wondering if parrots had heels and if so how she might get at them, way up there on the mantelpiece, nailed to a mossy log and sealed beneath the enormous bell jar, Betty realised he meant the statue of the beleaguered saint outside the bedroom door, whose heel was slightly lifted in anticipation of his imminent flaying. And there she found it, and there in the bureau the prize: an antique, if not ancient, ring of luminous gold with a procession of twelve round-cut Indian diamonds, given to Martha on her wedding day. It had slipped on easily enough last night, but now, this morning, here in the steaming kitchen, with the heat, the stress and the sheer claustrophobic panic, she couldn't take it off. Nor did she really wish to. For now that Martha had it back, she was not about to give it up.

She had stopped trying to interpret Jack's response. She

supposed it meant that all talk of Oliver was somehow not part of the conceit. When she had phoned Nora later that night, Nora claimed to be unaware of the conversation but declared that the boy – 'Yes, Oliver, well done' – was hardly the mystery Betty would have him be, and was currently staying with Martha's sister, Victoria, in San Francisco. Furthermore, it was not appropriate to talk to Mr Drake (as she was back to calling him) about anything that Mr Drake did not want to talk about, and why was that difficult for her to understand? After all, Betty was not being asked to actually *replace* Martha, but merely to *present* a version of her, as one might approach any other role, superficially, for a short time, and for a specific purpose. Betty objected to the word 'superficially', whereupon Nora objected to Betty objecting to anything, and why didn't she just go home to the rain and cold if she was so affronted?

And as for alcohol, continued Nora, now her claws were out, did Betty think it was appropriate for a professional actress portraying a drunk on the stage to actually be drunk on the stage? No, said Betty, she did not, and was moved by Nora's truculence to apologise, though she was quietly consoled by detecting some glee in Nora's tone as she referred, if only obliquely, to Martha as a drunk. She wasn't sure she believed anything she had to say regarding Oliver, though it was true that Martha did have a sister called Victoria living in San Francisco, but none of that explained why there was so little evidence of the child in the house, why everyone was being so evasive, and above all why there was no mention anywhere of Martha Lear as a mother. It felt like she now had this in common with her subject: there was afoot some attempt by family, friends and even the media to rob them both of their children.

She was aware it had been wicked of her – the word was not too strong – to bear Paul's child when, even as the child took shape inside her, she knew she would not stay with Paul. This foreboding sense of wickedness was not shared with him, nor the fact that throughout twelve hours of labour it was another man who occupied Betty's mind – an older man, a less handsome man, less ambitious, poorer; yet a less possessive man, a more loving, funnier, freer, cleaner man, who never made her doubt herself, who thought of her before himself, who wanted to be with her always and forever (though Betty knew that this too was out of the question, for there would surely be, once she had tired of him, other men, and so there had been). But none of this had given her pause as the child grew within her and was, with Paul's warm hand in hers, identified as a boy, and therefore named after the young man who had taken her virginity, which she knew was wicked, and that the word was not too strong.

Once more Martha had been the first one up that morning, and this time had made it downstairs, for Betty had awoken to discover herself wearing Martha's red kimono and a very large straw hat, playing Beethoven's 'Ode to Joy', which seemed tartly ironic. Not to say that Betty did not know how to play the piano – she did – but it was a discomfiting return to consciousness and one that she could have done without. She had however stayed in the kimono and the wide-brimmed straw hat and still wore them now by the side of the pool, though the hat was in peril from the building mistral, its brim flapping back and forth, sometimes blinding her completely. After concluding her bitter exchanges with Paul, she had dialled Clara's number from the landline – to say what, she did not know, and indeed in the end said nothing, since a formal male voice had asked her, in French, to leave a message.

One thing she had succeeded in doing, and behind Nora's back to boot, was obtaining a copy of Jack's script *Unburied*.

It had not been too difficult. Her dear Urbain Grandier had been an absolute angel to his little devil, Sister Agnes, and yes, yes, he'd said, he had indeed been sent a copy after that last night at the theatre, and no, he had not been offered the part, but had heard rather that Drake himself had taken on the role of his own father, which they both supposed was a bit much, but what the hell, that was show-business. And so within the hour the PDF was with her, and so, with her feet in the water, beneath an enormous yellow parasol and her gigantic straw hat flapping like a fucking pterosaur, she settled down to read it, mainly to see if things could be any stranger. She was not disappointed.

Jack could have answered her question in a hundred different ways; he could also have ignored her, he could have hung up and had his faithful guard dog, Nora, warn her off. But to utter, in this self-consciously enigmatic manner, that Oliver was not yet born was both tiresome and baffling. In the first instance, it surely violated their code, such as it was, for was it not reference to the thing itself – the stratagem, or whatever he preferred to call it these days? It was also provocatively obscure and would more likely cause her to pursue the peculiar matter even further. How, from now on, was she expected to broach the issue? What was or was not to be said? If she was called upon to portray Martha prior to motherhood, then by how many years was she expected to regress? As things stood, Betty was seven years younger than Martha had been at the time of her death, and six or seven years seemed to be the age of the child; but if this figure was relevant and the date of all these calls was tacitly presumed to have been six or seven years previous and she was supposed to have taken this into account when talking of the world, then why was this never made clear from the outset? For if Betty was not – as she had always assumed – playing Martha alive in the present, as though she had never died, then she must surely be playing some other, reimagined, historical Martha, a Martha for whom motherhood and suicide still loomed. In which case she had an abundance of questions. For example: did Martha want to be a mother? Plan to be a mother? Relish being a mother? Was Jack chosen to be the father? Did he want to be a father? *Is* Jack the father? Are there other children? Other fathers? And back once again to the primary question, the question that grew louder each passing day, the question Betty could never banish from her mind as long as Martha lived so vividly within her, the question she was certain she had been sent here to answer – for wasn't that the purpose of this game, this stratagem? – why did Martha kill herself?

For it occurred to her now, as she gazed at the mountain as Martha must have daily gazed, that Jack did not know.

But there was no call that night. And since Betty had been left behind in the bedroom, it was Martha who ate the last of the stew and the cheese. It was Martha who, furnished with Bartholomew's backstory, knocked him from his perch on the mantelpiece, Martha who stayed up till three, smoking and drinking, floating in the pool beneath a slice of moon. And it was Martha who made it into bed before Betty could stop her and so dreamed deeply inside her, so selfishly and so indelibly that it would be impossible for Betty not to remember her. And when Martha was, once more, up before her, she would take great care to show Betty the best way through the woods, and there to whisper into her ear exactly what should happen next.

CHAPTER 24

INT. BEDROOM — NIGHT

Eleanor is seated by the bed. It is two days
after the miscarriage and the bump is no longer
in evidence. Sam, now in his sixth day of
decomposition, is looking worse than ever. A
number of flies buzz around the room. Eleanor
swats them away with her red Bible as she
speaks. Through a crack in the door we can make
out Jack with his camera, unseen by his mother,
documenting everything.

> ELEANOR
> I don't want anyone to think I'm doing
> this out of love, as though I can't let
> you go. I can let you go, Sam. I can
> certainly do that. In fact, there's
> nothing I would like more. But just a
> few final things, before you drop away
> forever. You didn't give me much of
> a chance. You didn't give me much of
> anything. All you ever gave me was my
> boy. And how much did that cost you?
> Your permission not to get rid of him?
> Were we not enough for you, Sam? Jack

and I? Or is it that we were too much
and you wanted less? Is that what she
gave you? Less? Maybe I did something
to deserve this. Not in this life. I
know I could not have done anything
to deserve such agony in this life. I
am not a monster. But perhaps I was
something monstrous in another life.
And perhaps that sort of thing gets in
everywhere, and it found its way into
that moment between you and her, as you
moved towards each other for that first
kiss, and you felt it unimportant to
resist. So perhaps it was my fault, or
rather the fault of someone I once was,
long, long ago. What do you think, Sam?

Eleanor removes her wedding ring and places it
upon Sam's chest, the diamonds anomalous atop
the squalor. Jack hides behind the door as she
leaves. When he is sure she has gone, he enters
the room and walks over to his father. He takes
a photograph. After some consideration he picks
up the wedding ring and gently places it into
his pocket.

After the first take had been cut short by an errant fly finding its
way into Eve Parnell's mouth in the middle of the monologue,
she and Jack agreed that the second take was worth consideration, but that she should try one more, and it was therefore
concluded that the third take would ultimately be used, with
perhaps the last few moments of the second. Billy played his
brief scene with fitting pathos, delighting Jack, though Solomon struggled to light the ring, failing to evoke the rare lustre
of the original.

    After Eve and Billy were wrapped for the day, Jack declared
he would need only thirty seconds for his close-up, which

was about as much as he anticipated being able to endure. As the camera began to roll, Douglas Proctor, the bug wrangler, placed one frozen blowfly on Jack's cracked lip, two on his cheek, one on his neck and another on his chin. After a few breathless moments, the warmth of Jack's rotting flesh revived the petrified flies, who then – newly invigorated but still a little foggy – tottered back and forth across his cheeks and chin, before eventually taking wing and cheerfully exiting the frame.

For the past two days Jack had been losing faith. He felt it pouring from him like a wound in water, changing the colour of everything around him. He had no passion to go on with the film. It was, he conceded, an abominable story. No one sane would want to see it, and he had no more strength to tell it.

'We should never have encouraged each other,' he said. 'We're bad for each other, Nora.'

It was early dusk and Nora walked with him down by the river, imploring him to persist, employing all her tested tricks, trying to convince him that it was by far his finest work, causing Jack to flap and scoff, as she knew he would, for nothing she could do or say would steer him from this stubborn malaise.

For her part, Nora was not inordinately concerned. She had endured so many of these slumps over the years; she knew it would soon pass. She reassured him that the worst was almost over; this dreadful episode he distrusted so much, this despicably intimate interaction with comparative strangers, ingrates, delusional fools. In short, the sheer hell of the shoot. Soon it would all be a bad memory. But for now, she knew, it was better to allow him his fit of doubt.

'You haven't spoken to France for two nights,' she said, changing the subject. 'Shall I let her go?'

'I don't understand what you're saying,' said Jack, his eyes fixed on the mud and shingle. The river's tide was so low they were walking the beach between the bridges of Blackfriars and Waterloo, kicking over filthy old rope and stones, bending, squatting now and then, as they were fond of doing, to turn over some scrap of nothing in their hand.

'We have a week to go,' said Nora, 'and if she's no longer important . . .'

'I don't have to talk to Martha every day,' said Jack. 'She doesn't expect it.'

Nora stopped and poked at something sharp and white with the toe of her boot. 'I know,' she said, and, certain that he couldn't see, shook her head. 'I know, but if you've changed your—'

'Why were you speaking of Oliver?' said Jack, interrupting, stopping, turning to face her.

'Oh,' moaned Nora, throwing up her eyes, 'did she tell you I was speaking of Oliver?'

'Well, she knows about Oliver, so—'

'Well, I didn't tell her,' Nora protested. 'She was asking about him and I said he was with Victoria, in America. What's wrong with that?'

Jack said nothing. He turned away and carried on walking.

'He's not left, has he?' said Nora. 'She asked and I told her. I said you didn't want to involve him, simple as that.'

Jack stopped again and kicked a small stone into the rising water. 'I don't want to speak like this,' he snapped. 'It's confusing. It's very confusing, Nora, and you know it is, so I don't understand why you . . .' He ran his hand across his face and closed his eyes. 'From now on, let me deal with it.'

'That's fine with me,' said Nora.

'Good.'

'You know how I feel.'

'Good.'

'I can't bear the woman.'

That was it. Jack had had enough of her. 'Shall we turn back?' he said, implying they should not. 'Or are you going for the train?' implying that she really should.

'I'm going for the train,' said Nora, as though it was her idea. 'Will you be all right?'

'Of course,' said Jack.

'The tide is rising. You should get back up on the bank.' She leaned in and he let her kiss him on the cheek and squeeze his hand. 'I'll see you in the morning.'

'Sorry,' Jack said, and nodded. And so she went; climbing the steps towards the National Theatre, where Jack could make out, on a torn poster, the face of an actor he detested and had thought long dead, but alas not, for there he was, scowling across the South Bank, as though it meant something. It meant nothing. He could see Nora, so small now, up on the bankside, making her way through the masses, a grey speck.

He had been coming down here, to the wet green wood, to the red mud and bricks, from an early age, and had once – one Tuesday afternoon, while walking home from school – found an Elizabethan jawbone, which had made him briefly famous, before the bone had been taken from him and placed in a glass case in a museum far away. He was neither thanked nor paid. It was a bad memory for him. A small, seemingly meaningless episode that still moved him to tears, even now, all these years later. It had, he supposed, something to do with loss. But he had, in his time, lost far more than that. Indeed, there had been occasions when he felt like he had lost everything, and that there was nothing left to lose.

But then something would come along, some fresh hope, some new blood, like now for instance: a new life, a child – a boy, they imagined – not planned, at least not by them. A child not yet born, making his move at last (after centuries some-times, it was said) and choosing them. It was not unheard of.

There were many who subscribed to such a notion. Not so very common perhaps, not all that often, but, argued Martha, just as some blighted souls might choose the time and cause of their death, so might not a child choose the time and cause of their birth? If that was what it would take, thought Jack, to carry Martha through this pregnancy – a condition that seemed to terrify her; as though she were 'horribly infected' was how she'd described it the other night – then he was willing to talk in such terms. If she had to fully embrace aberrant doctrines of karma to sustain the burden of this thing inside her (she had called it a 'thing' from the start), then Jack would embrace them equally, at least in her presence, at least until it was over and the child grew old enough to tell them they were lunatics.

The brown tide was rising. He looked out across the water to the dome of St Paul's and thought of Martha. He was resolute. He would not call again tonight. No. Not until the package had arrived.

CHAPTER 25

It would be difficult to say who had the harder time leaving the house that morning. Martha wanted to, but could not, and Betty could, but did not want to. Martha had dressed, a little incongruously for her purpose, perhaps, in a pastel Versace minidress and a black baker-boy cap, but Betty had no quarrel with that. She still wore the wedding ring and added the Givenchy clutch for her phone, her fags and a small Dupont lighter. Neither of them really chose the heavy tan walking boots, but there they were somehow, refusing to cross the threshold, and Martha furious with Betty's feet, as Martha's hand on the door frame pulled them both through and over, Betty retreating and falling back and both of them half screaming, half whispering at the other in two or even three different voices. Sometimes it was a chilling jumble that gave way to something neither of them had heard before, whom one of them called Marty and the other referred to as Bertha, and then they both laughed and tried to get through the doorway all over again.

At one point Georges happened by and shook his head at the dance, but thought nothing of it. Having lived with the germ of this aberration for two weeks now, he had learned not to ask questions, and so went about his business, preparing the various rooms and driving into town to fetch sustenance for the poor suffering creature. By the second hour Martha had made it into the open air and was spinning in the garden, making the occasional break for the front gate, while Betty, lying low and scarcely breathing for fear of detection, would suddenly leap up and march not back inside, but down to the far west corner of the house, past the garage and across the long back lawn, thinking that if she could just make it to the pool, she could hurl herself in, and that perhaps the shock of the water would extinguish Martha's exuberance.

But then Betty was confounded by the truth that Martha was simply more fun, and so finally gave in. She allowed her to run back past the house, up the path, out the gate, down the road, past the postbox, past the horse, towards the mountain and into the woods. But then later, almost lost in the low light of the smothering trees, Martha began to weaken and her breathing faltered, and her eyes grew sore, and Betty's heart began to beat and Betty's sweat began to flow, and Betty, finding it almost impossible to swallow, had to curl up on her side and turn face down. The sharp earth grazing her cheeks. Shards of fractured leaves sticking to her lips. Slick bugs, like tiny black violins, swarming on her hands. Then, lifting up her face, her feeble, empty English voice, hardly there, whispered: 'This isn't fair, Martha,' but knew instantly she should not have said it, for a haze of pale sparks seemed to crackle and scatter at the back of her skull. As the sun climbed up through the trees, the mistral began to shake the branches and the sun, and to bend every thought, until Betty picked herself up and walked, emerging at last into the full light, bewildered.

There before her was the open throat.

The roaring lung of the railway tunnel. The sun on the rails, and the smell of the rails in the sun and the smell inside the open mouth, and the open sores on the rusty bricks. Betty reached out. The heavy boots walked her in. Beguiled by the dark, she lay down. Her fingers clutching at the gravel and gripping till they bled. The smooth steel on the nape of her neck. Was this the last thing she ever saw? thought Betty. This black ceiling, barely visible, or was she deeper in? Could she see anything at all? Or was it only her heart by now, keeping count, winding down in the dark?

Betty closed her eyes and realised that the two women were, astonishingly, for the first time, side by side, and that if she offered her hand, she would feel Martha there. So certain was she of this that she did not reach out for fear that Martha would take her hand in hers and keep her there till everything that had once spun so beautifully would be fixed in position for the rest of time. It is not the worst thing, thought Betty; it is not the worst thing, to die. And as she lay there, on her back, her neck on the rail, her skull filled up with thunder and the rails began to boil. She saw herself from above and scrambled up and onto her hands and knees and pushed herself to standing, and from there staggered back, stumbling on the bolts and stones, her bleeding fingers feeling for the broken wall. The furious train bellowed like a falling mountain and its blazing eye spat out its lightning, passing in and through, faster than gunshot but never-ending, blasting her against the bricks, pulling with all its might at her bones, the breath sucked out of her lungs and smashed backed down, and the dreadful, unbelievable, unendurable sound, like a district of hell passing through. She felt it would go on forever. Perhaps she had not survived after all. Perhaps death was this. Not frozen, as she had thought, but eternally moving. Scraped out and coughed up by some ceaseless colossal rage. She huddled there and took it, punched in the face over and over, harder and harder, louder and louder, and then fell down, softly, simply, like a pin, like a pea, like a beetle from a shelf.

And lay there in the silence. Mindless. Forgotten. Martha's tiny watch ticking on her trembling wrist.

Her phone rang. She reached into her bag to find Paul's small face smiling, and his eyes shining with what must have been, back then, affection. She did not answer but put it down on the stones until it stopped. It rang again, lit up again, stopped again, and then once more, and once more after that, and stopped, and after a minute a low-pitched plop to tell her a message had been left. She took it up and listened.

'Hello, Mama.' His voice was faint against the sound of bells and drums in the background. 'It's Freddie, Mama. Me and Papa are calling, and Edie and Lakshani. I'm on holiday, Mama, and I saw elephants and a leopard, a monkey, peacocks, twelve peacocks, and a flying snake. Lakshani is my friend. She's only five, but I like her. She's a bit bossy,' he laughed, as though tickled, 'and naughty. Her mama is pretty like you. She has a dog called Bebi who licks my nose. Did you know snakes can fly? They can. You wouldn't like it here because you don't like snakes and you don't like flies. I miss you, Mama. Bye. Papa and Edie say hello and bye bye. And Lakshani is pulling her tongue out 'cos I told you she was naughty.' More laughter. 'Bye bye, Mama.'

Betty put down the phone and spun it across the stones and into the side of the rail. She could see her black cap outside in the sun, caught up in the branches of a tree. He hadn't said 'I love you'. Sometimes he forgot. Peacocks were his favourite bird. She'd painted his face once as a peacock feather and he didn't wash it off for a week. She wondered how he was coping in what she imagined must be stifling heat. It was his first time. Had they let him on the plane with his chickenpox? What on earth was he eating? Did he like Lakshani because she was bossy and naughty and only five, or in spite of all that? What was Edie like? Betty really had no idea. Perhaps she was the loveliest girl in the entire world and deserved everything the world bestowed upon her. Did Freddie love her? Did he tell her? He said he loved a lot of people. And sometimes he forgot. Forgot to say it or forgot the people. It was an easy thing to say.

The sun nudged up, clear at last from what appeared as several acres of cloud, and lit up the bricks, the rails and the crushed white stones, and one stone stood out, rounder, smoother, whiter than the rest. Betty crawled, ripping her knees and hands. Taking the white pebble into those bloody hands, she turned it over, and held it up to the light. It was the size and shape of a small potato, but white like bleached bone, and smooth as glass. On one side there was a perfect black penny-sized circle, and in the exact centre of the perfect black circle a single black dot. Betty stood, picked up her bag and her phone. Keeping the pebble in her raw red hand, she took out a cigarette, and as she walked, at last, out of the tunnel, she lit the cigarette, and stood in the sun. She stared hard at the white pebble until it seemed, with its black circle and its black dot in the middle, to be staring back.

She hadn't asked her to come in, but that hadn't stopped Isabelle from making it all the way through to the kitchen, and she hadn't asked to hold Tomas, but he'd been thrust upon her as his mother bent to unbuckle the packages from the baby buggy, his tiny feet kicking her in the hips and a sticky wet hand patting incessantly at her face as though he were trying to revive her. He seemed less irritable than on their previous encounters; he was even smiling. Perhaps he'd had a few things explained to him. Betty had only been back for an hour and still bore the scuffs and scars of her ordeal; the hem of her dress was hanging down and her eyes were still red from crying all the way back through the woods. She was tired of crying in this country, in any country, day and night. Betty cried, Martha cried, Betty cried to feel Martha inside her, and Martha cried for being brought back to life.

'Your gate was locked,' said Isabelle, placing the two packages on the kitchen table, 'so Clémence left them with me. *Clémence c'est la postière.*' She was dressed in a yellow bathing suit with a cheesecloth shawl tied about her waist, and that was it. Even her feet were bare. One box was book-sized, addressed to Georges, and the other larger – an eighteen-inch cube – heavily taped, sent from England and addressed to Betty.

'Thank you,' Betty said. 'Would you like a coffee?'

Isabelle's face lit up. Her eyebrows emerged very briefly from beneath her thick round spectacles before disappearing into her fringe, and her strange teeth looked stranger than ever against a new, thicker, pinker lipstick. '*Ah, oui, merci, s'il te plaît. C'est très gentil, merci.* But after, I must go. My husband is sick.'

'Oh no,' said Betty. 'What is wrong with him?'

'The scabs, you know,' said Isabelle. Betty didn't know and didn't pursue it. She thought she should perhaps offer Isabelle her baby back, but he was as light as a bird, and she was comforted by the feeling of his soft, warm body against her skin.

'He likes you,' said Isabelle. 'Tomas, do you like Betty? *Ah oui,*' she said, in a voice that Betty thought hardly suited him. '*Bien sûr. Elle est belle!*' He sounded like he smoked too much.

'*Merci, Tomas,*' said Betty, pecking the top of his head and laughing. She sat him snug on her hip, holding him in one arm as she set about pouring coffee from the press.

'You ran away the other day,' said Isabelle, affecting a look of concern.

'Yes.'

'I think I scare you.'

'Yes,' said Betty, placing Isabelle's coffee before her. 'Yes, you did.'

'*Désolée*. I get too excited.'

'Excited?' said Betty; it was a strange choice of word.

'Yes.'

That was it, just yes. Adding nothing further, Isabelle picked up her coffee, took a sip and looked nosily about the room, standing up to afford herself a better view.

'Yes,' she said again, smiling, as though that explained everything. 'I have never been in the house. It is very different to mine.'

'Is it?' said Betty, knocking back her coffee and sniffing Tomas's fuzzy blond head. 'How?'

'Well, this,' said Isabelle, 'is a very strange house, it looks. And mine is normal. I am normal.'

Betty nodded.

'But these people are strange.' She paused, and corrected herself. 'Were strange. He is strange, I hear. Clara says so. But Clara is strange too,' and she threw back her head and laughed.

'How is Clara strange?' asked Betty.

'Oh, she's not,' said Isabelle. 'I am kidding.' Then she smiled wide with the long grey teeth all the way out. 'Or am I?' and winked. She seemed to think she was more endearing than she was.

'When was the last time you saw her?'

'Clara?' said Isabelle. 'Long, long time. Year?'

'Was that the last time you saw Oliver?'

'*Oui*. My God, Betty, *on dirait une femme flic!*'

'*Désolée*,' said Betty, confused. '*Plus lentement.*'

'Like the police with your questions every time I see you.'

'*Pardon.*'

'It is OK,' Isabelle said, stepping forward to take back Tomas. Betty took one last sniff, kissed him on the cheek, fondled his fingers, tickled his feet and let him go. She could have held him all day.

'If you ever want a babysitter . . .' she said.

'Oh, but you are very busy.'

'Not really.'

'What is it you are doing?'

'Oh,' said Betty, unable to remember what Georges had told her. 'I am doing tests.'

'Tests for what?' said Isabelle, suddenly serious as she buckled Tomas into his buggy.

Betty picked up the large box and was surprised to find it lighter than she had expected. 'Er, tests for camera,' she said.

'Tell me,' said Isabelle, standing back up. 'Like what? What do you mean? I am curious.'

Betty opened a drawer and took out a large pair of scissors. 'Well . . .' she said, 'Georges, who you met, is a cameraman. A lighting cameraman, as they say in the film world.'

'You are also in the film world?' said Isabelle, her excitement growing.

'Yes,' said Betty, 'sort of. I'm an actress.'

Isabelle put her hands to her face, wide-eyed and mouth agape, as though she had never heard anything so wonderful in all her life. 'Like Martha?' she said. 'You are famous?'

'No,' said Betty, as she began to cut into the tape on the box. 'No, not at all. I am not at all famous.'

Isabelle stepped forward, a little too close. She looked carefully into Betty's eyes and whispered, 'You know what?'

'No. What?' whispered Betty in return, concerned at the look on Isabelle's face. Why were they whispering?

'You look like her.'

'Who?'

'Martha,' said Isabelle.

'No,' said Betty.

'You are the sister, yes?'

'I am not the sister.'

Isabelle took a step back to appraise Betty full length. 'You even dress like her. Your hair. The way is your make-up.'

'Really?' said Betty, turning quickly away, continuing to hack at the cardboard layers of the package.

'No one ever said it?'

'No one ever said it.'

'Ooh,' said Isabelle, pulling off a pantomime shiver. '*J'ai la chair de poule.*'

'The what?'

'The flesh of chicken.'

'The what?'

'Chicken skin,' said Isabelle, smiling, and rubbed her arms.

'Still not getting it,' said Betty, opening the box flaps and seeing it was packed with polystyrene peanuts.

Isabelle stepped forward once more and showed Betty her bare arm. 'Look, I'm not joking, for real. It do this.'

'Goosebumps!' said Betty, realising at last. 'We call it goose-bumps,' and tried to remember the French for goose and whatever a bump might be, so that she could mistranslate it back to her.

'Goosebumps!' shouted Isabelle, and again, louder. 'Yes, I will remember this.'

Meanwhile, Betty dug her hands into the box and stopped. Something in there was soft and clammy and slightly sticky, not unlike chicken flesh, in fact. She parted the white peanuts to see what it could be and, gaining just a brief glimpse, immediately pulled her hands out in horror. It was the colour of chicken flesh. Any flesh, actually, not necessarily chicken. Very likely not chicken. Whatever was in there looked and felt very much like flesh. She began to sweat.

'Is everything OK?' said Isabelle.

'Yes,' said Betty, stepping back from the box.

'What is it?'

'Oh, nothing,' said Betty. 'Just something I ordered.'

'What?'

'My God, Isabelle,' said Betty, laughing, ushering her towards the door, pushing the buggy with one hand and Isabelle's shoulder with the other, 'you are like a *femme flic*. Is that how you say it? *Une femme flic.*'

'Yes, yes,' Isabelle said, allowing herself to be pushed and delighted to feel she had taught Betty something useful. '*Une femme flic. Très bien. La femme flic.*'

'Don't forget your husband's scabs,' said Betty.

'You're right,' said Isabelle. 'I must go to *la pharmacie*, before it close. Thank you, Martha.'

Betty froze. 'Don't call me that,' she said, sharply.

'What?'

'You just said Martha. Don't ever call me that.'

'No, of course not,' said Isabelle, disoriented, ashamed. 'That is terrible. I'm sorry. I get excited. I'm stupid. And look, again,' she held out her arm, 'the *chair de poule*. The goosebuds.'

'I don't care,' said Betty, her voice rising. 'Go now. Goodbye.'

Tomas, feeling the heat no doubt, began to wail. Betty had had enough of them both. She pushed the squawking baby and his ridiculous mother all the way over the threshold. 'I'm really so sorry,' said Isabelle, taking control of the buggy. Betty tried to smile but could not, and so closed the door in her face. 'Sorry, s-sorry,' stuttered Isabelle once more, and scampered away up the path in her bare feet, with tiny Tomas now as red and loud and outraged as ever.

Betty pressed her face against the window to the side as she watched them go, her heart pounding. She walked back to the table, cautiously circling the open box as though it were a bomb about to blow. Just as she was ready to take another look, she saw Georges ambling across the back lawn from the direction of his little house beyond the pool. He was wearing only shorts, while struggling to pull on, over his wet head and torso, the same T-shirt he had worn for three days in a row now. She was happy to see him. Much of the time she avoided him, finding their conversations so painfully stilted that she too often lost patience with him and sensed that he felt the same, but right now – in the state she was in, with all the confusion and complexity of her life in this house, in this job, in this brain – she felt comforted to see him limping towards her, adorably dishevelled and three-quarters still asleep. As his head emerged through the top of his shirt, he looked over to catch her looking back at him with a strained smile on her face. He waved awkwardly, half-heartedly, and Betty waved back, comically overenthusiastic, wiggling her fingers and grinning, making him laugh.

'*Bonjour,*' he said, smiling, kissing her on either cheek, as was his custom, heading straight for the coffee pot.

'*Bonjour, Georges. Ça va?*'

'*Oui, pas mal. Et toi?*'

'*Oui, tout va bien.*'

And so on. She handed him his package and opened a new pack of her own cigarettes, before she was tempted to accept one of his.

'*Merci.*'

'What is it?' said Betty.

'We'll see,' he said, sinking one small cup and pouring another. In the next moment he held in his hands the package, a packet of cigarettes, a cigarette from the packet, a lighter and the small cup of coffee, which he managed to drink while preparing the cigarette for lighting, while beginning to tear open the package and placing the cigarette packet back in his pocket. It was all very Georges and made Betty want to play him one day. 'Ah,' he said, taking out two books and dropping the packing into the kitchen sink, 'they come.'

'What are they?' said Betty, stepping forward.

'Here,' said Georges, smiling proudly, handing her both books at once. 'One is for you. One is for me.'

One book was called *French Conversation Made Easy* and the other *Parlez Anglais Naturellement*. She was so touched, she leaned over, kissed him once on his unshaven cheek, then hugged him tightly, pressing her face against his chest. '*Merci, Georges. Merci bien*. That is just . . .' She held her book out before her and riffled through the pages, stopping here and there as one did. 'It's just . . . the best. Now we can talk.'

'Yes,' he said, grinning, 'now we can talk.' He thought about it, and added, 'Well, soon.'

'Yes, soon,' she agreed, and they both laughed and smoked their cigarettes and drank their coffee and tapped their ash and laughed a little more.

'We both will study hard,' he said, nodding, riffling through the pages of his own book.

'Definitely,' said Betty, 'definitely will. Yes.'

'What is yours?' said Georges.

'My what?' said Betty.

'Your package,' he said, gesturing. '*Un cadeau?*'

'Oh,' said Betty, wishing he hadn't brought it up. 'No, no. Well . . . actually, *en fai, je ne sais pas.*'

'*Non? Mais c'est ouvert.*'

'Yes, it's open, but . . . *C'est un peu étrange, je crois.*'

'*Pourquoi?*'

'*Je ne sais pas.* Will you look?'

'Me? I will look?'

'Would you? Will you? Please. *S'il te plaît.*'

Georges rested his cigarette on the lip of the ashtray and pulled the box across the table towards him. He stood and scooped out a few handfuls of the polystyrene packing, then he plunged his hands back in and, making contact, grimaced and poked out his tongue, aping distaste. He frowned as he peered in to see what it was, and as he lifted it, his brow grew heavier and heavier until Betty could barely see his eyes.

'What is it?' she said, leaning back in case there was a smell. She could feel her heart thumping in her breast. As he lifted it clear of the box and the last few peanuts fell away onto the table, they both stared blankly at what appeared to be an amorphous lump of flesh-coloured rubber, or jelly, or . . . Suddenly Betty thought she recognised exactly what it was, but she had no idea what on earth it was doing here, in France, in Georges's thick dark hands. It was Sister Jeanne's silicone hump, which Betty had been gifted on the last night of *The Devils*.

'Well . . .' said Georges, '*c'est bizarre, n'est ce pas?*'

Betty reached over to take it as Georges offered it up for closer inspection. It was indeed silicone, and weighed the same, with the same straps and the same smell, but then she remembered that Rebecca, the actress who had worn it, had signed it for her, and there was no evidence of that here. She looked again at the writing on the box, but did not recognise it. And then as she let the hump hang down, flop out and unfold, she felt as though she had been stabbed in the spine with a spear of ice. This was not Sister Jeanne's hump. This was not a hump at all. It was the wrong size, the wrong shape. It had a bulbous navel. It was not a hump to be worn on the back. It was a bump to be worn on the belly. A label inside said *Eve P.*

Betty threw it down on the table, appalled. It had not been cleaned and there was still a smear of old Vaseline along the inside. Closing her eyes and holding her hand over her mouth, she fumbled her way out of the room and into the fresh air of the garden, leaving poor perplexed Georges to poke at the thing with his finger and wonder what on earth it was that had so upset her.

CHAPTER 26

Her new man was treating her to a special weekend, and Eve Parnell was almost breathless with excitement: young Billy and Jack were being furnished with all the details. Billy, seated beside her on the sofa in the library, and Jack, sitting alone in the dark in the utility room, eating red grapes, wearing paisley pyjamas and a pair of headphones. The actors' radio mics were live and he could hear every word.

'Bill,' said Eve.

'Like me,' said Billy.

'No, never Billy,' said Eve. 'He hates Billy; always Bill, he's very strict about that.'

There was a long silence.

'He's taking me to Brussels for a few days,' said Eve, starting up again.

'What's in Brussels?' said Billy.

'What do you mean, what's in Brussels?' she said. 'Lots of things are in Brussels. Beer's in Brussels, chocolate, waffles, Tintin, Magritte, the Manneken Pis.'

'What's that?' said Billy.

'He's a plumber,' said Eve, 'but he wants to be a singer.'

'Who?'

'Bill.'

'Oh . . .'

'Musical theatre.'

'A plumber?'

'But wants to be a singer. He has a beautiful voice.'

They both fell into another long silence, and Jack popped in three more grapes, listening to the actors breathe noisily through their noses, with the occasional sniff and clearing of the throat. He was just about to take off his headphones when Billy said, 'Did you not know about the baby?'

'What about the baby?' said Eve.

'Losing the baby.'

'Not until yesterday,' she said, disgruntled. 'He told me about an hour before my scene.'

'I didn't know until this morning,' said Billy. 'I only just saw the new pages.'

'He didn't want us to know.'

'Why not?'

'Because our characters wouldn't know,' said Eve.

'But our characters wouldn't know anything before it happens, so what's the point of having a script at all?'

'Exactly,' said Eve. 'He's making it up as he goes along. I think it's weird, killing the baby for the sake of it. As if this story isn't weird enough.'

'I heard about his wife,' said Billy.

'You know she was originally going to play this part?'

'No way.'

'Until she . . .' Jack heard a strange noise he could not identify. No doubt some tasteless gesture. Eve had not been cast for her resemblance to Eleanor, but with each passing day a resemblance emerged, and the more accomplished she became at infiltrating his mother, the more Jack disliked and distrusted her, in the same way he had disliked and distrusted his mother. It would likely have been a disaster with Martha in this regard, and he supposed he should be thankful that it had never come to pass and that she had, of course, received that better offer from elsewhere – a much longer commitment, more permanent, more complex, meatier, a leading part in her own drama. He bit one of his last four grapes in half to make it last.

'Did you ever meet her?' said Billy.

'Of course,' said Eve. 'I knew her.'

'What was she like?'

'Well . . . she was a contradiction,' said Eve.

'What do you mean?'

'Well, she could be very warm and make you feel like you were the only person in the room.'

'Right,' said Billy.

'Unless you actually *were* the only person in the room,' said Eve. 'Then she could be very cold and make you feel like you were the least important thing in her life.'

Jack had never heard it put in this way, but as he mulled it over, picking at a stubborn pip with the nail of his pinky, he considered it a fair assessment.

'And she killed herself?' said Billy

'Killed herself,' said Eve.

'In front of a train.'

'Yes.'

'I saw a man do that on the internet,' said Billy, confidentially, in a whisper now. Jack turned up the volume. 'His body went flying down the platform and crashed into two other people and they had to go to hospital with broken skulls and ribs.'

'Oh God.'

'And that's what she did?'

'Yes. They could only identify her by the serial number on her false hip.'

'Her false hip?' said Billy, suddenly animated. 'She had a false hip?' as though this was the most interesting thing he'd heard all day. 'How old was she?'

'Forty-two. It was titanium.'

Jack took off his headphones, walked out of the dark, down the hall, and into the now elaborately lit library, where the two actors sat waiting for something to happen.

'Morning, Jack,' said Billy, standing up.

'Morning, Jack,' said Eve, rising to her feet and kissing him on the cheek.

'Morning, Eve. Everything all right? No problems?'

'Everything's fine,' she said. 'I really like this new scene.'

'I didn't know till this morning,' said Billy, 'that she lost the baby. That's so cool.'

'Well, it wasn't so cool at the time, I can assure you,' said Jack, and then, plucking at a fine black wire peeping out near Eve's collar, he called out, 'Dennis, can we take a look at Eve's radio mic? I can see it.' He walked off towards Solomon, leaving the two actors to think about things.

'Oh my God,' said Billy, 'did you hear me? So cool, I said.'

'Yes,' said Eve.

'So cool.'

'Shut up,' said Eve, hitting him on the arm with her script. 'Let's get on with it.'

'What an idiot,' he said, shaking his head. 'What a complete idiot. So cool that the baby died.'

The oppressive heat made it one of the most difficult days of the entire shoot, with everyone growing increasingly irritated. There was certainly a sense of resentment from the actors that they had been thrown into the deep end – expected to learn, interpret and perform new, difficult material of which they had been given no warning. Jack had been made to feel as though

211

he should justify if not apologise for his methods. Had Godard, employing similar techniques, suffered such insurrection from his actors? Had Tarkovsky?

The heat had sustained into the early evening and Jack's heavily made-up fingers were sodden and caked with sweat, encrusting the computer keyboard and mouse with a sticky blue-brown glaze. Even the paper of his yellow pad was damp through several leaves, causing the ink to bleed, rendering his already erratic scribble practically unreadable, forcing him to type and print out the new voiceover. At his request and direction Nora had already put together a rough assembly of the relevant shots. He scribbled a note and pinned it to the board, sticking in a second red pin to emphasise its importance, as was their custom. Over a total of twelve shots of empty rooms around the house – concluding with the infernal room at the end of the landing – Jack, in devout and solemn tones, read the words out loud:

ADULT JACK
The best hope for an ugly man if he
craves the sexual attention and sincere
devotion of a beautiful woman is if
he, by some propitious kink of fate,
resembles her father. That my mother's
father was as hideous as my own father,
and furthermore compatibly so (the
same flattened nose, the same twisted
lip), was my father's good fortune, if
anything that befell him or my mother
subsequent to their ill-fated union
could be described as such. I include
myself in this. I doubt my father ever
saw me as either good or fortunate.
Perhaps in the early days, the very
early days, before I could speak or
disappoint, before anything resembling

a character might be extrapolated
from the squalling blob at the end of
the bed. As soon as I could express
my failure to express, my cowardice,
my insufferable clumsiness, then all
was lost in the eyes of my father.
Sometimes he would gaze upon me with
immoderate contempt and then proceed to
calibrate his observations and, in the
process, punish both of us. My mother
did little to protect me, until it was
too late. It occurs to me now how much
more, in death, my father resembled my
mother's father in *his* death, for I had
watched my grandfather in his coffin,
perched close to the mantelpiece.
That's right: I watched him. The dead
must be watched carefully, and if
necessary, as my mother well knew, one
must have a word with them. And if
you have the imagination, then one's
dead are interchangeable, as I believe
was the case with my father and my
grandfather in the eyes of my mother.
I believe that if such a thing were
possible, she would have liked to have
hauled all her dead men up into that
room and left them there to get on with
it. Defiled, unsanctified, unforgiven.

Jack was busy scribbling amendments, intending to lay down an abridged version, when the call from France came through. He snatched up the tablet, rushed out of the room and down the stairs. He was immediately thrown by the fact that Martha was a good deal closer to the camera than usual, wearing a dusty black cap and red plastic sunglasses. He was familiar with the apple-and-lemon summer dress that was just visible on the tops of her shoulders: it was hardly suitable, given what he had presumed might be the circumstances. Her lower body was hidden from view. He suspected something tedious was afoot.

'Good evening, Jack,' said Martha, forcing her mouth into the shape of a smile. Then into that mouth passed the usual cigarette, already lit. She was still wearing the ring.

'You're smoking,' said Jack.

'Is that a problem?'

'You tell me.'

'Why should it be?' said Martha. A large tumbler was lifted into frame, something thick and brown, with bricks of ice clinking against the crystal as she tipped half of it to the back of her throat. She took another drag on what – now he could see it better – looked like a French cigarette. No doubt a point was being made.

'I don't want to speak if there's going to be an argument,' said Jack.

'Is there going to be an argument?' said Martha, adjusting her red glasses with mock astonishment.

'How drunk are you?'

She took a last swig, finishing it off.

Oh Christ. 'Martha, we haven't spoken for three days, I don't want—'

'I still can't see you, Jack,' she said, almost shouting, cutting him off. 'You want things to be real, but you're only willing to go halfway.'

'Martha,' said Jack, noticing her accent slipping, 'be careful.'

'Oh fuck you,' she snapped, and then laughed. 'If I'd been careful, I'd never have married you. Let me see you,' she said.

He paused, pretending to consider it. 'On the next call.'

Martha took a last drag on her cigarette. 'You're hiding things from me,' she said.

'No.' Jack had hoped for something more palliative than this, more playful, and he felt assailed, as though she were building up to something intended to devastate. He certainly wasn't in the mood for that. 'You don't sound like yourself tonight, darling.'

'I don't understand what you want from me, Jack,' she said, staring down the lens with a curious blend of desperation and sedition.

'Well, I want you to stop drinking and smoking, for a start.'

'Why?'

'You know why.'

'Oh fuck this!' she rasped, and threw her glass across the floor. 'I'm sick of all this, Why can't you ever say what you mean? Why do you have to speak in riddles? You're a director. Just fucking direct me.'

'All right,' said Jack. He could see that his hands – and therefore Martha's face and voice – were shaking. 'I don't think you should be drinking and smoking when we're going to have a baby.'

'Really? What you mean is, I'm going to have it and then you're going to take it.'

'Why would you say that?'

'You mean I'll cook it and push it out and cut it and wipe it, till it's ready for you and some other little bitch who wouldn't know what to do with a baby if it bit her in the cunt.'

'That's it!' said Jack sharply, rising to his feet, furious. 'You need to watch yourself. Do you understand?' He wasn't sure to whom he was speaking: Martha was far too much in shadow tonight, and this woman – whose name now reared up inside him – too much in the light. He had miscalculated. His requirements had clearly become too esoteric for the likes of her, who seemed more suited to the debauched and fatuous elements of Martha's character.

'Do you understand?' he repeated. He was met with more silence and a deep, dead, medicated stare, as though the creature

215

didn't know where nor who nor what she was. It was broken. 'It's over,' said Jack.

'Goodnight, then,' she sneered, dripping with insolence.

'No,' said Jack, 'not goodnight. Goodbye.'

'Whatever.'

'I mean it's over. You can go home now.'

'I am home.'

'No you're not. You're in *my* home and I want you to go.' Her expression didn't shift. 'That's it,' he said. 'Goodbye.'

And with that, he tapped the screen firmly with three fingers and her baleful gaze dissolved into the smudged and yawning black of his own reflection.

CHAPTER 27

Betty had dreamt she was a baby given birth to by Martha. Not to say that she was Oliver, nor really herself, but rather Martha. That is, more of Martha coming out of Martha and growing very fast. So fast that it hurt. And then in her turn giving birth to yet more Martha, who then grew beside the already growing Martha who had been Betty at the dream's outset, but tormented by even more pain. And so it went on until at last out plopped a tiny incomplete foetus. A headless thing. Slippery and pink. More like a chicken. Mouthless and eyeless, of course, but crying all the same.

She had known it wasn't the best idea. The name was familiar, she'd heard it bandied about in American TV dramas. She understood it was some sort of tranquilliser, but it had scarcely fulfilled its promise. On the contrary, it had wreaked considerable havoc, not so much a balm as a small bomb. She should never have taken two.

She woke up in the night to the sound of someone swimming, she thought, in the pool, in the dark. She stood at the window but saw nothing, save for a splinter of moon pricking the horizon and the impossibly tall poplars bending in the rising wind. She thought she heard herself talking to herself but could not fathom what was said, and a short time later she discovered herself kneeling naked by the pool, gazing down into the water at a teaspoon she had fumbled the previous afternoon. She saw ants on her thighs and felt many more on her face, and must have washed them off in the water, for later there were small puddles on the bedroom floor and the spoon was dipped in a glass of milk on the nightstand. The bed was stripped to its yellow mattress and covered in photographs of Martha. They had been separated, it seemed, into different ages and scattered into loose piles. One pile of eight photos she found placed away from the others, on the small white table by the window seat. In these Martha wore her hair severely short and blazing red. She was almost always turned away from the camera, which was perhaps why Betty had set them apart; she couldn't recall. The other noticeable feature was that Martha was wearing, in six of the eight, the same dress – even if, judging by footwear and accessories, the photos were not necessarily taken on the same day – and this dress, now that Betty looked carefully, was clearly one of the maternity dresses she had found hanging in the closet. So here was Martha, pregnant with Oliver, and yet not once was the bump proudly displayed for the camera. Was this just chance, or, as Betty suspected, were there other photos that had been suppressed?

As she descended the staircase, she sensed the spectre of earlier expeditions all throughout the previous night. There was her handprint on the wall; there a lost slipper; there a pair of scissors she now kicked aside, and books on the tiled floor with their pages torn out and torn in half and half again.

Georges was in the kitchen, mopping the floor. His mood was rarely what one might call blithe, but this morning's was a new level of misery, as he struggled with the difficult combination of a rich, slippery bouillabaisse and shattered crystal. Since he did not reciprocate her mumbled salutations, Betty presumed she was the focus of his indignation.

'I am not paid for to be your cleaner,' he said, as though talking to the mop.

'I know,' said Betty, though in truth she did not, for he cleaned every day without complaint and he was apparently paid for more than shifting a few light stands once in a while.

'Look at this.'

Betty looked at it. 'I know,' she said. 'Was that me?'

'You lose your mind.'

She couldn't argue with that. She began to walk towards the fridge.

'*Attention.* There is . . . *Il y a du verre brisé.*'

'What?'

'*Du verre cassé,*' he said, nodding at the floor. 'I don't know how you say.'

'Say it slowly.'

'*Attention!*' he snapped, pushing her back with the wet head of the mop, but it was too late: she had stepped onto the glass with both feet and, falling to the floor in shock, was lucky not to slice open her palm on a shard lying in wait in the spilled stew. 'I say it,' protested Georges. 'I say be careful, be careful, you see.'

'Yes, I see, thank you very much,' she said, trying not to move lest she cut herself further. Looking around, she saw that the whole floor was glistening with shattered fragments of what must have been champagne flutes – she could see the docked stems, alongside crushed crab-claw and mussel shells, lined up on the counter top. She felt the fine cotton of Martha's nightgown sticky against her belly where she had been poked with the wet mop. She stank of fish. Here and there the black spines of breached sea urchins reared up, sharper than glass, from the surface of the glutinous soup. Georges offered his hand, pulling her to her feet, guiding her to the coast of the spillage, laying down a clean cloth and sitting her on a chair before she did any more damage. Stepping back to afford a clear look at her, he shook his head and laughed. 'Oh my God,' he said, and, '*Merde!* Look at you. What did you do?'

'I said I'm sorry,' she said, with scant contrition.

He began to circle her in a broad orbit, regarding her head as though it were on a plinth. 'You look now the real maniac at last, wow.'

He looked at her with such scorn, as though she were wearing a ridiculous hat, which, as far as she was aware, she was not, but she put up her hand just to check. Nothing. No hat. But then, another kind of nothing, or rather, something less. Hair. Less hair than usual. Much less. She spotted a steel saucepan to her left and raised it up. Well, that couldn't be right. Horrified, she threw it down and turned to the mirror on the far wall. Wow, indeed. Disregarding whatever had happened to her face in the night – all the eyeshadow around her lips and the lipstick around her eyes – it was the hair, or rather the lack of it, that drew attention. It was not gone altogether, but gone enough to shock. My God, she thought, what vandalism. She put her hands through the thickest part of it, relieved that nothing came away in clumps. She wondered where the rest of it was. In the bathroom presumably, in the basin or the bin, flushed down the toilet perhaps and now on its way beneath the fields and hills to the open ocean.

'Don't you like it?' she said.

'What is it?' said Georges.

'What do you mean, what is it? What does it look like?'

'Like everything here. *Un bordel.*'

Betty didn't know what that meant, but she knew it wasn't a

compliment and was about to tell him to fuck himself when she had a better idea. 'I want you to dye it for me.'

'Die for you?' he said.

'Yes, die for me,' said Betty, in her best Blanche DuBois, somehow managing to smile. 'I want you to die for me, Georges. Would you? I've always dreamed of a man who would, but they've all been too chicken.'

Georges turned, taking up his mop. 'Die for you. Two chickens. I never know what you talk about.'

'You're hilarious. Wait there.' And suddenly remembering her bloody feet, she set off, on the backs of her heels, out of the room and towards the staircase.

Her hair was neither in the bin, the basin nor the ocean, but piled up in the bathtub like a squashed kitten. The shower head, for some reason, was unscrewed and dangling out of the open window like a phone left off the hook. On the mirror, with a thick eye pencil, she had drawn a large black circle with a small black dot in the middle, seemingly copied in her nocturnal delirium from the polished white pebble, which was now set on top of the cistern.

Sitting on the floor, she took a pair of golden tweezers to the soles of her feet and began removing the splinters of glass. She had a long shower, rinsing away as much animus and panic as was possible. She towel-dried her hair into something presentable, before cutting what was left of it into what might be described as a fashion, referring all the time to the photos of pregnant Martha. On her knees, she rummaged in the low cupboards for sachets of tints and dyes she'd seen a week ago. Finding something resembling Martha's tone at the time of her maternity, she pulled on an old T-shirt and concerned herself, on the way back to the kitchen, with how she could articulate to Georges what was now required of him.

As it transpired, Georges was more than up to the task,

handling the brush and applying the pungent thick paste with more dexterity and sensitivity than she had anticipated. He had obviously been making good use of his English language book, for he was sufficiently relaxed and eager to attempt a conversation. His father, as far as she could understand, had been or was still – Georges's tenses were erratic – a respected painter of landscapes, and his mother a wheelchair-bound botanist. Georges had married in his early twenties a woman (Marie) in her late twenties, who had left him after three years for a woman (Elise) in her mid forties. By another relationship (another Marie) he had a ten-year-old daughter (Simone), whom he had not seen for five years (not spoken to for two), since she now lived in Vancouver with her mother and a stepfather (Vincent), who was, or Georges believed to be, or Betty understood that Georges believed to be, a tree surgeon, or possibly just a surgeon. Georges had, in his time, been a mechanic, a locksmith, an electrician. He had played double bass in a jazz band and had spent a year in Iraq working as a photojournalist, almost dying of dysentery. On the day he was due to leave, he had lost his left foot. He offered to furnish Betty with a demonstration, but by then it was time to rinse off the paste – though she'd be perfectly happy, she assured him, to take a look at his ingenious prosthesis if, after lunch and a swim, he would help her to fasten the straps on hers.

As she waited for her hair to dry in the blazing sun, she saw that she had received, at four in the morning, a message from Ruth that read simply: *What is wrong with you?* A quick check of her call log from the previous night revealed nine outgoing calls. Eight of them had lasted no longer than thirty seconds, but the ninth and final call had sustained for a worrying seventeen minutes.

All this time, as Betty waited for her head to come to the boil, Georges had been pacing the length and breadth of the garden with his phone pressed hard to his ear. Sometimes he arrived at a complete standstill and listened at length, moving not one whisker, and then suddenly he was off again, nodding, throwing back his face to the sky. His rubbery foot was out in the open, sandalled for the first time in a fortnight. As he passed and paused she could hear that his quarrel, or his seduction – with these French it was difficult to tell – was winding up. Either way he was getting nowhere, for in its closing moments he seemed suitably chastised and contrite. When at last it was over, and the phone tossed onto a soft patch of lawn, he cursed and spat and set off on two more lengths of the limestone path.

'*Qu'est qu'il y a?*' said Betty.

'*Qu'est qu'il y a?*' asked Georges. '*Qu'est qu'il y a?*'

'I suppose so, yeah,' said Betty.

'I think you know.'

'Know what?'

He put his arms out to the sides, spread his fingers, opened his mouth and his eyes as wide as they would go and let out a groan of such immense exasperation as only a Frenchman could produce.

My darling Jack, I think you're being foolish with all this. I'm sorry for the way I spoke to you last night and I don't even know what you meant by reacting like that, telling me such things, but there was no need. My darling, I feel him kicking! I feel him kicking. Imagine! I wish you were with us. Don't be such a sourpuss. Be the Jack I love and I'll be the girl you adore.

Was sourpuss too much? Did anyone say that sort of thing any more? An hour passed with no response. She tried again.

Can we speak later? I know it's your day off. In an hour? Two hours? Can I call? I have something to show you.

Though what did she have to show? Her hair, presumably. Which was now passably chic and fiery bright, a sort of scorched

223

iridescent copper. Wouldn't he realise she had gone that extra mile? And if it meant strapping on, with Georges's help, this ridiculous prop, then wouldn't it be worth it not to have to go home, not yet, not now that she was getting so close to the woman? Not now that her heart was in sight. She would not drink, she would not smoke, she would not swear nor question her man. Whatever Jack wanted, Jack would get. Whatever Jack needed, Jack would have. That was how it would go, at least for now.

Poor Georges had been furious to discover that she had jeopardised his position. She had no idea he'd been having such fun. It wasn't like he gave much away. But, as it turned out, his time here had been precious, he said. *Précieux*. The peace, he said, misty-eyed. The isolation. What else? The company? Perhaps. Perhaps she ought to embrace the flattery. They had sat out in the sun for another hour, snacking, talking at the onyx table. Onyx according to Georges, who seemed to know such things. It was, he announced, the same word in both tongues. They had looked it up. '*Ah oui!*' he cried, his finger on each letter. 'From the Greek, meaning *griffe ou ongle* – claw or fingernail – onyx!' She had asked him about the white pebble and he told her the circled dot was a traditional symbol for the sun. It was also, apparently, protection against the evil eye, a labial click, an ancient representation of the metaphysical absolute, or an instruction to tumble-dry at a low temperature.

'Why do you do this?' he said, indicating her hair, as though she were turning it red by sheer force of will.

'So we don't have to go home.'

'I mean this job.'

'It's a job.'

'It's a strange job. You must be this woman who is insane and dead. I'm watching it.'

'You're not supposed to.'

'How can I not? It's bad for you to be her so much.'

'It's no different to any other part. Once I played a woman who starved herself, so I starved myself. Another time it was a woman who slept on the streets, so I slept on the streets.'

'But this woman, Martha, kill herself.'

'Maybe that's not the most interesting thing about her.'

'What is?'

'She was a mother.'

'She was a bad mother.'

'Why do you say that?'

'Because she's not here.'

'You're not with your child. I'm not with mine.'

'But we're not dead.'

'Not yet.'

'My God. You've been here too long. This is the most French thing to say.'

At three o'clock, Georges received another call, sending him off back down the limestone path and twice around the pool, his posture less combative, his expression not quite so besieged. The talk had obviously been reconciliatory, for he returned to their blanket beaming. She had been granted, it seemed, a last-minute reprieve and was to appear within the hour, in the study, no nonsense, no conditions, fully prepared, in good spirits.

'In good spirits?' said Betty as he helped her fasten on the bump. 'Were those his words?'

'*Oui,*' said Georges, '*de bonne humeur. Alors, sois prudent, Betty Dean; sinon, je vais te tuer,*' and he smiled.

'You'll kill me?' she said, clutching her pearls and fluttering her lashes. 'Georges, we've had such a delightful afternoon, don't spoil it by being sinister.'

'There,' he said, tightening the straps and patting the belly. 'She is ready for the take-off.'

'He,' said Betty, cupping the warm silicone fondly. 'We're going to have a boy.'

'*Pas de surprise, aucune condition, absolument prête, et de bonne humeur.*' He held up four fingers, one for each command, and then leaned in close to her ear, almost whispering. '*Et ne scie pas la branche sur laquelle tu es assise.*'

'You are so French,' she said. 'I've no idea what that means. Now leave me alone to warm up. I know that sounds a ridiculous thing to say in this heat, but it's an acting thing, darling. You wouldn't understand.'

'You are so English,' said Georges, walking away, waving his hand. 'I have no idea what that means, darling.' And then he laughed more than she had ever seen him laugh, which made her laugh, which was wonderful, and she felt like hugging him. Then she caught sight of herself in the glass door and Martha wiped the smile off her face. 'Come here,' she said, marching her over to the front of the house. 'I haven't slept. I feel like shit. I look like a pig.' *De bonne humeur*, thought Betty, letting go, *de bonne humeur*.

She wandered about the house, upstairs and down, knowing she was forbidden to flee the grounds and so passing from one luminous mirror to another, turning side on in the sunlight, or bent over, backlit in silhouette, her hands resting on the mound. Perhaps he had changed his mind. He was not going to call, and she was not forgiven after all. There were only so many ways she could resist her instinct to escape. She did not feel herself. Is it me? thought Martha, pausing briefly before the small mirror outside the guest room. I'm too small to see. Why doesn't he call? He doesn't want this baby. He doesn't want to speak. He doesn't want to know. I don't want to know. I don't want this. Is that it? Why doesn't he call? I am not forgiven. I am not forgiven. Why am I not forgiven? Did I say too much? I cut my hair for you, Jack. Look at me walking up and down the stairs, passing from room to room, waiting for the phone to ring.

She put her ear up to the wall and listened. She could hear someone coughing, something kicking. She could see scissors now beneath the bookcase. She ran down the corridor and out into the garden. The wind was rising. The trees were bending. The enormous yellow parasol was turning somersaults across the field. Her feet were bleeding. She turned and pressed her face against the glass. A parrot was looking. One black glass eye concealed a camera. Why doesn't he call? Will he ever call? Did he ever call? I cut my hair, Jack, and painted it the colour of . . . what? Wasn't it your father who said? The phone is ringing. Inside the house, the phone is ringing. She rushes in. It rings once. It rings twice. It's a white phone on a white wall.

'Hello? Jack?' she said.

'Hello?' said the woman.

'Who is this?'

'Martha?' said the woman.

'Yes,' she said, glimpsing herself in the mirror above the bureau.

'It's Clara.'

Her grip on the receiver tightened

'Somebody called me.'

'Yes.' She closed her eyes for a long time. 'Did I?'

'There was no message, but I had a call from this number.' Her English accent was very good, only the slight schwa gave her away. The voice was sullen and curt.

'How are you?' She felt as though she had awoken from the deepest of sleeps, only to discover herself consumed by the air.

'I am the same.'

It was a reasonable answer. Whatever it meant.

'Why did you call me?' said Clara.

Didn't she know? 'Where are you?'

'I'm in Paris,' said Clara, almost defiant. 'How are you?'

'I am the same.' Whatever that meant.

'Why did you call?'

'I wanted to talk to you.'

'About what?'

'About Oliver.'

There was a long silence. Perhaps a cigarette was lit.

'What about Oliver?' said Clara.

'You know.' She searched a hundred words. 'Arrangements.'

'Arrangements?'

'Yes.'

'What did you tell people?' said Clara.

'Nothing.'

'Nothing?'

'What should I have told them?'

'The truth.'

She looked down at the swelling beneath her yellow dress. In this light, the flowers looked more like owls. She could feel her own pulse inside the dull silicone. 'I have told the truth.'

'I doubt it.'

The silence was so long and pure, she thought it was over, but then: 'Is Jack there?' said the nanny.

'No.'

'I should come to see you.'

She lifted her chin and allowed an insipid smile, as though she could be seen. 'Yes. Would you?'

'Only if you confess,' said Clara.

The parasol could be seen tumbling at speed back towards the house.

'Will you confess?'

'I'll confess,' said Martha. And the line went dead.

Curious, that, she thought. One does not say the line died, one says the line went dead.

CHAPTER 28

To begin with, the yellow dress – the much-loved yellow dress with the blue flowers and grey-black bees – broke his heart. He wasn't expecting that. This man Georges had excelled tonight, seating her on a plain stool, somewhere in the copse of laurel, with a small moon fed gently through the leaves so that her tender neck shone as if it were a lantern, lit from within. And the hair now – just look at that, like blazing coals. And some low, soft amber light, perhaps from the window of a candlelit room, or the stained glass of the vestibule, smoothed out over the rounded belly beneath the bees and flowers, and Martha's calm hands, fingers interlocked, resting there, the gold ring glinting. Her eyes closed and a slight red smile pulling at her lips. This was more like it.

He'd sobbed in the night, sobbed uncontrollably. He could think of no other word. It had left him breathless and stunned that its violence could sustain for so long. Pressing his sodden cheeks into the sheets of his father's bed. Eventually he had put on his coat and boots and walked the streets, resting, when he had to, against the walls of small black alleys. His awful convulsions echoing off the bricks. It hadn't happened like this for years. Not even this past year with all its bold agony and loss. So why now? Because he had told her to go, rather than her going of her own accord? Because he had given up trying to save her? Because, this time, it had been impossible to win her love? Why had she seemed to despise him so? Perhaps in death – for he had now to be honest – perhaps in death, seeing all, knowing all, she had found no good reason to admire him. Quite the opposite. But this? This awful bellowing in the back streets of London? The stars no more than bullet holes. The moon a bitten pill. The sound of the river climbing the Embankment in the dark, creeping up Peter's Hill. Finding its way into the deep pockets of his overcoat. Seeping into his boots and bones, then turning him over to face the ground.

He'd told Georges to prepare the car, to print her ticket, to throw out the food, to drain the pool, to help her pack, to lock every door and window. Throughout, he had managed not to utter her name, and Georges had understood. He was loath to say it himself, it seemed. Jack had thanked him for his time and his art. He had stressed his satisfaction, and that his quarrel was not with him.

Nora had called at four to tell him they could expect the silicone corpse by Tuesday afternoon, just in time for Wednesday's hanging. While Monday and Tuesday would be spent on location at the school, exploring Miss Marsh's world of red brick and chalk, back at the house the wall between the entrance hall and the library could be taken down and the floors and architraves fixed up in time for the shoot. It had come to Nora's attention that the wretched squatter in France had been granted a car to take her from Heathrow to her home, and she wondered if she was really deserving of such a courtesy. Jack had stated irreconcilable creative differences and left it at that, which Nora took to mean that he had finally discovered the tedious creature to be the haughty and ungracious scoundrel

she really was, and perhaps he had come to his senses and realised that the much-vaunted resemblance to Martha was hardly
remarkable and would not pass the test with most sane people.

But only one minute after finishing the call to Nora, Jack's
phone whistled out and there it was: Martha's fussy apology.
Overdue, yes; apt, certainly; but thankfully not uncharacteris-
tically contrite. A sourpuss, she had called him, a sourpuss. Just
listen to that. And better yet, the baby was kicking. He hadn't
expected the news of this tiny assault to be delivered with such
glee. *Us*, she had written, *I wish you were with us*. Perhaps this
was just the thing. A kick. A literal kick. Perhaps the gloom had
been lifted and the black dog put down. He hadn't responded
straight away, but rather took stock of his impetuosity and
prescribed some time with himself, to ascertain faithfully what
his heart had to offer. Another appeal came through within
the hour. She would call him, if that might be permitted. She
had something to show him, and Jack, for ten playful minutes,
enjoyed a bright game of guessing what it could be. But then a
wet bug of distrust crept in, putting him back on the floor with
his eyes to the ceiling, and then the footsteps on the ceiling
and the sneezing of the pipes and the flies in the chimney stack
talking. No, he would not call. He would not fall for it. It was
not his fault. He had done nothing wrong. He did not need to
be forgiven.

But then later, back out in the streets, in coat and boots, away
from the walls, he had called Georges and requested a change,
and it was Georges – good old stolid, resourceful Georges –
who had suggested an exterior. Something of a speciality of his,
apparently.

And here she was: the perfect Martha. The radiant mother, glistening in the lyrical glow of the early evening. This, then, was
what she had to show him. Hope. Expectation. Even bliss. Hair

as bold and ablaze as one only sees in the paintings of Rossetti. Her pale head tilted back, red mouth a little open and eyes fully closed in rapture.

'Martha?' he ventured, scarcely daring to wake her. 'Martha, are you with us?' A rich smile blossomed on her lips, slowly, knowingly, but her eyes remained inside. Her fingers twitched and a foot shifted in its scuffed blue shoe as she played her little game, barely able to contain herself. Everything would now be all right, thought Jack, everything would now be as before. She is back. They are with me. I am with them. 'Martha?' he repeated. 'Are you with us?'

'What do you think?' she said, eyes still closed. 'Do I please you?'

It was a touch theatrical, this, but what was Martha, after all, if not a touch theatrical? It was the soul of her. And so . . . 'You please me very much, my lady.'

Well, that was it. That was the end of that. The Rossetti was knocked from its stand and replaced by a mocking, snorting, giggling girl, playfully applauding and rocking in her seat, her eyes bright open, that blue shoe kicked up and off. She leaned forward, beaming, bug-eyed down the camera, pointing her finger and shaking her head. 'My lady?'

'My lady,' said Jack, hoping she could tell that his smile was as true and wide as his whole happy face. 'Too much?'

'A little too much, Jack,' she said, regaining her composure, wiping her eyes on the veins of her wrists. 'I don't know where we could have gone after that. I'm sorry. I'm not making fun.'

'You started it.'

'I know. I'm sorry. I'm just feeling a little giddy.'

'Well, that's about the best news I could hear. It's a long time since you've felt giddy.'

'Is it?'

'I wouldn't say,' said Jack, 'that you've felt anything close to that for about six months.'

'I see,' she said, and rearranged herself on the small stool, peeping out, for a brief moment, of the perfect light. 'Well, that's good to know.' Her face was recomposed into something more pensive and deferential.

'I'm just saying . . .' said Jack.

'How was your day?' said Martha, butting in, ever so politely.

'Oh, just fine,' said Jack, smiling, 'just fine. You know . . . Not long to go now.'

'Are you talking about your baby or mine?'

'My baby?'

'Your film.'

'Martha, come on . . .' said Jack, hesitating.

'Jack, I know you were talking about the film. And that's all right.'

'I wasn't . . . I meant . . .'

Martha sat up and ran her fingers back through her new hair, keeping her eyes on the dark open sky as she spoke. 'Well, that doesn't make sense, Jack, because there *is* long to go, isn't there? There's three months to go, though perhaps that doesn't sound like long to you. But you'll make three months sound like three years when you're shooting. And yet how many days' shooting do you have left?'

'Three.'

'Exactly, three days. So you were talking about your baby. Not mine.'

'Ours.'

'All right,' she conceded, sighing. 'Your baby, not ours.'

'Martha . . . where has all this come from?'

'I'm sorry I'm not giddy any more,' Martha said, and leaned forward to put her blue shoe back on. 'It didn't sound like you wanted me to be anyway.'

233

'I think we're getting a little confused, darling.'

'Well, that's happening a lot recently, isn't it?'

'Right,' said Jack, sternly, 'just take a breath. Let's both just take a breath.'

He watched Martha do exactly that: gripping the sides of the stool, tilting back her head and closing her eyes, in an attitude reminiscent of the call's inception, but now scarcely in rapture. He too took a moment to calm his racing heart.

'Like this?' she said, as her breast rose and fell and her belly quivered beneath the shimmering dress. 'Is this what you mean?'

'Things flew off a little quickly just there, don't you think? Let's not have words tonight. Not after the last time,' said Jack.

'All right,' she said, opening her eyes and sitting straight in her seat. 'I'm sorry, I'm sorry. What do you want to talk about?'

'Names,' said Jack, cheerfully. 'You know, for the baby.'

'Oh,' said Martha, lifting one eyebrow and then, as was her custom, pressing one finger on top, as though to stop it from rising any further.

'I thought of Véronique, for a girl,' he said. 'Or Simone. Or Iris.'

'And if it's a boy?' said Martha, cautiously, her finger still in position.

'I don't know,' said Jack. 'What do you think?'

Martha shrugged, a perfect French shrug. '*Je ne sais pas.*'

'I thought you said you had something in mind.'

'Did I?' said Martha.

'Go on,' said Jack.

'Go on what?'

'Tell me.'

'The name?'

'Yes, the name, of course the name. Go on, say it.'

'I don't—'

'Say the name you've got in your head,' said Jack, a little too crisply perhaps. 'Say it, Martha.'

'If it's a boy?'

'If it's a boy.'

'Well . . .' she began, 'I was thinking . . .'

'Yes?'

A too-long silence.

'Say it,' pressed Jack, leaning over the screen. 'Say it.'

'Er . . . Oliver?'

'Perfect,' cried Jack, throwing up his hands and grinning. 'Just perfect.'

'OK,' said Martha, taken aback.

'Like your father,' said Jack.

'I suppose so,' said Martha.

'Oliver it is, then. Oliver Drake.'

'If it's a boy.'

'Which I'm sure it will be. I have a feeling for these things.'

'Do you now?' said Martha suspiciously.

'Well, it's not something I get to show off all that often,' said Jack, relaxing, determined to enjoy himself.

'Do you think I'll ever work again?' said Martha. 'Do you have a feeling for that sort of thing?'

Jack gripped the tablet a little tighter. 'What a thing to say. Of course you will. You'll never stop working.'

'I will if people forget me.'

'How could anyone forget you?' said Jack. 'You! You're unforgettable.'

'Well, I haven't left the house for months, have I?'

'Haven't you?'

'You know I haven't. I haven't been anywhere since this happened,' she said, lightly patting her yellow bump.

'I don't think that's true.'

'Well, you just have a look, Jack. See if you can find any

235

pictures of me. Just one single photograph of me. Out for the night, out for the day. Out anywhere, looking like this.'

'Well . . .' said Jack, treading carefully. 'Well now, that has been your choice, hasn't it, Martha?'

'Has it, Jack? I'm just checking.'

'You make it sound as though I've locked you up.'

'I'm just stating facts.'

'Listen. Listen closely,' he said, as much to himself as to the face on the screen. 'Yes, you haven't left the house in months. But that was your decision, Martha. It has nothing to do with me. Is that clear?'

'Like I say, Jack, I'm just checking,' said Martha. 'Just making sure that I understand things properly. I think you know what I mean. I think you have a feeling for this sort of thing, do you not?'

He looked away from the screen and gazed out across the large darkened room in which he was sitting. 'You know,' he said, much calmer, scarcely audible, 'I was born in this house.'

'I know,' said Martha.

'Conceived, more than likely.'

'That,' she said, 'ranks pretty low on the chart of crazy shit to have gone down in that house, wouldn't you say?'

'No doubt.'

'Although given what you've told me about your parents, I'm sure the occasion was at least worth the price of admission.'

He pulled the tablet closer and studied her carefully. She had retreated now into almost complete shadow. A fleeting green eye. A flared nostril. A wet red lip and a spark of hot copper catching in the moonlight as she shifted back and forth. 'Martha?' he said.

'Yes?' she said.

'I do adore you, you know.'

'I know, Jack,' she said. 'It's a shame for you.'

'You know, if we wrap on Wednesday, I could be with you by Thursday afternoon.'

'What's left to shoot?'

'Oh, a couple of scenes at the school. A few pick-ups. The hanging.'

'You know, I was thinking about your father,' said Martha.

'Oh?' said Jack, intrigued. 'What about him?'

'He wanted to be exposed.'

'Go on.'

'That's why he bought you the camera.'

Jack wondered how she knew such a thing, but of course she was familiar with his story – she was his wife.

'And you drove Conrad Ripley away,' she continued, 'because you were always going to play your own father.'

'You've given this a lot of thought,' said Jack.

'You think that if something doesn't happen in front of a camera then it doesn't really happen, and it isn't a real thing. Look at us. You're terrified I might disappear if you don't catch me on your screen.

There followed a long silence. Jack clearing his throat, just to reassure her that he was still watching.

'Is that it then?' she said at last, sitting forward into the crafted light. 'You have nothing more to tell me?'

'What is there?' asked Jack, rather dumbly.

'Well, here we are. There you are, in the house in which you were born. And here I am, in this house, in which I fear I may die. And here is this thing inside me. Here is this baby, who will be a boy, whom we will call Oliver.'

Jack felt a fat tear of sweat race down his neck from the back of his ear to his shoulder.

'You know there are pictures in the living room, Jack. Pictures all over the house. Paintings of old cardinals, farm girls, soldiers in armour, women in habits, women in bonnets, naked women. There are photographs. I can see them from here,' she said, leaning towards the light of the window and peering in. 'Photos of, let me see: Picasso, Truman Capote, Simone Signoret. Stravinsky, Gershwin, Frida Kahlo, Eartha Kitt. Anne Frank, Albert Finney, Bertolucci, Dr Seuss. Charles fucking Manson over there by the harp. Felix the Cat. There is a parrot in a bell jar. But I tell you this, Jack: let us never display a picture of this child, this child inside me now – who will be a boy, whom we will know as Oliver – anywhere in this house. Ever. And if either of us ever catches the other putting up such a thing, then it will be up to the other to take it down. Can we agree on that at least?'

'Martha . . .'

'Can we agree on that at least?'

'What on earth are you talking about?'

'Can we agree on that at least?'

'Stop saying that!'

'Can we?'

'Fine!' shouted Jack. 'Yes! If that's what you want me to say, then yes.'

'Good.'

'For the love of God.'

'Ha!' she said, and rose out of the light and into the perfect dark. Only the womb now was lit, a dim nicotine globe of fading yellow, and then even that was gone. Switched off by an unseen hand. Then footsteps, blue shoes on a limestone path. Then horrible laughter. Then more muffled laughter. Then silence.

A long silence, before the sound of something unhappy, moving slowly through the water.

PART THREE

CHAPTER 29

Around the age of ten, there was nothing Betty liked more than taking a bullet in the back. She was so fond of being shot that her father was called into the school to discuss this upsetting hobby. Why would any child in their right mind wish to simulate the trauma and agony of being shot? Not to mention the supplementary acting-out of death pangs and the declarations of whispered devotions that often followed. She didn't mind who shot her. It could be a Croatian assassin, tearing out of the downstairs toilet with a silenced revolver, or perhaps a lone sniper picking her off with a long-range infantry rifle from an open window above the fishmonger. She might be blindfolded before a firing squad. Permitted one last prayer and a sherbet cigarette. Or best of all, go down heavily in a hail of sub-machine-gun fire while running for dear life across the no-man's-land between Mothercare and Woolworths. Her father could not fathom her, and Ruth, upon finding her sister mortally wounded at the bottom of the stairs, twitching and groaning, would more often than not kick her in the buttocks and tell her not to be such a show-off.

It wasn't unusual for an eleven-year-old girl to pass an idle afternoon by squeezing a small balloon beneath her jumper and cracking jokes about who the father might be. But Betty once kept the balloon up there for a whole weekend, even sleeping with it, two nights in a row, and might have carried it on through into the next week had it not burst with such a godawful, heartbreaking bang late Monday morning. Betty had been inconsolable and carried the shreds of green rubber around in her handbag till the end of the summer holidays. It was very concerning.

Perhaps that was why, all these years later, she was now loath to take off this bloated clod of silicone. No, she had not slept in it, but she had spent the night beside it, and upon waking at sunrise she had wasted no time in fixing it back in position. This had been done with great tenderness. One might almost say love.

Betty herself might almost have said love, and so what if she had, she thought, as she poured her coffee; what if she had said love? Stranger things had happened at sea. Now that she was out in the garden, she didn't know who to be: glum, despond-ent, bitterly expectant Martha, or equable Betty, blooming and smitten. She put up the bare feet of one of them and took her time to choose, drifting painlessly between the two. Martha was in a stinking mood and wanted to chew on her own fingers for the rest of the afternoon, whereas Betty was happy to be happy, and happy to be Betty, bushy-eyed and bright-tailed, feeling a great deal improved for a night off the booze. Her first in an age, it seemed. She felt she could breathe without pressing down on her chest with a balled fist. Perhaps because she sensed an end was in sight. And whether or not she ever made any sense of what had happened here, now, in recent days or in the distant past, seemed of little consequence, for she had decided, after last night, that it was none of her business. At least for a few small moments. For what did she know after all, really, of these poor people's appalling lives? She'd imagined she would have been asked to leave on the next available flight, but had discovered Georges shifting last night's lights back inside the house, back into Martha's grand boudoir, where the whole thing had begun, suggesting that the fun was not yet over.

And so here she was, talking to herself about Betty's concerns, but in the caustic north-Californian drawl of Martha. Clenching her teeth like Martha. Bending like Martha to reach her drink. A peach and peppermint cordial with crushed ice, which was Betty's choice, since Martha had been refused her neat gin.

It was curious: Martha, who believed this baby to be real, would have gladly had it removed or subdued by whatever means necessary; whereas Betty, who knew this bump to be the clumsy prop that it was, wanted desperately to keep it. Holding onto it now, she walked unsteadily across the sharp grass and blazing stones in bare feet and flopping hat, down to the pool, taking Betty's glass and Martha's cigarettes, and settled herself with some masterful slapstick upon the inflatable flamingo. She finished her drink and smoked a cigarette, tapping the ash in the sticky glass. She took photos on her phone of the dazzling white house, her painted yellow toes, the flamingo's dopey grin. She took goofy selfies of her crazy new hair and her big daft hat to send to Ruth and Freddie. As though life was just fabulous and really very normal and there was nothing, nothing whatsoever to worry about, because here is your sister, here is your mummy on her peculiar little holiday, and she misses you both ever so much and loves you and she wishes you were here. She looked at everything twice, applied a few filters, checked her spelling, doubled the kisses and resolved to send it all when she was back in the house and could get a better signal.

She pulled her hat low over Martha's green Dior sunglasses and closed Martha's eyes and burped Betty's gas and smiled for the two of them. Now and then Betty felt moved to swat at a bug, but Martha let them land and crawl without caring. Is that wind in the trees, she thought, drifting into sleep, or trees in the wind? There was that tiny lizard on the other side of the blue field. There was the mountain, punctured, sinking down. Inside the house it was black and white. And look: there was Freddie. Freddie in Oliver's black cap. But as she moved closer, she saw that the cap was in fact made of thousands of tiny black flies and that Freddie was made, very shabbily, of silicone. He was saying something in a language she did not recognise, and so he spoke louder and louder, growing more and more frustrated. And when she protested that she couldn't understand, he said, 'But you're not even trying, you're not even trying!' And as Oliver clenched Freddie's eyes, like fists, Freddie opened Oliver's mouth, as if to scream, and his cap dissolved into a black swarm, buzzing and hissing, and the top of his head was open and full of . . . what? What was it? He wouldn't show her, and the closer she drew, the further away he seemed, until she had to move slowly in the opposite direction to stop him from disappearing altogether. 'Martha?' he said, though hardly at all.

'You mean Mother,' said Martha, and one of the flies bit her. A hard black horsefly, fat and heartless, bit her savagely on the calf, and she cried out and kicked her leg in the water, waking.

'Martha?' she repeated.

'Who?' said Martha, for she did not know.

'It's me,' she said, for Martha could tell it was a she, and could see, from beneath the brim of her hat, small feet in simple leather sandals and a shiny white vinyl shoulder bag set down on the stones. Through the tiny holes in the hat's tattered raffia she made out a young woman holding a cigarette in her mouth and searching her pockets for a lighter. Betty couldn't take Martha's eyes off her.

'What?' she said, her face still hidden.

'It's me,' said the woman, 'Clara.'

'Ah,' said Martha, and oh fuck, thought Betty, and, 'Yes. There are matches next to my goggles.'

'You're smoking?' said Clara, seemingly astonished.

'Yes,' said Martha, adding, 'for two,' for she was nothing, if not a scoundrel. The silhouette seemed to have stopped moving altogether. How long can I keep this up? thought Betty. For no good can come of this.

'What does Jack think about that?' said the silhouette.

'What makes you think it's his?' said Martha, but that was it, she didn't wait for a reply, for it was too late, too late now: Betty – taking firm control of the situation – had flipped herself over on the grinning flamingo and, leaving her enormous hat up top, disappeared deep beneath the surface and began swimming submarine lengths of the pool. Life had shifted into slow motion. Perhaps for Clara too, as she observed her former . . . what? Friend? Employer? Enemy? Nemesis? . . . This strange fish in a pleated white linen smock, this sluggish ginger maniac, whom she assumed to be Martha, gliding wearily from end to end for no good reason other than to provoke and confound. Silly of me, mused Betty. Idle of me not to have thought properly about this moment. And where was Martha when she needed her? Dead. Typical.

The uncommon buoyancy of her foam-filled rubber bump was beginning to take its toll. Pulling her towards the light with every kick of her legs, with every aching rotation of her enfeebled shoulders. Flipping over onto her back, Betty let out a long, loud moan, which must have risen in a bubble to the surface, giving fair notice of the despair to come. Her time was up. She tried another moan, but nothing came. Too late, she thought. Too little, too late, and so she fumbled for the rail of the ladder and pulled herself up with all her might. As she burst from the water, she realised her back was to Clara and she thought about making a run for it, but a run for what? Certainly not dignity, nor integrity, and so she turned in Clara's direction, slipping clownishly on the soaked tiles, and made a beeline for her goggles and towel. Sulking with a tucked-in chin, brows down, lip out, and eyes fixed unflinchingly on the ground.

'What are you doing?' said Clara. Betty snatched up her things and held them in a loose bundle against her wet belly. She wondered if Clara had noticed yet, and wondered when the punch might come. 'You,' she said, as Betty stomped off towards the house, and again, 'Hey, you!'

That's it, then, thought Betty.

'Stop!' shouted Clara, and Betty stopped but did not turn. She could see Georges in the kitchen, skulking in the shadows. She wondered if they'd already met. Had he let her in? Where had she come from?

'Turn around,' said Clara.

Betty complied, keeping her eyes fixed on the dry grass, and stood shivering, as though with shame. Her teeth began to chatter.

'Who are you?'

She looked up at last. Clara was standing with her white vinyl bag back on her shoulder, arms folded and peering at Betty over the top of a pair of small copper-rimmed, green-tinted sunglasses. She was a slightly aggressive-looking creature in her late twenties. The sort of face Betty supposed was called hand-some. Her mouth was closed, but Betty suspected long teeth. Her cheeks were bespattered with fierce freckles. She was taller than Betty, slimmer and, yes, stronger: if there was going to be a fight, Betty might have to bite, which she was not against.

'I said, who are you?'

'No one,' said Betty. 'I'm sorry.'

'What are you sorry for?'

'You'll see.'

She turned and began once again walking, slowly this time,

towards the house. She could tell that she had not left Clara behind, for she could hear her footsteps and perhaps her breath in the warm air at her back. She wondered if Clara could see the straps through the wet linen. Had she noticed the ring? The two women made it all the way to the shaded terrace. Betty threw her damp towel, her goggles and cigarettes upon the onyx table and slumped down in the chair, raising her head defiantly, regretting leaving her sunglasses at the bottom of the pool. Clara took a seat on the low stone wall and, seeing Betty's lighter, took it to light her cigarette. She was wearing white shorts, which made her legs look all the longer and all the more tanned. She crossed them and leaned her elbow on her knee, smoking like a professional Frenchwoman.

'How did you get here?' said Betty, shading her eyes with the flat of her hand and smiling pleasantly.

'The train,' said Clara.

'Ah,' said Betty. 'Yes, I know that train.'

'Then the bus.'

'Ah, yes.'

'How did *you* get here?' said Clara, blowing her smoke directly at her.

'Plane,' said Betty, keeping up her perky demeanour.

'I meant,' said Clara, not smiling at all, 'how did you get *here?*'

'I don't, er . . .'

'Who are you?'

'Yes . . . you asked me that.'

'Why did you speak like that just now?'

'Like what?'

'When I asked you questions, you answered like Martha, not in this voice you have now. With Martha's voice.'

'Did I?'

'You're British?'

'You have a fine ear.'

'Where is Martha?'

'She's not here.'

'But where is she?'

'I don't know.'

Clara stood up and crushed her cigarette against the wall. She held out her hand. 'I'm shaking, look.'

'I can see,' said Betty. 'Are you all right?'

'Did you call me?' Now her voice was also quivering. She sat back down on the wall.

'Yes.'

'You asked me to come here.'

'No.'

'What?'

'You said you should come and I said yes, would you? But it wasn't my idea.'

'But I thought you were Martha. You wanted me to think you were Martha.'

'Yes.'

'Why?'

'So we could talk,' said Betty, 'about Oliver.'

Clara's face became clenched and pink and her eye sockets glistened in the sun. Her lips parted, her shoulders fluttered and she began to cry, raising her hands to form a kind of visor, a thumb on each temple. She wore no rings. Betty had been wrong about her teeth: they were not long, but rather small and pretty, and softened her face a great deal, even in this rictus of grief, or whatever it was. She must, thought Betty, have a very charming smile, this Clara, and wondered, under the circumstances, if she would ever see it. It seemed unlikely.

'What is going on?' said Clara, through her tears. 'I feel like I am in a dream. This isn't what I expected.'

'What did you expect?' said Betty.

'I don't know.'

'A confession, you said.'

Clara wiped her cheeks and nose roughly with the backs of her hands and looked Betty directly in the eye, waiting, it seemed, for her to say more. Betty remained silent, but, discomposed by the damp smock, made a great show of removing it, leaving her exposed in her simple blue bikini and of course the anomalous synthetic bulge clinging tightly around her middle. So tightly, in fact, that she continued to unburden herself, removing, at length, the gelatinous bump and placing it ever so gently upon the table between them. Clara watched all this with mounting concern, staring at the fleshy lump with explicit distaste. 'What is that?' she said.

'Well, that,' said Betty, scratching her hips, 'is Oliver.'

'What?' said Clara. 'What did you say?'

'It's Oliver,' repeated Betty, thinking she might as well, for there was nothing left to lose.

Clara sprang suddenly to her feet and ran back across the grass and stones, all the way down to the pool. The first casualty was the flamingo, which was hauled out of the water by its beak and punctured repeatedly and vigorously on the sharp protrusions of the low green fence. She then knelt on the side of the pool and pulled out the enormous raffia hat and flung it into the building wind so that it spun out and up across a neighbouring field, catching at last on the branch of a distant fig tree. Betty watched all this with rapt fascination, standing on tiptoes on her chair as Clara laboured and grunted at the far end of the pool with the winding mechanism of the enormous tarpaulin. When enough of the cover was released, she continued to haul it, by hand, with brute strength, out and over the shining water, not satisfied till the whole pool was covered from end to end, length and breadth. And when it was done, when the water was completely hidden from view and the parasols folded and the pump disengaged, she knelt there in the setting sunlight, head bowed, not moving, for as long as Betty could bear to watch. At last she climbed down from her chair and took her bump, her towel and her dripping linen smock back inside the house. For the mosquitoes were once more at large and beginning to bite.

Georges had made a simple and oddly dry salad of beans, egg and endive, mindful that in the event of the evening meal ending up on the floor, it should not be too difficult to sweep up. He explained that he had not in fact met the young woman, who must have walked in through the open gate at the front of the house and directly down the side. When he suggested offering Clara some of their meal, they looked outside, down by the covered pool, but could not see her. 'Perhaps she has gone back to Paris,' said Georges. 'I could have given her a lift to the train.'

'Perhaps she has gone to see Isabelle,' suggested Betty. 'They were friends.'

Who knew where she was? Perhaps she was still out there somewhere in the dark, weeping behind a shrub. Wasn't there something moving down by the poplar grove? Or was that only a fox, or a small cloud of bats? Georges told Betty there would be no call from Jack at this time of night, and that he would therefore retire to the guest house, where he had other work to finish.

Betty washed the plates and forks and drank a glass of hot turmeric tea. She wiped the counter tops and closed the shutters. With still no sign of Clara, she went upstairs, ran a hot bath and listened to a half-hour podcast about parachuting dogs. She considered again her messages to Ruth and Freddie and was about to send them, but, finding them now a little too flippant or forgiving, thought better of it.

After the bath, while drying and combing what was left of her hair, she thought she heard footsteps downstairs, then a sigh, before the opening and closing of several doors. By the time she had brushed her teeth and put on her robe, Clara, whom she found on the couch in Jack's study, was already asleep – still in her white shorts and shirt, but now wrapped snugly in the brown silk jacket that had hung every day until now on the back of the door. Jack's door. Jack's silk jacket presumably. Betty lingered there a while before treading softly to the desk, where a candle had been left burning. With a well-licked thumb and fingertip, she nipped out the flame and crept back to the door, closing it softly behind her.

'Come in,' said Georges.

Betty smiled, stuck out her tongue and crossed her eyes through the yellowed glass, waiting for him to open the door. She wore a blue hooded anorak over her thin cotton robe and a pair of what she had to explain to Georges were called bovver boots. He had to check his dictionary: '*Les bottes déranger?*'

'If you like,' she said, 'but I've got a feeling you're missing the point.'

'What is the point?'

'There isn't one, Georges,' she said. 'Don't worry. What are you doing?'

'I am ready for sleeping,' he said, perching on the edge of his bed. He'd had to hop to the door, since his foot had been taken off and now stood, proudly, still wearing its thin purple sock.

Betty had never been down here, never inside. She'd never been invited and she'd never really cared, until now. It was a large ochre room, with a small kitchen at the far end and a double brass bed at the other. There was a couch, close to the door, two bentwood chairs, a large oak table and a tiled cast-iron fireplace. There was a strong smell of turpentine. Next to

251

the table stood a large, sturdy easel and, to the side, a trio of low stools bearing brushes, crushed paint tubes and a well-used wooden palette. What was presumably a considerable canvas (the whole set-up standing taller than Betty) was turned away.

'I didn't know you painted,' said Betty, moving towards the easel.

'Yes,' said Georges shyly, tucking his stump up and under the opposite thigh. 'Yes, I paint.'

'What is that you're working on?' she said, nodding at the easel. 'Can I see?'

'No.'

'No?'

'It is not finished.'

'Can I see your foot?'

'It's there,' said Georges, pointing at his foot. 'There is my foot.'

'I mean your other foot.'

'My other foot?'

'Your not-foot.'

'My not-foot?'

'Oh come on, Georges,' she said, sitting down on the bed beside him and pushing him to the side. 'You know what I mean.'

'Don't push me,' he said, smiling. 'I fall over.'

'You know, I had a boyfriend once,' she said, bringing her own feet up to kneel, bouncing a little on the mattress. 'His name was Reuben.'

'OK.'

'On the street where we lived, there was a one-legged cat.'

'Right.'

'I always called it the one-legged cat. But then Reuben pointed out that it wasn't a one-legged cat. It was a cat with one leg missing. So it was actually a three-legged cat. And that's what we should call it. But I could never get used to that, and so I carried on calling it the one-legged cat. And in the end that drove him so mad that he left me. Just because I wouldn't call this one-legged cat a three-legged cat, just because it had one leg missing and not three. Do you understand?'

'What was the cat's name?'

'Mr Hudson.'

'So call it Mr Hudson.'

'That wasn't an option.'

'This is the most crazy story you tell me.'

'Well, anyway, that's why he left me.'

'Maybe for other reasons.'

'No, no other reasons. Just for that reason. That was it. We talked about it a lot and it was definitely just that, he promised me.'

'So why are you telling me this now? This story about this one-leg cat?'

'Because you've got one foot.'

'Ah, I see.'

'Good.' And they fell to the side, half on top of each other, laughing.

'I think you need to see a doctor,' said Georges.

'I went out with a doctor.'

'Oh.'

'He made me sick.'

Again they laughed, and Betty – 'Do you get it? He made me sick' – made a grab for his leg.

'What are you doing?'

'You won't let me see your painting, you won't let me see your stump . . .'

'What is this . . . stump?'

'Will you let me kiss you?' she said, without thinking she was going to say it and not really worrying that she had.

'Of course not.'

'Of course not?' she said, pulling away. 'Wow, that's not even a no. That's very definite.'

'Why I would kiss you?'

'Why would you not? Why would you of course not?'

'Because I am sorry for you.'

'Georges!' she shouted, scrambling off the bed and to her feet. 'I'm only messing around. Don't make it all serious.'

'I am serious.'

'Oh my God, shut up.'

'I mean it, I am sorry for you.'

'Shut up, please.'

'And I don't think it is a good reason to . . . hold someone.'

'Really? Because I always thought it was a very good reason to hold someone. I think it's the best reason to hold someone.'

'That's why I'm sorry for you.'

'Right, well, goodnight,' she said, turning, zipping up her coat and then buttoning it all the way to the top.

Georges pulled his stump out from beneath his thigh. She didn't look. 'You don't have to go,' he said.

'I do. Goodnight.' She opened the door, and something nasty and black flew in, causing her to flinch and squeak.

'I think you are being silly,' said Georges.

'I think you are being horrible,' she said, and waited to see what he thought of that. He just stared at the floor, where the nasty black thing was crawling towards his shiny black shoes.

'You can look at the painting. If you like, you can—'

'I don't want to look at your stupid painting.'

He shrugged. 'OK. Well . . .'

'Goodnight.'

As she walked back across the lawn, she passed the fig tree and noticed the white floppy hat, still white and still flopping in the thick black branches. She loosened the tree's grip and plucked off one of its figs to eat before bed, then tramped across the limestone flags in her baggy coat, bovver boots and enormous hat, looking and feeling like a ponderous old mushroom. Through the holes in the hat she saw what was left of the moon, and realised that she was sick of the sight of it. Always there in some fucking form or other, ever since the day she was born, and no doubt long after she was dead. Like it thought it was some kind of big deal. Completely sick of it.

CHAPTER 30

Jack's old school was no longer a school, it was now a sparkling apartment complex not far from St Katherine Docks, but
Jack's location manager was able to find something similar,
much further north, near Cricklewood. With a reduced crew
and no actors – save for a mob of initially excitable, and later
profoundly disappointed, eleven-year-old supporting artists –
Sunday was spent shooting establishing shots of the playground.
The corridors and various drab interiors of small classrooms
were now dressed with splintered wooden desks, a hundred
old names scratched on their surfaces and the sticky brass ink-
wells packed with pencil shavings and bubblegum. On Monday
morning the same kids had been persuaded to return, but now
they were promised action and drama and real actors speaking,
and crying, and fighting, and the rumour was that one of them
(a lady, even) would be undressing, for this film was for the
cinema, and since they were all far too young to be allowed to
see it, they should make the most of it now and put away their
phones, not look into the camera, and though the food was delicious and free, they should use a little common sense and not
make themselves sick. Was all that clear? Any questions? They
all liked Charles, the first assistant director, because he knew

some famous people, and even though he was older than their dads, he was wearing shorts in solidarity with the boys, and in solidarity with the girls he'd put a ribbon in his hair, until Jack told him to take it out.

The first scene concerned Miss Marsh introducing the idea for a project in which the pupils were to share with the rest of the class, by way of a presentation, some aspect of their home life. To describe something about the house itself, the habits of the family, the occupations of the parents, family pets, hobbies of siblings. Maybe they lived with a grandparent, or a helper from overseas. Perhaps they lived, like little Brian Milligan, above their parents' shop – tell us about that shop. Perhaps one of their parents worked far away and was not always around – how did that feel? Perhaps their house was haunted – tell us about that. Bernadette Lowe, who was a natural with children, or so she claimed, was eager to be allowed to extemporise, to stick to Jack's script but not be put off if one of the children stuck up their hand and asked a question and she had to go off road. Jack told her that the children would not be sticking up their hands, nor asking questions. The only people talking would be the actors. She suggested that Billy, Young Jack, could ask a question, but Old Jack told her that Young Jack would not dream of it, and that he despised Miss Marsh and had (did she not remember?) thrown a horseshoe at her window at three in the morning. She had then complained again about the nostril mole.

'And the nudity,' she added, crinkling her nose.

'What about it?' said Jack.

'Must we?'

'You agreed to it.'

'I know, but now we're here . . . with all these children . . . well . . . must we?'

'We'll talk about it later,' said Jack, and put on his head-phones, implying, surely, that the conversation was over.

'Some of these kids go to our Billy's school,' said Phyllis.
    'Do they?' said Nora.
    'Him there,' said Phyllis, 'Micky London, he does.'
    'I see.'
    'Nice name that, innit? Micky London.'
    'Yes,' said Nora, who did not have headphones to put on.
    'Good old sort of a name.'
    'Yes,' said Nora, and she tossed a pill to the back of her throat, causing a tress of grey hair to fall out from beneath her cap and onto her cheek. Her dog had kept her awake all night with his sneezing, and she had a thumping headache.

'I went over to the house first thing this morning,' said Solomon,
    'Oh yes,' said Jack, flipping through the pages of his script while sinking his teeth into an apple he'd taken from the teach-er's desk. (No one gave Mary Marsh apples, except perhaps his father.)
    'They're knocking down the wall today,' said Solomon, 'for that shot tomorrow.'
    'And . . .?'
    'They weren't sure if it was advisable.'
    'I don't care. It's the last shot.'
    'Not in story order it's not.'
    'I don't care if the whole fucking house falls down,' said Jack, nipping off the stalk of the apple with his front teeth. 'In fact I hope it does.'
    'Not before the shot.'
    'It'll be fine.'
    Solomon frowned and stroked his chin with the pad of his

thumb, looking up to the ceiling and down across each wall as though assessing the structural stability of the classroom.

'Some of these kids go to our Billy's school,' said Phyllis.

'Do they?' said Bernadette, who was practising writing on the board with green chalk.

'Her over there. In fact those three over there: Kirsty, Kiara and the other one, can't remember her name. It begins with a K, though. There's a lot of Ks around these days. Not so many in our day. What are you? Forty?'

'I'm thirty-six.'

'Really?' said Phyllis, looking at her from another angle, in better light. She stretched a string of grey gum halfway out of her mouth and pushed it back in again. 'Green chalk,' she said.

'Green chalk,' said Bernadette, nodding and dotting an i like she was killing a fly.

'I hear you've got to get your kit off again.'

'Not if I can help it,' said Bernadette. 'I don't think it's appropriate. It's gratuitous.'

'Is it sex? Is it more sex?'

'No, it's in the boy's mind.'

'In my Billy's mind?'

'Yes.'

'Oh Gawd,' Phyllis said, snorting, catching her gum in the palm of her hand. 'Good luck with that then.'

'Martha had an interesting insight the other night.'

'I'm sorry?' said Nora, startled. Had he noticed her eye was twitching? 'Martha what?'

'Had an interesting insight the other night.'

'Oh, you spoke to her?'

'Yes,' said Jack. 'I've made some changes to the second scene in light of it.'

'Oh,' said Nora, fiddling with some geometric shapes on the windowsill. 'I see. What was the insight?'

'Sam wanted to be caught.'

'Wait a moment,' she said, suddenly realising. 'You mean Martha has read the script?'

'Of course she's read the script. She was going to play Eleanor.'

'I know, of course, but I didn't know that "Martha". . .' and she said it in a peculiar strangulated voice, 'had been given . . . the latest draft.'

'Yes,' said Jack.

I'll stab the bitch, thought Nora. I'll run her over in a side street. 'Oh. OK then.'

'Sam gave the camera to Jack because he wanted to be exposed.'

'I can't say I agree with that,' said Nora.

'Then why did he give me the camera? It's not like he was in the habit of lavishing extravagant gifts on me. I think it's a fascinating way of—'

'It's bullshit,' snapped Nora. 'She doesn't know what she's talking about.'

'Well . . .'

'Who the hell is she to know what your father was thinking?'

'Well, who the hell are any of us . . .'

'Crap!'

'. . . to know what he was—'

'But Jack . . . I mean, who the hell is *she*?'

'She's my wife.'

'Oh Jack, come on. We're at the end now. This was all so you could finish the—'

'Who the hell are you?'

'We wrap tomorrow.'

'I said, who the hell are you?'

'I'm Nora Flynn, Jack. And I'm flesh and blood.'

'What a bizarre thing to say,' said Jack, recoiling.

'Well, if you think that's bizarre, then I don't know what—'

'Is everything all right here?' said Charles, suddenly appearing, placing a tender hand on each of their shoulders. 'We're trying to get a light in here, chief. Do you two want to step into the chemistry lab next door?'

Nora shrugged herself free and stamped off out the door, towards the assembly hall, where she thought she might be able to scream. Her headache had now moved into her legs and fingers.

'I was telling Bernadette that you go to school with some of these kids,' said Phyllis.

'Were you?' said Billy, hoping that some of the kids he went to school with didn't see him talking to his mum.

'Yeah, Micky London and the girls.'

'Please don't talk to the actors, Mum.'

'The actors?' said Phyllis, chuckling. 'The actors? There's only Bernadette and you. I've already spoken to Bernadette. Am I not supposed to speak to you?'

'Keep your voice down.'

'She says that you see this naked woman,' said Phyllis, incapable of keeping her voice down, 'this naked woman in your head, and that it's her. Is that right?'

'Yes.'

'You never told me that.'

'I didn't know.'

'You didn't know? There's a naked woman in your head and you didn't know?'

'No, Mum,' snapped Billy. 'Please go away. I'm trying to get into character.'

'Oh you make me laugh, Billy, you really do . . . "Get into character". . . You make me laugh.'

As Jack walked by, head down, Phyllis caught him by the arm, stopping him in his tracks. 'I don't know what you've done to this one,' she said, pointing at Billy, 'I really don't. We're never gonna get his head back through the door at home.'

'Mum.'

'And it's a big door, let me tell you. Isn't it, Billy?'

Billy turned away, mortified.

'I'm sure you'll be fine,' said Jack, struggling to get away. Phyllis still had hold of his arm.

'I wanted to ask you a question, Jack,' she said.

'What's that then?'

'You know how your dad hanged himself?'

'Mum!' said Billy.

'Yes,' said Jack, finally managing to release himself from her iron grip.

'And Billy tells me you thought he did it when he did it because he wanted you to see it.'

'Yes,' said Jack.

'Well, why didn't you see it then?'

'Because I was late home from school.'

'Yeah, I know that,' said Phyllis, as polite as could be. 'But why? Why were you late home?'

'It doesn't matter,' said Jack. 'It would be too complicated to put in the film.'

'It's just, you see, I think everything happens for a reason,' said Phyllis. 'I do tarot, for example, don't I, Billy?'

'Yes,' said Billy, completely sick of her.

'I read palms and interpret dreams.'

'I see,' said Jack.

'So go on,' she said.

'Go on what?'

262

'Go on, tell us why. Why were you late home, Jack?'

Jack looked around, wishing he could find someone who needed his attention more than this lunatic, then finally surrendered. 'John Wayne,' he said.

'John Wayne?' said Phyllis.

'Who's John Wayne?' said Billy.

'He was a cowboy,' said Phyllis.

'A cowboy?' said Billy, now intrigued.

'He was a famous American actor,' said Jack, 'who played a lot of cowboys.'

'I don't understand,' said Billy.

'Well, let him tell us, Billy,' said Phyllis. 'Go on, Jack. John Wayne. I'm already getting something. The letter J. We'll come back to that.'

Jack closed his script and sat down at one of the desks. Phyllis pulled out a chair, seating herself opposite. Billy remained standing, ready to flee.

'In 1975,' began Jack, 'John Wayne made the only film he ever made in London. He played a Detective Brannigan. The film was called *Brannigan*.'

'Remember that, Billy,' said Phyllis, prodding her son. '*Brannigan*, we'll have to watch it.'

'And on the afternoon of my father's death,' said Jack, warming to his theme, 'they were filming a car chase on Tower Bridge. Well, I was already very interested in the cinema, and so my friend Clifford Croft and I stopped to watch what was going on, and we were lucky enough to see a grey Jaguar leap across a gap in the bridge as it was being raised.'

'A jaguar?' said Billy, frowning.

'It's a car,' said Jack. 'A real classic movie car.'

'But it's also a symbol,' said Phyllis. 'And so is the bridge, of course. Go on, though.'

'And then we saw John Wayne himself climbing out of a

bright yellow Ford Capri, which at the climax of the chase had crashed into a skip.'

'This is all perfect,' said Phyllis.

'I didn't get home till teatime,' concluded Jack. 'And by then my mother had cleared up, so to speak. So there you go: I have the Duke to thank.'

Phyllis closed her eyes and spread her fingers on the desk. 'The jaguar is you, Jack. JackYouAre. The fearless cat crossing the divide. The Duke, the ruler, is your father, obviously, and the car – yellow, the colour of cowardice and deceit – in the skip . . . What did you say it was, the yellow car?'

'A Ford Capri,' said Jack, now mesmerised.

'Capri, yes Capri, meaning goat. Symbol of sexual desire and bad judgement. Gullibility. In the skip. Therefore thrown away. That which is no longer needed. The yellow Duke tossed in the dustbin. It's all there, if you know where to look.'

'Who's this Duke?' said Billy, now looking completely lost.

'They called John Wayne the Duke,' said Jack.

'Why?'

'Because it was his dog's name.'

Billy shook his head. 'Why did he have his dog's name?'

'Because he didn't like his real name,' said Jack.

'John?' said Billy.

'Marion,' said Jack.

Billy snorted. 'Is all this just a wind-up?'

'Watch the film,' said Jack.

'We will,' said Phyllis. 'We definitely will now, won't we, Billy? Fascinating.'

The much-discussed exposure of human flesh was, when it came down to it, a fleeting affair. In the middle of Miss Marsh's monologue, Billy glimpsed her for a mere flash of a moment, fully naked, full-length, with only her bony buttocks bared.

To spare Bernadette's blushes, Jack had cleared the classroom of all children and superfluous crew and allowed her to deliver those few lines of speech turned to the blackboard, scraping out the word 'copulation' in green chalk, which was, of course, another concoction of Young Jack's flustered psyche.

The second and final scene of the day detailed Eleanor's downfall, Jack's own downfall, the downfall of Miss Mary Marsh. Indeed, the downfall of all concerned. For as it turned out, Young Jack could be a dedicated student when he put his mind to it, and had listened well to the remit of the class project as described in the first scene of the day. He had paid close attention, despite Miss Marsh's sallow bottom, to what was required, and if the naked Marsh woman wanted a candid account of what family life was really like in the House of Drake, he was very happy to give it to her in full Kodak Ektachrome, as captured by one of the finest cameras available in 1975. In the vast and precarious rock pile of Jack's memories, the day stood out like a dung-covered diamond, and it was only fitting therefore that he should leave it until one of the final scenes of his film to fix it in its rightful place.

After Tommy Shaw had shown off his mother's plate collection and delivered a jarring recital of 'Please Mr Postman'; after Norma Snoil had spoken at length of her father's passion for dog-racing and presented, with great pride, what appeared to be a papier-mâché whippet; after some dismal paintings, some interpretive dance and a rambling speech about British Leyland; after many tedious and concerning depictions of family life, young Jack Drake had struggled to the front of the class carrying several three-by-four-foot cards wrapped in black bin liners. Three minutes later, the whole room was in a spectacular uproar. Some of the more timid children had fled the scene. Some squatted in corners, hands over their faces, sobbing. Others lay sprawled flat on their young backs, having fainted in shock at what the awful Drake boy had uncovered and described in detail with a specially purchased telescopic pointing stick. He'd attempted to deliver a carefully written speech, but the horrified Miss Marsh had panicked and subdued the ghastly boy in a sort of stranglehold, with one of his arms hitched behind his back and his face turning puce.

It wasn't the shots of sexual congress, both oral and penetrative, that had so scandalised and revolted the class (though they had), so much as the photos and descriptions of his father's death and decaying corpse in its several stages of vivid decomposition. Day 3, for example: *First manifestations of autolysis. Father begins to bloat.* Or Day 5: *Putrefaction has commenced. Foaming blood from mouth and nostrils. Larval blowflies amass.* Day 8: *Father listens to Mother reading from First Corinthians, King James Version: 'Flee fornication. Every sin that a man doeth is without the body; but he that committeth fornication sinneth against his own body.'*

Jack had managed to land himself in a great deal of trouble that day. Several parents took legal action against the school for conspicuous exhibition of what amounted to obscene images. Many children, in fact almost all the children, required and were administered long hours of counselling. Miss Mary Marsh suffered not one, but possibly three breakdowns over the coming weeks, and subsequently left her husband, her home and the teaching profession to live in the suburbs, where she opened a small shop selling ornaments and fancy goods. Law enforcement showed a keen interest in Jack's presentation, and by the end of that day were taking many compelling photographs of their own, though with, in Jack's opinion, far inferior cameras. Eleanor Drake was caught unawares and was escorted from the house in the firm embrace of the relevant authorities, citing, as she trudged down the front steps, the First Epistle to the Thessalonians as a rationale for her actions.

All that would be shot tomorrow, back at the house. But for

now that was a wrap on Bernadette Lowe, who was applauded with gusto as she beamed and bowed and peeled that foul black mole out from under her nose with great ceremony. When she was asked if she would like to keep it, she politely declined.

Nora drove Jack back to the house in near-total silence. She in a sulk she was too long in the tooth to carry off, and he so desperately lost in the past he felt he might never find his way back.

'Be careful when you go in,' she said as she dropped him at the front door. 'Remember they were taking the wall down today.'

'Of course,' said Jack, putting his key in the door and waving her off.

'I don't know what kind of state things will be in.'

'I'll be fine.'

'And just so you don't die of fright . . .'

'What now?'

'I hear that your corpse arrived today,' she said, beginning to pull away. 'I expect he's out of his box.'

'Thank you,' he said, stepping over the threshold.

'Just so you don't die of fright.' And with that she drove off, one hand aloft in a flamboyant farewell.

I wouldn't mind dying of fright, thought Jack. Don't we all die of fright in the end? He felt his way through the dark to where the large double door frame had stood, in search of a light switch that was no longer there. Nora had been right on both counts: the wall was very much down and the corpse had arrived. He could see it in bold silhouette, backlit by the street lamp. By the light of his phone he approached the pitiful thing, the floorboards creaking, the enormous shadows shifting from one end of the room to the other with every step and bend of the wrist. The eyes and mouth were open as requested, but the tongue was far too long, too fat, and flopped out on the chin like that of a parched dog. It would be no great task to rip it out.

The moment he turned off the light and put the phone into his pocket, it rang out in the silence with its emphatic, alarming, heart-stopping old rotary phone ringtone. 'For Christ's sake!' He was sure he'd turned it off. 'Nearly died of fright,' he said, and, catching himself, smiled. Taking the phone back out of his pocket, he was met by Martha's beaming face. A photo he'd taken in Tuscany on her fortieth birthday. She'd been as high as a loose kite on cheap limoncello.

'Hello?' he said.

'Jack?'

'Martha, what is it?'

'We need to talk.' She sounded distraught.

'Now?'

'I want to see you.'

'I've just finished work,' said Jack, and felt his heart pounding, his hands shaking. 'I've just walked through the door.'

'Call me straight back,' said Martha. 'On this number, from your phone, so I can see you. I'm scared. There's someone in the house.'

CHAPTER 31

At the precise moment on Monday morning when Jack Drake was telling Phyllis and Billy about his encounter with John Wayne, Betty Dean, passing the bathroom mirror – naked, save for one black sock – had paused to jam her fingers deep into her knotted orange hair and lift it high and wide, out at the back and sides, where it stayed, lending her the appearance of an electrocuted clown. She smudged what was left of last night's lipstick, crossed her eyes and puffed out her cheeks.

Martha was nowhere in sight. Not even close. She had, at last, left the house. Standing at the window, looking down across the garden, Betty could see Georges already hard at work, picking figs from the grass and placing them onto a green plastic sheet in the shade of the tree. When she opened the window, she could hear him whistling a repetitive ditty that had been a favourite of her mother's. Now she saw Clara walking back from the direction of the poplar grove at the far end of the grounds. She was still wearing her white shorts and shirt, but had removed Jack's silk jacket. As she passed Georges – only a few feet apart – they acknowledged each other with nothing more than nods. Perhaps they have already spoken, thought Betty. Perhaps everything has been explained. Why was she still here? Did she really believe that Martha would make an appearance? Or Oliver? Or was it Jack she was waiting for?

Suddenly, as though she had felt the burn of Betty's gaze upon her, Clara lifted her eyes from the path and looked directly up to the window where Betty stood, still naked, save for the sock, her face and hair still an awful fright. Neither of them moved for an absurd few seconds set to the soundtrack of Georges's whistling. It was only when Georges, distracted by Clara's defiant posture, looked from her to the focus of her gaze that Betty took a step back into the shadow and closed the window. Clara, meanwhile, did not shift. Her eyes remained fixed, as though Betty might re-emerge.

In the darkened bathroom, her phone woke up on its white shelf, illuminating Martha's phone beside it. It was an overly plucky, dutiful message from Arnold Plack asking her how *all this bonkers* was shaping up, and how she felt about *Ibsen, Cardiff, Hedda Gabler, September to December – thoughts?* She had none. Then she noticed another alert that must have come through in the night. She did not recognise the number.

Dear Betty, in more ways than one I am writing this in the dark. I cannot sleep. Your beautiful boy is also awake at the end of the bed. I can hear his breathing and his eyes opening and closing. I can almost hear his heart beating – breaking. Paul is asleep. I took your number from the phone beneath his pillow. This is over for me. I know what you think of me. I understand. Why wouldn't you think those things? I am writing to tell you that on Wednesday Paul has to go to New York until next Tuesday and I know he hasn't told you. He wants Freddie to stay here with me for a few days, but with your consent I will leave here and bring him back to you. Not because it is inconvenient for me but because it is the right thing to do. This has not been discussed. I know he would disapprove, but as I say, this is over, as is, hopefully, your contempt for me. I am not that woman, Betty. Please let me know where I can find you.

Betty's eyes shifted from the screen to the floor. Nothing moved, except perhaps the whole house. She was about to read it all again when she heard footsteps in the corridor.

'I see,' said Clara, suddenly appearing in the doorway, taking in the state of the room.

Betty was still naked, but with the composure of an actress who had tolerated long years of backstage exposure, she walked with little haste to pick up her robe from the back of the chair. She put the phone in the pocket but could not release it from her grasp. 'You see what?' she said, not looking at Clara.

'You're sleeping in his bed.'

'You're sleeping in his clothes,' said Betty.

Clara took a moment to comprehend the implications of this violation. 'Are you fucking him?'

Betty pulled the robe together and took her time to tie it, fussing with the knot for no good reason other than to prolong the silence. She found her sandals beneath the bed, clawed off her sock and tinkered with the tiny buckles. 'No,' she said at last.

Clara strolled across the room with her hands clasped behind her back. She looked down into the garden. 'Who is this man?'

'He's a painter,' said Betty, eager to tell the truth whenever it was useful, which right now, in this scenario, seemed to be hardly ever. 'He's a famous French painter,' she lied. 'His name is Claude.'

Clara moved away from the window to sit on what both women understood to be Jack's side of the bed. She placed her hand on his pillow and smoothed it out to the corners. 'Where is he?' she said.

'Who?'

'Jack.'

'You seem much more interested in Jack than in Martha,' said Betty.

'Well then,' said Clara, forcing a smile, 'where is Martha?'

'She's with Oliver,' said Betty, and Clara recoiled as though something had been thrown at her.

'You're lying,' she said.

'Why?'

Clara looked first at Betty and then at the painting on the wall behind her. 'This is not fair. You asked me to come here, and now—'

'I didn't ask you. You suggested—'

'Yes, you said that,' said Clara, holding up her hand to stop her. 'The point is, I came here because of you. No matter what you say, or said, or pretended to be, if it wasn't for you, I would not be here, and now I am here, you have done nothing but taunt and insult me. And now you're lying to me. I don't even know your name.'

'Your English is perfect.'

'It should be. I teach it. I said I don't even know your name.'

'Betty.'

'Right, Betty, what has Jack told you?'

Betty pulled out her cigarettes and offered one to Clara, who took it, lit it and passed her her lighter. '*Merci*,' she said, gobbling her first puff.

'He's told me very little.'

'What has Martha told you?'

Betty took a deep drag and sent it out across the room, sinking the weary Christ in a grey fog. It was a good question. 'Everything,' she said, and then couldn't stop herself. 'She's told me everything. There's nothing I don't know.'

'I'm sure that whatever she told you,' said Clara, 'is not the truth. You don't know as much as you think you do.'

'I could say the same of you,' said Betty.

'Well go on,' said Clara, hardly bothered. 'Test me. What don't I know?'

Betty stared at the legs of the bed and counted the knots in the wood. What was it? Maple? She should know. Paul would know. Paul knew his wood. She turned suddenly and bumbled into the bathroom to fetch the soap dish, which she carried high on her palm, flicking her ash into the suds, before setting it down on the small stool between them. She scraped her painted nail against the cigarette's filter until it began to peel. I'll say it, she thought. Why not say it? She didn't see any advantage in withholding it any longer.

'Go on,' said Clara.

'She's dead.'

Outside, Georges was still whistling.

Clara showed no reaction.

They both kept their eyes fixed on the tips of their respective cigarettes. 'I mean Martha,' said Betty, in case there was any confusion.

Clara stood, walked to the window and stepped out onto the balcony. She stared out across the garden, or perhaps her eyes were closed. She must have been devouring that cigarette, because it looked, from where Betty was sitting, as though her head was pouring out smoke. At last she turned and stepped halfway back into the room, leaning against the door frame. 'When?'

'Three months ago,' said Betty.

'How?'

'Suicide.'

Clara crossed to drop her dead dog end in the dish and made to leave. Before she walked out into the heavy shadow of the corridor, she turned. 'Why did you say she was with Oliver?'

Betty felt no further animosity towards the woman. She pitied her. 'I don't know. I was trying to find out where he is.'

'Where do you think he is?'

Betty looked around and up, as though the answer were

written somewhere on one of the walls. Eventually she shrugged. 'San Francisco?' she said, conceding in her tone that the answer was very likely flawed.

Clara emitted a brief sniff of derision and shook her head. She lingered a little longer, looking again at the painting. 'Was it a train?' she said.

'How do you know?' said Betty, standing.

'Was it?'

'Yes.'

'Good,' said Clara. And with that she turned and disappeared into the shadow. Betty listened to her footsteps grow fainter and fainter along the corridor and down the stairs. After a short while she could hear them again, this time from far behind her, and she rushed to the window to see Clara striding back across the lawn and over to where Georges was now raking out the grass. She caught his attention and stood a few feet away with her arms folded. Eventually Georges laid down his rake and shook her hand, smiling shyly. Though their conversation seemed, from a distance, amicable, there was much nodding and shrugging and waving of hands. Standing out on the balcony, Betty tried to listen, but they were too far away, and speaking too softly, too quickly, and of course, too selfishly, in French.

If Freddie were to die, thought Betty, if one day his little heart simply ceased its beating, or if some unfathomable calamity were to befall him, would that therefore, inevitably, be the end of her? Or if he were taken away in fine health, forever, or even only indefinitely, could she go on with her days and still consider herself sane? And so she wondered if Oliver had been snatched from Martha, just as Freddie had been snatched from Betty. Was he now in London, with Jack? Or else lodged in Paris with this pitiful mistress? Or was he, as Betty was beginning to understand, beyond salvation?

Either way, something had been so insufferable to Martha as to drag her down into the woods to surrender at last by stretching herself out on the steel. When Betty had told Clara that Martha was with Oliver, it had been a piece of mischief; she had meant nothing by it. Clara had flinched and called her a liar. But now that Clara knew of Martha's death, might not this be true after all? Yes, thought Betty, yes. Oliver is surely dead. And with that thought, she pulled her suitcase out from beneath the bed and began to pack.

This tragedy, or treachery, or whatever it was, was none of her business, and she was going home now to some quaint tribulations of her own. She had no time for all this. She felt the eyes of Christ and the eyes of the painted coquette upon her, gratified by her promised departure, as if their work here was done. They had seen it all. Noticing that it hung on its nail by a small leather loop, she was able to turn the crucifix to the wall. On the back it said *Made in Spain*. Yes, thought Betty, Oliver is surely dead. It was a house filled with dead things. Dead birds, dead faces, dead gods and saints. The whole house was dead. But it would not put its rope around her. She considered stealing a few shabby accessories: a cotton scarf, a plastic belt, the floppy hat, but her suitcase, for some reason, was fatter than four weeks ago. Everything now bundled and rolled, nothing folded, stuffed with all the sweat and stress. All she would keep was the polished white pebble, which she dropped into the pocket of her jeans. She laced her boots, buttoned up her bobbled cardie and pulled her old grey beanie so completely, so thoroughly over her hair that her whole head and face seemed suddenly grey. She took one last look in the mirror. Would Freddie still want this woman for a mother? Would he still want to hug her? Was she pretty enough? Was she honest enough? Clever enough? What was the point of her? What was she for?

Enough of that, she thought. She turned and gave the glass one last look at her back and left it there all on its own. Trapped on the wall in the big white room. Staring at the door.

'I have an open ticket,' she said. 'Business class. I can go on any flight.'

Picking up figs from the lawn must have exhausted Georges, for he could barely open his eyes and his hair was all up at the crown, like he'd been hung upside down and spun. 'You still have to book,' he said.

'I don't care,' said Betty. 'I'd rather sort all that out at the airport. I don't mind if I have to wait. I'll spend the night there if I have to.'

'But why now?'

'Because, Georges, I want my life back, thank you. I'm tired of being the dead mother of a dead child.'

'What dead child?' said Georges.

'I saw you talking to Clara,' she said. 'What did you talk about?'

'Why did you say my name is Claude?'

'Because I couldn't remember your name,' said Betty. 'So what did you talk about?'

'She asked me if it is true.'

'If what is true?'

'Martha is dead. I say yes. She ask why we are here. I say.'

'You say that we're doing camera tests?'

'Well, yes, I tell her that and she say is bullshit, and I say yes it's bullshit, and she is a little angry and a little crying, and so I say what we do. The truth.'

'And what did she think to that?'

'She think it's strange anyway. She thinks we are all crazy. And it's true, I think.'

'Where is she now?'

'I don't know. Maybe gone.'

'Well, good, me too, so it'll just be you. You'll have some peace.'

'You can't just leave.'

'Why do you care? You don't want me here. You don't like me.'

'It's not true.'

'I'm going.'

'But it's not finished. There is maybe call tonight, tomorrow night. The last night.'

'I think they've forgotten about us, Georges. We've been left here to rot, like everything else.'

'Rot,' said Georges, frowning. 'What is rot?'

'Never mind. Look, don't worry, I'll take the train to the airport. I hear the train is very reliable. Always on time. Goodbye, Georges. Good luck. I won't kiss you. I know you don't like that.' And she turned, as she had turned from the mirror, for the same reason: to hide the tears. By the time she reached the terrace, the whole world was so bubbled and blurred she could barely see where she was going. She listened out for the sound of the door closing, wondering if he would at least have the decency to watch her go. If he didn't watch her go with some little pang of regret, then there was something wrong with him and he deserved to have one foot. She heard nothing, no last words, nor the door of his little house closing. But then she was sobbing so thickly and perhaps he had closed it very softly, just to be polite. For say what you like about him, she thought, Georges had always been a perfectly polite man.

And then she did hear something, but not the right sort of thing, and not from the right direction. It was the sound of something heavy but soft landing with a dull thud in the long grass to her left. She wiped her eyes on the sleeve of her cardie and watched the pale pink silicone belly rolling down the slight incline, picking up speed, in fact, before bumping into and bouncing off the small wall at the foot of the hill, coming to rest in a shallow ditch next to a coiled hosepipe. Retracing its trajectory, she arrived at last at Clara, who was sitting at the large onyx table with her back to the pool. Her eyes were fixed on the house as though she had nothing to do with the absurd thing that had just happened.

Betty stopped and waited. Was Clara looking for a fight? Did she expect Betty to throw it back? She decided to let it pass. After all, what was left to say?

'You don't look anything like her,' said Clara, not moving, still staring at the house. 'I don't think so. Not even your friend there thinks so.'

'OK,' said Betty, baffled.

Clara wasn't finished. 'Who thinks you look like her?'

'Well, Jack, apparently,' said Betty.

'It's all in his mind.'

'Perhaps.' The two women were still not looking at each other.

'I wouldn't like to be in that mind,' said Clara.

'No.'

'Nor Martha's. Poor you. Though Georges says you were very good.'

'I fooled you,' said Betty, walking closer, deciding she might not go in quite such a hurry after all.

'Congratulations. What a triumph.'

'I'm sorry,' said Betty, taking the chair opposite, letting Clara see – if she didn't already realise – how truly upset she was. She wiped away more tears with the bulb of her wrist bone. She noticed Georges still standing in his doorway. Had he been lamenting her departure, or only bemused by the flying belly? The point was, he was there, thought Betty, and left it at that.

'Are you going now?' said Clara.

278

'Yes. I have to get back to my son.'

'How old?'

'Six.'

'Six,' said Clara fondly, and smiled. She sat back, took off her sunglasses and placed them softly on the table, casting two short smears of green light across the smooth onyx.

'About the same age as Oliver, isn't it?' said Betty.

'Oliver would be seven by now.'

'Would be? Or would have been?'

'What's the difference?' said Clara.

'Would be could mean that he is, but you haven't seen him for a while. Would have been means he never will be.'

'Yes, you're right, of course,' said Clara, looking up into the dancing branches of the cherry tree, taking note. 'So . . .' she began, and looked Betty in the eye, 'would have been.'

Both women allowed the silence to do its work. Over Clara's shoulder Betty could see Georges, now wearing his battered panama, moving away from his door and over to the fig tree.

'What she told you is a lie,' said Clara at last.

'She didn't tell me anything,' said Betty. 'I never met her.' She took out her phone and, bringing up the finest photo of Freddie she could find, passed it to Clara. 'Freddie,' she said. 'That's my Freddie.'

'He looks like a Freddie.'

'He's the Freddiest of all the Freddies,' said Betty, managing a small smile, though her heart was not in it.

'He looks like you.'

'Don't you think he has Oliver's eyes?'

'Not at all,' said Clara, with some distaste. 'It's all in your mind.'

'I suppose,' said Betty. 'I'm sorry. You wouldn't want to be in my mind either.'

At that Clara simply shook her head and looked again at the photo. 'His eyes are happy.'

'Was Oliver not happy?'

'Nobody knew. He didn't talk.'

'Why not?'

'He couldn't talk,' said Clara, handing back the phone. 'He was not well. He was born not well.'

'Is that why they hid him?'

'Do you think they hid him?'

'Don't you?'

'Yes, of course.'

'You said what she told me was a lie. What did you think she told me?'

'Nothing.'

'About you and Jack?'

'What about me and Jack?'

'You were sleeping in his jacket.'

'It's a nice jacket.'

'It's not that nice.'

Clara smiled. 'That was not the lie.'

'How did she find out?'

'There were photographs. He took photographs. She found them.'

'Perhaps he wanted her to find them.'

'Perhaps *I* wanted her to find them.'

'Why?'

'Because I am not nice.' Clara crossed her arms on the table and set her head down upon them.

Betty took the opportunity to pick up the green sunglasses and try them on. She looked back at Georges, who was still tending to the figs. 'Was Martha a good mother?' she said.

Still with her face to the table, Clara snorted, 'Not at all.'

'I know she didn't like being pregnant,' said Betty.

'She hated to be pregnant,' snapped Clara, lifting her head and sitting up. 'And she hated to be a mother.' She pulled her hair back from her face and tied it in a band of blue elastic. 'And of course she hated me. But not at first. At first she needed me, because their child is not right, and so she can work. So they can both work. The work is what they really love – this stupid work, this dressing up and . . . well, you know all about it.' Betty shrugged. 'I'm sorry,' said Clara, 'but I don't think it is so important. It is not the most important thing.'

'I agree,' said Betty.

'The important thing,' said Clara, 'should be this boy she does not love, she cannot love. Who does not speak. Who cannot speak. Who never smiles and sometimes screams with no sound. But with his face and his eyes he is screaming loud, and he is screaming at her. And he also, like me, has taken her husband away from her. They both lost their happiness, they say, because of this silent screaming boy who they don't understand and do not like, but whom I love, and whom I think loves me. I have a tattoo, look.' She placed her upturned left hand on the table between them. There on her pale palm was a perfect circle with a black dot in the centre. The flesh of Betty's face began to prickle.

'What is that?' she said.

'It means Oliver. It was his sign.'

'What do you mean?'

'I taught him to write his name: a big O, then a small l, i, v, e, r. But when I put the dot over the i, he never liked it there. He was cross about that. He became anxious. He would make me rub it out and put it in the middle of the O, which was where he preferred it. And so that became the way he wrote his name, always: just an O with a dot. And that's the way everybody wrote it – me, Jack, Martha. So when I went back to Paris, I did this to remind me.' Clara closed her hand and put it back beneath the table, out of sight.

'How did you know about the train?' said Betty.

'Because that was the thing she would say, always: "I will throw myself before the train." When she found the photographs. When Oliver screamed. When Oliver was silent. When she had not slept. When she put on weight. When she did not get the part: "I will throw myself before the train, you will see." And so now . . . Well, it was not one of her lies.'

'What did you want her to confess?'

Clara took out a tissue from her pocket and blew her nose. 'Does Jack love you?' she said. Her voice seemed to have grown weaker.

'Not at all,' said Betty, bemused. 'He doesn't know me. I promise you, that's not the story.'

Clara looked behind her to see Georges, who was kneeling down on the green tarpaulin, seemingly sifting the good figs from the bad and tossing the bad into a bucket. While her back was turned, Betty reached into the pocket of her jeans. 'Show me your hand,' she said, and Clara turned away from Georges, back to the table.

'What for?'

'Just show me the hand you showed me before.' Clara lifted a tight fist from beneath the table and held it out. 'Turn it over, open your fingers.' Clara did so. And as tenderly as she was able, Betty placed the white pebble on Clara's tattooed palm, thus replacing one perfect circle with another.

'What is this?' said Clara, barely able to breathe. A fat tear plopped down and trickled along the smooth edge of the pebble.

'I don't know,' said Betty.

'Where did you find it?'

'In the tunnel.' Clara looked at her askance. 'In the tunnel where Martha waited for her train.'

Clara set the pebble down with great care in the centre of the table. A solitary ant crawled out from beneath Betty's elbow, and as it neared the pebble, Clara put her face down close to the surface, her lips almost touching the tiny creature, and blew it all the way off to the edge and down to the bright white gravel. She then settled herself back in her chair, folded her arms and stared at Betty with a calm yet pathetically forlorn expression. Betty stared back in silence, then for a short while she watched Georges as he pulled the green tarpaulin of figs out of the sun and into a patch of shadow close to the pool. When she looked back, Clara's expression had not changed and it felt like this might go on for the rest of the afternoon, which would have been fine, thought Betty, if that was how it had to be. From somewhere deep inside a distant laurel bush, two toads were talking. Otherwise all was silent.

At last Clara looked away and up at the eaves of the house. 'She was sitting where you are sitting,' she said. 'I was sitting where I am sitting. Right here. Can you see the pool?'

Betty made a clear show of looking over Clara's shoulder. 'Yes,' she said.

'Yes. Very well?'

'Yes.'

'So this is how it was,' Clara said, and took a deep breath. 'A few days before, she had found the photographs, in Paris. They had an apartment. I was here with Oliver. Always I was here, alone, with Oliver. She left Jack in Paris and came back that morning. And in the afternoon she brought me out to sit here. She told me that she would like to kill me, but that I was not worth it. She said that when she had asked Jack if he was in love with me, he had laughed and laughed, like it was the most ridiculous thing he had ever heard. And perhaps that was not one of her lies. Perhaps that was true, I don't know. She told me I was not the only one. That I was the least of all of them.

I had left Oliver playing by the fig tree. Right where Georges was just now. As she was talking to me, I could see her eyes watching him. Like you were watching Georges. And I know right now, from watching you, that Georges is no longer by the tree. And so after a little while I thought Oliver was no longer by the tree, for her eyes had him just over my shoulder, which was, well, a little close to . . . And I turned my head to check, but before I could see him, she grabbed my face in one hand.

'Martha had very strong hands. Your hands are all wrong. She took my face in her hand, her right hand, and gripped my cheeks and jaw between her thumb and four fingers. Her nails and rings were digging into my skin. My lips were pulled into an ugly shape, showing my teeth. And she must have liked that ugly shape, because she held me there, fixed like that for a long, long time, while she told me how worthless I was. What a whore I was. What a piece of filth I was. How I had destroyed her life, me and that boy behind me, who, although I didn't realise it then, of course, had already wandered too close to the edge, as he was not supposed to, for he could not swim, but loved to look at himself in the reflection. And as she gripped my jaw tighter and tighter, I watched her eyes dance back and forth, calling me every dirty name she could think of, for as long as she could keep it up. Words I'd never heard. And by now he must already have been in the water. Had I known, I might have watched for it in her eyes. She had been cold enough to remove her sunglasses the moment it had come to her. The moment she realised what might be possible. The moment Oliver started walking from the tree towards the water, off came the glasses and up came the claw, to fix me in place, and the dirty words, hag, slag, slut, bitch, cunt, kept coming louder and louder to drown out the sound.'

Suddenly Clara stopped, catching herself. 'Ha!' she said '"To drown" is a bad word, of course, in this case. I should simply say to stop me from hearing the terrible sounds of the water. I don't know how long it took. Perhaps it was quick. Only she could have told us that. But to her such a thing never happened; she would never admit it, not even to me. I knew the truth: I did not see it, of course, but to see the look on her face and in her eyes was to know exactly what she had done. And then, when she was sure that it was over, she let go of my face and slapped it, hard. More like a punch. And I took it. I deserved it. I cried out in pain, and when she was satisfied that I was too upset to notice what had happened, she ran off and through the house and up to her bedroom, and stood there at the window, halfway out on the balcony, exactly as I saw you standing this morning.

'She was already on the phone. To whom, I don't know. To Jack? Someone. Anyone who would say they were speaking to her by the time I came to my senses and ran off in search of my darling boy and found him there, face down. There was a bubble of air beneath his shirt, and on the hill of the bubble a butterfly. And his black cap banging against the filter like it was trying to get away. I jumped into the water and lifted him out and did all the things I knew to save him. But I could not. He was not to be saved. And when I tried to scream, I could only scream like him, with my wide eyes and mouth and nothing coming out. And when I looked up, there was Martha on the balcony, looking down, blank, with nothing in her eyes. Looking down at me and her dead boy like she was looking at . . . what? A chair. A hole in the wall. At thin air.' Clara bowed her head and stared at the ground. 'At nothing at all.'

An unbroken trickle of tears ran from her eyes to the tip of her nose and dripped to the bright ground, enough to turn the white gravel grey. 'And then, out of this silence,' she continued, 'it was Martha who screamed. Not like a mother who had lost her baby. Like an actress. Like it was her work. Then she

285

took a good deep breath and screamed again, for the telephone. Louder this time. Take two.'

As Betty watched Clara shift and clutch and gasp for air, she felt certain that she herself had drawn not one breath, nor had she blinked, nor had her heart roused one beat. She had surely turned to salt. Georges now stood motionless by the pool, his hat to his breast, his eyes in the shadow of his brow, fixed in their direction as if he had heard poor Clara's every word, though Betty knew he had not.

After a few moments of tireless silence, Clara continued. 'I said I will call the police, and she hissed in my face and said, "Go on." She said it was she who would call the police, and who would they believe? Who was the one paid to be in charge of the child? She said it would be the end of me. I was training to be a teacher, and did she think it would be possible to carry on with that? Who would want me? Who would trust me? And now it was me who was spitting the names. Every word I could think of: *salope*, *diable*, *monstre*, *meurtrière*. Every name for as long as I could keep it up. She called Jack in a rage of tears – more theatre – and told him he must come back, something unthinkable had happened. He must come back from Paris. And at the same time she told me that I must go to Paris. "Get back to Paris," she screamed. "Get the fuck back to Paris." That she would take care of things, but that I must go, immediately, and never come back. Never. Go and wait to hear what I should do.

'And so I went, and I did wait, but I never heard. I never heard anything from anyone, not her, not Jack, not the police, *les services sociaux*. No inquiry like I thought there must be. And all this time, I told no one. Not my mother, my father, my brothers, my friends, no one. It is the worst thing that has ever happened to me. It will always be this, no matter what, the rest of my life. All this time I cannot work. I do not go out. I do not study. I do not sleep. I do not eat and I think I will go insane. I think I will die. I never heard anything from anyone, till I heard from you, and didn't I say? Didn't I say she must confess? That I will only come if she confesses is what I said, and you said yes. And here I am. And here we are. And here is this.' She held up the polished white pebble, turning it on the tips of her fingers. 'Here is this,' she said again, and with the plain, unpainted nail of her thumb began to scratch at the black dot to see if the marking was indelible, and seeing it to be the case, she set it down on the table, where it seemed to tremble for a short time before settling, suddenly still, as though dead.

'Have you seen this before?' said Betty. Her voice crept out dry and broken. She felt like she had not spoken for days.

'No,' said Clara.

'Do you know what it is?'

'I know where it belongs,' she said. And easing her chair away from the table, she stood and walked around to the other side. 'Come with me,' she said, picking up the pebble, taking Betty by the hand and pulling her gently to her feet. 'I'll show you what I found last night.'

CHAPTER 32

As the great seventeenth-century poet John Donne lay dying of stomach cancer, he commissioned a sketch of himself, girded in his knotted shroud, so that he might stage-manage and sensitively appreciate posterity's vision of him: memorialised as he was, and indeed still is, in a corner of St Paul's mighty cathedral. Thus Jack Drake – a great devotee of the poet, and a frequent visitor to his grave – pulled up a plastic chair to sit in silent contemplation of his own silicone cadaver in its crimson pyjamas, its face (now that the tongue had been snipped out with a pair of workmen's pliers) practically beatific, were it not for the bulging eyes and sagging jaw. No matter: it offered Jack the chance to imagine the glory of what lay in store for him one of these dark nights, should his snarled, ungrateful heart elect to attack him in the small hours. They had made a fine job of it in the end, at least from the neck up. Each minuscule whisker had been punched in by hand, each pimple faithfully painted, his flesh tones perfected, the deep dry red of the rope burn in a ring about his broken throat, each yellowed tooth in its proper place, each crevice and hollow, each bone and blood vessel, pored over for hours, no doubt, by the looks of things. Yes, they had made fine work of it, and he lingered there transfixed,

twirling the long rubbery tongue. Twisting it in his fingers between his thighs, which was not quite right, he thought, not
really quite right.

He had not called her back. What had she meant, there was
someone in the house? He had intended to go straight upstairs
to his studio and call her from there, to regale her with stories
from the day, to embrace the end of it all and take stock of how
far they had both come since the idea for this whole thing had
first presented itself during an evening walk by the river, as they
had discussed his father's deferred funeral by the light of the
festooned bulbs of the South Bank. But now the idea of such
a conversation had lost all its charm and turned into his least
favourite of all things – a drama.

It was a curious thing: he had given up smoking twenty years
ago, and yet seeing a packet on the base of an upturned bucket
over by the front door, he was tempted to take one. What
difference would it make? he thought. What harm would it
do? He looked around to see how he might set light to the
thing should he pursue the matter further. Finding nothing in
easy sight, he stood and wandered, ever vigilant, towards the
kitchen, where he supposed that at least the gas ring might be
up to the task; but, for the duration of filming, the kitchen had
been reduced to a cluttered dump room. He began wrestling
chairs and poles out of his way, trying to reach the source of
the sacred flame as though his life depended on it. And that
was when he heard his phone ringing from the other room.
Blasting out like a school bell and setting his heart beating. He
had to climb out of the wreckage, tearing his left leg in the
process, catching his cuff on another stray nail and putting his
shoulder out. Before he could make it, the ringing had ceased,
and all he could catch was a glimpse of Martha's raddled face
snapping back to black. He lay down on the floor and thought
once more about the cigarette. It had become an obsession.

He had, in the space of five minutes, transformed from a reasonable man with a commendable intellect to a complete idiot. The telephone rang again. He picked it up.

'I'll call you straight back,' he said. 'Straight back. I've had a fall.'

'I was just checking you were all right,' said Nora. 'How did you fall?'

'I didn't,' said Jack.

'You just said you did.'

'I thought you were Martha.'

'Martha's dead, Jack,' said Nora.

'Goodnight!' snapped Jack, and skimmed the phone across the polished wooden floor until it crashed and rebounded off the skirting and into the depths of the vestibule, where it lit up the walls for a short time, showing the painting of the girl on the mountain. Jack marched over to the upturned bucket, snatched up the packet of cigarettes and found nothing but a dead bee and a rolled-up ball of silver foil.

'I can't see you properly,' said Martha. 'Lean back into the light.'

Jack was sitting at his desk, and when he moved back from the monitor, as instructed, he angled the lamp to better illuminate his face, which he had washed, and his hair, which he had brushed. Martha was in the garden, speaking on her phone in almost complete darkness. Only the faint glow from a few distant oil lamps showed that she was there at all. 'I can't really see you,' said Jack, tilting his monitor.

'It doesn't matter,' she said. 'You know what I look like by now.' There was no kindness in her voice tonight.

'How are you, Martha?' he said. 'You sound a little fractious.'

'That doesn't matter either,' she said. 'I just wanted to say goodbye.'

'What do you mean?'

'Well, it's our last night, is it not?'

'I don't know what you're talking about, Martha.'

'It's your last day of filming tomorrow . . . yes?'

'Yes.'

'And you wanted me here while you were filming, so you could concentrate on the work?'

'Not precisely.'

'Well, that's what I was given to understand,' she said, rather grandly. 'So then that's goodbye.'

'It'll never be goodbye, Martha.'

'Oh, but it will, Jack.'

'We'll always be together.'

'Well, that's just the thing, Jack. That's what I wanted to talk to you about.'

'Martha, you're beginning to frighten me.'

'Good,' she said, and smiled. 'I'm glad that I frighten you. That's a very good start.' She was walking around the garden rather erratically. Carelessly tipping the phone this way and that.

'A good start to what?' he said. 'What is it that you want to start?'

'The end,' she said, and stopped abruptly by a nearby lamp, making sure that he could see her eyes.

'Are you not feeling well?' he said

She began to walk again, tilting the phone straight up in the air so that all he could see were the branches of the trees racing by against the blue-black sky.

'How is the little chap?' he said cheerfully, imagining that he'd steered things back on track.

'He's very quiet,' he heard her say.

When at last she had stopped walking, she set the phone against a ledge or wall so that he could see more of her than just her face. She was sitting on one of the chairs near the edge of the covered pool. She was dressed in a simple white skirt and green cap-sleeved top. Her belly was flat. She sat in such a way as to assure him of that. In fact, she now leaned forward, towards the camera, in a posture that would be difficult, indeed impossible, for a mother-to-be. He must already be born, he thought. She had moved things along. Good for her.

'What did you mean by your message?' he said. 'That there was someone in the house? Did you mean Oliver?'

She put her head all the way down to her knees with both hands on top to keep it there. She began to scratch at her scalp.

'But then you said you were afraid,' said Jack. 'Surely you can't be afraid of Oliver.'

She lifted her face and looked once more directly into the camera. 'Aren't you afraid of Oliver?' she said.

Jack shifted in his seat. He thought again about the cigarette he had not found.

'Why on earth did you bring me back?'

'Back?'

'You should have left me in my grave,' she said.

To his great consternation, he noticed something moving behind her. The shape of a woman walking from the gate at the end of the pool and off across the garden in the direction of the poplar grove, which also seemed softly lit by an unknown source. 'What's that?' he said, bringing his face close to the screen. 'There's someone there.'

Martha nodded. 'That's her.'

'That's who?' he said, his voice trembling.

'The woman.'

'What woman?'

'She was at the top of the stairs the first time I saw her, look-ing down,' said Martha. 'Then I heard her talking to someone in the boudoir. I hear her walking around in the middle of the night. One day I followed her out into the woods and spoke to her. She says you know her.'

'How should I know her?' said Jack, baffled.

'She says you brought her here,' said Martha.

'No.'

'She was wearing my clothes, Jack.'

'Stop.'

'She says you said she could. She says you said she must.'

'Stop it, Martha.'

She paused to light a cigarette, and then whispered, 'She's been sleeping in our bed, Jack. Wearing my clothes, sleeping in my bed. What are you two up to?'

'I'm ending this.'

'Do you think I'm expendable?'

'No.'

'Disposable?'

'Martha!'

'Do you think I'm replaceable?'

'Stop!'

Jack dragged his chair back from the table and stood up.

'Sit down, Jack,' snapped Martha. 'I'm not finished.'

'I am,' he shouted back. 'I'm finished. This is finished,' but he made no move to turn her off.

'Do you know what she told me this evening?'

He moved back to the desk but remained standing, gripping the back of the chair.

'She told me there will be policemen in the morning.'

'Policemen?'

'At the end of the garden.'

'I see,' he said, his voice fading.

'Down in the poplar grove.'

'Very well,' said Jack, sitting back down. 'If that's how it must be.'

'That's how it must be.'

'Very well,' he said, and bowed his head.

'She said to tell you that it's been a fine game, hasn't it? That's how she said it: "A fine game, hasn't it?" She said she can't say that she's enjoyed it, but that she doesn't suppose that was the point. She wonders, what was the point? I said, I wonder that too. She said that perhaps the point all along was to have me confess? "Confess to what?" I said. She said, "Oh, you know. You know very well what I'm talking about, and so does Jack." Is that right, Jack? Do you know very well what she's talking about? She said that I was to tell you that the girl had nothing to do with it. Clara – she's talking about your Clara. Tell him that it was you, she said. Even if he thinks he knows, she said. He just needs to hear it from you, she said. Do you think so? I said. She said yes, Martha – and that, she believes, has been the point. Tell him, she said, that you did it to the girl as much as you did it to the boy. And in fact to you, Jack, of course. And then to myself, apparently. I said I don't understand a word you're saying, dear – it must be the accent. She said that I wasn't to worry and that Jack will understand and that's all that matters. Is that right, Jack? Is she right?'

'Yes.'

'Did she do well, Jack?'

'Yes.'

'Good.'

'Yes, tell her she did very well.'

'And will you let her go now?'

'Yes.'

'Can she say goodbye?'

'Yes.'

She stood up and straightened her skirt. 'Goodbye,' she said.

'Goodbye, Martha,' said Jack.

'Goodbye, dear,' said Martha, and she turned, crushing out her cigarette with one last twist of her pointed toe.

'Betty,' said Jack. The woman froze. 'Betty,' he repeated, a little louder.

Betty turned, taking off Martha's hat, tossing it to the floor. 'Yes?' she said.

'Goodbye, Betty,' said Jack. 'Thank you.'

'Goodbye, Jack,' she said. She turned back away from the camera and, kicking off her shoes, walked slowly, barefoot, towards the house, leaving the phone leaning against the wall, capturing her every step all the way back to the open terrace doors. That's all been carefully worked out, thought Jack. She certainly knows how to make an exit. She is an actress, after all.

They had endeavoured to make the mound of white pebbles not too explicitly what it was. Down there in the poplar grove where the boy had loved to play. Not with his father, no, nor with Martha, but play he did, apparently, by himself or with Clara. It was a small shadowed patch of tapestry lawn, as far away from the house as one could get. There had been one of those circles carved into the bark of the tallest tree there. 'Over a hundred and fifty feet high,' Jack had told him. 'Imagine that.' And perhaps he had. Or perhaps he didn't need to, for there it was. No imagination required. It had been a foolish thing for his father to say. Either way, he gave no response. Martha thought that in another life the boy must have said too much. In another life his words must have caused tremendous pain, she said. And then he chose us, she said. Imagine *that*.

He'd sent early word to Nora that he was profoundly exhausted and therefore had no stomach to shoot the morning's work, and that it would be no great hardship for her to take the helm. And so he watched his cast and crew from the high window of his mother's old sewing room, bringing out the bagged body of his rotting father as a frolicsome mob of seventies extras heckled unconvincingly and a handful of flared-trousered photographers held their cameras like rank amateurs. The policemen – there were four of them – were too slovenly. His young self had not stood out in the light like that but hidden in shame, in the garden. His mother had not wept like that; she had not wept at all. It was difficult not to stick his beak in, but that was as it must be now. He would hand the entire thing over to his poor, staunch and indefatigable Nora, who would make of it all what she could. He had, he hoped to dear God, prepared her well.

As he buttoned the bottom button of his flannel pyjamas, he thought fondly of the woman he had once addressed as 'my sublime Clara'. She'd thought it a little much and asked him not to. She said she didn't believe him. She said it wasn't even love, as he professed, and that soon he would leave her. He'd told her that nothing could come between them, that to lose her would be to lose everything. She said he didn't know what he was talking about, and she had been right of course, for who in this world knows what they are talking about? Although he did, as he had promised, lose everything. He wondered if she had at last, wherever she had gone, come to know that. He wondered where she might be right now. As he put his feet into his slippers, he was saddened to realise that he could not recall her face. All he knew was that it had been a kind face, one of the few. Freckles. Yes, he remembered freckles.

Lunch was in the grounds of the church, but he had no appetite and so did not join them. Besides, who could eat anything with that poor soul looking down from his cross? Half naked, half starved, scarred flesh, blood everywhere. Jack had never been able to keep even the plain wafer down. 'I'll take a nap,' he told Nora. 'It's a long afternoon.'

'It certainly is,' she said. 'A long last afternoon,' and kissed him fondly on the tip of his nose, leaving him there on the maroon chaise longue. One slipper on, the other off, set down on the floor with his phone tucked inside. 'Can I bring you anything from catering?' she said.

'Just a banana,' said Jack, 'and perhaps a few grapes.'

'A banana and grapes,' she said, 'a banana and a few grapes,' repeating it as she left him, as though she might forget it. 'A banana and perhaps a few grapes.'

Solomon, reliable as ever, had anticipated the first shot of the afternoon and put on a twenty-eight-millimetre lens, but Jack — now that he could see things clearly, with no one but Vladimir the parrot cluttering the frame — replaced it with his favourite thirty-five. The new corpse was dangling splendidly. Far better than the Ripley disaster that had landed them here in the first place. The feet seemed about right, the arms not too taut, the neck twisted nicely and the face tilted down, glaring at the floor, the jaw lifted a little as he had requested, with just one tooth out on the lip as had been suggested by Charles. It was a nice touch, but now that he saw it again, perhaps a little much, and would be forgotten for the close-ups. He made a note and stuck it to the camera.

There had been many discussions in heated production meetings about the right chair, as though it was one of the most important elements in the whole story. Historically it had been a three-legged stool, painted blue, which his father had found down in the cellar and for some reason brought up to fit the bill, as though it had been a question of taste (which perhaps it had been, after all: consider the pyjamas). A three-legged stool, painted blue, did not look good beneath the red slippered feet of a doomed man. In the end they had settled for a simple oak sabre-leg side chair, modestly upholstered with a green velvet seat to contrast the clownish apparel of the deceased. When it falls, thought Jack, it should land with the plush green at forty-five degrees to the lens. He set it so and walked back to the camera to take a look. No, no, he thought. It should land facing away, exposing the chair's underbelly, which was nicely aged, with its tattered hessian hanging down. He ran the camera for thirty seconds on this configuration. The light was too intense on the left of frame and so he repositioned a pair of flags and put up an extra scrim to diffuse the glare on the noose. Not content, he climbed a stepladder and dusted the rope with a handful of fuller's earth, working it well into the fibre with a dirty rag, almost falling as he made his way down. As he came level with his cold dead face, he took a moment to kiss himself, as Nora had done, fondly, on the tip of the nose.

'I think Billy's more upset than he's letting on,' said Phyllis.

'It's always sad to finish these things,' said Nora. 'Everybody feels it.'

'He nearly cried when they clapped for him.'

'Lots of people do cry,' said Nora. 'Grown men.' She was peeling one banana while balancing the other on a plastic plate filled with wet green grapes. 'I always cry. You just watch me this afternoon, though I won't be getting any applause.'

'Well, you should,' said Phyllis, opening the library door for her. 'You deserve it, darling. We all do.'

Jack was back on the chaise longue, fast asleep, at last. One slipper on, the other off, set down on the floor, as before, with his phone tucked inside.

'God knows how he can sleep,' said Phyllis, 'with that bloody parrot squawking like that. He's the one thing I won't miss. Bloody nuisance. He went for me this morning.'

It was true that Vladimir was making quite a racket as they

298

passed into the main room, shrieking like a maniac, flapping wildly from one end of the library to the other. At one point he crashed slap bang into the hanging prosthetic, causing it to swing like an absurd red pendulum

'I'll just put these down for him,' said Nora, setting the fruit on the long table, 'and then I'll go through that list of casting agents with you.'

'Thank you,' said Phyllis. 'Our Billy will be ever so grateful.'

As Nora walked softly away from the table, turning to check on Jack, mindful not to disturb him, she noticed something peculiar about his hair: it was slightly askew, hanging down over one ear. As though he were wearing a toupee. Then she realised he wasn't sleeping at all; that his eyes were wide open and fixed on the ceiling. As she drew closer, she felt as though her flesh had hardened and her bones had turned to milk. She was still chewing on her banana, a detail she would never forget, and always mention when asked to recount – as she often was over the years – how it felt to be the woman who discovered the incredible scene of Jack Drake's famous suicide. She never ate another banana for the rest of her life; that was another thing she always told them.

As soon as she realised that it was merely the silicone facsimile of her dear man lying there, stiff, on the maroon chaise longue, she knew exactly what he had done, for she knew well the workings of the great man's mind. It was not the squawking and the flapping of the parrot that had caused the hanging man to sway and spin, but rather the hanging of the man himself that had set the parrot squawking and flapping. The camera, of course, was still running. As for Phyllis: once the gravity of the situation had been explained to her plump and astonished face, 'Oh my God!' was all she could say, over and over and over and over. 'Oh my God!' as though she would never stop saying it, as though that was her state for the rest of her life. It wasn't long before the screams of the two women and the shrieking of the bird brought other members of the crew barrelling in, and as the stepladders were put in place to bring him down from the ceiling, it was he who brought the ceiling down.

And then down they all came: Jack, Solomon, Charles, Rex, all in a heap of dust and rope and blood and rubble. And there was Billy over by the vestibule with his cumbersome Rolleiflex, peering down into the viewfinder, moving up to go down and right to go left, and in the end just putting it aside and filming the whole thing on his phone.

Nora was still standing by the prosthetic, who was, from the comfort of the couch, oblivious through it all, utterly unconcerned. His one tooth on his lip and his glass eyes wide to the ceiling. One slipper on, the other slipper off, set down on the floor with his phone tucked inside, and the phone now ringing out and above the terrible commotion of the crumbling room. And there on the screen was Martha Lear's flushed and drunken face, shining pink in the Tuscan sun.

Nora Flynn toed the slipper and its tiresome passenger to the edge of the rug and kicked it, with all her strength, as far as she could across the polished wooden floor. Past the parrot, past the camera, past the scrum of panicking men, all the way to the other end of the room; then, since no one else, it seemed, had thought to do so, she took out her own phone and dialled 999.

CHAPTER 33

The two women had knelt in the grass there beneath the poplars, the pile of white pebbles cold beneath the burning sun. No words. No birdsong. After a long silence, Clara had leaned in, gently blown the dust from the small hollow at the crest of the mound and set the smooth stone back where it belonged. It fell into place with a dull click. Why Martha had taken it with her into the dark of the tunnel would remain an enigma. Perhaps it was merely a piece of shabby theatre.

Policemen did not come in the morning. Clara was not ready for that and asked that she might spend those precious early hours in peaceful contemplation of the past and of the dreadful complications to come, when all this would be known by people who had no business to know. People who would only now know Oliver by name and two or three bleak photographs. He had despised cameras. He imagined – with good reason, thought Clara – that their dead black eyes did not love him. That they wanted, more than anything, to hurt him. She had his drawings to prove it.

'I'll come back if you need me to,' said Betty. 'I'll bring my son.'

'This is no place for him,' said Clara.

'I mean to Paris,' said Betty, 'when everything has calmed down.'

'*D'accord,*' said Clara, smiling.

'I'll also stay with you now if you change your mind.'

'No,' she said. 'This is not your problem. I'll wait until you've gone. I may even wait another day. Give Georges time to get to wherever he's going.'

'No one knows where Georges is going,' said Betty. 'No one knows where Georges has been. He's a man of mystery.'

'I don't want him involved in all this.'

'But don't stay here on your own after that.'

'No, I'll be with Isabelle tonight. She has a baby now. I will love to see her baby.'

'Yes,' said Betty, 'I've met him.'

'What's he like?'

'Well . . .' said Betty, looking for the words, 'I've always found him to be delightful.'

In her time in the theatre, Betty had grown accustomed to a restless and peripatetic existence. To making and shedding friends at short notice, and in time turning those friends into acquaintances and those acquaintances into strangers; to moving into and out of distant towns and rooms and keeping one's eye fixed always on the next town, the next room. She'd grown accustomed to living with, around, beneath and inside other people. And she'd learned to let go of those odd, strangely clothed, strangely conflicted, complicated souls once they'd done what they had been created to do and everybody had made good use of them.

But nothing had prepared her for this. The strangely clothed, strangely conflicted and complicated soul of Martha would be difficult to exile. These painful few days would remain with her for years. This home, that she had first thought so exquisite, now seemed anything but. It was, she realised, an ill-conceived house. Poorly constructed, full of cracks and leaks, leaning backwards, scrappily painted, with creaking boards and crumbling walls. It resembled the people who had blundered and fumbled within it, a thing so preoccupied with pretending to be something else that it ended up being really nothing at all. She would not miss one brick of it. She imagined it would not survive to see another summer. Wasn't it typical for sites such as these – the scene of some infamous wickedness – to be torn down in the name of decency? After all, who would want it now? Who could find peace on this ground knowing what pitiless souls had walked it?

'Let's try this again,' said Betty, putting her nose round Georges's open door. She was already wearing her English coat, which was a lousy idea. She could feel the sweat slipping off her back.

Georges set down his brush and wiped his hands and arms on a scrap of rag. He hadn't had time to turn his painting to the wall. '*Comment?*' he said, though he'd heard very well what she'd said.

'Let's try saying a proper goodbye,' she said. 'I'll try to be almost pleasant. You try to look like you're bothered.'

'But I will drive you to the airport,' said Georges, pulling his old shirt off over his head, revealing paint even on his chest and back.

'What is that?' said Betty, looking at the painting behind him.

'An experiment,' said Georges, embarrassed, standing in her way. There was a sort of face, or faces. Two, maybe three, all in the same face. Something like eyes either side of some sort of nose. Where the mouth should have been was something that looked nothing like a mouth and more like something that had been burned or melted and later spilled and spread. If it was human, it had no hair. If it was not, then it should not be wearing earrings. She had a creeping suspicion it was supposed to be her.

'Those are Martha's earrings,' she said.

'Really?' said Georges.

'One of those eyes is mine.'

'Maybe.'

'I don't know about the other three.'

'Well . . .' said Georges.

'Where is she? In a cave?'

'In a field,' said Georges. Betty frowned. 'On a mountain,' said Georges.

'Oh.'

'In a field, on a mountain.'

'I like it,' she said. And she did, though it was possible she would one day wish she had never seen it. Perhaps as early as later that afternoon. 'I've already said goodbye to Clara.'

'OK,' said Georges.

'I've put my case in the back of your car.'

'OK,' said Georges. He had still not put on a clean shirt and stood there with his hands on his hips. She could see a few of his chest hairs twitching, close to where his heart must have been beating. 'Why?'

'Why what?'

'Why did you put your case in the car, if you will say goodbye now?'

'Because I won't say goodbye now. I'll say goodbye at the airport. Keep up, Georges.'

She held her own phone in her hand, but it was Martha's phone that cheeped first, and by the time she had pulled it from her pocket, the other phone had lit up and she saw that she had two different texts from the same number. Jack's number. But when she opened them up, she saw that it was in fact the same message: *One day you realise you will never leave your country ever again. Another day you realise you will never leave this city ever again. Another day it's the house that holds you fast. Days later, a room. A bed. You will never leave this bed. You turn to find your final position. Now, all there is left to leave is this life. And all that remains of its grand ambitions is a fragment of desire to die in reasonable health.*

She recognised it at once. Somewhere near the beginning of act two. It was the note Jack's father had left on the pillow in Eleanor's bedroom, fixed in place beneath a bronze and hickory crucifix. Overcome by a vertiginous feeling of foreboding, she called him first from Martha's phone, and then, receiving no answer, tried again from her own phone, once more without success. She looked at her watch. It was a little after two.

The drive to Marseille was this time in daylight, and Betty sat not in the back, but at Georges's side, with her bare feet on the dash and the window down. She even asked if she could drive, but Georges just laughed in her face. In fact, Georges laughed for most of the journey, which might have made their last hour together touching and memorable were it not for the fact that he was laughing with some other woman. A few minutes after pulling out from the house, and in the middle of Betty telling him about her family holidays, his phone had rung and a loud, excitable, childish and high-pitched chatterbox entered the car, speaking far too quickly for Betty to catch anything but the most obvious words, though she was apparently completely hilarious, since the normally mute and lugubrious Georges now flung both himself and the car this way and that with the irrepressible vigour of his mirth. Betty had never seen him laugh very much at all these past weeks, and so was shocked and baffled now to see him so entertained and so voluble in himself, so eager to be heard, and apparently so enormously witty in return, for the woman laughed as much with him as he did with her, and the more they laughed, the more Betty fought back the tears, and buried her nose in her phone. She took her bare feet down from the dash, wound up the window and pushed her boots back on. She loathed the whole journey and wished she'd taken a taxi. To make matters worse, as he arrived at the airport, parked the car and walked to the terminal, he carried on giggling with the phone now pressed to his ear. With his other hand he tried to help Betty lift her case, but she snatched it away from him and walked ten paces ahead, pretending that she had a call of her own, from an equally entertaining idiot. Though she doubted that he noticed. It wasn't until she had checked in and had the ticket in her hand that he finally hung up. She felt like punching him.

'Right then, Claude,' she said, looking around at the signs to see where she should go next, 'thanks for the lift. Have a safe drive back, and good luck with everything.'

'What's the matter?' he said.

'Nothing. Is it this way? My ticket says A1. Where's A1?'

'Over here,' he said, and began walking so that she had little choice but to follow him. 'Am I bad?'

'Yes, Georges,' she said, 'I think you are bad. To spend the whole trip laughing like that, after what's happened. I think that's insensitive. I think it's thoughtless.'

'Has something happened?'

Betty stopped walking and turned to look at him. She thought Clara had explained. 'Ask Clara.'

'What has happened?'

'I said ask Clara.' She set off walking again, leading the way, checking that he was still behind her.

'I'm sorry for phone call,' he said, his head bowed in shame.

'She's been on holiday. We didn't speak since a long time.'

'You're sorry for *the* phone call,' said Betty, correcting him tersely. 'You didn't speak *for* a long time.'

'For a long time.'

'*Qui?*'

'*Comment?*'

'Who, Georges. *Qui.* It's a French word. Who haven't you spoken to for a long time?'

'*Ma mère.*'

Betty stopped and turned again. 'Your mother?'

'*Oui, bien sûr.*' He looked completely forlorn.

'Your mother makes you laugh like that?'

'Yes, of course,' said Georges, brightening now that he could see Betty's growing smile. 'She is very funny.'

'You told me she was a botanist,' said Betty.

'She's a very funny *botaniste.*' He took hold of her case and wheeled it the last few metres to the departure gate.

'You have my number,' said Betty, 'so if you ever come to London, you can call me.'

'I will come to London,' said Georges.

'Yeah, yeah, we'll see,' she said. 'So anyway—'

'In January,' he said. 'I will come in January.'

'What for?'

'I have an exhibition of photographs.'

'I thought you were a painter.'

'I am. I have an exhibition of paintings in Avignon, in March. But first is January, London.'

She looked into his eyes for a little too long without saying anything. She removed his hand from her case and wheeled it away from him. 'Well, maybe in January you won't feel sorry for me any more.'

'I don't feel sorry for you now,' he said with a sigh. 'I feel happy for you that this is over.'

'But you still won't kiss me?'

'No, of course not.'

'Stop adding that "of course not",' she said, pushing him in the chest. 'Just "no" will do fine.'

'Sorry.'

'I should think so. Maybe you'll kiss me in January.'

'Maybe.'

'There you go, that's more like it.'

'You're funny,' he said, roughing up her hair. She couldn't believe it.

'Like your mother,' she said.

'Yes,' he said, with his best smile yet. 'You're like my mother.'

'OK! Goodbye!' she yelled, turning. 'That's it. Goodbye.' And grabbing her case, she ran towards the security booths, which due to the rat's-maze of staggered barriers took her far longer than she would have liked for that refined and noble farewell. Georges stood and watched her all the way, laughing wonderfully, laughing like he'd laughed in the car, gasping for breath, wiping his eyes on his glistening wet wrists.

'*Au revoir,*' he called. '*Au revoir, Maman!*'

CHAPTER 34

It was almost impossible to sustain three people beneath one small umbrella when bags had to be hauled, phones answered and a wheelchair navigated across the slick and ruptured kerbs of a bustling Brick Lane on a Saturday afternoon. They had therefore taken shelter in the doorway of a derelict curry house till the storm subsided. In the gutter, a deflated beach ball bobbed and lurched on the surface of a filthy torrent, well on its way, it seemed, to the corner of Old Montague Street. From the wall opposite they were being closely watched by a large and colourful painting of what looked like Buster Keaton in a gas mask. A sudden burst of lightning lit up the dull windows and puddles, and seconds later came the stomach-turning thunder, as though the whole of nearby Bishopsgate had crumbled to the ground. Betty pulled Harold's feet further into the doorway, where they shared their shelter with a young mother and a baby who sat slumped and damp in its tatty brown buggy. Harold stared at the baby. The baby stared at Harold. Neither was impressed.

'A fragment of desire to die in reasonable health?' said Ruth, passing the phone back to Betty. 'What the hell does that mean?'

'It's from his film,' said Betty, slipping it back into her pocket out of the rain.

'Why did he send it to you?'

'In the story it's his father's suicide note.'

Ruth looked at the nearest puddle, and then another larger, deeper puddle, and then back to the first. 'I don't like the sound of this film,' she said at last. 'What's it called again?'

'*Unburied.*'

'I'm never going to see it.'

'I'm not sure anyone will now.'

'It said in the news that he filmed his own hanging.'

'I know.'

On any other day such behaviour might have made it onto the front page of the *Standard*, but since some enterprising genius had thrown acid at a TV astrologer, Jack's fate had been relegated to page five and therefore passed unnoticed by Betty when she arrived back in London on Wednesday evening. It wasn't until the following morning, when she received an in-appropriately jocular text from Arnold Plack – *Hope this had nothing to do with you – heartbreaker!* – and a link to the BBC's version of events, that she learned the full gravity of what had come to pass. She had sent a brief message back to Plack telling him that if he wished to retain his ten per cent, then he should do so, but that all other payment should be either refused or returned, and that she wanted nothing to do with it, nor any requests for comment. He did not reply.

'You know,' said Ruth, 'I was thinking.'

'What?' said Betty.

'I look more like her than you.'

'Who?'

'Martha Lear.'

Betty looked at her sister. Her claim hardly bore scrutiny. She was dressed in a fluffy brown coat with a fluffy brown hood. The hood had ears. There might even have been a tail of some sort. 'Well, you should have mentioned it earlier,' she said.

'But I could never have done the voice,' said Ruth. 'Do the voice again.'

'No,' said Betty.

'Why not?'

'I'm never doing the voice again.'

Betty had not yet told her sister the story of Oliver. It was, at least for now, to be kept between Betty and Clara. Not even Georges had known at the end. She would not reduce such agony to gossip. That would be left for untold others, any moment now, no doubt, though it had been three days. Apparently Clara had not yet made her move.

'What will Freddie think of that hair?' said Ruth.

'He won't see it,' said Betty pulling down her black cloth cap to cover every last lock.

'Why not?'

'I'm picking up some dye on the way home.'

'Well, get some for Dad,' said Ruth, looking down at Harold's grey roots coming through at the crown. 'I've not done him for a month.'

'You've not shaved him either,' said Betty.

'Well,' Ruth said, snorting, 'let's see how you get on with that.' She ran her fingers through her own hair and, catching her reflection in the whitewashed window, messed it up till she could only see out of one eye, which was the way she liked it. 'Apparently,' she said, 'Sean Porter's shaved his whole head.'

'I don't care what he's done,' said Betty.

'According to reliable sources,' said Ruth, 'he was spotted on a bench in Swedenborg Gardens snogging the teeth out of some bird in knee-high black patent leather boots with a balloon tied around some feather wings that were hanging off her shoulders. According, as I say, to reliable sources.'

'Who?' said Betty.

'Me,' said Ruth. 'I'd followed him. The wings were filthy.'

They fell into a long silence broken at last by another blast of lightning, which set the baby off screaming. 'I hope all this doesn't delay the flight,' said Ruth.

Betty looked at her watch. 'It shouldn't be long now,' she said. 'I'll check,' and she pulled her phone back out of her pocket. 'You know she offered for me to go round there.'

'To her place?' said Ruth.

'So I could see where she lives.'

'Why would you want to see where she lives?'

''Cos that's where Freddie was staying. So . . .'

'That's weird,' said Ruth.

'I think she meant it in a nice way,' said Betty. 'Reaching out.'

'Reaching out. Listen to you.'

'She was just being—'

'Oh, you love her now.'

'I don't.'

'She's your best friend.'

'Pack it in.'

'She wants to know if you want to move in with her.'

'Ruth.'

'And you do.'

'Anyway,' said Betty, calming her sister down, 'I said no. I thought it was better for Freddie to bring him straight round.'

'Of course it is,' said Ruth. 'He wants to be home.'

'Yeah.'

'Did you talk to him?'

'Yeah, briefly. It was a bad line.'

'What did he say?'

'He asked if he could have an elephant. I said no. He said just a baby elephant. I said no. He said what about a pig? I said what about a pig? He said a guinea pig then, and I said I'd think about it.'

'If you get one,' said Ruth, 'you'll have to get two.'

'Why?' said Betty.

''Cos guinea pigs hate to be alone. They go mad. In Switzerland it's illegal to have just one guinea pig.'

'How the hell do you know that?'

'I read a lot.'

Betty looked long and hard at her sister, smirking, and then burst out laughing. She kissed her on the cheek.

'What's that for?' said Ruth.

'You,' said Betty. 'Shall I tell you what else he said?'

'What else did he say?'

'He said he was glad that Grandpa was out of hospital and that he couldn't wait to see him.'

'Ah.'

'I said, "How do you know that Grandpa's out of hospital?" and he said because Auntie Ruth had told him.'

'Oh,' said Ruth, nibbling on her thumbnail.

'"Did she?" I said. "Yeah," he said. And he said that Auntie Ruth had called him quite a few times. I said, "Did she?" He said, "Yeah." He said, "She called me to tell me how you were, and what you were doing, and that you loved me." "Did she?" I said. "Yeah," he said. "That was lovely of her," I said. "And that's how I knew you weren't dead, Mama," he said.'

And that was it: Betty's lips and chin crumpled, and her whole face was suddenly as wet as the pavement, and she turned, pressing her cheeks tight and snug against her sister's fluffy arm, and began to shake. The baby stopped screaming. The mother smiled and looked at the old menu in the side window of the deserted restaurant. Even Harold seemed to notice and tried to look up. Ruth said nothing, but just stroked the top of her sister's damp cloth cap before slipping two fingers beneath the band to massage her scalp. This went on for some time.

313

'You're always crying,' said Ruth eventually. 'Why are you always crying?'

'It's something to do, innit?' said Betty, standing up straight, wiping snot on the back of her cuff and catching her nostril on a sharp button.

'Well,' said Ruth, 'shall I tell you something else to cry about?'

'What?' said Betty.

'I'm going to Cornwall.'

'What do you mean?'

'Well, when you said you'd have Dad for a few weeks, I thought, I'll go to Cornwall with Elaine Blott. Remember Elaine Blott?'

'The Buddhist?' said Betty.

'The Buddhist. Well, she's gonna come with me. Stay in a caravan. Do you hear that, Dad?' shouted Ruth, tapping her father on the shoulder. 'Staying in a caravan.' Harold had no opinion on the matter.

'Where in Cornwall?' said Betty.

'St Agnes,' said Ruth. 'Near the cliffs there.'

'Where we scattered Mum?'

'Where we scattered Mum.'

And off went Betty again, right back into the side of her sister's fluffy arm.

'There you go,' said Ruth, 'always crying.'

'Always crying.'

'Why's he wearing a gas mask?' said Ruth.

'Who?' said Betty, lifting her head up.

'Buster Keaton.'

'Dunno.'

They both looked at him for a long time, as though a solution might present itself if they thought about it for long enough. Eventually their gaze was broken by a black taxi pulling up to let out a small man carrying flowers, who paid his fare as quickly as he could before running off through the rain at great speed, almost falling as he passed the old school. The taxi lingered, its engine ticking over, and a mesmerised Harold seemed to explore every part of it. Lost in the deep black of it. As though the whole of outer space itself had just rolled into town.

The rain had finally stopped, which was just as well, as Ruth had caught a bus into the West End to buy walking boots and sheet music, leaving Betty with Harold and all Harold's bags, and there was no reasonable way of steering his chair and chattels down the Whitechapel Road while at the same time holding up an umbrella. As she pushed him along, she tried to tell him about where she'd been, but found him so unresponsive as he sank deeper and deeper down into his chair that she might as well have been talking to the chair itself. Every now and then she had to stop to hoist him up, or make sure his hands didn't hang down by the wheels. She found herself staring with great melancholy at the top of his head, realising how it reminded her of when he used to carry her on his shoulders. He had more and darker hair back then, of course, and his shoulders were not these sloping, broken things, and these twisted fingers were not so feeble. What, she wondered, was going on inside that head now? In his taxi-driving days, every street in London had wound its way through there. Every name and number, every turn at every junction, every square and crescent, every park and circus. She wondered if all that knowledge still prevailed, or if that vast plexus of terraces and avenues had since seared into one unfathomable clod.

She wondered therefore if he'd noticed that they were no longer heading west, towards Tower Bridge and home, but that they had, at the end of Osborn Street, just turned left instead of right, in the direction of the old Whitechapel bell foundry, the

East London Mosque and the enormous blue hospital rising up from the bones of the old Georgian one. The hospital where his girls had been born and where, not really so many years later, he'd arrived too late to say goodbye to their mother. She wondered if he cared. Not that these things had happened, but that they might happen again if the building came any closer. But it was too late now to turn around. There may come a time, thought Betty, when Freddie will push me towards a hospital. Perhaps this hospital. Almost certainly so. And perhaps, from up there on my shoulders, he will wonder what remains inside my head, this head once filled with sonnets and soliloquies – with Euripides, Lorca, Ibsen, Pinter – and whether one syllable still endures or if all has been reduced to ticks and whistles, as had recently so nearly been the case. Perhaps he would never forgive her the past six weeks and wish her, mercifully, to the grave, once she was too bent out of shape to be of any use or fun. Perhaps he would say that the damage was already done, Doctor, and that the dead lady never really left her and so died within her daily, and if one could open her up on the day when she herself finally dies then you would find that dead lady there inside, still dying till the end of time. Yes, and maybe he would wonder if *she* had noticed that they had turned left instead of right, losing north in the direction of the distant mountain. In the direction of the empty pool and the poplar grove. And wonder if she cared, not that these things had already happened, but that they would never cease to happen if she drifted out any further. And the poor boy foreseeing perhaps a time when his own recalcitrant child would push him, pushing his mother, pushing her father, and he in turn, somewhere in time, pushing his own father as they drew closer and closer.

And as they all now turned right, instead of back, in Betty's burning head, into the anaemic procession of the hospital approach, poor Harold had begun to hum and to rock, making the chair difficult to steer. But Betty, having none of it, lifted and then slammed down hard the back wheels to bring him to heel. And once they were through the bright glass doors and into the lobby, he'd completely stopped his nonsense and sank back, chastised, as Betty rebalanced all the bags and parked him by the vending machine to study the chocolate. He watched her then, his little girl, with building anxiety as she walked, slowly, removing her black cloth cap, as though nothing was wrong, to join the queue at the reception.

There had been no shortage of reports, popping up both in print and on newsfeeds all over the internet, but each report was so hurriedly compiled and so soon after the appalling event that the details were essentially the same, coming as they did from only a small handful of reliable sources. It was of course of interest to Betty that there had been no mention of the house in France, though France was mentioned in the expected context when it came to speculating upon the reasons. Of course, everything pointed to the tragedy of his late wife. There was a photograph of Martha on the BBC, wearing a black-and-white chequerboard minidress, the same dress Betty had worn the day she cycled into Pontelle for the first time. She recalled her bold reflection in the bright windows of the town. Beneath the photo the text told the tale of how the poor woman had entered a 'picturesque Provençal tunnel' in early spring. No one knew why. She had been so beautiful, they said, and rich and talented, and always well dressed. She had been, however, they hinted mindlessly, in her forties and childless, with her career in decline. She had not been seen in public for a number of years. Since Mr Drake had left no note, it was difficult to ascertain the true motivation for his actions. The whole thing had been captured on film by the great man himself, perfectly staged and lit 'in glorious Technicolor', said one tabloid, as though it was 1950. It was thought that the footage was intended to be used in the finished film, though it was unclear if this would in fact be the case. This detail from a Miss Nora Flynn, the film's producer, who was said to be in shock and thoroughly inconsolable. She was sixty-four and lived alone. A Mr Solomon Monk BSC ASC, sixty-seven, said he had nothing to say and then said it was all so very unexpected, though to be honest not completely out of character, and therefore perhaps foreseeable after all. He would now retire, he then added, shaking his head.

It was a Mrs Phyllis Rigby, forty-two, mother of one of the actors and a former nurse, who had saved the director's life. If indeed it could be saved. It was too early to tell. Mr Drake, a resident of Clerkenwell, was at the time of writing under intensive care at the Royal London Hospital, Whitechapel.

What then had it all been about? she thought, as the lift doors rattled shut. Why had he sent his note only to her? Was it punishment or gratitude? Had her only job been to somehow teach him some kind of lesson? But what, after all, had she ever taught him but something he had already learned from his father: how to dangle from a piece of string? And what – at the end of a bad day – was so very difficult about that?

Why on earth had he brought *her* back? What horror, to set that head back on its spine. To peel back those eyes. (There were no mirrors in this lift. Had anyone reported that?) She looked at her left hand and held it up, turning it back and forth in the light, before dropping it down to her side and banging it over and over on the cold steel wall of the lift, harder and harder, until her father began to whimper. 'They must think I'm a dirty one,' she said. 'Therefore I must be a dirty one. Therefore I must roll in the hot street and on the wet floor of the public bathroom.' Harold tried to turn around. 'I long to be approached by some intriguing stranger,' she said. 'Someone not quite pleasant. I long to be talked to as though I don't deserve to be told the truth. I don't care if it's a man or a woman. I don't care about age. I don't care about any of these things, simply because I have always cared so much about these things. The only important thing is that whatever happens next should in no way resemble what has usually, all my life, happened next. I don't even care if it hurts.'

When the doors finally opened, she froze and gazed out into the freshly mopped white corridor, silent, still. There was a white clock on the white wall. It seemed to have stopped. Just as the doors began to close, she thrust the chair forward to force them open. Harold began to rock. She wheeled him to a quiet corner not far from the nurses' station and left him there, staring at a cage of gas bottles. In a daze and sucking a smudge of blood from her knuckle, she followed signs round two corners till she found a brown door.

He was either sleeping or still unconscious. There were several drips in his arm and a mask over his mouth. Hubs and monitors on either side of the bed. The sheets were folded down and wrapped tight, tucked across his chest, his bare arms straight down on either side, both palms up, as though meditating. His gown was open at the throat and she could see that the neck was heavily bruised. No one had shaved him. Even behind the mask and tubes and pallor and stubble he looked younger than she had imagined. She thought of his face on that final night and how it had moved her to look into his eyes for the first time. She thought of his voice and how it had seemed to buckle with every syllable.

There was another bed close to the window, where an upsettingly skeletal old gentleman with two black eyes and a bandaged hand slept, snoring gently, with his mouth wide open. Next to him, seated in a wheelchair by the window, was an elderly lady wearing a green overcoat and matching headscarf. She was gazing out at the old hospital's immense incinerator chimney. She was not to be disturbed.

Betty approached Jack's bed and stood close enough to smell him, though he did not smell of much: sweat and polyester beneath a twist of lemon and a dash of bleach. She reached into her bag and set a white envelope containing a handwritten note on the nightstand: *To Whomsoever It May Concern,* in blue ink and her best italics. A brief explanation, should Mr Drake not awaken. She looked up and noticed a small plastic crucifix stuck to the wall with sellotape, its tiny pink Christ no bigger than a cockroach. Just as she moved over to take a closer look, a young nurse appeared in the doorway.

'Can I help you?' she said.

'No,' said Betty, startled. 'Everything's fine. I was just about to go.'

'You're not supposed to be in here.'

'I know,' said Betty. 'I realise that. I was just leaving something for Mr Drake. I'll go now.'

The nurse looked over at the sleeping man and at the old woman by the window. She glanced once more at Betty, smiled, nodded and left.

In the chill hospital air, and aided by a squirt of sanitiser, the ring slipped off her bruised finger with almost no effort. She felt the pleasing weight of it in her palm, gave it a quick polish with the corner of her cardigan and set it down on the nightstand, next to the envelope. She reached out her hand, thinking to touch him, perhaps on the face, but then she could not.

Then, 'Jack,' she said softly. It was only one word of one syllable, and so difficult to know for certain which of them had spoken. No matter. He did not stir. She walked over to the open door and turned to take one last look.

'Goodbye,' said the old woman suddenly, turning from the

320

window and wrestling her wheelchair away from the wall.

'I'm sorry,' said Betty, putting on her cap. 'I didn't mean to . . .'

The woman had a blue blanket across her lap, and resting on it a large red leather-bound book with a black cross embossed on the cover. She stood up out of the chair, taking the Bible into her hands, allowing the blanket to drop in a heap to the floor. Slowly she hobbled over to the side of Jack's bed and, glancing briefly down at her old ring, took his cold grey hand in hers. 'You can go now,' she said. 'It's over.'

But Betty had already gone.

ACKNOWLEDGEMENTS

Hermine Poitou for her important contribution to the story, for listening tirelessly night after night and her invaluable help with the French language.

Régine and Jean-Pierre Poitou for allowing me space in their nutty house, and a bed in the basement of a thousand books and toys.

Clifford Ashcroft for being the first person in my life to encourage me to write anything. Mike Leigh for being the first person to encourage me to write a novel. Atom Egoyan for encouraging me to write this novel and for giving me the confidence to stick at it.

Seamus McGarvey for cinematographic advice. Erik Gosselin for prosthetic advice (and some scary photos to pin above my desk).

Jonny Geller, my very patient agent. Lisa Babalis for all her early work on the first draft. And of course, Federico Andornino for making this possible and real and for doing it all with great charm and humour.

Help us make the next generation of readers

We – both author and publisher – hope you enjoyed this book. We believe that you can become a reader at any time in your life, but we'd love your help to give the next generation a head start.

Did you know that 9% of children don't have a book of their own in their home, rising to 13% in disadvantaged families*? We'd like to try to change that by asking you to consider the role you could play in helping to build readers of the future.

We'd love you to think of sharing, borrowing, reading, buying or talking about a book with a child in your life and spreading the love of reading. We want to make sure the next generation continue to have access to books, wherever they come from.

And if you would like to consider donating to charities that help fund literacy projects, find out more at **www.literacytrust.org.uk** and **www.booktrust.org.uk**.

THANK YOU

*As reported by the National Literacy Trust